D0974993

NECESSARY
OBJECTS

Lois Gould

NECESSARY OBJECTS

Random House   *New York*

Library of Congress Cataloging in Publication Data

Gould, Lois.
    Necessary objects.

    I.   Title.
PZ4.G697Ne [PS3557.O87]   813'.5'4   72–2696
ISBN 0–394–46847–3

Manufactured in the United States of America by Haddon Craftsmen, Scranton, Pa.

First Edition
2 3 4 5 6 7 8 9

For Bobby—in the best possible way

The Pleiades are . . . essentially a constellation of cold weather. On a hazy night or when obscured by city lights they may seem blurred, like a pale smudge of light stolen from the Milky Way. On clear nights they appear distinctly, six tiny brilliant stars. Sometimes one can just distinguish a faint seventh, The Lost Pleiade.

Especially widespread is the connection of the Pleiades with death . . . The Aztecs cherished an ancient tradition that all creation had once been destroyed on a night when the Pleiades culminated at midnight—and that the calamity would eventually repeat itself. On that night all fires were extinguished and a sacrificial victim made ready. A human victim—a token offering, the death of one, that others might be spared. It was considered a great honor to be chosen as the sacrifice.

The Arabs, the Berbers and even nineteenth-century astronomers looked at the mysterious cloudiness of the Pleiades and believed that there lay the center of the universe . . .

In the Amazon Valley it is believed that only during the months when they are visible is the bite of a snake poisonous.

The Polynesians call the cluster "Little Eyes," and believe that long ago they formed a single star, the most brilliant in the sky— beautiful, conceited, ill-mannered and objectionable. One dark night [it] was smashed into six little pieces. The fragments . . . no longer dare boast aloud how beautiful they are, but when the nights are dark and quiet they still lean down close to earth to see themselves in the mirror of the oceans, and then they know that they have no equal.

In Greek mythology the Pleiades were changed into stars because they grieved so unconsolably over their father, when he was made to bear the weight of heaven on his shoulders. Another account has it that they were passionately pursued by Orion the hunter, until Jupiter placed them all in the sky, where the chase continues . . .

There is nothing else like them in the whole world of stars. Knowledge of the Pleiades long antedates any record or legend of them . . .They were familiar to the earliest men who ever watched the skies.
—Peter Lum, *The Stars in Our Heaven*

NECESSARY
OBJECTS

One

I

N THIS AURORA-PINKISH

lighting, everyone said, even the *boeuf en gelée* looked younger. And so at first glance the Lowen sisters had a way of gleaming like a controversial portrait of some exiled royal family. Luminous cultured-pearl faces loosely fastened to the black velour banquette. And wearing those faintly significant smiles during the seating process, in case anyone had forgotten the line of succession since their last public appearance.

The first thing each sister did, unconsciously, the way most people unfold the napkin, was unpack the necessities from her handbag. Setting everything out on the fresh white cloth, in precise order, with a slight catch of breath, as if she were lining up ivory chess pieces for a tournament match, or counting marked bills before paying the highest ransom ever demanded for a kidnapped child.

This object lesson could not really qualify as a shocking display of wealth. In the first place nothing really qualifies any more—not in the strict sense, as, for example, French lace did when its price reflected the number of French orphans who had gone blind embroidering it. Heirloom lace, so called. So that at least the well-traveled creatures who knowingly folded yards of it into their trousseaux did so with care. Highly cherishable. Each fragile square a keepsake swaddled in soft tissue against yellowing time. Hankies neither for showing nor blowing, but to be tucked once in twenty years into a daughter's white sleeve, and once again by the daughter in turn, in another twenty. A barbaric tradition, at an unspeakable original cost, but mellowed by all that ignorance and old age, not to mention redeeming foolish sentiment.

Whereas the precious nonsense assembled here had not cost a single eye, and would certainly not outlast the current season. It was merely stuff which the Lowen sisters would cart proudly around in snug suede pouches, as they had once carried their new jacks, until the shine wore off. In a few months Mai would probably sell her new old-Etruscan-looking compact; it was the kind of thing too many other people would want one just like. Elly (Elly to the world; Ella to their father and the Passport Bureau) would leave her hammered-gold cigarette case in a cab; Alison's tiny malachite pillbox would be at the bottom of her summer scarf drawer (she would know it was somewhere, though, unless the maid). And Celine, the practical one, would pry the cabochons out of her little perfume flacon, because maybe they could be used in her new bracelet.

4

All for no better reason than to keep this luncheon ritual from becoming even more of a bore.

It wasn't their fault; Amos Lowen had raised them to be consummate consumers—the kind of women who would think of the nearest branch of Lowen & Co. as an extra walk-in closet, roomy enough to get lost in as often as possible. Amos Lowen taught his daughters carefully that poor was a curse word, and that if money couldn't buy happiness —a point he never conceded—there were still plenty of other selections.

Hardly anyone remembered any more that Lowen, the retailing czar, stores in ten, twelve major cities now, had once literally peddled rags along Jewish neighborhood streets in Indianapolis. "Ragman to riches," a magazine cover story had once said. Lowen's blistering letter to the editor was printed in its entirety, which he triumphantly mistook for a retraction.

Besides rich, the only other thing Amos ever wanted to be was unpredictable. His two brothers and three cousins had all shortened the Lowenthal to Lowe: Amos refused to part with his final *n*. The family never quite forgave him, either, because no matter how many Lowes he tucked nepotistically into key executive slots at every branch store, the name of the chain was still Lowe*n*.

And later when Leona kept getting pregnant, people assumed that Amos was after sons, a pride of merchant princelings who would oust their *n*-less uncles and cousins from their rightful leather swivel chairs. Daughters they had. Not even good-looking daughters—although Amos could fix that when the time came. Six or seven they had, two stillbirths or one died in infancy—something like that.

But the real tragedy, everyone thought, was that he couldn't get a single store president. (Not even he would have predicted Alison's ending up as anything but a customer.)

Anyway, as it turned out, he'd wanted daughters all along— or so he said. A houseful of useless girls. Most people didn't believe it, but Amos could persuade them it was true. Daughters were proof that he could afford anything, even an overstock of children purely for decoration.

As for the necessary alterations, Amos cheerfully took care of those when each girl reached her early teens. The nose jobs turned out so well that Leona wanted one too, so Amos gave it to her for their twentieth anniversary. For years his favorite joke was to show off the family to strangers, boasting loudly: "Damn good thing the girls got Leona's nose, hey?" But at least they had kept the noses longer than anything else Amos ever bought them, or taught them to buy for themselves.

Such as the inconstant inventory on the table. Boxes. Despite the changes, it was a collection of boxes. Things to hold other things, all with clasps so ingenious that it usually took several nails before one got the hang of it. And the ones for pills were always so small that it was amazing how much saccharin they could hold. Alison's now was made with two tiny compartments, to keep the saccharin from spilling its bitter sweetness on the tranquilizers.

None of the sisters owned a cigarette lighter, and none of them ever noticed the restaurant matchbooks so thoughtfully furnished with the ashtray. The captain provides a light if one is lunching without an escort. Something masculine about lighters, and a ridiculous nuisance besides. Like ballpoint pens; no matter how expensive, not one ever works. Nuisances were anything one had to keep remembering to do something about —filling or plugging in or putting the top back on. Alison had so much on her mind, and only the one maid now. The others

6

had husbands who . . . well, not the kind of husbands who offer to do that for you. There were enough *serious* needs unfilled in those marriages. The kind of filling that wasn't included in the dowry that came with every one of Amos Lowen's daughters, on every one of her wedding days.

Mai, Celine and Elly always studied each other's new acquisitions in thoughtful silence—making their private evaluations. Then they would turn to Alison. Her treasures had to be approved by the full committee. When the inspection was completed, all dutiable items declared and customs paid in the Lowen currency of devalued superlatives, there was the abrupt chorus of leather purses snapping shut, and the sisters arched their backs slightly for a better view of the restaurant. Who, each of them needed to know, is here besides ourselves.

They would order the shirred eggs and one plain broiled sole, or the brains in black butter and, always, poor Elly's plain sliced tomato ($3.75; it was outrageous, and she brought her own dressing). They sighed resignedly for her and turned their gazes inward again. Alison was squinting. Elly looked surprisingly well in that bright red, didn't they think?

Elly plucked happily at the chiffon scarf around her neck. "Really? Isn't that funny, I'm usually terrified of red."

"But I'm not sure about the hair," Alison went on methodically.

Mai elbowed Celine to watch Elly's crest begin to fall. Her slightly puffy face sinking softly into its round self like a perfect cheese soufflé whose golden moment never was meant to last.

"No," Alison decreed, without benefit of jury trial, shaking her own arrangement of frosted ringlets in lieu of a genuine halo. They knew perfectly well she would never let it go at that. "The more I look at it the more I hate it. Look at how they put in those streaks—like a Spanish flag! Doesn't she look like a Spanish flag?"

Alison flung questions like gauntlets; she never asked anything rhetorically. Mai and Celine crunched rolls and began chewing very hard, as if to speed up the getaway car. Oh, just one time not to have to take sides. Alison's side, that is. One sided against Alison's verdicts at one's peril. I thought I *liked* the streaks, Celine mused. Thank God I didn't put it in writing. She flicked her slightly soiled beige gloves into her lap. Never can tell when Alison is reading one's traitorous mind.

Mai was the only one whose hair never came up for discussion. She touched it now with protective fingers, just to make sure. Like a heavy mass of rich brown silk, it rose from her brow in a single smooth wave, and coiled into thick round knots at the back, like bunches of exotic dark fruit. Although it was her hair*line* that people noticed first. It had always seemed too perfect, like the front of a wig. Perhaps she pruned it into shape like bonsai, or possibly even had it transplanted, strand by carefully tweaked strand, from the heads of retired geishas.

In any case, since hair was today's topic, Mai could calmly sip her not too spicy Bloody Mary and remember that Alison couldn't help the way she carried on. She was like a medical missionary who believed passionately that lack of chic was a disease. That God created some persons with absolute taste (like musicians with perfect pitch) which made them immune; that she was one of those, and therefore that she had a sacred duty to tend the less fortunate. Florence Nightingale for the fat and frizzy-haired, the pimpled and rumpled. Curing them of their fatal unattraction. In the street she often stared in open horror at strangers whose clothes or figures offended her. Not only stared, but demanded that anyone with her stare too. "Did you see *that?*" she would exclaim. "And my God, look at this one coming—no, you *have* to look!"

So those close to her, especially her sisters, had long ago learned what to expect when Alison examined them. Any symptom she spotted must be lanced at once with her sharpest instrument; otherwise, there was no telling how fast the virus could spread.

Mai watched Alison applying her surgical skill to Elly's unfortunate head. It was unlikely, she decided, that Alison was even dimly aware that Elly was on the verge of tears. Somehow poor Elly had never learned when not to quite hear her eldest sister.

Luckily Celine's attention had wandered. "Isn't that," she whispered excitedly, trying to point with her chin, "no, over *there*—isn't it Ira's ex-wife? The one with the huge diamond flower I can't tell if it's real from here but I'm positive—don't turn around *now*, Mai, for God's sake, she's looking."

"Oh, how could it be," Alison snapped irritably, squinting. "That girl is maybe twenty-four, *tops*. And wasn't Susan Wolf in Mai's class at, where was it, Smith? And the kids are what —ten, twelve?"

"Goucher," Mai said.

"What?"

"Goucher. I went to Goucher. Smith was where Papa knew a trustee who wasn't able to be of much help."

By now every one of them had crossed Alison's threshold of annoyance, which had been even lower than usual lately. Next Friday was her thirty-ninth birthday. Suddenly she wished they would all choke on their flaky croissants.

"But I didn't *mean* Susan," Celine threw in. "I meant Tessa Whozit from Ohio, the *first* wife—she paints or something. Anyway, never mind her any more. What about the man she's with, isn't he—"

"Yes, you're right!" Alison exclaimed, distracted at last. "Chad . . . isn't it Chad? . . . Bachelor, oh, not Bachelor, but Batch-*some*thing, and he *is*. Divorced. Or anyway pending. And isn't he the head of—"

9

"No, he isn't the head of," Mai cut in, treading carefully. "Why is it you always assume every man is the head of. He's a vice-president of some public relations company. Not bad, not great." She shrugged.

"Not bad is absolutely great this year," Alison retorted, but her dander was safely down. They had managed to deposit her on an intriguing patch of neutral territory, leaving poor Elly to lick her superficial head wounds.

"I thought Mai was bringing Cathy today," Celine said into the silence. "Hmm?"

Mai flinched. Not that she hadn't expected one of them to ask. "Oh, Cathy wasn't feeling . . . quite up to it after all," she replied evenly, through one of her clenched smiles that for some reason looked dazzling in newspaper photos.

"I thought you said she was—"

"Oh, she *is*—*much* better. We're mad about the new doctor, I told you, marvelous man, head of that new clinic where Molly Squires' daughter. He really is the *first* one we've felt any confidence about at all. And he's sure all Cathy needs is a little time. Now that the baby. Well, obviously. With a baby she just has to *begin* to grow up. He feels, this Dr. Weissman, feels that Ira and I ought to go ahead with our trip now. That it would *not* be good for her, in fact, just the opposite, if we just went on baby-sitting all summer. Of course, there's no way to predict how she'll . . . but Weissman knows what kind of strain we've been under. Ira and I. You saw how Ira looked the other night? The two of us, it's been . . . well, I don't want to go into it, I'm sure you can guess. And he needs the trip more than I do; we've postponed it twice, you know. It's just unfair to ask, well, *any* man, to spend the whole . . . and she is much better, I talked to Weissman for an entire hour last night. It's only been six weeks, don't forget."

"Does he think," Elly ventured timidly. "I mean does anyone think she . . . Cathy might just want"—Mai's look was not encouraging, but it was too late not to finish— "just want her . . . husband back?" Elly ducked behind her raised demitasse, not that she thought it would really ward them off. Mai's mouth fell open unattractively, but she didn't say anything.

"Elly is still a romantic," Celine observed softly, dropping another saccharin into her cup. "And here we all thought she outgrew that the first time she got sued for alimony."

Elly's face turned a color that made the bright red shade less becoming.

"Sandy Rossbach was a ridiculous choice for poor little Cathy," Alison reminded them all. "Mai and Ira knew damn well the child couldn't handle—"

"Oh, who makes anything but a ridiculous choice at the age of seventeen? Remember how Papa had to get rid of Celine's first—"

"Oh God, Elly, *please*. Papa bought Celine a nice clean annulment. *That's* what I call a *choice*. Cathy was four months gone before the little stinkers even told us!"

Elly attacked her face with a powder puff. Alison sat back, squinting toward the table where Chad Batch-something was sitting. Not the head of, she thought, but so what.

Mai sighed. If it had been fifteen degrees cooler last Saturday, she reflected bitterly, I guarantee not one of them would have batted an eye. Much less called it a Southampton war atrocity. Whatever that means. I still don't see what kind of a crime I committed, heat or no heat. The boy had visitation rights, so I let him visitate. On *my* property, my country house. Which wasn't even part of the settlement.

Maybe if I hadn't locked Cathy in her room. Although what was I supposed to do—let them claw each other to shreds in front of a houseful of guests? People should see what goes on

11

when just his rotten *name* comes up at the dinner table
. . . the child carries on as if . . . well, God knows how long
the *help* will stand for it.

So what did I do that was so terrible? Sent the nurse down
to the lawn with the baby. Instead of what—delivering him
myself? Present my grandson to that little creep—like dessert?
A reward for six months' stud service? What should I have said:
Here, Sandy, and thank you? Because we all appreciated your
little stay with us? And wasn't it nice that you got to use your
black marble john before you left? Oh, Sandy *loves* black,
Cathy said. Oh, couldn't we do his john in black marble? He'll
love it.

My God, a hundred and thirty thousand we sank into that
apartment for them. Where Sandy resides until the night his
baby is born. And then excuses himself from the family. Deposits his bride in the maternity ward and calls to say goodbye. He
had a date to go skiing in Kitzbuhl—or was it Zermatt.

My poor baby Cathy, going on eighteen she looks like a
thirty-five-year-old degenerate; you'd swear she had something
venereal. Won't even pluck her eyebrows. Drag her to the
beauty parlor, it's like throwing out the eighty dollars. And not
a damn does she give about anything. The baby doesn't exist,
I don't, Ira—I've never seen Ira so nervous. Nothing moves her
except the damn pills, I don't even know where she gets them,
we closed every one of the accounts. We never know in the
morning if, God forbid . . .

Anyway, that was all it was, that was the *entire thing*. Those
damn columnists! As if not using my name makes it all right
to say I staged a . . . Roman circus. That I made them . . . made
my *son* and the baby sit on the burning grass while I lounged
on my terrace jeering. Eating and drinking with my guests
while the Christian martyrs rolled around in the broiling heat.

Roman circus! Children dying of thirst while I swilled frozen daiquiris! I haven't had a frozen daiquiri in two years.

Ah, poor Grandma Mai. Hmm, what about *Grandmai* for short? Celine reached over to bestow a fluttery consolation pat on her sister's black Dior sleeve.

Mai was not especially soothed. "I see you're wearing your giant economy-size ring," she observed. A truth for a truth. Celine deserved it. And they had tried so hard to stop her from wheedling that kind of *dreck* out of Ned. (*Dreck* was one of the few lower-class Jewish words they permitted themselves to use, at least with each other, because sophisticated fashion writers often used it in print now, which took the curse off. Of course, the Lowens always said it in italics, with an aristocratic smile, to show they were slumming.) Much good it did. You could lecture Celine about diamonds until you were blue-white in the face. "But who *cares* about flawless?" she would argue, with the calm illogic of a ten-year-old. When for the same price she could light up a whole room by just waving hello.

This particular ring was pure Celine. Which meant that it was the kind of ring you see in joke stores, with a rubber bulb on the back that squirts water. It was all too real, however, and flawed near its center with a glaring black speck like an imploded birthmark.

"I can see that flaw from here, it's disgusting," Alison had told her. "Reminds me of those ten-dollar lucite paperweights with the trapped insects." Infuriatingly, Celine had replied that the flaw was what made the thing such an incredible *buy*, didn't they understand.

They did, of course; that was the trouble. And it was pointless to appeal to her husband Ned's better judgment. If he had his way, Ned Greenstone would get her two of them, two for ninety-nine if slightly imperfect, an even more incredible buy. The pursuit of vulgarity, especially at a discount, was one of Ned and Celine's most deeply shared marital pleasures. Celine's sisters assumed she had picked up the habit while living in California, where it probably grew wild around free-form swimming pools, like some noxious weed. It was a theory that neatly avoided the nagging possibility that Celine might have become a hopeless *dreck* addict anywhere, and that, by extension, so might they.

Celine missed California. There were even times, such as right now, when she wished Papa had let her stay married to Jay Harvey Martin, the director, though she never admitted that to her sisters. She was convinced they still resented her short, glamorous fling at a movie career. It had not *quite* been a career, but she had appeared in three films, one a two-million-dollar-budget production and one with feature billing: ". . . And Introducing Celina (sic) Lowen as The Girl." She had gone to all kinds of Hollywood parties with all kinds of men, and she had actually eloped, with Jay Harvey Martin. Although at the time—eighteen years ago—she had startled herself by sighing with relief when the registered letter was slipped under the door of their honeymoon suite the day after they arrived. (Amos Lowen's fatherly hand having followed at a discreet distance.) "My dear Celine, Please understand that annulment proceedings must be taken at once. I have enclosed an air ticket for you. Your mother joins me in sending you our deep affection at this time."

Celine had loyally called her mother to protest in tearful clichés: they had never even *met* Jay Harvey Martin; she was *in love*; they were *happy*. Quietly her mother reminded her that Papa never decided such things in haste, and therefore never made a mistake. That was true, and so Celine had obediently annulled everything—love, happiness, Jay Harvey Martin

14

and her movie career. Although no one, not even Celine, ever really understood why. The columnists wisely cracked that Papa had simply threatened to disLowen her. But eighteen years later, seventeen of them acceptably married to the sort of man Amos Lowen preferred for his sons-in-law, Celine still had this recurrent nightmare about her aborted first marriage.

Not the marriage, exactly. The week before the marriage, when she and Jay Harvey Martin . . . In his one-room apartment absolutely bare except for the bed in the middle like an exclamation point, so huge that you had to hug the wall to avoid it. No room for two people to pass without touching it or each other. How had she got there in the first place? She couldn't remember, never had remembered, no matter how many times she tried. Picked him up at some party, was all she could think, though she had never done that. Come over for dinner, she remembered him saying. On the phone? No . . . and he hadn't *said* it; he had commanded. Never a dinner like that either. One enormous blood-rare steak. Period. They ate on the bed, and when it was gone he had picked up both their plates to lick the blood. Slurping. Turning the plate around slowly, playing it on his tongue, like a machine playing a silent LP record. Absolute silence the whole time, like in one of those surrealistic French movies where you don't know which part is reality and if so whose. And then he announced that he would do that to her. She couldn't remember what it sounded like when he said it, only that his eyes flickered like matches trying to stay lit in a high wind. No, she had said thickly. They were still on the bed, and he was neatly folding the spread, or rather rolling it, down, and the pillow case was grimy. She had tried to get up, mumbling stupidly about going home now, but his laugh stopped her. She hated being laughed at. And so.

Look, he had said. Look at us. Watch me. In front of a

mirror, where had that mirror come from, she didn't remember it before, a full-length mirror. And he was kneeling with his back to it and she was standing facing it. Are you watching me. Yes . . . yes. She had been afraid not to. Tell what you see. I can't. Of course you can. I see . . . your feet, she had said finally, and still remembered how her voice sounded, as if she were suffocating under that grimy pillow. The bottoms of your feet . . . look so pink. Like monkey feet. Zoo monkeys with their toes curled around the trapeze bar.

And he had laughed again, a piercing terrible laugh that made her feel embarrassed and afraid, the way she felt at dances when boys suddenly thrust her away, just holding her distant hand, expecting her to dance out there alone, and she had never known how.

He had turned them both sideways, so that they were profiled in the mirror, and bowed his head, hiding his strange sad face against her. Now tell me.

You look . . . as if praying. To—

To your—

To my body.

Say what. Say what I'm doing.

Like the steak plate.

He made the same noise. Just like that. Please, I want you to stop.

You do not, you're a liar.

No, please. And she had started crying. But why? To make him feel sorry.

Now do me, he said.

What.

Do me, I said.

No I won't. I don't want to, I can't.

But he pulled her by the hand firmly back onto the bed, as

16

if escorting a small child to the bathroom. You have to make weewee now, you have to.

No. But she did everything the way he told her, upside down with her face caught like a walnut between his hard knees. And he was still making those . . . noises far away inside her. Terrible, thinking Terrible, how soft the inside of her own thighs must feel, like great overripe plums. As if fingers pressed against them would form permanent finger-shaped indentations.

Was she just eighteen then? Younger than Mai's Cathy. Poor sick little Cathy who reminded her a little of that old— that young—Celine. The only one of the Lowen girls who had never kidded herself that maybe she would enjoy motherhood. Biggest mistake a woman can make, Celine had decided long ago: kidding herself that maybe she would enjoy . . . anything.

"Batchelder," Alison said.

"What?"

"Chad Batchelder. The name of that—" Alison stopped abruptly, embarrassed at being the only one who cared. She ventured an indifferent shrug, not quite successfully. "I just happened to think of it."

Elly, whose lacerations had healed nicely, decided to reenlist. "Why don't I invite him to the party Thursday. Alison? He knows Mopsy Taylor, and it's in her honor. So there's nothing awkward—"

"Mmm, all right." Alison nodded carelessly, because why should Elly suddenly have such power over her social life. As if to restore the balance, her eyes snapped back to Elly's deposed crown. "And I hope you're not going to wear your hair that way."

"Oh, Alison, shut *up*," Celine cried, but of course that made it her turn. "If. I. Shut. Up," Alison replied, discarding each word like a manicurist snipping cuticles, "you would *all* be walking around like freaks. Dangling earrings, clothes that show every . . . your idea of sexy. Or glamorous. God knows what. And what you look like is somebody's colored maid on her night off!"

"Chad Batchelder seems to be looking this way," Mai observed. "Would that call for a temporary ceasefire?"

Alison ceased.

I'm too honest, she scolded herself. Why do I *bother* any more? They don't even appreciate it that I care how they look. Not one of them. You'd think they'd thank me, but nobody wants to be told the truth. I'm probably the one person in the world who goes on telling it.

Look at Dr. Szabo. The best nose man in New York, charges two thousand dollars with a Hungarian accent. I bring Jill in. I know *exactly* what he charges. And I know exactly how small a difference it would make, in her case. Attractive, of course she'll be attractive anyway, once she loses the weight. But why not a great beauty? If a child has a chance to be—perfect? This is a man with a professional *commitment* to help a woman be as beautiful as she can. Isn't that what it's all about? The cosmetics, the clothes, whole industries that exist because we *need* . . . and here is a mother willing to spend two thousand dollars. Not that it's a bad nose, I never said it was *bad*, not even noticeable, like mine was, or even Mai's.Papa would call it semi-prominent. Just that slight little downward turn, it's not even a straightening, what it needs. Even the child—for once even Jill admits I'm right. Right in his office, in front of the mirror, I put my finger right on the point where it needs . . . Just right there, I said. You see the difference?

You must be crazy, he said. I would not touch that nose, it is an *excellent* nose. But don't you think just . . . I still had my

18

finger pressing it, you'd think I was ringing for the elevator—
and Jill is in tears all of a sudden. No! he shouts at me, I
definitely do not think. What I think is you should take home
your daughter and not waste any more of her time, or mine.
Can you imagine? Right in front of the child.

Rummaging in her bag for the other mirror, the magnifying
one, Elly's hand brushed against the long crisp envelope from
Horace T. Ambruster, Headmaster: "Regret to report that
despite all our hopes, Jason is showing no improvement whatever this term. That in fact his performance has deteriorated
in several key areas, so much so that the faculty is forced to
admit that St. Stephen's has apparently failed Jason . . ." (none
of the schools ever put it the other way any more; that was nice)
". . . and would she and Mr. Berliner arrange to come as soon
as possible, in view of . . ."

A good military school, Elly's husband Ralph had insisted,
arguing on the phone with Jason's father, Ted Birnbach. Jason
needs that kind of discipline, Ralph said. But for once Ted
agreed with Elly. Military school seemed so . . . well, passé. But
maybe Ralph was right.

Jason had gone to boarding schools since he was nine. It
seemed to make more sense for a boy than a governess. Ted
didn't even seem to want the kid in the summer, after all the
legal fuss he'd made. Typical. And then Elly was . . . between
marriages. And, well, Admiral Farragut Academy—the name
even sounded like a salute. A lovely green campus all neatly
trimmed and fresh-smelling like the boys' hair. Parade grounds
and bugle calls and tightly tucked blankets. Jason had gotten
to be such a pig, his underwear lying around in figure-eight-
shaped rolls with brown streaks in the middle. He must do that
deliberately, to keep her from ever setting foot in his room. But
a brilliant pianist, she knew that. Incredible talent for a boy of

19

fifteen; it almost frightened her. Must take him to some top musical person who can tell if he's actually a genius. In which case maybe a military school wouldn't—though what if Admiral Farragut had a marvelous music department?

"What's that snide smile for, Mai? Look at her; she's had that smirk on for five minutes."

"Was I?" Sweetly. "Can't even slip a smile past Alison, can we? Anyway, nothing. Just thinking about the party. And yours, Alison, the other night, was so divine. But Frieda . . . I can't get over her leaving that open Kotex box in your bathroom. And I started to put it away before I realized."

"What Kotex box?" Alison fidgeted. "I haven't the faintest idea what she's talking about."

Mai released one of her mischievous giggles, floating it like a trial balloon. "I should have guessed right away—she left it there on purpose. A fanatic housekeeper like Frieda? Oh, Alison, come *on;* only Frieda would dream up a number like that. An open Kotex box. She wanted to tell the company what a little girl you still are!" More giggles, bubbling and foaming now. "In case any eligible male who wandered in there had the slightest doubt!"

Alison blinked defensively, like a child ducking a water-pistol fight. She couldn't quite decide how to arrange her face; which feature to use, to register which emotion. Celine was laughing so hard that her mascara had begun to sting in the corners, and Elly, struggling against the laughter, had given herself hiccups. Alison finally settled on a stiff upper smile, teeth decently covered.

"What a cute thing for a maid to do, though!" Celine gasped finally, dabbing her clotted lashes with a wet napkin.

"Frieda hates to be called a maid," Mai replied dryly, making it sound like a paid political announcement. "Every time

20

I phone Alison and Frieda answers, I have to hear the full run-down on what she goes through there that no maid in the world would put up with, and would I mind telling her why she stays when she could get a job where somebody would appreciate it once in a while. That housekeeper in *Rebecca*—what was her name, Mrs. Danforth? Judith Anderson, that's right. Only if you could picture Judith Anderson being a Jewish mother on top of everything else—Danvers, that's it—you'd get Frieda. Almost. Am I right, Alison, or not?"

"Alison calls her a maid," Celine said in an injured tone.

"Of course she does," said Mai triumphantly. "Alison would call Judith Anderson a maid."

They all laughed again, so Alison kept her pinched smile in place, like a pair of dyed-to-match dancing slippers that couldn't be exchanged.

"I bet Judith Anderson would quit, though," Elly said, having finally decided it was safe to play. "Can you imagine Frieda leaving Alison? She can hardly stand to take her Sunday off, she's so worried whether Alison can survive till Monday."

Alison never knew what to do when they kidded her, except to argue back in deadly, interminable earnest, like an elderly trial lawyer. "I don't know why you have to exaggerate," she began. "So what if Frieda is conscientious? After twelve years why shouldn't she be? She takes her days off like any normal maid—like anyone. Only if I'm not going out, she fixes me something on a plate and leaves it. What's wrong with that? So all I have to do is turn the light on under the coffee. And last week, that reminds me, there was no—she *forgot* to make coffee. When I turned it on, the whole pot burned, almost started a fire, you should have heard the knockdown fight we had Monday. She's screaming at *me*, can you imagine? Why don't I look in the damn pot! she says. Did you ever hear anything so ridiculous? I wouldn't even know how to take the lid off. I was so nervous by the time I got to my office. Sometimes my nerves, I tell you it's as bad as having a husband . . ." She laughed quickly, in case that sounded peculiar. But nobody was listening.

"I still don't know what to wear Thursday," Elly said. "I wish I liked myself better in pants. Every time I put on pants I end up taking them right off."

"So *that's* why she does that," Mai murmured.

"Hmm?" Alison didn't get it. Alison never got anything smutty. It was a point of pride, like not having had sexual relations in the ten years since her divorce.

What makes you think Chad Batchelder won't be more trouble than it's worth, she was already thinking darkly. They all are, it's beginning to look like. Elliot Nadler, anyone would throw in the sponge after that. Palm Beach millionaire with an only son who never leaves his side. Why wasn't I suspicious? I mean, why wouldn't it *dawn* on me to be suspicious? The boy is seventeen, the father never remarried, I just thought it's natural for them to be close, with no mother. After all. Who starts right out thinking something is abnormal? A rich, attractive widower with a son that age. I think I even mentioned it to him once, how refreshing it was to see such a wholesome kind of relationship for a change, between a father and son. Compared to what's going on in so many families these days. I don't even remember who started that story—how strange that they were always traveling together. That Elliot dragged the boy to every party, that he never lifted a finger to introduce him to people his own age, to girls. And that he had no plans to send the boy to college. Maybe the boy didn't *want* to go to college, I said. I was so annoyed. Maybe Elliot couldn't get him into a top college, is there a law that he has to send him to some third-rate . . . It's not as if the boy needs a degree to get a job, I mean Elliot must own twenty-six newspapers. But what are you driving at? Until finally somebody said I think the boy is a pansy. Something queer about them both. It must have been Mai who told me—yes, I can still hear that little sniff of hers at the other end of the phone. Like a tic, after every sentence, so you know her lip is curling a thousand miles away.

Not that Mai was the only one. All of a sudden, in fact, it got to be the favorite topic. Wherever I went somebody was dying to fill me in. That the boy Ricky wasn't even his son; Elliot had adopted him at the age of twelve and *trained* him to be a deviate. (To herself Alison still pronounced it devi-eight, though Mai corrected her every time she said it out loud.) A couple of fairies living together impersonating a father and son. All right, I should have seen it myself, should have seen *something*. The boy did look . . . well, soft. And no color in his face, unhealthy, like a prison pallor. Nobody in Palm Beach looks like that. Elliot himself looks like an ad for Palm Beach on color television. And what about the pinky ring—platinum with a big star sapphire—What kind of a normal seventeen-year-old wears a ring like that? He was polite too; I remember Frieda couldn't get over it. Even his voice was soft and pale—not that he ever said anything. But there I was arguing with the whole world. I don't *agree* with you, I said. I know a million pansies, I can *always* tell. Jealous, I thought. Spiteful gossip. Until the two of them disappeared. A whole month it's this big romance—and then pouf. Batman and Robin. Nobody even knew if they went back to Palm Beach. I can't think of one person who didn't call up to ask what happened. Of course, I have to say, of *course* I knew all along.

Like Celine, Alison hated to be laughed at. The Nadler fiasco had horrified her mostly because so many people knew how naïve she had been. It was so important to maintain dignity and other people's respect. To know that the elevator men never talked about her, that Frieda was the only maid in the laundry room who never had a spicy story to tell about the madam. The only tidbits Frieda could offer were the dates of birth of her madam and the other Lowen sisters, their husbands and ex-es, and their husbands' ex-es, and theories about why Alison was the only one who couldn't seem to get herself married a second time in spite of all Frieda's efforts.

It was a difficult question, though Frieda was sure she knew at least half the answer. "Your mother," she would scold Jill in the kitchen, "doesn't know how to play up to a man. Look how she keeps them waiting for dinner. A man is entitled to get fed up."

"Oh, is that ever not it," Jill would reply, groaning with pubescent disgust.

"Then what, you tell me, you're so smart from private school."

"It's a waste of time," Jill would say, but she sort of liked philosophizing over Frieda's head. Eating incredibly sugary pineapple upside-down cake that was supposed to be for supper, and picking surreptitiously at her face, which stared at her greasily from the kitchen knife. "My mother should never have got married to begin with. All she ever needed was a tuxedo. An inflatable tuxedo! That would fold up small enough to go in her evening bag. Prop it up on the seat next to her and nobody'd ever know. Except she'd probably forget how to blow it up."

Frieda didn't understand that kind of talk; she only knew it was fresh. "That's how they teach you in private school, to talk fresh about your mother?"

"What mother?" Jill would retort cleverly, and Frieda would have to clatter dishes so as not to hear that.

Like most lonely young daughters of glittering, distant

women, Jill constantly squinted up at Alison, searching for her source, making small, incomplete discoveries. She was quite right about Alison's inability to discern any appreciable difference between a husband and a properly attired male dinner companion—or, for that matter, between a male dinner companion and any other evening accessory. But it had never occurred to Jill that her mother might know all about the differences. That maybe she only pretended not to.

Nude on her massage table, with the Baroness, her masseuse, kneading away the flaccidity, Alison was aware of her body as one is aware of the silver needing attention. Except for these thirty minutes of truth three times a week, she was aware only of her *figure*. Unlike other women, studying their naked selves with thoughtful worried eyes, conjuring silently the judgment of lovers or potential lovers. How does he see this; would he like the shape of this; is it all right for nipples to be so pale; I wonder if the stretch marks show in lamplight. And the coarse hair; in novels the heroine always has silken hair, even there . . .

Alison would study her nude reflection, censoring it like a lurid advertisement that must be cleaned up before her retina would consider printing it. When you hold a kitten up to a mirror and say see the pussycat, it will stubbornly refuse. Stares right at it and won't acknowledge it. What pussycat?

Alison was acutely conscious of the lines, though: midriff, waist, upper hip, derrière, female anatomy as dissected by *Vogue*. If the girdle pushed a roll of flesh beyond its established border, Alison would notice that. And report it at once to the Baroness: this needs attention.

The Baroness did have a whole name when she first came —Erica von der Nordestern—but Frieda saw no point in wasting all that time on a woman who went around giving massages. Every time she arrived, Frieda would announce "the Baroness" loudly, with a disdainful sneer, so Alison would know that at least *she* was not taken in for a minute.

The Baroness had a lush but solid figure. Incongruous—a Rubens model who jogs. She wore a starchy white uniform and carried a black satchel like a lady doctor. It contained a golden wax depilatory which gave a very smooth finish to the legs but took forever because of having to be slowly heated before application, and then having to dry while the Baroness sipped coffee, making sour critical faces because no one made Viennese coffee here, and describing between sips the current fatty deposits of her other elegant clients. Alison didn't have the patience—she had enough trouble spacing appropriate "Reallys" and "Mm-hmms" during Frieda's monologues—and she couldn't stand the pain when the dried wax was peeled off.

Nude on her narrow slab of a massage table, flesh puddling off the small-boned frame. The victim, not criminally assaulted, still at the morgue pending positive identification.

Alison had redone her bedroom twice in the years since Bob Landau had moved out. The first time she had merely tidied up after him—reupholstering the dual headboard in a marvelous creamy-gray heavy satin, with a matching king-size spread and great swooping tieback drapes. The second time, two years later, she'd gotten rid of the two beds (one of them was just taking up room, after all) and found a single monastically slender antique cot, perhaps two inches wider than the massage table. The quintessence of feminine with its white dust ruffle and canopy, according to the glossy photographs in three magazines. Like the cocoon of a glowing pre-debutante, swaddled in crisp chintz with immense cabbage roses swagged across the huge windows. The quintessence of feminine, designed for single occupancy. No man entering Alison's boudoir ever failed to understand, though Alison surely didn't mean to imply . . . It had only seemed sensible, it made the room larger, and

26

it didn't look so . . . incomplete, as if it were frankly waiting for a second husband to materialize. In which case she could always do the room over again, couldn't she?

Alison had no theories of her own as to why one hadn't materialized by now. While her sisters seemed to have no trouble going through one after another. In a way that made it easier to rationalize: My sisters show no discrimination until after the fact. I guess I'm just a perfectionist. It was impossible to imagine her married to an Ira Wolf, for instance. A jaunty little press agent whom Mai had beached in the Hamptons two summers ago. They had managed to peel him quickly out of his seaweeds—impossible iridescent silk blazers; nubby pink slacks—and to make him public relations director for all the Lowen stores, but Alison still considered him the kind of catch you toss quickly back, not the kind you clean up, hoist on its tail and pose with.

Like most press agents, Ira had an incurable case of name-dropsy, but he would never simply *say* the names. Instead he trickled them out of his pockets in a silent Xeroxed stream of coy press releases—WOLF HOWLS, he called them—about himself and his clients, now including the family, whom he dubbed his Lowen-laws. (The New York store he persisted in calling Alison Lowenland.) No one ever shook Ira's hand and came away without a fistful of assorted HOWLS. People who knew better than to shake hands but stood within ten feet of him would find at least a CRY WOLF! calling card in their pockets when they got home. It was remarkable that his pockets didn't bulge any more, but Mai had the suits specially made. He still wore pointy-toed lizard shoes with tassels and talked very fast, as if he were taping messages for his telephone recorder, but after two years of marriage to Mai, he had begun to lapse into abrupt silences, and once in a while a stranger would feel his hand fumbling in a pocket, creating some embarrassment. Even the pointy shoes looked blunted—squashed, as if someone had done it deliberately. No, definitely not Alison's idea of a husband. Not even in the old days.

Ned Greenstone, on the other hand, was not squashable, even if Celine had ever been so inclined. But Alison found Ned's defects infinitely more serious. The vulgarity, for one. He was one of the few men who could look uncouth in white tie. Heavy blue-black jaws hanging like dirty storm clouds over the custom-made ninety-dollar dress shirt. Oil-slick hair, and what her daughter Jill called Siamese eyebrows—inseparably joined in the middle.

As for Elly's current husband, Ralph Berliner, Alison would say he was certainly more pleasant than the last one. Which would mean that were he not married to her sister, he would be the kind of man Alison could never remember having just been introduced to. "I only know what I'm not looking for," she was fond of saying. I'll try again when there's more of a selection.

The one husband Alison had picked, Robert Landau, had at least been memorable. Attractive and even moderately rich in his own right. His family owned a fair-sized commercial laundry business in Cleveland. For a change even Papa had approved, though Alison was very young and Landau was still at Columbia. Lowen had not approved when Alison had her first abortion, but he hadn't interfered. After all, there was certainly plenty of time to start a family, and since Alison had her heart so set on learning the retailing business first.

The second time, however, Papa forbade it, Landau refused to make the arrangements, and Alison decided to take care of it herself with a sterilized knitting needle. It would have been all right except that she punctured the uterine wall and nearly died of peritonitis. The following year Jill was conceived and Alison reluctantly had her.

Bob Landau consummated his marriage with Alison perhaps a dozen times altogether. Each time, like the first, came as an unpleasant surprise to both of them. He finally stopped trying sometime in the middle of the fourth year.

Before marriage, Alison had no clear notions about sex at all, and her fantasies were based on old movie close-ups. Two perfectly made-up faces meeting with shiny closed lips and eyes, and then parting carefully so that nothing smeared. One did not see the bodies, just as she did not see hers (perhaps that was how she had learned to do that). Paul Henried would hardly think of asking a woman to open her lips or eyes, or to put her hand on parts of him that were not to be released by RKO.

Before marriage, Bob Landau hadn't thought of asking for that kind of thing either. He took Alison dancing and to movies or to visit stiffly with relatives, and there were the requisite number of well-dressed firmly closed Paul Henried kisses in front of the elevator with the cab waiting. But then the wedding night. Not that he demanded much of her; he was only slightly less ignorant than she. It was just that how could such an activity itself ever be anything but ugly? *Ugly.* Even in the dark there was no way not to be aware of the dark curly hairs everywhere—chest, arms, legs, even tufts on his shoulders— that made the skin in between so ghastly white. A frightful fleshy mass of strange clumsy shapes slung carelessly under the torso, the way flounces or bows are tacked onto cheap dresses. Alison remembered male deities in classic white marble, the pubic ringlets neatly carved in tiny new-moon crescents, lapping neatly one over the other like waves at low tide. And the . . . organs themselves, almost poignant, so roundly nestled in the smooth stone foliage. But this . . . collection of his bore no resemblance; how could it possibly be the prototype. Unappetizing vegetable stew, he offered her. Grayish pink, flopping,

pinned on, like a dead orchid corsage. And erect, rudely pointing, swaying slightly as if it must be too heavy without some
sort of additional support. Not . . . well *designed*. Not orderly.
A woman's organs are at least folded up and put away. Even
in use, they don't tumble out sloppily like dirty clothes from
a drawer. There must be some mistake.

Mostly Alison thought that how she felt about it was right.
That other women must be lying, pretending not to find it
horrid—pretending for obvious reasons. She could well understand why: to please a husband who pleased them in other
important ways. A rich, indulgent husband. Or to make such
a husband out of a rich, indulgent lover. Some women are
willing to . . . compromise, to close their inner eyes only, so
desperate must they be not to be alone.

But it was better to be alone, Alison was quite sure. If other
women were really honest about it, they'd see it just as she did.
Though in some ways, she would concede, for some women the
compromise was unavoidable. And perhaps for some the price
was not quite so high. There are men who respect, who don't
force their . . . needs on a woman. Men who can if necessary
curb such needs because the woman means more to them. She
had certainly heard of marriages where this was clearly understood.

And what about the husbands who chase after other women,
didn't that prove something? About their wives feeling the
same way she did? That was *exactly* what it proved. The wives
didn't even mind if the . . . problem had to be handled that
way. Or knew enough to pretend they didn't mind, which
seemed a sensible arrangement, she thought. Wasn't that what
went on in European marriages? Where the wife obviously
makes it clear she would prefer not to . . . indulge that particular appetite of his, and if he is unable to curb it. Or unwilling
—mostly it must be unwilling, because Alison could not really

believe that a man was physically *unable* to control himself. Some men, though, apparently can't, or say they can't. Anyway, a civilized compromise. The only time it would get out of hand was in a case where the husband might be carried away. Where it was allowed to become something more important than fanny-pinching. Or else if some . . . dame decided to make trouble, to use a man's weakness for her own selfish purposes. There were plenty of women like that—unscrupulous. Alison would say it boiled down to a matter of maturity. People in this country were still very immature, for the most part; in spite of our technical brilliance, there were certain things Americans hadn't yet learned as a race.

On Jill's last birthday Alison had of course invited Bob Landau to dinner. At one point when the child was out of the room, they were talking about themselves, and Alison had impulsively asked, "Do you think you've matured these past years? I mean, enough to understand a woman like me?"

"God, no," Bob replied, smiling. "Thank God, no."

It's starting again, Elly realized, squirming against the warm sudden rush of blood. Primordial ooze, which still astonished her every time, as if by never stocking up on sanitary napkins she might prevent it from ever happening again. Be unprepared. And so she was forever getting the curse in movie theaters or stores, and once when she was seventeen at a boys' school dance, that awful snaky crawl of thick wet warmth down the inside of her thigh. In a mauve organdy formal, and she knew there was nothing anywhere to stop it with, and what if she sat down; she couldn't possibly sit down, or else. Keep dancing like the ballerina in *The Red Shoes*. If there was a machine, it was empty; if there was a drugstore, it was closed. And every time she'd have to settle for stiff john paper wadded up crunchily in her underwear, maybe Kleenex if she was lucky, and walking funny in halting steps to keep it from sliding sideways, hoping desperately nobody could tell. And what if it already showed in back, she would have to ask a friend, whispering the awful confession, the plea, the question: "I'm leaking! Walk behind me, can you *see* anything?"

Yet she never learned, never remembered when it might strike again, never believed that it had to, because every time it was over she was absolutely sure it was a mistake, that it had only happened this time through some ghastly clerical error and wasn't addressed to her at all. And the next time she would be crushed all over again, truly crushed, as if someone she trusted had somehow betrayed her. Her body, which had promised so many times to be immune, was the Judas within. Joan of Arc never got the curse; why do I have to?

Elly had had a contraceptive loop implanted three years ago, and never once bothered to check whether it was still in place. Blithely, doggedly ignoring the doctor's whole careful speech about how to feel for the tiny green plastic threads, because if you didn't find them, there was a chance the loop had slipped out. Since she'd been wearing it, the periods of bleeding had begun to last longer and longer, and seemed to come more and more often. Ralph finally complained angrily that she was *always* getting it now, and what the hell good was a contraceptive that only worked because you couldn't lay a hand on your wife for twenty-five out of thirty days? He thought it was supposed to help their sex life; some help. Okay, she didn't have to mess with the diaphragm she hated so much, and okay, she was afraid of the pill business, but bleeding like a stuck pig was an improvement? In the old days he hadn't minded screwing her during her period; there was hardly any mess. She used to try to hold onto the Tampax string, like a child with a precious kite. Fist clenched tight around it, shielding it with her body, don't let go, otherwise he'll end up driving it all the way in. And tomorrow she'd have to fish for it with her whole hand, with a flashlight and a mirror, terrified that it was swimming around someplace disintegrating in the wrong pipe, probably wrecking the whole plumbing system. And what the hell would he care.

Today was not like a normal period though; it was worse. Carefully she got up to go to the ladies' room, trying not to walk that way, trying to sail past the iron matron with her dish of three cemented quarters, as if she didn't really need to use any salmon-pink metal cubicle but was just passing through. Carefully selecting the one on the end because it had one solid wall that went all the way down. The floor was dry, thank God. She took off everything, hanging it all up on the one measly hook, and scrunched down on the freezing tile, bracing against the solid wall, feet up on the opposite side. Must be careful to place the shoes facing front so that anyone in the next booth glancing down would assume there were feet in them—unless they leaned way down. Surely only a very snoopy person would lean way down, to check the label.

Elly sighed and began to clean up with the rotten little squares of stiff john paper. She felt very tired of fighting everything—husbands, sisters, child, self. She was hungry too; she hated tomatoes. She wasn't even fat, hadn't been fat in years. Some people thought she was painfully thin. Painful it was, but there was no choice. She weighed exactly ninety-six pounds, as a matter of principle. Besides tomatoes, she ate lean meat and skinned chicken, drank only champagne, and weighed herself nervously three times a day. She had bad dreams about gaining weight, about waking up to find that her face and body had reverted to their old selves, with age lines superimposed upon the baby fat, radiating from the pre-surgery nose and the uncorrected bite. She was hysterically self-conscious, breaking out in beads of sweat if she had to fill out a confidential cosmetics questionnaire. "Age——. Enlarged Pores——. Acne as a teenager——. Occasional blackheads——. Oiliness or pimples during menstrual period——. Fine lines around eyes——. *Deep* lines?" She also panicked if her hairdresser noticed brittle ends or dry scalp. Obsessed with mirrors, she derived no pleasure from them, but confronted her reflection in any surface as if it were an enemy in ambush waiting to destroy her. Store windows, salt shakers, silverware, automobile bodies, other people wearing sunglasses.

Sometimes Elly looked into people's eyes so carefully that they became uneasy, wondering what on earth. But she was only searching the surface for reassurance. For confirmation of her worst fears. Anti-narcissist: one who loathes her own image and can face nothing else. If Narcissus wasted away from unsatisfied desire, how could the gods possibly punish Elly? In the ladies' room she closed her eyes again, waiting for there to be a little less of everything.

Two

CHAD HEARD the telephone from the third-floor landing, but with two more flights to go, he decided the hell with it. There was a time, not all that long ago either, when he had relished this little challenge, leaping at the signal like a second-string player whose team is in trouble. Lately he had begun to consider this reflex in a more sensible light—something akin to old men shoveling snow off their sidewalks or dutifully mounting, if not surmounting, their wives twice a week. Two wrongs making a conjugal right.

He still took the steps briskly two at a time, however. If one did that routinely, he believed, one exerted just enough stress to wind up the old . . . ticker . . . without busting . . . any essential springs.

Once upstairs, one cracked the *Christian Science Monitor* with a double chaser of Johnnie Walker Black. A mixture not specifically recommended by the makers of either product, but Chad thought that in cases where one couldn't quite draw the requisite comfort from the one without the other, it was more than likely they would both understand. A certain strength, he would argue cheerfully, lies in giving in to one's essential weaknesses. And in giving in to them, when necessaary, without a debilitating struggle.

The pile of unread *Monitors* on the mahogany humidor was a little high, though—nearly a week's worth. Whereas the level of Scotch in the bottle indicated he was somewhat ahead of schedule there. Frowning, he eased off the loafers and used a long-handled pigskin shoehorn to slide into the crewel-embroidered opera slippers his last wife had lovingly needled. As she had him. As they all had him, eventually. He sighed. It always took about four years to become unbearable. A cyclical phenomenon, like menses or federal elections. Not a bad rhythm if one understood it beforehand, and thus approached each assignment intelligently, like a career ambassador preparing for a series of sensitive posts. No career ambassador disposes of his permanent residence, for example, upon being named envoy to Kuala Lumpur. He has absolutely nothing against Kuala Lumpur, you understand, never having been there, but at the same time he'd be a fool to plan on remaining there on more than an interim basis. One hopes, one is entitled, to home leave before being . . . reassigned.

Which was why keeping this apartment, this two-room sanctuary, had always made the essential difference. Having your return ticket in the strongbox along with your passport; flight guaranteed in case an outbreak of hostilities. A fifth-floor walk-up in an unchic but eminently affordable East Midtown location. Most of the women he married made the pilgrimage here once, just to check it out for signs of sin, corruption, undeclared income, whatever. And they were invariably reassured, he knew, by the solid, frayed-elbow ambience, the honest, expensive smell of his specially blended Dunhill tobacco. Comfy old bachelor disarray—exactly the right degree of mess (proving that he really did need a woman's care) without a speck of basic dirt (proving that he was not *au fond* just some species of unwashed bohemian). There wasn't an insidious or seductive accessory in the place; no suede divans, light dimmers, zebra-skin rugs. And no sexually suspect touches either—those carefully dusted, exquisitely arranged groupings of crystal obelisks or baby-deer antlers that were always such dead giveaways in a tasteful masculine penthouse.

No conscious style of any kind. Nobody ever realized that this was precisely the point. It was supposed to be just a rather drab but cozy little place owned and operated in an offhand way by an authentic male person—the sort of man who would fill it with just such slightly rumpled, quality merchandise according to no particular design. Each thing belonging there only because it must have pleased him. One could tell he had read all those books, heard all those records, and was fond of them. That he burned genuine logs in the genuine fireplace and put his genuine feet up to warm them. Still, there was something not quite . . . well, sincere.

Possibly just the purposeful anonymity of it. The eclectic furniture, eclected over many lives and now brought together not in harmony but in guarded peace. The entirely too easy chair covered in worn real leather with a defiantly unmatching footstool. Algonquin Hotel-lobby warmth, pretending not to be the sort of air you put on, but the kind you breathe. Perhaps it only seemed so. Or was meant to seem so.

Anyway, each of his ladies would make the one visit and be relieved. He would charbroil a steak for her in the fire, and she would fold herself up uncomfortably on the sofa whose cushions had the punished look of people who have lost a great deal of weight on doctor's orders.

She would always appreciate the special flavor, chewing the burned part carefully in case the middle really turned out to be raw. And he would make her listen to Bach or some scratchy vintage jazz, she growing fidgety and glassy-eyed with heroic attempts to make realistic smiles out of yawns. And finally he would take her someplace more her style.

She would never visit him there again. Every time he married, there was at first a tussle about his giving up that dreary little place, which *They* would obviously never have any use for. With Barbara he would be moving out of the city, in fact— to Bucks County, her lovely estate. And though of course they'd be coming into town for theater and things, this would hardly . . . Not even a closet for her to hang anything in, and the bathroom . . . Surely he could see how impossible . . .

Still, he would argue gently, for me, for my things. I don't want to clutter our home with all that tired old . . . It's enough that you let me clutter it with my tired old self.

But darling—

Ah, I've lived with it all so long, sweets. How can I consign all those years to the sanitation man. *You* understand, dearest. Most women wouldn't, but *you*. And I promise, scout's honor, I shan't even trouble our help to come clean it. Call it my closet. Where I keep my . . . skeleton.

All right, my poor sentimental love, but then she would— Barbara and Elaine would, anyway—want to pay the place another duty call. Barbara suggested bringing her maid up from

38

Bucks County to give it one good going-over, but he put his foot down at that. Just if you insist, darling, in going over it yourself, though I can't imagine why you bother. Well, she thought just in case he might feel like bringing a favorite chair or something along. Books . . . she hadn't really exam—— looked at everything all that carefully. And his wardrobe, she certainly ought to go over his wardrobe.

And so there would be a careful search, to confirm that there were absolutely no mementos of other . . . assignments. Curiously, she would not find a single photograph, letter, shred of forgotten lingerie, not a stray bobby pin or Tampax in the medicine chest. Odd, considering the multiplicity of pasts. Not even a trace of Chad as a child—snapshots of parents, brother, the home in Wichita, class rings, school yearbooks. But none of them was ever bothered by this. They found it somehow flattering, as if it proved he had sprung full-grown from their foreheads.

The drawers of the desk were crammed with clippings from the *Christian Science Monitor*, all neatly scissored, no hastily torn edges. An informal collection of reasoned arguments for living more sanely, more in truth, from now on. All very Mary Baker Eddifying. Amos Lowen would not have liked the smell of it, Chad was well aware. Amos would have had him investigated, and the report would have been none too satisfactory. Thirty-two shaky thousand a year, hardly impressive, possibly not even passing, packaging TV shows. Well, maybe if he had his own agency. Still, iffy, and that would demand a damn sight more ambition. No, not *more* ambition, come to think of it, just not his sort.

Bucks County had had its points. The dogs alone, great shaggy beasts yelping and bounding at his heels. Shetland tweeds and servants to pour the Johnnie Walker. On the other hand, Barbara . . .

Alison Lowen was as far a cry from Barbara as he could imagine, within his by now well-defined marital boundaries. A city girl, this one; a career woman, but equally sleek, equally self-possessed. His women seemed always to have floated smoothly to the cool bright surface of some private, well-stocked artificial lake. To have beckoned him, each at a precisely right moment. Alison Lowen was even the precisely right age—just past, but not noticeably, his own. And well wrapped, as they had all been, in furs or other richly insulating materials, to ward off any sudden extreme of emotional climate.

The Lowen landscape was well charted; he had been there several times, yet he still found it exotic. It still delighted him that he could speak the language fluently, yet that no one would ever take him for a native. It was a preposterously unreal place where, ironically, the natives were always more lost than the tourists. Chad could still tell himself that he pursued such unreal worlds in order to conquer them from within. A Christian Scientist never merely ignores the unrealities of sickness and sin. He overcomes them, he *forsakes* them. God knew Chad had forsaken them, but as with the Johnnie Walker Black, not quite yet on a permanent basis.

He sighed again and tried to picture Alison Lowen's puzzled face when she came to call on him here. That could be, he guessed, quite soon. He hadn't even thought about remarrying until the moment he saw her in the restaurant. Though it was high time.

Elly much preferred other people's parties, especially if there was some kind of lively music—not a piano particularly, but one of those one-man-band contraptions that looked ridiculous until the musician plugged himself in and everything went off like rockets, beating and pumping, kissing and stroking and throbbing, rhythm and blues and drums and horns and gypsy violins. Then she could kick off her sparkly rhinestone heels to dance, holding the glass of swirly champagne in one hand and the hem of her swirly chiffon skirt in the other. Gathering it way up in soft folds as if she were going wading in very deep, on tiptoe between the ridges of the carved carpeting, so that her legs would flash long and silky-nude in the pink party light. Eyes closed under the long fur lashes; auburned, softly set curls tangling—The Barefoot Contessa through sheer sandal-toe nylons. At such times she could dance past a mirror without seeing anything wrong. The others would all stand back and clear a little magic circle, and clap the rhythm for her and love how she moved because she was the gayest and freest with just a little music and one glass of champagne. Wonderful that she could feel so . . . intoxicated.

Whereas at her own parties it always took so much longer to begin dancing, and so much more champagne. Even then she had to concentrate, humming the lyrics carefully to herself to drown out the nervous sense of being responsible for everything, and of so many things that were probably going wrong over there and there and God knows what they were doing in the kitchen. Grease spot on the bartender's rented satin lapel, and the wrong flowers on the piano, half of them dead even before the guest of honor arrived. Trite little canapés; they charged twice as much for shrimp and so she'd ordered shrimp and they were perfectly all right except that no one ever noticed what she served. It seemed so . . . dinky. Meaningless dry or soggy little nonsense that everyone else had gotten tired of serving hundreds of parties ago—why was it she never could catch up?

Tonight all the usual disasters had already happened; one of the bartenders wasn't even coming and her husband had called to say he'd be late, naturally, and the masses of pale yellow instead of coppery-gold pompons had been stuffed brutally into one small bowl, so that all the stems were crushed and dozens of their tiny grief-stricken heads were bowing over the glass walls. Somebody had neglected to polish the big silver platter, there was no parsley around anything, the quiche was just plopped on a tray without paper-lace doilies under it and there were scrawled messages all over the telephone pad that made absolutely no sense. "I'm going in to lie down," Elly announced in too high a voice to the scurrying black uniforms in the pantry. Bugs or nuns. Why did it have to smell so terrible in there? They always seemed to be cooking something that she couldn't possibly have ordered. "I don't want to be disturbed until six. *Six.*"

She fled into her silvery bedroom where the mirrors met in corners repeating all her secrets. Undressing as fast as she could to avoid having to rivet attention on certain figure problems, but then noticing anyway, watching herself shivering and dropping things, watching herself sneak under the pink velvet spread as if someone were about to catch her skinny-dipping.

Until this bleeding business Elly had loved her late-afternoon nap. Lying naked under the velvet caressing her own naked sleepy velvetness. Or sometimes for a change on the smooth satin chaise longue which was not longue enough to quite lie down, so she would doze reclining. Olympia by Manet with a hand delicately poised between the thighs—and a Negro maid barging in with the flowers. Elly always took a long-handled mirror to bed. She liked to study her breasts, holding the mirror so that she could see them from underneath, like pink minarets. Onion spires on a Turkish cathedral. Mosqued balls.

The mirror was so fundamental. Using it should be considered a bodily function. There should be reflective nail polish so that one could be less obtrusive performing it. One had to make do with rings and bracelets or the distortion of table silver, windows in cars or trains which could not be expected to give any sort of accurate accounting. Elly traveled with fingers resting lightly on a small silver-backed mirror inside her handbag. Her aide and discomfort; her personal misfortune teller.

Before the bleeding business she had watched herself like this every afternoon, masturbating herself to sleep, such a nice deep sleep in which telephones always rang but never interrupted the thread of the dream. There was always some way to work it into the dream.

Sarah. She would dream about Sarah. Sarah Saxon who majored in physics and so was always curled over her desk in her pitch-dark room except for the dusty cone of light from the gooseneck lamp. Curled over her books, with her smooth cap of Prince Valiant blue-black hair lying thick and glossy like a horse's mane, a solid curtain of hair that Alison would never approve of. It hung heavily down the sides of her angular Indian-looking face until it veered inward, sloping like a tentative smile, a gentle low arc cupping her chin. Elly could never understand why she found that so beautiful, the way Sarah's hair hung, especially since she had always, until Sarah, believed that girls' hair should consist of long gold separate curving strands, twisting to catch the sun. Elly had never even followed the Prince Valiant comic strip; she thought the characters talked too much in the balloons, though they were all beautiful. She had always known that was how people should look.

And Sarah did. Even her golden olive skin, even her rounded shoulders, even her cowboyish slouch and the wide pale mouth that was not designed to wear lipstick—the whole face became strange and ugly under lipstick, as if the mouth had swallowed all the other features. Sarah wore glorious beat-up clothes: ancient torn work shirts once her brother's and genuine farmhand jeans genuinely faded from scrubbing with strong yellow soap on a washboard in the dry brown heat of her Tennessee farm. It wasn't really the clothes, it was how she wore them; her body seemed always in the process of shrugging them off. Tennessee farm clothes still smelling of sun and hay and cows that Sarah knew how to milk. Sarah and her brothers, who always cleaned their plates of steaming exotic mixtures. Okran-tomatoes served and pronounced together, and for all Elly knew, grown that way too.

Five o' clock in the morning, an hour that existed nowhere else except on Sarah's Tennessee farm. Sarah reaching under hens to gather warm eggs. Feathers tickling the back of her hand, hay scratching the palm. Animals with soft enormous tongues, lapping. Sarah showering with a garden hose, icy water poured thin and clear over her like any precious tonic with power to cure dirt and thirst and tiredness and the ache for a pure colorless stream of simple joy.

Riding without a saddle, Sarah on a brown satin horse, like a girl centaur, her black mane and his pointing straight behind them, like the teeth of a comb parting the tangled cornfield. All in a beautiful foreign country for which Elly had no visa, and could never get one except in her mind. Yet she could smell and touch the rough-textured truth of it, like Sarah's good coat that her family had selected from the fall mail-order catalog. Picture Sarah in the Better Coats Department at Lowen's. Picture Prince Valiant's hair styled with a compli-mentary make-up on the fourth ("Beauty") floor. Sarah kicking off her pale frayed tissue-thin jeans in the fitting room. A Lowen's saleslady relentlessly zipping her into something "becoming." If you'd only stand up straight, dear.

Ah, no. Not Sarah Saxon. They would never strap gold kid sandals on Sarah's bare brown feet. Sarah would be forever bent over her desk, hair curtaining her face, doing her endless physics homework with a leaky black pen. Left-handed. No one in the whole Lowen family was left-handed; it was unheard of, not allowed, and therefore strange and wonderful, like double-jointedness and noticeable scars.

Elly spent the first eight months of junior college majoring in Sarah Saxon. Sketching her as she worked, writing her name and crossing it out. Copying her loping walk, her terrible posture, trying to look like that in jeans. Nobody else looked like that in jeans. Memorizing her hillbilly records, T. Texas Tyler singing "Dad Gave My, Gave My Dog Away." And then finally—how did it ever finally begin?—sweet sad kisses on Sarah's salty mouth, the salt of Sarah's running tears. Sarah could not believe she was so loved; there could not be such a thing. And trembling Elly tried to explain it to both of them. Sarah clinging to her like a frightened child rescued from drowning in the deep end of a swimming pool. Sarah shuddering, Sarah turning all golden gooseflesh, little-girl unformed breasts and soft moans and silent tears. Beautiful. How is it, how ever can I do this? Elly would wonder. Elly would always wonder. How was it that I could make her feel whatever it was I made her feel? Mystified by her own powers, like a hired magician at a child's birthday party who truly doesn't know where the red silk handkerchief came from, or the blue or the green or the yellow . . . Wonderful, and what does it mean?

If she knew it, Sarah never revealed the answer. She herself did not have the power. At least she never touched Elly with her hands, except to clasp them tight around Elly's neck, while Elly carried her to safety out of the deep end of her pool of tears. Elly never wondered about this; it seemed natural, proper. Sarah was the beautiful one, the valiant; Elly merely was someone whose love had been accepted. Only Sarah's sweet tearful mouth gave kisses; the rest of her received. In June when Sarah graduated, Elly still had not learned what Sarah had received.

She visited Sarah once, in Tennessee, and fed the animals and rode the brown satin horse through the cornfield, and had okrantomatoes for dinner. And slept at night in a narrow single bed with Sarah, hearing the snores of Sarah's thin-lipped father through the wall, and Sarah's Grant Wooden mother sleeping beside him with her hair still in a bun. And Sarah so wide awake under Elly's loving, inexplicably magic touch.

A good girl goes to sleep with her hands *outside* the covers; you must put them there on top like this and now we'll tuck you in. Very nice and snug, with the hands right on top so we can see them.

The governess slept in Elly's room, because she was the youngest. Elly could never fall asleep until the governess did, but she learned at four or five how to make her breathing sound as if she was asleep. Then she could hear forbidden radio programs, and finally roll over and pull the covers out and put her hands underneath, and there. And watch Nanny undress, through barely fluttering, cautious lids. Nanny, who would lock her sobbing in the closet if she caught her, who would wash her face with the underpants she wet in school, wagging her finger and saying *Shame.* Who would give her an enema if she did not move her bowels. In junior college Elly gave herself enemas after meals; lots of girls did. That way you could eat desserts and never gain one ounce, they said. But it didn't seem to work for Elly. By the time the butterscotch puddding worked its way down to where the enema was, the whipped cream topping had already congealed on her hips. Life was measured not in coffee spoons but in fat globules and their rate of travel through her bloodstream. If only one could chew everything once and spit it right out before getting attached to it.

After Sarah there was Millicent, and it was Millicent from

whom Elly at last received what she had given. It was, she discovered, nice to be loved back. Not necessarily *better* to receive, but nice. Both were nice.

Millicent lived in Vermont. Flowered china in cupboards, two dogs and a cat, four-poster beds and wallpaper with tiny designs. Sun through the kitchen window, angel food cake, hobnail chenille bedspreads, thick red rugs and fireplaces that worked all winter. You could hear snow crunch under your feet, and you could run through real woods with the dogs yelping. Every road had legible tracks; one or two sets of snow tires had traveled there before you, so that you knew the trail had been blazed, that some other intrepid traveler had gone first, and that you would surely like him if you met. All gone, poor animals, Millicent had told her the last time they met. Eight years ago? With a low gentle laugh, surprised that Elly should remember all the animals' names. All gone.

And Millicent too. With her blond crunchy curls, blue-china eyes like the flowered dishes. She had always turned her collar up, the points of it sharp and dark against the peachbloom baby face. And a tiny space between the front teeth, to put one's tongue inside her smile and warm it there.

After which Elly got engaged to Ted Birnbach, who said, "I kiss the dollar signs inside your eyes." His mother was a dental technician; his father, a podiatrist. Professionals, but with a very lower case *p*, in Amos Lowen's alphabet.

How much will we be getting for a wedding present? Ted had asked Amos Lowen with what he thought was refreshing candor.

What kind of a question is that? Elly's father had thundered. Who asks such a question?

I didn't mean to be rude, sir, Ted said. Poor Ted had no

idea that nothing he could ever say would undo the damage. I only asked because I . . . because we need to make our plans. For Elly and me.

What I give—*if* I give. Comes after the wedding, if the wedding comes. Nobody makes plans from a gift. In my family nobody makes such plans.

Later Amos confronted his daughter. You love this man, Ella. He said it minus the question mark.

Yes, Father, Elly said, not looking up.

What is in him to explain your love?

It was extremely hard to lie to Amos Lowen. Elly was the poorest at it, flinching at the voice and evading the hollow black eyes that saw precisely what no one wanted them to see, and nothing else. How can I tell him I do not love this man, of course, that I will never love any man more or less than this one? That I will marry him, however, so as to have been married, because one must have been married in order to live as one likes. I will not be the Lowen girl who "never married, you know." "Why do you suppose she never married?" "Hmm." Even Caesar's *ex*-wife would be above suspicion, but not Amos Lowen's unmarried daughter.

So it was to have been very simple. Married, then formerly married. Having been given in marriage and then returned. At Lowen's, merchandise received as a gift is returnable, provided the tag has not been removed. See, Papa, Ted and I have this agreement. We're going to live together for a few months, maybe a year, as man and wife. But only in name, as the saying goes: in *his* name, on *your* money. A simple deal, a simple handshake, like gentlemen or businessmen. And a nominal sum, a wedding check, just to establish good will. That's my end of the bargain—to establish Ted in something. I don't know, he doesn't care really, maybe a Carvel stand at a good location. Who cares what, so long as he can support his awful wedded wife, until a decent interval. And next year, see, I can do as *I* please. Renounce my throne for the womaan I love. Millicent and I think we might like to travel. Maybe buy a little house somewhere—Capri, Raritonga. You could pick the spot yourself, Papa, someplace you'd like to come and visit.

Aloud she had said that of course she loved Ted. Loved his honesty, like a child, so blunt and genuine. A little like you, Papa.

The answer was good, smooth and credible, but Elly looked away too quickly, and Amos noticed only this. I'll not give a wedding check, he replied quietly. Nor a wedding. And he sighed like Solomon wielding his reluctant silver sword to cut the child in twain. Later, of course, Amos had relented, after they'd had Jason for him. But he hadn't relented quite enough, Ted didn't think, which was why they finally had to part so unpleasantly. And by then Millicent was gone, and Elly had begun to make her own kind of uneasy peace with loveless marriages.

The shame of it was that Ted Birnbach was the only husband who ever gave her so precisely what she wanted of him, and that he *wanted* to give her so precisely that—not a penny more or less than her suggested retail price.

It was not one of Elly's most dazzling parties, but then, none of Elly's parties ever was. Somehow Celine found herself trying for nearly an hour to ignore the woman now sitting next to her, a lacquered brunette whose emeralds dropped like tears shed over her declining bosom, or fortunes, or years. Her name was Melba Dee Fox; all the Lowen girls had known her slightly, which was more than enough, for ages; she always seemed to be in Reno or Mexico or the Dominican Republic at the same time they were, as if she set her divorces by theirs.

At first Melba's eyes had been riveted on Celine's neck,

around which hung the terrible weight of her newest piece of jewelry. A fat rope of gold tying up a handful of rubies in lumpy sailor's knots. Amusing. Fifteen thousand, Melba estimated, and the rubies look like used throat lozenges. She switched her attention to Celine's dinner plate. Frowning slightly and occasionally swiveling around to peer at the buffet table, as if to verify her findings. Celine began to wonder uncomfortably if she'd put something in one of the curries, and if so, which.

"How old are you?" Melba demanded suddenly. Startled, Celine dropped a shrimp diavolo in her satin lap. Melba lowered her iridescent lids over the gleam in her eye, like a considerate driver or a veteran basilisk who hardly needs to prove anything more about looks and killing.

"Thirty-six," Celine replied unhappily, retrieving the fallen shrimp. She didn't think Melba would have a constructive suggestion for removing the chutney sauce.

"Oh, come on, honey," Melba exclaimed with an unpleasant chortle.

She was very drunk, Celine realized now, as the face lurched toward her. Could those eyelashes be shot like porcupine quills? "I *am*. Thirty-six." Celine winced at her own voice; she was whining. She daubed again at her lap, as if to wipe away the sound.

"Believe me, dear, I couldn't care less." Melba's lids had rolled back up; the eyes were cobalt-blue, like Tiffany china. Copied from unearthed relics of some ancient, corrupt dynasty. "You never had children, did you?"

"No," Celine said softly, wishing her sister's last decorator hadn't stuck a four-hundred-pound glass cocktail table with dangerous metal corners in front of this sofa. Melba Dee had her carefully wedged in.

"Or a career either—I mean, since you, uh, *retired* from Hollywood?"

"No," she said again, more firmly, sliding, she hoped imperceptibly, toward freedom. "But would you excuse me anyway, I've spilled something—"

"Did you? Well, I happen to know you're *well* over thirty-six." The voice had acquired a cutting edge as sharp as those metal corners.

Celine knew they were attracting a faintly amused audience now. "Look, I'm sorry, really, Melba," she offered, with a winning starletty smile. "I'd love to be older for you, honestly." A helpless glance toward the ring of bored faces now trained on them. Liveliest show in the room. "I only wish I could be fifty, if it would help in any way."

"Mmm," said Melba huskily, closing her eyes again. "Isn't that darling of her?"

There were several responsive snickers. No way to tell for or at whom.

"Well, how old would you settle for—thirty-nine? Forty-three?" Celine hoped she sounded light-hearted now. Think of it as a game.

"Oh, *no!*" Melba shrieked delightedly. "I think thirty-six is *per*fect! I think you do thirty-six mag*nif*icently! I would definitely stick to thirty-six if I were you! My God, thirty-nine! Forth-three! Who on earth would believe that? With *those* rubies?"

The audience roared. Cheeks inflamed, dress sopping, Celine finally excused herself, slicing her knee open with the edge of the table. Melba was fast asleep.

"What time do you think we should call Cathy?" Mai whispered.

Ira was annoyed; she had pulled him away from a well-known baby-food manufacturer who was rumored to be considering a shift in his PR account.

"I mean, I only want to call once; you know how she gets if she thinks we're checking on her. And then I won't sleep again. Remember the last time? With the car? Ira—"

"Crissakes, Mai, you're beginning to sound like a nut yourself. Go call—get it over with! But give me a night off, will you?" Ira shrugged his wife's hand off his suit, patted the pocket with the press releases and elbowed back toward the baby-food account.

Mai started for the bedroom, but Alison intercepted her at the door. "I was just looking for you. I wanted to show you my broadtail coat."

"Yes, Alison, in a minute. I just have to call—"

"I had it shortened and added the silver fox border. Hmm?"

"Yes, it looks—"

"—instead of buying another fur coat this year? Don't you think?"

"Umm, it looks—"

"—wearing so much black lately—" Alison stopped and turned suddenly. "Why do you look so tired, Mai? Every time I see you—"

Mai brushed defensively at her eyes.

"It's not just your *eyes*," Alison snapped, "it's your whole— I mean you've got to do something. This business with Cathy —"

Mai took a deep breath. "What would you suggest?"

"What would *I*? What about the *doctor*? Doesn't he—I thought you had such a marvelous new doctor. I thought he saw a decided improvement." Alison went back to study her own reflection in the mirror. "Where does Elly keep her belts, do you know? In here?"

"I don't know," said Mai. She made a move toward the telephone.

"Oh, here. Look, how do you like it with a belt? I had it shaped so I could wear it belted or not. Hmm?"

"Well—"

"Not with this kind of a belt, though. Obviously. But just to give you the idea. Don't you think?"

"I don't know. Yes. It's all right belted."

"Mmm, but what about the doctor? You didn't answer me."

"I didn't realize you expected—" Mai changed her mind. "Anyway, I don't have an answer. By now every psychiatrist sounds like the last one did just before he gave up. He sees an improvement, I don't know if it's decided or undecided, then the next week, the next *day* sometimes, boom . . . she's back in the hospital. Unconscious. Drunk, stoned . . ." Mai paused. "Nobody ever knows what sets it off; every time it's something else. At least nobody tells *me* what. I never have the slightest *idea* what. You think the doctors know? If they do, I'm the last person they tell. God knows what she says to them. This one, if I dare call him up, he gives me some kind of runaround— it's between him and her, he can't tell me anything without her *permission.* As if it's none of my damn business. As if I—I mean, who does he think sends the checks every month? Don't ask about the checks either. You wouldn't believe what they charge—not that it means anything, what it costs, who would *care* what it costs if they ever got anywhere with her? But like this . . ." Mai trailed off, suddenly embarrassed that Alison might really be listening.

She wasn't, though. She had just been waiting for the pause. "Well, *I* couldn't live with that," she began. "Psychiatrists. I never had any faith—I still say they encourage a person to be weak. It stands to reason, doesn't it? The more helpless she is, the more she needs the psychiatrist?"

Mai picked up one of Elly's brushes and began stroking her

hair, up from the roots, up and out and back to the intricately pinned system of knots. Her arm flew like a veteran bandleader's, caught by its own rhythm, yet so accurate, so controlled, that not one strand of hair ever moved.

"I still say," Alison declared, "she'll snap out of it. Some new clothes, new friends, a *party*—"

"Cathy does not need a party," Mai said coldly, "and God knows *I* don't."

"Then why don't you just sell that apartment you bought her?" Alison flared. "Instead of saddling yourself—"

"And do what with her and the child? Move them in on Ira? He's not nervous enough?" Mai's voice had begun to rise. "We have to build four new storage cabinets for his *pills*."

"Just listen to your voice, Mai, you sound—" But Alison wanted to stop. There were no more belts to try with the coat, and what if Chad Batchelder arrived while she was in here squabbling? She offered Mai her last piece of good advice anyhow. "Get Cathy a competent *maid*, at least."

"Thanks a lot, darling." Mai glared at her sister. "Maybe you'd like to donate *your* maid?"

Alison looked away quickly, in case she was serious, but then felt a small compassionate twinge. Poor Mai was being sarcastic, that was all. "I was only suggesting . . . because I'm more worried about *you* than about Cathy. You say Ira's nervous? Mai, you can't even *discuss*—"

"I don't have to discuss," said Mai very calmly. "*I* came in here to use the phone."

Alison's twinge passed abruptly. "If I were you," she announced, "I'd put that girl in a hospital once and for all. And give the baby to what's-his-name; let *his* mother—"

"*His* mother is almost sixty."

"So what; you're not twenty-two either."

"And 'what's-his-name' doesn't *want* the baby."

"If I were you—"

"Thank you, Alison. I'll think about—"

"—instead of saddling yourself—"

"I said *thank* you." Mai sat on Elly's bed, with her back toward her sister, and began to dial Cathy's number. Alison flung her coat on the bed, not quite grazing Mai with the silver fox border, and stalked out of the room. She broke stride only in front of the last of Elly's bedroom mirrors, to be sure nothing was out of place.

For some reason none of them spotted Chad Batchelder's entrance, though they'd all been arranging their expressions for it half the night. He must have arrived with a full elevator and simply homed into the bar and out to Alison on the terrace, as if he'd been programed. Because suddenly there the two of them were, studying each other like pen pals who had once exchanged blurry snapshots.

"Of course," he exclaimed, snapping his fingers.

"Of course what?" She steeled herself for some mistaken, or more likely phony, recollection. No, it couldn't have been Cannes.

"Of course you'd be here, and of course that was why I was so pleased when she asked me. Your sister. I don't even know which sister it is, do I? Are they all here? Anyway, that was it. Of course." He laughed delightedly.

Alison had no idea how to handle it. "Is that a compliment?" she asked coyly. "Why, thank you, sir." Making a sort of curtsy in her seat.

"Let me get us one more of these," he said, "and find your marvelous sister to thank her. And then of course you'll have dinner with me. Unless—" He stopped, searching her eyes for unlikely disinterest.

"—Unless of course," Alison finished for him breathlessly.

Did she actually sound witty? They both laughed, and he stopped first. "Alison Lowen," he said. A simple declarative statement. And went to get their drinks.

She felt light-headed, watching him stride through the huge crowded room, pausing to say charming things to Elly and Mai and Celine and Ned and Ralph and Mopsy Taylor, the guest of honor, and assorted others. Receiving his bunches of printed matter from Ira, like a visiting President accepting flowers from Girl Scouts at the airport. He was inches taller than everyone. He was the most attractive man in the room. He was . . . *winking* at her over all their heads.

At me. But of course. Alison smothered an idiotic giggle.

They were all clustered in the bedroom, like young girls on blind dates. Freed for a minute to giggle, to *tell*.

"Well, what do we think of him?" Elly exclaimed.

"Do you mean generally or in this case?" said Mai irritably.

"Both!"

"I think he's interesting, if true," Celine volunteered.

"Too interesting? How many wives did you say?"

"I didn't. Four, though, I think. But only one or two at a time, *on dit*."

"I heard five, but never mind the number, it's the quality one needs to know. Consistently high, from what I hear."

"I've heard that about him too."

"Oh, we've all heard that. But I meant his marital standards."

"His standards before marriage, or during?"

"After is the only time that counts," Elly murmured.

"Which means what?" snapped Mai.

"Oh, poor baby," Celine volunteered. "She means he divorces divinely."

"I see." Mai shrugged. "Except I still don't."

Celine sighed gently, like an overworked kindergarten teacher. "He divorces like a dream—without issue, without regrets, without a backward glance—and so far without paying a red sou in acrimony."

"Four times? Five? Oh, I just don't believe that."

It was Celine's turn to shrug. "Once he had a stepson that wanted to come with him. Age five or six, I think. Named George . . . no, I guess that was the mother."

"One child? The others were all sterile?"

"Barren, I think is the word. As in earth. Fruitless. No, I think most of them had served a term or two. Previously. The children, by the time he latched on, uh, became available to their mommies, the children were someplace appropriate— someplace else. I'm guessing."

"I don't much care for the type myself," Mai said, yawning. "Boyish charm with charcoal pin-striped temples. Even the laugh crinkles look as if he applies them."

Elly giggled. "No, they're permanent. He had them installed, though. Commissioned a well-known chiseler who specializes—"

"Oh, I know—Cris Crinkle."

"—And for the same price he put the scuff marks on those new Italian loafers. But who do you think taught him to button his cardigan sweater wrong?"

"Oh, Mai, you bitch! I think the cardigan looks adorable buttoned wrong. Gives him a kind of lost genius look, like Lenny Bernstein with his hair mussed."

"You're all insanely funny, but nobody's answering the question. What do we *think*?"

"I think a smallish wedding, and Alison in something pale and floaty. Organdy. And carrying fresh English roses from Mai's country garden."

"And little Jill as the flower child."

"*I* think any caterer but Elly's. I couldn't handle another shrimp diavolo."

Cathy had not been left alone with the baby since Sunday, the maid's day off. The last maid; this one hadn't had a day off, but she hadn't shown up this morning. That was usually a sure sign she wouldn't last the week.

After Mai's call—Yes, Mother, I'm fine, Mother, yes, *really* —Cathy took her glass into the baby's room and sat in the rocking chair near his crib. Strangely, she didn't feel like sleeping any more herself. She was now sleeping an average of fifteen hours a day.

He was very pretty, the baby. She gazed through the bars at him dispassionately, like an estranged wife on visiting day at the penitentiary. How's things at home, Bessie? What do you say when the kids ask about me?

Look at his feet that have never been used, Cathy mused aloud. If I had thought of it, I could have refused to stand up and walk. Then mine would still be new like that. Look at that skin. Miracle nonwoven stretch fabric, so much a yard. Recover worn bodies like new.

She reached in and pulled open the snaps of his terrycloth sleeper and the crackling plastic pants. The diaper was hot and soggy, and underneath, the soft toy genitals lay like a tiny bunch of pale flowers somebody picked and forgot to take home.

Remember when he was this hard ball inside and my bellybutton popped out. And I thought of Buddha, contemplating his all the time even though it would never do that. Maybe that was his problem; maybe he kept expecting it to.

But she didn't want to *own* a baby. She didn't want. She left him unsnapped and sat heavily in the rocker. She could smell herself. It must be over a week since the last time her mother

58

noticed and made her bathe, ordering her to clean herself up, like a child or a mental patient. Or a whore.

She hated the powdered oil smell they put on the baby. Rubbing away all his natural sourness and anointing him with foreign substances that were all ironically labeled *Baby*. So that he would never recognize his own body in the dark, the way she could recognize hers now. Small victory, discovering your acrid identity after eighteen years. Buried alive under thousands of layers of powdered oil.

Three

"SO YOU'D BE JILL."

"Not if I had a choice, actually," Jill replied, not even bothering to smile. The first time they came to the house was always the worst. After that she could stay locked in her room or mumble "Oh, hi" and duck past him into the kitchen.

"I didn't expect you to be so pretty." (Affable.)

"Then it's okay if I'm not, right?" She thought she'd better throw a smile now.

"Bright, I did expect, though." He smiled back. (Crinkly.)

"No, not too bright either. Too bright is bad for little girls."
Jill began backing out of the living room.

"Would you consider being friends at all?" He stuck his hand out. "I mean, as long as we're up."

She shook hands solemnly. "I'm not very good at it. Being friends with my mother's escorts, I'm afraid."

"Suppose I turned out to be different."

She paused, as if seriously considering. "I really don't think it would change anything. *I'd* be the same."

"But you might feel—"

"I don't think so," she said, politely now. He might have been offering her candy. Never take from a stranger. "But you're certainly welcome to try," she added. Holding out her hand again, with a sudden disarming grin. "I think my mother's coming out now. El Morocco time."

"Jill—?" he said, not ready to concede.

"Mr. Batchelder?" she countered, over her shoulder.

"It's Chad, you know."

"Yes, I know. Whatever Chad is."

Quarter past three, oh God. Alison decided maybe another Seconal. She almost never did that, one right after the other, but there was the store's damn Christmas theme meeting tomorrow, and she had already postponed it once. Tomorrow was June 20. One more week and the electrical union would go on vacation and nobody would take any more orders for anything. No other store in New York waits this long.

Damn Christmas. She rolled over again, cursing the satin hairdo-protector pillow. Hot as hell, and what good was it anyway in this lousy weather. I can actually feel the hair frizzing up on my neck, and that damn air conditioner is on full blast. She turned once more. Maybe if I pull all the hair straight back and lie on it like this, and press *down* . . .

Alison sighed. Not one idea for Christmas, not *one*. Except just please not another disaster like last year. Most spectacular thing we ever did, with that winter-wonderland forest all over the main floor and the windows. Those frosted branches I designed, we almost put that terrible little man's lighting place out of business, he said. Branches made out of thin white neon tubes—nobody ever saw anything like it. Some out of business; I made him famous! Overnight he's the biggest supplier in town, Lord & Taylor's, Bendel's. He should be doing Lowen's for nothing this year, but just watch, I won't even get him on the phone.

The branches—and what about the animals! Enormous Lucite creatures with lighted eyes peering out of those dazzling trees. Museum pieces; like permanent ice sculptures, I don't even remember what they cost.

But why I insisted on the damn carpet, God knows. Insisted. Wall-to-wall white carpet over the entire street floor. I must have been out of my mind. Even Ralph said that, and I could have killed him. Ned, Pembroke, I had to fight every one of them. Why not just spray something? Foam, even plastic sheeting. It all looked tacky. I *knew*; it had to be carpet. Thick and soft, like a real forest snowfall. The silence, I screamed at them. Otherwise the whole tone, the whole mood is nothing! Bleaching thousands of yards of Ozite. Bleaching it! Four times until they got every last little black speck.

Out of my mind. But it *was* gorgeous. Would have been. The damn rain! Why couldn't it rain the day *after* the *Times* comes to photograph it. Thousands of yards of filthy slush. Wall-to-wall indoor-outdoor filthy slush. And those damn porters, double-time pay to drag the mess out. The carting company bills. Clean it, how can you clean Ozite? You replace it. Re*place* it—the biggest Christmas volume we ever had. Wiped the floor with the profit sheet, Ralph said. Just took a little carpet beating, ha ha. Only next time don't be so stubborn. Papa always said ninety percent right plus a little rotten

62

luck makes a hundred percent crazy. Only next time . . . All right, Papa, not so stubborn next time. God, I promise. Tomorrow I'll listen to them. Even if I'm a hundred percent right.

Papa always said what does Alison want to be so serious, anyway? For fun, all right, and she'll maybe learn something. She's got a personality, an artistic bent, my oldest one, in a store, who knows, maybe she'll even add something a little lively. And the publicity, he had reasoned shrewdly, couldn't hurt.

But did I learn, Papa? Were you proud of me in Hartford? What about how hard I worked? And in Newark, didn't I surprise everybody? Didn't I prove . . .?

Alison could never really prove. She knew. Even if Amos was proud of her in Hartford, in Newark. Even though he said so —to her, anyway. Wouldn't have made her a president otherwise, he said. Except not to the others, not to anybody else. The employees, the press, even the rest of the family, her sisters, their husbands who worked with her. *For* her. To them he said it different. That she had begged, Please, Papa, make me a president. And that he hadn't had the heart to be sensible. Have you been a good girl? Well, then what kind of papa wouldn't make you a president? Whatever it costs me, so it'll cost me.

But I did earn it, Alison blurted through incredulous tears. I did *so*. And with every silly mistake she ever made thereafter, Papa would wink over her head. Was winking still.

She felt the back of her hair again, knowing it was worse. All limp little waves and fuzz, like a 1920's permanent. Even the wiglet wouldn't cover it now; she would have to hide it all. The whole wig, no matter how she hated it with that evening dress. Not to mention how it was going to feel in this heat. I'll probably suffocate. I'll pass out from—what does the maid call it?—from the heat frustration.

Oh, damn Christmas.

She had been alone in her office forty-five minutes, stretched out on her stomach across the huge glass conference table. The pain was still unbearable.

It would not be the first time she had had to direct a staff meeting this way. Prone and in agony with this very same pain. No telling what it was—gas, tension, lack of sleep. (It's nothing, she would snap at them, it goes away by itself. Leave me alone. Groaning and clutching herself while they talked, never certain which of her noises meant pain, which displeasure.) Every other time she'd at least had the sofa, which God knows was more dignified, but now the damn thing was out being re-upholstered. Her whole office seemed to be out, in fact. For weeks.

Whenever any other part of the store needed redecorating, all they had to do was surround the area with fresh white filigree Indian screens and post a "Pardon Us—We're Changing!" sign, and somehow it seemed to get done almost overnight. But Alison's office always took forever. Swatches of fabric and wallpaper samples stayed Scotch-taped to the walls until they curled and changed color, while Alison considered. Paintings stacked in corners got their gilt frames chipped and protective glass shattered. The beautiful old fruitwood desk disappeared under piles of papers, their final resting place until the file cabinets were resprayed, with the exactly right shade of parrot-green.

No one quite understood how she made such lightning decisions—for good or ill—in every other area of the store. It was just that her own office frightened her. Deciding what to say about her executive self. How to express the quintessential, presidential Alison.

She tried to get up, but it wasn't any better. She'd have to do something about the chairs, though; they couldn't all just sit around this table while she lay on it like a roast beef dinner. Clutching her crisp linen abdomen, she stood up and began rearranging the furniture, then buzzed the secretary to send them in.

They were dressed for the icy blast of her air conditioner, which everybody knew she kept ten degrees cooler than the rest of the building. Bundled in heavy sweaters over their sleeveless minidresses and goosepimples. Why are you bundled up like that? she would always demand irritably. I hope you're not parading through the store in that.

Only the homosexuals looked right for this time of year. Bodies bonded to body shirts, molded trousers and contoured behinds, heat-formed like fiberglass art objects.

"My God, Ali, what—"

"It's nothing. It's just one of my stomach aches. If someone could just get me a pillow, though. This place is like a deserted warehouse."

"Why don't we move into my office?" Ralph Berliner offered. "At least you could lie on a couch."

Alison smiled weakly. Elly's husbands were always the most considerate. "Never mind," she sighed. "I don't want to move anywhere, let's just start so I can stop talking. It kills me when I talk." She grimaced. See what I get for promising God I'd listen to everybody else for a change.

Finally she turned over on her side, grunting. Papers shuffled in laps, and then both her brothers-in-law cleared their executive throats. Ralph pulled out a drawing. "I think you're gonna love this, Ali. This is what we thought for the front of the building. We sheath the entire face from the second floor up in shiny red Mylar, I've got the sample here, it's specially treated for outdoor use, very heavy. And then we tie it up with a big gold ribbon. All the Christmas wrap we order to match, even the shopping bags."

"What's the gold ribbon, Mylar too?"

"Sure."

"Why not lights?" Alison sat up. "A great big ribbon of gold lights, with an enormous bow. Where's my pencil." She began sketching it on her memo pad, still clutching her tummy with the other hand. "Fat round loops, see? Maybe they blink on and off? Doesn't that save electricity?"

"Alison, you're talking thousands—"

"Every loop you got there'll cost you in the neighbor-hood—"

"Ali, please—we have to go easy this year. Don't forget last—"

"Oh, please yourself! There's no *point* in having a dinky little bow. Don't you see that? *Any* of you? If you're wrapping a building, it's got to look like it's worth opening!"

"Well, *I* don't think we should wrap the goddamn building at all." Ned Greenstone, who had been a merchandise manager even before he'd married Celine, fervently wished he were back at Macy's, where they put up a plastic Santa, stuck a few snowflake lights in the windows, and got back to merchandis-ing. "Electric loops, for crying out loud. We'll be over the budget before we hang a wreath in the windows."

Alison smiled and settled back on her stomach. "Ned," she said, "I think you just solved the problem. *Nothing* in the windows."

What did she say?

"No windows! We wrap the whole store, down to the side-walk."

"Alison dear," said Ned hoarsely, trying to muffle his rage with heavy irony, "this is not The Museum of Contemporary Crafts, right? This is a *store*? We sell *merchandise*? You want to cover up a million dollars' worth of street-level display space. During the Christmas season. With red Mylar."

Ralph scratched his head. "He's right, Ali, we can't do that."

"Craziest idea I ever heard." Pembroke Wittenberg, the display director, chuckled. "I love it."

Alison closed her eyes. "What *kind* of a store is Lowen's? What *are* we selling here?"

"Oh, for Chrissakes," Ned exploded. "Clothes."

"Wrong," said Alison. "Wrong, wrong, *wrong*. We are selling elegance. The idea of elegance. Throwaway chic, we are the last *word* in throwaway chic. Every other store crams its windows full of sequined can openers and mink doggy bags. *Macy's*"—she paused to glare at Ned—"*Macy's* has to unload ten thousand dolls that make weewee, and a thousand washing machines. Why do *we* have to act like . . . rag peddlers?"

"Because we are, dammit!"

"You are, Ned. I'm not."

There was an embarrassed silence. Flushing angrily, Alison raised her voice to fill it. "We have an image. I have. Either we can afford to be subtle, either we live *up* to the image, or we're just another tacky dress shop. I mean, if we've got it, I say we don't *have* to flaunt it."

"So we go with the red Mylar?" Dodie Mason, the new assistant promotion manager, was not used to the pace of Alison's staff meetings.

Alison hoisted herself on one elbow and turned to peer at her. Pretty girl. Terrible hairdo. Puckered nylon T-shirt, for heaven's sake. "Yes, nylon," she said. "I mean *Mylar.*"

Everybody scribbled.

"Down to the sidewalk," Pembroke whispered to Ned, rubbing it in.

Alison nodded. "And the biggest, loopiest electric bow we can get."

"From that thief in Jackson Heights who did the neon branches?

Alison hesitated. Ned was gazing pointedly out the window. "What do you think, Ralph?"

"Only if he gives us a break on the price. The thief."

She nodded. "Otherwise let's find another thief. We'll design the bow—Pembroke?—all he has to do is make it light up."

Pembroke nodded, scribbling happily. He was the only one.

"Okay, everybody? We should get estimates in by the end of the week," Ralph said. "Any questions?"

"If I'm not being too crass," Ned began, bowing slightly toward Alison, "may I ask what we do for an encore inside? I presume we're not clearing the place for a charity ball."

"Knock it off, Ned," Ralph said nervously. "Counterproductive."

"I'd like to say a word, if I may." Harley Davis, head of the accounting department, looked as if his alarm had just gone off.

"Yes, Harley?"

"This Christmas," Harley began, reading from his notes, "we cannot afford another, er"—he glanced uncomfortably at Alison—"item such as the infamous white carpet." He coughed elaborately before going on, as if a piece of Ozite had stuck in his throat all year. "Our receipts last year . . . I won't recount the unhappy figures, but as we know, the receipts were disappointing, despite the publicity and the traffic. People came to see us, but unfortunately—"

"Harley," Ralph cut in impatiently, "let's not dwell—"

"—My point is," Harley went on, "to borrow an image from last year's theme, if I may, that the public could not see the merchandise for the trees."

"Hear, hear," Ned muttered.

Alison, propped up now on one elbow, was doodling on her note pad. Harley Davis smiled proudly, thinking she might be jotting down some of his thoughts. Although she'd never done anything that sensible yet.

Ralph called on each of the department heads, three of the senior buyers and several executives from advertising, promotion and sales. Everyone had come armed with at least three ideas. As usual, Alison doodled busily as they talked. She drew elaborate paisley patterns with women's faces inside the teardrops. Each of them was carefully woven around geometric abstractions of her monogram, A.L.L. She had dropped the name Landau immediately after her divorce, but not the initial. A.L.L. was such a lovely monogram. Like the Z on the fancy Zeckendorf hotel china, years after Zeckendorf lost his hotel empire. Impressive and solid, that Z. And for Alison, divine to have it ALL, even if only on linens, silver and parrot-green memo pads.

She sighed impatiently in somebody's mid-sentence. Ralph motioned whoever it was to stop. It had all been only a formality, Ralph knew perfectly well. She would not like anyone else's ideas at all, even if she heard them.

"Dull, dull, excruciatingly dull," she said. "Not just you"— she looked up quickly to see who it was—Miss Mason, to whom she flashed a conciliatory grimace—"your suggestions aren't even excruciating. I mean, the biggest sensation of this entire meeting is *my* stomach ache."

Ralph recognized the symptoms. She was clutching her belly again, fidgeting and irritable.

"Anyone else? Is that all?"

Two or three hands started to go up, but Ralph shook his head almost imperceptibly, and the hands fluttered down.

"Now," said Alison, "here's what we're going to do inside." She had just thought of it. "We're going to clear the main floor, just as Mr. Greenstone suggested. Although *he* was joking." She smiled at him, and he rolled his eyes heavenward. "But we're not going to have a charity ball." She paused. "What we'll have is a continuous *performance* of our Christmas merchandise. Live models in Christmas tableaux, wearing, holding, demonstrating all the marvelous things we have for sale throughout the store." She paused again, as if for applause. Nobody said anything, but everyone glanced furtively at everyone else, noses testing the air for reactions. Ralph sighed.

Ned finally spoke in a hoarse whisper. "What happens to impulse sales? No boutiques? No salespeople on the entire main floor? No browsers? No service? We've got four elevators in the place, and you expect every woman who walks in to go stand in line for an elevator before she can spend a nickel. At Christmas!"

Alison went on as if he hadn't opened his mouth. "Models in skiwear and accessories; maybe a sled with reindeer. Fill the sled with samples of the catalog items, and even dress up the reindeer in whatever from the pet boutique."

"Antlers—we could hang costume jewelry from the antlers."

"Santa's workshop!" Dodie Mason, the promotion lady, cut in eagerly. "Elves in children's wear, and a work table full of little suggestions for under ten dollars."

"And Santa—"

"Santa," said Alison, firmly regaining control, "will have to be slim."

"Oh, my God," said Ned Greenstone.

"Ali, darling—" said Ralph.

"No fat Santas in Lowen's," said Alison sharply. "As I said before, we sell an image here, and fat Santas are not it."

"Why not lady Santas?" Pembroke offered. "Marvelous Auntie Mame types dripping diamante bibs instead of snowy beards."

"Auntie Santas?" somebody said. There were scattered giggles.

"—Glorious red hostess pajamas from the Chez Nous Department!—"

Alison smiled. "That's *not* bad. All right, we'll consider that."

"But don't we still need some male figure to dress up?" Pembroke asked. "How do we show our men's gifties otherwise?"

"How about—" Ralph began thoughtfully—"well, it's tricky, question of taste, but how about a tableau of Wise Men, bearing gifts for the, uh, Child. I mean, couldn't the Wise Men be elegant?"

"In Cardin blazers? Are you kidding?" Ned groaned.

"Well, why not?" Pembroke retorted. "It's a Wise Man who gets a Cardin blazer. Only thing to wear for star-following, if he wants to impress the heavenly host."

"Jesus!" said Ned. At which everyone roared.

"Wait," said Pembroke, "how about shepherds in imported lamb's-wool sweaters? Or a sheep? Even a sheep follows better in a sweater."

"*Live* sheep?" Ralph asked doubtfully.

"Marvy," said Pembroke. "A sheep in sheep's clothing!"

"I hate to bring this up," said Ned, "but I hope to God you're not considering a Virgin Mary."

"Looking *divine*, in one hundred percent virgin acrylic!" said Pembroke.

"I don't think—"

"Chez Nous in the manger. I mean, some fabulous robe like in a Byzantine painting. Why not, for heaven's sake? Didn't Mary know company was coming?"

"Look, Ali, crazy is all right, but not sacrilegious. I think we'd better stick to Santa—at least he's non-sectarian."

"I don't know, we'll have to work that out. But I don't want to clutter the floor—"

"By all means," Harley Davis interjected, "this year we've got to keep the floor clean."

"What about a tree?"

"Oh, I'm so bored with trees. There's no way to make anything fresh-looking out of a tree."

"We could use a bunch of dancers in green leotards. Wearing strings of lights as belts."

"Mmm."

"Or holding candles? No, probably against the fire laws."

"Shiny balls hanging from strategic parts of their bodies?"

"*No*, Pembroke."

"At least a live tree can be decorated with real merchandise. At least it's a natural display prop."

"Dead," said Alison. "A live tree is dead."

"Okay, no tree."

"I didn't say no tree. A tree of dancers just *might*—though how much like a tree can a bunch of dancers actually look? What if they just look like dancers in green leotards?"

"Why don't we just try it and see," said Pembroke.

"God bless us, every one," Ned muttered, wondering if a Lowen man could ever go back to Macy's.

Elly and Ralph were spending Easter in Curaçao again, so Jason would spend spring vacation at Aunt Alison's with his cousin Jill. Jason's father had had him over Christmas. It was always hardest for Alison to say no, even though she worked. Mai had the "Cathy problem." But Celine had a terrible aversion to children. She might even be allergic, she thought. What she said was she'd really love to have Jason, or Jill sometime, when things weren't quite so hectic. No one ever pressed for an explanation.

The fact was that most days Celine fled from her house before ten in the morning, and wandered through stores, in various stages of panic, until five-thirty P.M. Searching for things to buy instead of other things that she had to return. Recycling. I have a million *lists*, she would moan, rattling her shopping bags. I just bought this yesterday and it looked fine in the store, it fit *perfectly*. Until I tried it on at home. I don't understand it, do you?

The shoes, she simply collected. About ninety pairs, most of them worn just once, and therefore unreturnable. Dozens of painful souvenirs, from foreign countries as well as every shoe department in New York. Something must happen to my feet, she would complain; these never seem to hurt in Italy.

So Celine could never take a child during vacations.

The last vacation Jason had spent with them, Jill had wanted to shave her legs in his honor. Alison had never given her permission to shave. Once you start shaving, two hairs grow for every one you cut. And blacker and coarser, so you become a prisoner for life. But you do it, Jill had argued. Alison had shrugged impatiently. Prisons are for grownups.

A way to change your body forever. Like irrevocable surgery. Jill had once read about a girl who had two inches cut off her legs at the ankles, so that she wouldn't be taller than her blind dates.

Jill had considered her body disgusting since it was nine years old. She had this hideous raised freckle on the back of her left wrist, for instance, and for six months she had worn a Band-Aid over it. Irene Stanislaw, her best friend, said there was an actress who always wore little lace mitts in the movies, or long sleeves with big cuffs that covered her whole hands. In the indoor scenes she always stood behind a big desk, or else everything she wore had pockets. Even her evening dresses had pockets. Nobody knew if she had any hands. Maybe she only had a raised freckle. Well, at least it wasn't in the middle of her nose; Mary Jane Bodley had one there. She couldn't even wear a Band-Aid.

Irene had a big space between her front teeth, though, so she hardly ever smiled, and when she had to laugh she would do it behind her cupped hand. She was a big laugher too.

Irene's grandmother lived with them, and didn't speak any English. It always smelled like cabbage in their kitchen, and there was laundry hanging everywhere. Thick orange stockings and enormous pink corsets with laces. Jill thought Irene was probably poor. They had linoleum on their floor. Not vinyl tiles but linoleum, which came in one piece and was printed to look like a flat shiny flowered rug. They had to walk up creaky stairs, and her mother did alterations in a cleaning store. But the worst was the grandmother who lived there and always stared at them in Polish.

Jill usually went to Irene's after school; they locked themselves in her room to play blind date. Okay, suppose he does this—and you grab the other person and try to feel something. Then the one who's playing the girl tries to stop him. They would wrestle, tossing around on the bed, giggling. Okay, but then what if he—

Irene had had to start wearing a bra when she was ten. Boys never looked at any other part of her, even now. They would just stand right in front of her and punch each other and laugh.

Okay, what if he—

Two years ago Jill had told Irene she wouldn't mind if her cousin Jason felt her there. Except not right on the front. Not in the middle. If you touch the middle it shrivels up and gets hard and sort of pointed. I don't think a boy would like how that felt.

Once she had unhooked Irene's bra, right through her sweater. Part of the game was to unhook it fast, so fast you catch the girl off her guard and she can't even feel you doing it. The way a boy would. It took a lot of practice. Usually Irene caught her and struggled free, and sometimes she'd slap Jill. Not a hard slap, because part of the game was not to make him think you really didn't like him. You want him to call again. You want him not to say you're a tease. You want him to go on kissing and things, but not too many. A few, though.

Flushed and perspiring, Irene would sometimes get so out of breath she'd start panting. Jill could see her underwear, and once when she had garters. If that happened, the game was over; you weren't supposed to let him see your underwear.

Irene's grandmother sitting three feet outside the door could never have imagined what kind of games. Neither, of course, could Alison Lowen have imagined. Boy, what would your mother say if she knew you could soul-kiss. Do mothers soul-kiss? Did they have that then? I bet they never even *heard* of it.

And then Jill had discovered that Irene shaved. Where do you stop, though? she demanded. You have to stop somewhere! You do the whole knees?

Sure, I do all the way up.

What about those little ones on your toes?

Just in the summer, Irene said.

Under her arms too. Jill had had trouble deciding about that. What about French women? All those books where the hero likes that she has hair there. Musky fragrance. The whole deodorant industry is against musky fragrance. There was a girl in their class who even wore dress shields.

Suppose everybody refused to shave there. Roll-ons wouldn't roll, aerosols would stick to it. Spraying it would probably be poisonous, like DDT on plants. Creams—imagine cream-coated little curls in there. Or does it get curly? Maybe it would grow in long wisps like on the back of your neck. That's probably what it does in France.

She decided not to shave under her arms. Jason wouldn't see anyway.

After Alison left for work, Jill would go into her closet. Not necessarily to borrow anything, but just to stand there. Her mother's clothes always smelled so nice. It didn't seem to be perfume, either; she just had this naturally better smell. Even her underwear in the drawers. She kept sachet ribbons draped over it, as if it had been decorated for bravery.

Jill was convinced she would never smell like her mother. Still, every time Alison lent her a dress or a blouse she hoped something chemical would take place. *Eau de mère*, seeping into her pores. Chemical exchange bank. But the opposite invariably happened; Jill would perspire and ruin the dress. Why are you so careless? her mother would demand. I never perspire.

Alison persisted in lending her things, just the same; in dressing her up, like the store mannequins. Another toy Alison. She would even try to lend her shoes, though their feet were four sizes apart, Alison's long and narrow, Jill's stubby and wide. Jill would try, and her heels would bleed and the insteps would be rubbed raw. But she would tell herself that maybe— maybe the chemistry happens through the feet.

Once at the age of five Jill had seated herself gravely before the altar of her mother's dressing table. She would perform the rites and change herself into the beautiful Mommy Alison princess. Solemnly dusting her small freckled face with the huge powder puff that looked and felt like a giant feathery dandelion you were only supposed to wish on and blow away. Atomizers squeezing magic golden juice and mysterious purplish-blue creams like soft bruises in silver jars. And then suddenly footsteps clicking in the hall, and she had jumped in terror, knocking over a tray of perfumes. Crystal nightmare in a house of mirrors, fragile toppling bottles spinning into their own reflections, hurling themselves at the huge wall mirror in its gilded frame, shattering and weeping rivers of squandered gold. On the big mirror amber tears flowed slowly down a giant spider web of jagged cracks. Jill had stood frozen with her creamy bruised eyelids, her dusty nose, her unspeakable crime. She was not punished because she'd gotten sick from crying. But she would never forget the overwhelming scent in that room. The essence of her mother's beauty which she had only wanted, which . . . well, all right, she had tried to steal. What had happened was an official warning.

To Frieda, most boys were snot-noses until proven otherwise. In Jason's case the description had always been unfortunately accurate. His nose was forever running; either there was a small wet streak zigzagging down his long upper lip, or else something had recently completed the journey, leaving its unmistakable track. Some day it would carve a permanent groove, like a dry riverbed.

He always had other dreadful things wrong with him too—like infected cuticles and breaking out. And he used to stutter, but they'd spent a fortune on elocution lessons and now he did it silently. You could still see him pushing the first syllable around in his mouth, and then he'd give up and breathe deeply and find an easier word to begin. I h—— I don't like girls.

Present company excepted? Jill had asked him once. N—— not quite, he had told her bluntly.

Despite this, and because he was really a musical genius,

probably, Jill went on considering everything about him interesting, except for the runny nose, and maybe he was over that now. So far it looked pretty dry today.

"Do you still hate your mother?" she asked, watching him unpack his military brushes.

"Of c—— sure, don't you?"

Jill was studying his crumpled jockey shorts in the suitcase. "Is that the kind of underwear you wear?"

He pulled the shorts out and stuffed them into a drawer. "Why don't you go play with dolls or something?"

Last year, Jill reflected, she could never have ignored that. "Were you ever in love, Jason?"

"Sure."

"You were? Who?"

"Miss F—— My first piano teacher."

"No, I mean really."

"Miss Fish. *Really.* Until I r—— I tore her st—— nylons moving the piano stool. And she walked out in the middle of my Khatchatourian."

Jill sighed impatiently. "You know what I'd like to do this vacation?"

"I don't think so. Could you get off my toilet kit?"

"I'd like to have sex."

"Oh. Say, have you got any chocolate around?"

"I thought you broke out from chocolate."

"Yeah, and it makes my mother nau—— sick just looking at me." He grinned.

"What about what I said, though?" She persisted. Last year, she would have just dropped it. And cried later.

Jason shrugged. "What for?" he said. Very blasé.

"Well—for practice. I need, I mean, I just want to, uh—"

He looked at her curiously, and she turned her head toward

the window. "Oh, forget it," she said. He thought maybe she was going to cry.

"You know that dumb friend of yours, Ray Tooker?" she said in a small voice. "Remember how I saved my entire allowance two years ago, to buy him an expansion watchband for Christmas? Well, there's this boy in his class that I met. You know what *your* friend Ray Tooker told him? That I have blackheads . . . and that my stomach sticks out farther than my . . . bust. Which is—" she turned around to face him with it —"a rotten lie. *Two* rotten lies, in fact."

Jason shrugged again. "Did you say you had any chocolate around, or you didn't?"

"Listen, Jase, I really was kidding before. About—"

"No you weren't," he said. "Anyway, it's okay with me if you want to."

"You mean *you* want to? Oh, but we can't tonight. My mother's having company. Unless you want to . . . I mean *now.*"

Jason blinked. "N—now? I pr—— I told Ray Tooker he could come over and play poker."

"We can stop when he gets here. We don't have to do the whole *thing* now, we could just—"

"Look, *I* know what to do. *I* don't need any practice."

"You don't? I thought you didn't like girls."

"I don't. What's l—— what's that got to do with it?"

"You mean you do it with a girl when you don't even—" He laughed. "Sure."

"But she likes *you?* That's not fair!"

"I don't know if she likes me. Maybe she likes f—— practicing."

"Oh."

"You still want to?" He looked at his watch. "Ray said—"

"Well," she said, suddenly wary. "You won't do . . . anything funny, will you?"

"Funny? The whole th——It's *all* funny. Sex is stupid and funny. Like girls."

"Present com——" Jill began, and then caught herself.

"You know what a twat is?"

"I'm . . . not sure."

"You ought to be! You are one!"

"I am not. Anyway, what is it?"

"It's that!" He pointed at her lap, and she flinched. "It's what you want me to practice—"

"I do not!" she cried. "I didn't ask you to do anything there. I never said—"

"You did so," he jeered. "Only now you're ch——scared! Never mind, I wouldn't touch it anyway."

She really was about to cry now. "Jill? Oh, come on," he said, and kissed her. "Look, I'll let you practice on me, any way you want."

"I don't—" But she stopped sniffling.

"It's easy," he said, pulling her hand.

"I don't care, I don't *want* to any more." She pulled it back.

He kissed her again and put both his hands under her sweater, which was okay; in fact, she was about to unhook her own bra to help him when he suddenly let go of her and started unzipping. Then he grabbed her hand again and pushed it—

"I said I don't—Let go, Jase, I mean it."

"Uh, hi, Jason." Ray Tooker was standing at the foot of the bed, staring.

Jason pushed Jill's hand away to tug at his zipper. "Uh, we were—"

"Frieda's here too," Ray observed uncomfortably. In fact, she was standing right behind him.

"Frieda, we were just—"

"Pl—— it was a game, Frieda, we were pl——"

"Frieda? You won't tell my mother, will you?"

"Or mine?"

Frieda spat. "No wonder they're sending him to military school! Reform school, he needs! If they can even reform a snot-nose! And you, what kind of a tramp? With her first cousin!" She spat again. "I only pity your mother, she should know what she's got here in her house."

"Frieda, you won't—"

Frieda turned and marched out of the room.

"You ready, Jason?" Ray Tooker said.

The two of them left to play poker in the den and Jill could hear them starting to laugh as soon as they locked the door.

Four

H E RECOGNIZED

Mai immediately. That perfectly straight horizon where the dark crest of hair met the white curve of brow. Couldn't be two women with hairlines like that. So the girl with her must be Cathy. Lovely sad brown eyes. Ordinary hairline. "Excuse me," he said, gently elbowing. The elevator was jammed.

"Then it's true what they say about Lowen's," he whispered just behind Mai's ear. "Only beautiful women shop above the main floor."

She half turned. Was he talking to her? Wasn't the voice

familiar? "Chad!" she exclaimed. "I was about to jab some masher with my pocketbook!"

"And this is Cathy?"

"Yes, this is," said Cathy.

"You're here visiting Alison, or shopping?"

"Shopping," Mai said. "Cathy needed—"

"Cathy didn't really need," Cathy interrupted. "Cathy's *mother* needed."

Mai squeezed the girl's arm and smiled.

"Alison promised me the deluxe tour," he said, ignoring it. "Why don't we meet somewhere and I'll take you both home? About an hour?"

"Lovely," said Mai. "Front entrance." Still squeezing Cathy's arm, she nudged her out at "Young Lowen's" on the fifth floor. Just before the gates closed he saw Cathy shake her arm free; there were four distinct fingermarks.

Alison was draping things on herself. Piles of jewelry and shoes on the floor, clothes heaped on the conference table. Propped up in a corner, a new window dummy, naked, waited for her to dress it up, like an overgrown Barbie doll. The dummy bore a startling resemblance to Alison, and Chad realized suddenly that all the Lowen's window mannequins did. Idealized, of course: the long waist lengthened, the bosom even smaller and higher, the large dark eyes larger and darker. Still, all Alison except for their silky modacrylic hair, which must be, regardless of variations in color or style, the kind of hair Alison wished she had.

"You really are marvelous," Chad said, watching her choose and reject. "It's your absolute sense of self that makes this store. I never imagined. It radiates you."

She tried not to gulp his reactions like a greedy child.

Flushed and breathless, she led him everywhere to show him. And to show *him*. Like a divining rod, he discovered all the touches that were hers, all the ideas she was proudest of. The only man, she found herself thinking, the only man who ever saw so clearly, who ever instinctively *saw*. His delight in her seemed to spring from some deep natural source, as if he were not even controlling it, not pouring it; as if he did not realize that she was there thirstily holding out her cup.

He did realize, of course, but in a way, it was also unconscious. Chad was hardly a strategist; his impulses were right, that was all. He had long ago mastered this field, true—but only in the academic sense, not the military. A gentleman, a scholar. Having won the scholarship and working his way through. The kind of student who displays a genuine passion for his complex subject—each of his complex subjects. The kind of student who earns every last A, and wouldn't dream of skating by on charm, experience or audacious cheating. (Though by now he could, surely. One really had to give him credit.) But also the kind of student who secretly dreads graduation.

The three of them settled into a taxi, the first stop Mai's apartment house, five blocks from the store. None of them ever walked more than half a block on purpose, though Alison had been known to trudge ten or fifteen in spite of herself, in no direction, looking for a cab in a rainstorm. Chilled and furious, she would tell about it at boring length later, and then look bewildered if someone asked why on earth hadn't she hopped on a bus. But how would I know which one to take, she would exclaim irritably. And anyway, I was *late!*

"So tell me more about Lowens," Chad said.

"I thought you just had the deluxe guided tour," Mai replied, while Cathy leaned her head back on the seat and gazed listlessly out the dirty cab window.

"I didn't mean the store; I mean *these* Lowens."

"We're a very close-knit family," Cathy murmured, not really trying to be helpful.

"Alison looks simply radiant these days," Mai said, leaning forward as if that would render Cathy inaudible. Or invisible. "I guess you must be the tonic, Chad."

He shook his head. "She looked simply radiant the first time I saw her. Now I've noticed it runs in the family."

"You live in the upper Fifties somewhere?" Like Alison, Mai squirmed under flattery. But Alison always felt obliged to utter a thank-you note, whereas Mai studiously ignored compliments. Pay no attention to them; maybe they'll go away.

"No, the lower Forties," he said, smiling at her. Letting her know that with him she couldn't quite pay no attention.

"But then we're going way out of your—"

"Nonsense, I'm having fun," he said. "And nobody needs me till seven-thirty. Which is when Alison will be almost ready in a few minutes."

"Oh, but then at least let us give you a drink. We'll just drop Cathy, she's too exhausted—" Mai reached over to stroke the girl's forehead. Cathy promptly removed the solicitous hand, depositing it gently back in her mother's lap, the gesture of a convalescent still too weak to throw a tray at the nurse. "Shopping wears her out," Mai went on apologetically, grasping the handle of her pocketbook tightly, as if both hands now needed an alibi. "Shopping even wears me out. Well. Anyway, Ira would love a chance to see you."

"You're very sweet," Chad said. "I accept."

Cathy was half out of the cab when her mother's hand fluttered at her again. "Sure you're all right now, darling?"

"I'm sure she's superb," Chad said firmly. "See you, Cathy."

The girl slammed the taxi door behind her, but then turned suddenly and tapped on the window. "Chad? It was"—she smiled shyly—"sort of nice meeting you."

"It's a wonderful apartment."

"Ira's very fond of yellow," Mai said defensively. "I'm so sorry he won't get home in time. He would have loved—"

"Alison tells me you're newlyweds. Two years?" She nodded. "I'd have sworn fifteen."

"He's been so marvelous with Cathy. I don't know how—"

"She's lovely," he cut in, sensing some comment about the girl's . . . illness.

Mai misunderstood at once. "You mean you are attracted to her?"

He hesitated only a split second. "I would never have noticed her if she hadn't looked exactly like you." She frowned and got up abruptly to refill the glasses. He wondered what she had expected him to say. "You're very direct, Mai. I admire it."

"Although you prefer to be indirect," she said, smiling. He noticed she usually smiled without using her eyes.

"I guess I am," he said. "I find it gets me where I want to go. Indirectly is often a much more scenic route."

"Mmm," she said, considering it. "I wonder if Alison would know the way?"

"I hope she will," he said, sounding like a small boy crossing his heart. "I hope sometime I can give her the deluxe guided tour."

"Well," she said, yawning, "I wouldn't count on Alison being much of an Arctic explorer."

"A warmer climate," said Chad, suddenly uncomfortable, "may make a difference."

That peculiar smile of hers flashed again. "You make it sound very pleasant, for a change," she murmured.

Mai had never thought of herself as the second-born, but as Amos Lowen's first disappointment. He had apparently forgiven Alison almost at once for being female. God, Papa must have reasoned in his usual matter-of-fact way, had decided the boy would be next time. Next time.

And later, when Elly and finally Celine appeared, he had obviously realized that it must be a joke God was playing on him. In his infinite wisdom, Papa slowly learned to appreciate God's sense of humor. Winking at each other, he and Our Father. But with Mai, the first startled bitterness never quite disappeared. She had somehow always sensed that.

In some ways Mai had turned out to be the most striking of the four. Tall and slender, with those aristocratically angled bones and the delicate eyebrows perpetually in flight, and the hairline. But she could also look like a sullen chipmunk when she pouted—the eight years of orthodontia notwithstanding—and as she grew older, that pout appeared more and more to be her most comfortable expression.

Knowing she was the least favorite, Mai had never really trusted anyone to give her a fair share. Sly and secret, she would crouch behind her squirrelly cuteness, her small shackled teeth aching for the hard dry bits of pleasure the others must have gathered—must be hiding from her. Alison especially; what right had Alison had to be first? But the others too; Mai knew none of them would ever tell her what they had stored away. No one else's word could ever be taken. She could never believe that anyone tasted food or saw colors the same way she did. Delicious! What do you mean, delicious? Does your blue look like my blue? Her long burnt-almond eyes would narrow into thoughtful rectangles. How do *you* know what my blue looks like?

She sat now, studying Chad intently for perhaps five seconds, slowly draining her colorless vermouth, waiting for the last trace of liquid to disappear in his Scotch. Then she got up, as if there had been a signal, and left the room. For a moment Chad thought he had missed the ring of a doorbell or a telephone; then he realized she had gone into her bedroom, and with a start, that she had meant for him to follow her. That in fact she would regard any other act as an affront. And finally, that whatever the final cost of such an affront to Alison Lowen's sister, particularly *this* sister, it was unlikely that he could afford it.

He paused at her doorway. "Mai?" Tentatively. Perhaps he had figured it—figured her—wrong. Gliding toward him with both her hands outstretched, like a gracious hostess. How very nice to see him after all this time. He kissed her, holding her hands awkwardly, as if to restrain her. She withdrew one slowly, and he felt her fingers pressing at once against his body. There you are. Pressed between his legs like a floral keepsake. He could feel them waiting to be pressed back. An obligatory response. One must at least acknowledge the invitation. R.S.V.P. indicating that one would of course be delighted to attend. Ah, good. Then she may look forward with great pleasure.

He reached for her again, still uncertainly. She shifted slightly into his embrace, but the hand remained fixed, those cool, graceful fingers curving against his flesh like a protective shield, still waiting for another signal. Her eyes gazed steadily into his, conveying no emotion that he could read. Mai transmitted and received only in code. Her own code.

The instant his body stirred under her touch, she moved away from him and began to undress, but in a way that women do when they are alone. Hanging things up, folding, placing in drawers and hampers, removing make-up with tissues.

Finally she stood naked in front of her mirrored closet door, not offering her startling whiteness, but presenting it impersonally, with the air of an experienced model for advanced life-drawing classes. He stood just behind her, searching her reflection for clues. Then he clasped her breasts, thumbs tracing arcs lightly across the small erect nipples. Sweeping rhythmic movements. Like, oh God, she thought, windshield wipers. And sighed, stifling a rude giggle, already wishing she had not begun this after all. Knowing it would be the same in bed; those precise motions of a skilled mechanic, routinely checking parts. A tune-up. Generator, carburetor, spark plugs, points. Lube job. Grease . . . monkey.

Silence and precision movements. A twenty-seven-jewel Swiss watch. His eyes would never open; hers would never close. We shall try each other on, she thought. Like clothes. How does this fit, how do I look in this? Even one's own clothes feel strange in a try-on room—limp and familiar, broken in. All the creases and the . . . natural folds. Never can stand my own . . . clothes once I take them off in a store . . .

Even the way he breathes—look, timing it with his strokes like a swimmer. In goes the . . . bad air. Twenty laps and he's hardly winded. Must be very fit. Compared to Ira, anyway. Ira heaving over her like someone being sick. She shuddered. Ira moved rhythmically only on his little lizard feet. With the tassels shh-shhing, Arthur Murray studio tempo, a-one, and a-two. Ira still sneaked over to Arthur Murray every chance he could get. Daily now, for all she knew. Disgusting need to rub himself against some little . . . instructor with fuzzy hair. Who smelled of bubble gum, that's what *he* smelled of, their bubble gum. Little . . . instructors with sharp little satin tits that matched his pointy shoes. She could see Ira shutting his eyes, shh-shhing his tassels, and rubbing . . . Trying not to ejaculate before she at least taught him the step. A-one and ah . . .

God, wasn't he finished yet, Chad? Yes. Now. Mai adjusted her body impatiently, twisting it slightly away from him. Free of him. They never gave her enough room. With a resigned sigh, settling under him, she freed one hand to work with. She glanced only once, furtively, at his closed face. Asleep? Good. Now . . . yes. Mine.

She remembered to breathe very carefully; sometimes they would notice something otherwise, and try to . . . help. Nuisance. Explaining. Apologizing. For what? Well. Just. Remember to breathe slowly, like early labor. Just before that great . . . yawn. The same enormous yawn, like a door never fully opened, suddenly forced . . . so wide. God. The frame of it . . . stretched and bending out into some giant O. Oh—and the moan that could be moaned from there. Hollow and resonant . . . voice of a screeching child making echoes in a tunnel. O . . . Edvard Munch's portrait of *The Shriek*. Concentric black o's circling from the mouth, little snakes of pain. Empty in the middle. Carlsbad Caverns. Grand canyons. Ohh.

Chad stirred, and Mai turned on her side, fitting herself against him. Now, this way . . . Think about—petrified stone ribs. Mem . . . branes. Tightly strung. Reverb . . . erating. Tremor. Tem . . . blor. Why doesn't it rumble, then? Or emit . . . volcanic lava. Vol . . . canic lava!

When he rolled toward her, waking, she fended him off gently. Not interesting enough, after all. She would just need . . . just . . . Where was I? Lava. Menstrual flow should be hot too. Life . . . stream. Wouldn't it . . . tell what one is really doing. Viscous Liquids. Vicious! Mucosa turning pink. Sun . . . rise. There. She sighed, still carefully, pretending sleepy contentment. Finished, Alison. Your turn.

Chad's eyes opened at once, again as if they had signaled

each other, and he slid out of bed. "Chad?" she called. It was the first word either of them had spoken.

"Washing up," he called back lightly.

She didn't move when he stopped again beside the bed, ready to be dismissed. Her hands were clasped behind her head, the hair uncoiled in enormous swirls, and she was smiling, this time including her eyes. "Chad?"

Like a beckoned child he bent to kiss her, but she turned her head a fraction, so that it just glanced off her chin. "Welcome to the family."

"Which hanky do you want, Mother? With the gold lace, or all white?" Jill stood at the door of Alison's dressing room. There were three evening gowns under consideration, but Alison hadn't tried on any of them yet; she was still in a towel from the waist down, assembling her face. The fluorescent bulbs gave everything a violet cast, even her nipples. Jill stared, fascinated.

"White, I guess," said her mother, shaping the words with some difficulty around her lipstick brush. "I wish I knew what to put on. Did I just hear Chad come in?"

"Yes. Want me to go talk to him?"

"Yes . . . no . . . answer the phone, will you, Jill? Whoever it is, I've gone. Who is it? *Who?* No, I've gone. Oh, I knew I should have had Frieda touch this up with the iron, look at it."

"I can't see anything."

"What time did you say your father was coming?"

"Any minute." Jill had learned long ago that there was no point in telling her mother time in hours and minutes. Alison grasped only broad general concepts: just enough time, not enough time, late and very late.

Bob Landau still came over every Friday night for dinner

before taking Jill out for their movie "date." Alison always thought how much nicer it was for them to visit comfortably at home, where Frieda could serve them a decent meal and it would at least seem like family, even if only once a week, instead of forcing Bob to take the child out to strange restaurants. There were ex-daddies who took their ex-children to parks and things on weekends, but then Bob's golf . . . So it became Friday nights.

Jill was almost fifteen now, but the subject had never come up again for discussion. Frieda still kept reminding Alison to look how thin Mr. Landau was getting; probably the only time he ate a decent meal was when he came *home* on Friday. And Frieda still kept outdoing herself with her briskets and lemon meringue pies and comments about how lonesome it must be for a man looking forward all week to this one night *home*. (Since Alison clearly had no idea how to get him back, Frieda assumed the assignment was permanently hers. Nobody could deny that she succeeded, either; wasn't he still coming back *home* every Friday for ten years?)

The custom did seem peculiar to Alison's escorts, especially since Landau had developed the habit of greeting them at the door, genially introducing himself and showing them around like the eager proprietor of a tennis club that needs new members. Often Alison would rush in from somewhere, twenty to thirty minutes late, kiss everyone hello and ask Landau to fix whoever it was another drink while she dressed. And Jill would be summoned inside to "change my bag"—the elaborate substituting of evening powder cases and hankies for the daytime ones which were larger and not so shiny or lacy, and therefore thoroughly unsuitable for carrying after five o'clock. Even though Alison's day could never be measured in hours or even in engagements; for her nothing ever counted so much as the dressings-up or down *between* engagements. Preparing herself was Alison's erotic foreplay, which always yielded more than the act itself. Exciting, exhausting, hurried, tense, and never to be sacrificed for the sake of arriving anywhere on time. Alison would gladly give up any play or party—or escort—that interfered with the dressing-up. Things had to be tried on with other things, after all; decisions had to be made. Silently, humbly, in grave conference with mirrors and jewels, the way one imagines an insane person pantomiming a monarch enrobing for the coronation. And she would emerge at last, well dressed to a fault. Not faultlessly, however; she always overdid it, but only just, never having quite absorbed the great teaching about putting everything on and then taking *one* thing off. Not fussy, quite, but fussed over. She was living disproof of the rule that no woman can be too careful about how she looks—too careful was exactly how she looked.

Usually, other women didn't see that; to them Alison exuded elegance. Every elegant thing she wore was so right with every other elegant thing. Women never failed to tell her how perfectly marvelous she looked, as usual. She took the flattery modestly but with huge pleasure, like a small girl accepting a nickel for keeping her white shoes clean in the park.

Jill had always understood that the preparation of her mother's evening bag was a sacred trust, usually left to Frieda, except of course on Fridays when she had to bustle in the kitchen over the meringue and brisket, muttering incantations about whether Mr. Landau seemed jealous enough of this escort, or whether she ought to drop some hints later about how every single night lately this escort was dragging Mrs. Landau somewhere; she never stayed *home* any more.

Christmas Eve, Friday or not, Landau also came for dinner, and to help trim the tree. Alison did not make another date that night if she could help it. And Frieda would remind Jill what to go in and tell her parents: that she didn't want any presents this year except for Mommy and Daddy to get back together again. She really wanted a UN-guide doll or a dark green velvet dress, but she wasn't to bring that up until Mommy and Daddy insisted. (Yes, dear, that's very sweet and we do understand, and we both love you just the same, and now really, what would you like from Santa?)

As for the escorts, they came and went like the Fridays, the briskets, the Christmases and Daddy. Jill knew them mostly by the cut of their dinner jackets (Peak-Lapel Peretz, Six-Button Samuels). Frieda knew them by the approximate cost of the flowers they sent, the frequency of their calls and, most important, by whether Alison paid for the theater tickets. And Alison herself knew them only to say good night to at the elevator with the cab waiting.

"Jill, did I tell you Aunt Mai brought Cathy in to shop today?" Alison asked, struggling out of gold lamé and into pink silk. "I helped them pick out—"

"Um, you told me. Did you want me to go talk to Chad?"

"I'm so worried about her."

"Who, Cathy?"

"No, Aunt Mai. You have no idea what this thing—"

"What thing? Cathy?"

"Of course Cathy. I can't imagine what I'd do in Mai's shoes."

Exchange them, Jill thought, for something with a little higher heel. Aloud she said, "I can't either."

"You wonder what gets into a child. Can you hook this for me? No, it's up higher. Have you got it? A child who has had every—I mean, if you didn't know what kind of a devoted mother Aunt Mai—"

"What kind of a devoted mother is Aunt Mai?"

"What kind of a question is that? Is that supposed to be—Jill, I told you not to stuff my bag so full, I don't need—What

did you put in here? Money . . . keys? no wonder it's all
stretched out of shape!"

"I'm sorry, I forgot. But I still think you should—I
mean, what if you had to come home alone? What if the
doorman fell asleep or lost the pass key?"

"Jill, please, I haven't got time for nonsense—I thought
you were going out to talk to Chad."

Jill sighed. "I am."

"Wait—do you think I need the pin too? Hmm?"

"No." Jill started for the door again.

"Just the long earrings?"

"Not those, either." This time she waited.

"I thought you were going to talk to Chad."

"Did your mother tell you she took me shopping at
Lowen's today?"

"No," Jill said, interested. "With Aunt Mai and Cathy?"

"Separate try-on rooms," Chad said quickly.

He seemed kind of jumpy, Jill thought. Maybe Alison
had begun to scare him off. Suddenly she hoped not, which
surprised her. It was the first time she had ever hoped not.
"Well, did you see anything you wanted?" she asked him.
The question came out funny, as if she were asking *for*
something.

"Nope." Chad grinned at her. Perhaps he hadn't picked
it up. "Only one thing I really needed," he went on. "Special item, one of a kind. Not available yet, but I have a
feeling that maybe when the spring line comes in . . ."

Jill grinned back. "I get it; you're looking for something
a little different in ladies' wear. The brain behind the
outfits!"

He laughed. Jill really liked it when Chad laughed, not
just the crinkles, but the whole shape of his silvery-blue

eyes changing. It was like getting a present, the sound of him enjoying something she said. Please laugh, she would whisper to herself sometimes, instead of crossing her fingers.

"You didn't make that up?" he asked her. "The brain behind the outfits?"

"No," she admitted, wishing yes. "Some magazine. Except they meant my grandfather. Obviously. I mean, obviously they don't write much about my mother's brain."

He didn't like that. Just for that he took away the little ends of the laughter and looked sternly at her. She knew he would. Not that he didn't make fun of Alison himself; Jill had seen him, lots of times. Whenever her mother would say something really dumb or crazy, about Negroes having porous skullcaps or that there was some link between this drug thing and all the homosexuals you see around. Then Chad would start cutting her up into little bite-sized pieces, as if he'd just been waiting for the excuse. He never argued with Alison; he was much too smart to get trapped into that. He just started coolly slashing away, right in front of Jill, or sometimes a whole roomful of company. Like a game. He'd give her mother this really sincere, interested look, and ask her, say, why she didn't write her views on that for *The New York Times Magazine*, seriously, because she could open a lot of people's eyes.

And Alison would say really? No, do you *really* think I should, or are you just kidding? I'm not much of a writer, would that matter, do you think? And Jill would wish he'd stop, oh, please stop, because no matter how much her mother deserved it, nobody really deserved it.

Until he would end it by laughing. Not meanly, but sort of lightly, as if how could he possibly even be laughing at her, as if it was just a sign of general cheeriness. So everyone else in the room could laugh too, even Alison, who wouldn't know quite why. And then he'd go over and kiss her very tenderly to show how perfectly okay it was to joke around like that when you're in love.

Actually, except for those times, which were really scary, Jill was fairly sure Chad did love her mother. At least he kept looking at her as if he did, and saying things that obviously pleased her. Bringing surprises, not in a phony way, but nice things. A picture he took of Jill and had framed. An antique quill pen he spotted in a window from a bus. He thought it was parrot-green, Alison's color, so he got off the bus to buy it. Alison said it wasn't exactly parrot-green, a little too olive. Jill would have cried and hated her for that, but Chad didn't even seem to mind.

As for her mother, Jill was a lot surer about her. Last week she had seen Alison cut an article out of the newspaper, just to ask Chad what he thought, before announcing what *she* thought. In her daughter's opinion, for Alison that could only mean love.

"Maybe they'll write about your brain some day, Jill," Chad was saying, having apparently forgiven her for slighting her mother. "Ten years or so—the brain behind . . . well, what?"

Jill shrugged. "Behind some man, I suppose."

"You don't really suppose that, do you?"

"Why not? I'm supposed to suppose it. My mother supposes it, don't you?"

He didn't answer, just shook his head no and poured himself another drink. "Jill?" he said softly. "How would you like it if I married your mother?"

Just like that. "You're kidding, you wouldn't," she said.

"Not kidding. I would if she would."

"Then you're—no, I don't believe you." She searched his face. He was smiling, but she couldn't tell what kind. She wanted to believe him. Didn't she? "You *wouldn't* marry her, would you?" she repeated. She wasn't even sure what she meant by the question.

This time it made him laugh. "You are a marvelous girl, Jill, you know that? And I never realized how protective you are. As if *you* were the mommy."

Why should she feel angry suddenly? He looked so smug, that was it, having figured everybody out. She stood up, sputtering. "You don't really love her, I *know* you don't! It's probably some crummy thing like . . . money. Which I don't understand—I mean I *do*, but I thought you . . . I *didn't* think you—"

"Which means," Chad cut in gently, "that we *are* friends, don't you see?"

He stood up too, as if he were going somewhere, and without thinking, she went over and hugged him. Almost before his arms closed around her, she was in tears. "Let *go!*" she cried. "I have to—there's the doorbell. My *father's* here."

This was the first Friday night Landau would be taking Jill out to a restaurant in over six months. Frieda had the day off to go to one of her weddings. She was constantly going to big weddings involving her nieces or her Irish friends' daughters. These functions, she assured Alison, or Jill if Alison was too nervous to listen, must have cost twice as much as the last lavish Lowen festival. Frieda also gave bigger wedding checks than Alison did, sent bigger bouquets to hospitals, from Alison's Park Avenue florist, and wore only the most glamorous number from Alison's last wardrobe. Whenever Alison bestowed a twice-worn dress on Frieda, she had to say it retailed for at least two hundred fifty dollars at Lowen's, otherwise Frieda promptly bestowed it herself on some poor person such as the super's wife, or one of the nieces or Irish friends' daughters whose husbands never seemed to be doing well after their colossal weddings.

"Are we meeting Aunt Elly and Uncle Ralph at the restaurant?" Jill asked her father.

"No, but maybe at the movie."

"Did you know Mother doesn't like us to meet them?"

"Doesn't she? I can't imagine why," Landau said, frowning thoughtfully. "Unless she's maybe a little hurt that we're still friends. Even years after a divorce, Jilly—"

"I know, the whole family can't talk to the other whole family. It's okay to talk *about* them, though, as long as you never say anything nice."

"Now, Jilly, you're exaggerating. I don't think either your mother or I has ever said—"

"No, you're the opposite; you still kiss hello and give each other birthday presents. Sometimes I think maybe you're not really even divorced."

"Don't you think it's"—Landau began uncomfortably— "nicer to have parents who act friendly?" He was always uncomfortable talking to Jill; he always had the feeling she might be clocking the pauses between reassurances. "I mean, for all I know," he hurried on, "if I didn't act friendly she wouldn't let me have dates with my best girl!"

Jill hated it when he started that stuff. His best girl; dates; necking. Let's get to the movies early so we can neck a little. Come here and sit on my lap.

"Anyway, how do you know she's upset about us meeting your Aunt Elly?" he asked.

"Oh, that. Well, she always complains when we go to the movies about how I smell afterwards. From the damn cigar smoke your father blows in your hair, she says. Why does he have to blow in your hair. So last time I told her it was from

Uncle Ralph's damn cigar because you gave up smoking. And she had this look—you know, when she's really too mad to discuss it. All she said, was, wasn't it some funny coincidence we were always bumping into them no matter what movie, and I said it wasn't exactly a funny coincidence because Daddy always *knows*—"

"I guess you shouldn't have said that, then." He didn't wait for her to ask why. "Well, what are we eating, roast beef?"

"Sure." She hated roast beef the way it came here, too big for the plate, so that the edges flopped over practically on the table. And it always had these wads of yucky fat. Disgusting. But that was her father's favorite thing here. She squirmed in the seat.

"That's my girl," said her father. "You and I like all the same things, don't we? Roast beef and movies—your mother never did like movies, she always fell asleep."

Jill didn't much like the movies her father picked either— Westerns and war pictures—but she certainly didn't fall asleep. In fact, sometimes she stayed awake the whole night afterwards, seeing the wounded guys holding themselves where they were bleeding.

'And we both like Aunt Elly."

"Yes, I like the way she laughs. Did you ever hear carillon bells? They sound like Aunt Elly laughing. And her teeth are beautiful, like those tiny Chiclets."

Landau laughed. "I'm not sure Elly would like that image —Chiclets are probably bad for teeth."

Secretly Jill wished Aunt Elly were her real mother; in fact, she secretly thought it was so. She had figured it out a long time ago. Jason looks sort of like me, doesn't he? And a lot like my father. Which means it's not even a Lowen family resemblance. He really might be my brother. Aunt Elly likes April Fool jokes, and I bet she wouldn't give back the presents I gave her and forget that's what they were. Alison was always coming across things at the bottom of drawers, all the leather link belts and hammered copper bracelets Jill had labored over in school, or the greenish-gold Statue of Liberty banks she had bought at the five and ten with hard-saved allowance. And offering them to Jill—What are these things doing in here, are they yours? I can't imagine where this came from, I was just about to throw it out but then I thought you might want it for your room . . .

Aunt Elly wouldn't make me take ice-skating lessons either. She'd listen if I said I hate it. Everybody else glides around to that carousel music, and I'll never be able to let go of the rail. Pushing one blade in front of the other, and then it turns over on its side. I can't help it, they just turn over like pie servers flat on the ice. The only person in the whole rink skating on my ankles. And there I am in a dumb red skating skirt that's supposed to make a little circle around you when you twirl around; it's supposed to stand straight out twirling around your legs, like the ballerina on a music box. But it never does, and I hate it and Aunt Elly wouldn't make me.

I remember once when I was half asleep and this princess came in my room. Any way, she smelled like one, from a fairy tale, and I just knew it wasn't my mother before I even opened my eyes. Her shoulders and her front were so white, I thought they must be coated with that stuff that glows in the dark. And this princess had a dress that stood up by itself with no top, like the portrait of Madame X in the Metropolitan Museum. Black velvet, and it looked like the top was just peeled back or carved away, the way you peel the outer layer of something, or the shell, and there's this soft milky-white inside. I couldn't understand how that dress would just stand up there otherwise. And her hair was dark and soft like fur or clouds resting on the white. And she leaned over and smiled and her teeth were like

101

those tiny Chiclets. And she kissed me, and it was Aunt Elly.

"You and I, Jilly, all the same things," her father said again, slashing at his fat yucky roast beef. "Someday we're going to live together, just the two of us. Aren't we? Maybe way out in the country, or on a ranch. You used to say you'd love to live on a ranch. And we'd have—"

"I don't really want to live on a ranch."

"Okay, then no ranch." He swished his bread around in the juice. "Anywhere you say, 'cause you're my girl. Your mother never appreciated either one of us."

"But why did she have me?" Jill had asked him that a million times. She had never once, however, asked her mother.

"Oh, that was my idea," Landau said, chewing noisily. "I was lonesome for a best girl, and I told your mother, if you won't be it, then I got to have a little Jilly." He beamed at her reassuringly. "Okay? We'll have dessert after, with Aunt Elly."

Jill was listlessly swirling the ice cream around in her soda. This was usually her favorite part, all of them going for ice cream sodas after the movie. Aunt Elly would sip her huge glass of plain ice water, and Uncle Ralph would sort of doze off behind his cherry Coke and cigar and paunch. And her father would order a great big black-and-white, two scoops for him, and a great big white-and-black, two scoops for her, and then he'd plow through it silently, scarcely hearing, or studiously ignoring, all the juicy secrets Jill had saved for Elly. Jill could tell her Aunt Elly about almost everything—school, boys, being too fat, everything except about wishing Elly were her mother instead of Alison.

Tonight, though, she hadn't said a single word. *They* were all talking across her, about the summer, and the club where they all played golf, and which houses they were renting this year. She went on swirling, letting it melt over the glass, even, just so they'd finally notice.

"What is it, Jill?" Elly asked finally, when she was about to give up.

"Nothing," she said, looking down into her foamy brown puddle. Meaning something very big. Meaning you better fish around for it and feel sorry you didn't ask before, because it's really serious and important and nobody's been paying any attention.

"Oh, no, you don't, Jill," Elly said, in her I'm-only-teasing voice. "I know that look! Last time you played with your soda like that—uh, oh, don't tell me it's another bad report card?"

Jill looked at her reproachfully. "I got straight A's. I showed it to you just last *week.*"

Elly bit her lip. "That's right, shame on me! Well, then, I absolutely give up."

"It's not some boy, is it?" her father muttered, trying to muster up interest.

"Oh, Daddy, honestly." An exasperated sigh.

They all looked helplessly at each other and shrugged.

"My mother's going to marry Chad!" She hurled it at them suddenly, and slumped back in her chair as if it had reversed itself and struck her instead.

They were gratifyingly startled; even Uncle Ralph's eyes opened part way. Aunt Elly glanced quickly at Jill's father. "Did your mother tell you that?" she asked softly.

"No, but she is. I mean, he said so—that he wants to." All of a sudden Jill didn't really want to talk about it, but it was too late.

"When? I mean when did Chad say that?" her father demanded.

"Tonight. He *confided* it." Jill began to shrink down behind her glass.

"I can't see why it should upset her," Uncle Ralph said. "I thought everybody was crazy about the idea."

Elly flashed a dark look at her husband. "Ralph dear," she said, very nicely, but digging her heel into his instep.

"You do like Chad pretty well, don't you, Jill?" her father asked casually. The tone was something of an achievement since he was the only one at the table who had been genuinely shocked by her announcement.

"Oh, sure, he's okay," she answered, shrugging eloquently. A tear plopped into the puddle. "I guess I don't want this soda. I don't feel—"

"Oh, I know how she feels," Uncle Ralph said heartily. "Big change in a kid's life, a new dad. I remember how my kids—"

"*Your* kids!" Elly exclaimed. "Were all in *college*, for heaven's sake."

"That was only the last time," he persisted. "All the other—"

"Oh, *please*, Ralph." The heel struck again. He moved his foot.

"We always managed to surprise 'em, though," Ralph persisted, smiling expansively, like a crack salesman recalling a few of the big ones. "Every damn time. Used to schedule it, whichever it was, marriage or divorce, over the summer while they were away in camp. Easier on everybody, I can tell you that. When they get home, the whole thing's done, even their clothes are moved."

"You will shut up now, won't you, dear?" said Elly, her remote-control system having obviously failed.

Jill's eyes were very full now. Elly put her arm around her and squeezed, which made it all spill over.

"I think maybe it's bedtime for us," Landau said awkwardly. He thought he probably felt even worse than the kid did, and he wasn't quite ready to think about why.

Recently Landau had gone to consult a psychoanalyst. Not because I need it, I never needed anything like that, and I'm forty-one. It's just that I have to get some advice about this one problem. Started to bother me lately, all of a sudden, maybe because of my age. Not business—no, I function just fine in business. It's my family's business, commercial laundries, I'm the president of the firm now. Clear about $60,000. Not that it was my lifelong dream, going into the family business. Making a bundle out of laundry, ha ha, people still kid me about it. Okay, when I was a youngster I thought something glamorous, like producing plays on Broadway. But I'm not sorry, I certainly don't kid myself about that.

No, what the problem is, it's this . . . situation I've been in for a number of years. Woman, yes. Twelve years, it probably sounds crazy, but that's how long. Since before my divorce. Only one divorce; I've only been married once. It's my wife's sister, my ex-wife's sister, name is Elly. We've been—you know, I think it's more like *fifteen* years altogether. Like a long marriage. Except she *is* married. In fact, she got married *again* a few years ago. Third time, I think. I didn't know the first one. Of course, we were off and on, the relationship, around that period. Between number two and three. When she married Ralph, that's the one now, the husband . . .

Originally? Well, originally it started very gradually. She just —she and her husband just did so many things my wife didn't like, or couldn't be bothered with. Golf, I don't know, bridge. Even the kind of vacations, and movies. Alison—my wife, Alison—is very social. Opening nights, Europe all the time. I went with her once and I just sat in the hotel—never been so miserable in my life. She still goes abroad maybe twice a year. So after a while it just got to be a habit, Elly and her husband taking care of me, in a way. Alison, well, we had almost nothing in common, and Elly just happened to be the answer. After a while I guess I just thought of her as my wife, and the other one was some woman who kept changing her clothes in my room. Sometimes when I'd run into her in the dining room or see her sleeping in the other bed, for a minute I'd forget who in hell she was.

And the night our daughter was born—we only had the one kid, she didn't want any—Alison didn't even bother calling me. I was over at Elly's playing bridge. Maybe she didn't remember where I was. I think we had an argument about my making the bridge date, and I just slammed out. Not that I was angry. But I didn't even hear about the kid being born until the next day. Heard it from Elly. I don't know why it should stick in my mind like this, it's probably not even important, I just mention it to give you an idea.

We got the divorce, it'll be ten years next month—that's right, the kid was going on five. It was really Elly's idea that I should divorce Alison. Not that I think I'd have gone on that way forever, the way it was. Though maybe I would. But I guess Elly was jealous. That's how I figure it now. She didn't want me to be married, even though *she* was married. Sounds cock-eyed when you say it like that, but at the time I thought it was nice she felt that way. Because I was really still her sister's private property. She wanted to switch me to a semi-private, I guess you could call it, considering the husband. Ha ha. And we were almost always together, the three of us. And her kid, a boy, and mine too whenever I had her. Summers, I always took Jill summers so Alison could go abroad. I'd take the housekeeper too, and we always rented a house at the beach, right near Elly's. Still do; I don't know why I make it sound like ancient history.

Did she know? Alison? About me and Elly? God, she must have. Though we never said a word about it, either of us. Maybe she didn't want to know for sure—probably easier for her. I never had the feeling she was hurt, though. I guess maybe that was easier for me.

Though other people . . . well, we didn't exactly keep it a secret all these years. We used to see all kinds of people who knew us all. And the other sisters—there are four of them, I forget if I mentioned that. But I doubt if they ever talked about it in front of Alison.

Not that it wasn't embarrassing sometimes. Uncomfortable. Sure, people at the club, looking at us and I guess cracking jokes. But I always *felt* married to her . . . It's hard to explain, nothing anybody said really got to me. And the husband, I really like him too. Is that crazy? I know it sounds—I'm supposed to want to kill him. Like a couple of love-crazy stags in *Bambi*, cracking their horns over Bambi's mother. I just never have felt that.

Maybe that's my problem right there: liking the husband, I liked the whole thing being three of us. Playing golf with Ralph and then all of us going out for a lobster. I don't . . . I guess I don't understand how married couples can talk just to each other for hours, it's got to be boring.

Afraid of being alone with her? I never thought of it that way. We were alone *sometimes*, obviously. But maybe any woman gets to be too much if you have to be alone with her all the time. Maybe Ralph feels the same way; if I don't come over one night, he calls up to find out what happened.

I don't *know* why it's bothering me now. Like I said, maybe it's my age. Maybe I just want to go home.

Five

THE DAY
the announcement appeared in the papers, Ralph Berliner
called a special secret meeting of all senior store officials except
Alison. Confidential memos had been fluttering in and out of
In and Out boxes for weeks, starting virtually at the first serious
blush of the romance.

In a dramatic reversal, though, Alison's secretary was
notified twenty minutes after the meeting started, following a
unanimous decision not to make it a surprise after all. One
never knew; she just might hate the whole idea.

They'd had a dozen blow-ups made of the two-column

Times announcement *(Miss Lowen of Lowen's Plights Troth),*
which carried a smiling three-year-old portrait of Alison wearing bangs and dark lipstick, another dozen blow-ups of the
Women's Wear Daily story, which had an impressionistic
sketch showing her current frosted hairdo and "trademark"
necklace of chunky gold beads. The *Women's Wear* story was
headlined 5TH AVE. HEARS LOWEN GRIN!

Not since Sybil Burton has there been such New York sales
potential in a second marriage, Ralph had noted in an early
memo—"And this one's in the family." The question was how
to milk it tastefully, but without letting a single drop evaporate.
That was the purpose of the meeting.

"Our President, the Bride" and "Our Bride, the President,"
were timidly raised and firmly dropped as possible window
themes. There were sketches of mannequins—more Alison-
esque than usual—wearing various second-time bridal cos-
tumes ("Not Sweet, Not Little, But Alison Blue Gowns").
Somebody thought that the blow-ups—all by themselves—
should be next week's windows, followed by yet another set of
blow-ups, this time of formal wedding invitations: "Lowen's
requests the pleasure of its customers at a storewide wedding
celebration."

"Oh, my God, I've got it," Pembroke Wittenberg squealed
suddenly, snapping two ringed fingers on each hand. "It all just
this *minute* came to me. Celebration—we simply give the
wedding here!"

"In the store? He's kidding."

"Talk about tacky and tasteless. Can you imagine Alison—"

"I can just see it—Lowen's gives the bride away—storewide
clearance!"

"I can guarantee you, she'll never—"

"What won't I ever?" Alison asked from the doorway.

"Ali, love, listen—before *anyone* says *any*thing!" Pembroke

109

pleaded. "Did *Breakfast at Tiffany's* tarnish their image? Did it so much as dull their vermeil?"

Alison shook her head. "Of course not."

"Well, then!" he beamed.

Ned Greenstone cleared his throat unpleasantly—what Celine used to call twanging his catarrh—and the movement set off violent ripples in his midnight-blue jowl line. "This would be entirely different. *Entirely* different," he intoned heavily. "This would—"

"What would?" Alison demanded. "Would someone please—"

Ralph signaled, and somebody from promotion held the blowups aloft. The rest of them burst suddenly into song: "Here Comes The Bride, All—" at which point Ralph signaled again, and they trailed off disconsolately. Blushing furiously, Alison made one of her awkward little curtsies, half tripping into a chair. "Well, thank you," she murmured, gathering herself. "But I still—"

Pembroke waved elaborately. "Darling, we're deciding how to do something glorious about your *nup*tials!"

"Pem's a little carried away," Ralph said, wincing. "We were thinking of ways to cash—to promote the, uh, happy family event. Without being, of course, undignified."

"I see . . . and you're all darling to do all—I mean, it almost feels like a surprise party!" Alison was struggling to pare the nervous guilt from her excitement, like a child who has been naughty just before his birthday. Whatever publicity scheme they had, wouldn't the whole world think it was her idea? Who would believe she was surprised? Because of course she never was, not even today. She had intercepted and read every one of the memos. She'd even sent one under Ralph's name, requesting the art department to draw up those Alison Blue

110

Gown sketches. They were, she noticed, barely controlling a frown, not quite what she'd had in mind.

"But I do see," she said demurely, glancing at Ralph, "it could seem . . . unladylike. Using our personal, my personal, private life to—well, to sell merchandise. I mean, people could look at it that way, couldn't they?"

"That's exactly how it'll be looked at," Ned Greenstone said dourly, "no matter what in hell you do."

"Not if we're careful," Ralph said. "But it's *got* to look as if you have nothing to do with it. Even if you . . . I was thinking you should take off—a little vacation for a few weeks. We'd do it all on our own then—really make it a sort of surprise party, like you said."

Wouldn't Ralphie just love me taking off on a pre-honeymoon junket? Alison thought. Just before the stockholders' meeting. And where's our charming Lady President, Berliner? Oh, you know how charming ladies are, gentlemen. She's . . . I can just see the gesture.

"No good, Ralph," she said aloud, firmly. "The public wouldn't know I was away, and even so, it's no alibi. I'm the head of the store! How could my staff plaster my name, all this . . . publicity about me all over the place without my *knowing?* Think about it."

"Ali, you still haven't heard *my* idea," Pembroke pouted.

"You mean *Breakfast at Tiffany's?*"

"That was just the *hint.*"

"Pembroke, I thought we—"

"Oh, let him finish, Ralph," Alison snapped.

Pembroke made a face at Ralph. Nyah, nyah, but he didn't say it. "Wedding breakfast at Lowen's!" he cried, closing his eyes. "Or brunch, or dinner! You *know* it's a knockout, Alison! On a Sunday, and no advance commercial chi-chi, not a *word.*

Just the wedding day itself, when *nothing's* for sale"—he paused, letting the nobility of it sink in—"and then we do all the windows, some outrageous nothing thing like, oh, glass slippers floating in enormous champagne goblets, rose petals all over the sidewalk. Whatever. I mean, you couldn't *be* more private and dignified. The store is absolutely closed!" He clasped his hands and dropped his voice almost to a whisper. "But then just think about the publicity on Monday. On *Monday* we all sit back on our little . . . dignities, maybe toss a quiet little bouquet—an Alison Blue sale here or there, without a line of advertising. I mean, we wouldn't have to run a nasty vulgar commercial line the entire *month.*"

"Pembroke is completely mad," Alison said. She was almost bouncing in her chair, like a first-grader who'd forgotten to go during recess.

"I knew she'd love it," Pembroke sighed.

"Shouldn't you at least ask Chad, Alison?" Ned Greenstone asked, bristling with revulsion. "I mean, what if—"

"*What* if," Pembroke retorted. "Isn't it *customary* for the bride's family to plan the entire wedding?"

"When it's in a Fifth Avenue shop window," Ned countered coldly, "I imagine it's *customary* to consult the groom."

"Oh, don't worry about Chad," Alison said airily, gliding toward the door. "I bet he'll love it too."

"I bet," Ned echoed darkly to Ralph.

"And *I* bet he'd better," Pembroke murmured behind them, winking.

". . . I don't understand why she insisted on having it here. We all offered. She simply—well, you know how Alison gets."

"Oh, but it is fun, don't you think, really. Such a dreary bore after a while, weddings."

"Simple good taste is never a bore."

"Mmm. Where was it you got married last time? In Las Vegas? How lovely—not even having to budge from the crap table!"

". . . gave his age as forty-two on the license?"
"Really, why did I think he was only thirty-seven."
"He *is!* But every time he marries one *d'un certain age*, he just raises his own—up to the level of everybody else's eyebrows. I just think there's something so elegant about that."

". . . actually upholstered the ceiling with flowers! But I can't figure out where they hid all the merchandise."
"My God, haven't you noticed? Her family's got it all *on.*"

". . . supposed to be a devout Christian Scientist. What is it they're against, besides calling in sick?"
"Dying; I think they invented passing away. More like passing through, in his case. Or out. And doesn't he have *any* family? Or friends? I haven't noticed a single guest that doesn't belong to Lowen's."
"Maybe with people, he knows when he's had too many."

"Where've you been, Jill? I wanted to talk to you!"
"I had to—I've been moving my dolls out of your den."
"Jill, you're not unhappy, are you?" Chad beckoned her into an alcove behind the bar.
"No, I'm really not, I think it's . . . I think my mother looks very happy. Like you're supposed to look when you feel loved. If you're a woman, I mean. I always wondered if a man's supposed to look any particular way."
"Well, look at me—do I look any particular way?"
"No." She studied him thoughtfully. "You look nice, though. But I doubt if that's what they mean."

"Jill?"

"Hmm?"

"You *do* believe I . . . love your mother, don't you?"

"I don't *not* believe it. I don't know how to tell. Besides—" She stopped.

"Besides?" Chad echoed softly.

"What if she doesn't . . . want you to, really. What if she doesn't want anybody to love her, because *she* can't do it back?"

"Now why would you imagine that?"

Jill smiled thoughtfully. "I don't think I'm imagining. And I don't think you're answering."

"All right," he said. But 'what if' questions are supposed to be hypothetical. I shouldn't really *have* to answer."

"Don't, then," Jill said. Her face looked as if it might crumple.

"No," he said gently. "I'll try. You may be right, with your imagining; half right, anyway. Not that she doesn't want to be loved, but that she's so *used* to not being. Maybe it frightens her a little, like waking up to too much sunshine. Maybe Sleeping Beauty felt frightened when the Prince kissed her hello. I think"—he paused, looking at Jill very seriously—"I think your mother could love beautifully once she sees it's worth a try."

Jill felt a leap of excitement. Yes, oh, please yes, save her. Because then I'll be safe too. I'll know. But she shook her head doubtfully. "My father says just the opposite. He says she couldn't possibly learn. That she can't *feel* love, either coming in or going out. He says she's not"—Jill hesitated, wishing there were another word, one that didn't hurt—"she's not *normal.*" The word hung there, like poisoned fruit. Jill thought of a horror movie she'd seen about people born without any insides, so that they look exactly like everyone else, but can never bleed or cry. Which in a way makes them superior—they never experience pain of any kind. But in another way, of course, it's terrible, a curse, because pain is your only protection. It's all you have to make other people be sorry.

Not normal. Some vital part or organ, invisible on the surface, but inside there, stunted or put in wrong, or possibly left out entirely. And so the gene for it—the x or the y—that the child needs to be whole, to feel the pain or love, the gene is wrong too. Or not even there to transmit.

"Chad," she said suddenly, recklessly, "how do you get frigid?"

He knew enough not to smile. "You don't," he answered firmly, " 'get' frigid." His silver-blue eyes, like bright steel magnets, kept hers from looking down. "*You* especially don't 'get' frigid," he said. "That's a promise."

"How do you *know?*" she challenged him, choking on tears. "What if it's in the *genes?* What if that's what my mother has?"

He hugged her quietly, stroking her hair, and didn't answer until she stopped trembling. "You know, there *is* a cure for it," he said then, in a light, by-the-way voice.

"There is? Medicine? A drug?" As if he could dispense the miracle, sprinkle her with the blessed water right this minute.

"Of course not," he said. "Much better than that. Much riskier, though. Lots of people don't even want to try it because of the risk."

"Oh, sure," she said, her face crumpling again. "I get it. You just mean love."

"Sure," he echoed, ignoring her disappointment. "But that doesn't explain how. First you have to get the person to *believe* in love, and then—the hardest part—you have to teach them to recognize it. To say yes, please, when someone offers it."

115

She frowned, testing what he said for depth, like an unfamiliar place to swim. "But what's the risk?" she asked.

"Just that there may not be any such thing." He tousled her hair and chuckled, to make a joke of it, and reached for her hand.

So she laughed too and followed him onto the dance floor. But she didn't understand, and it wasn't a joke, and she thought—she was positive—that he hadn't thought it was, either. Her new daddy.

"Have you seen Cathy?" Mai asked in a whisper. Ira sighed irritably. "I asked you," Mai went on sharply, "to help me keep an eye on her—she seemed to be drinking an awful lot—and now all of a sudden I don't know where she disappeared to."

"Probably just sitting in one of those alcoves—there's a million alcoves."

"I *looked*, where do you *think* I've been looking," his wife retorted. "And one of the bathrooms has been locked for half an hour, at least. Ira—"

"It's probably just busy—look how many people, with just two bathrooms—"

"Ira," she said, plucking at him nervously. "I know she's in there."

"What do you want me to do?" He was beginning to sweat.

"In five minutes I want you to get something and open the door."

"You're crazy," he said, jerking his black sharkskin shoulder out from under her curved nails. "There's possibly a good two hundred people in here, not counting reporters and those four snotty photographers. And she wants me to smash in a door! You don't even know who's *in* there."

"I know," she said, the voice rising unevenly. "If it doesn't open in five minutes and she doesn't come waltzing in from any place else, I know."

"Let me look some more," he said quickly. "It's so crowded, how could you even see if she's here. I'll go—" Pointing his new lizard dancing slippers, he glided off, a-one and a-two, heavy gold buckles jingling.

"In five minutes," Mai called after him, "I want the door—"

Now calm down, she said to herself. If she's even in there, couldn't she just be sick? You should have stopped the champagne, it's your own fault. And what if that's all it is, champagne, and you make a big scene. It'll be all over the papers. She shuddered, and then thought yes, but what if that isn't all it is, what then? It'll still be all over the papers, only bigger. That's what.

Mai looked around carefully, aiming bright targetless smiles at distant corners, sweeping the room like a tower beacon pursuing a crippled plane or a fugitive convict, then edged slowly toward the locked bathroom. "Cathy?" she called, smiling at the door. "Cathy darling?" The band was playing sweetish dancey versions of old Beatles songs. *All you need is love, love—*

"Cathy, I know you're in there," Mai called liltingly, almost fitting it to the music. *Love is all you need.*

"I am not in here," Cathy murmured, giggling. "I'm sorry, but Lowen's no longer carries any Cathy darlings. Unless— have you tried our Hopeless Miss Fit department? They just might."

She was sitting on the white tile floor with her legs stretched straight out, like a child in a Peanuts cartoon, surrounded by dollar bills, coins and a half-empty champagne bottle, which had been full when she had deftly lifted it off the tray of a passing waiter. She was trying to count the money, and also to figure out how to stuff it all in her ridiculous evening bag, which didn't even close over one lipstick and two bottles of pills. It was supposed to be fifty dollars, for supplying her little cousin Jason with some hash. She hadn't really given him fifty dollars' worth, but it *was* good hash, and it was all she'd been able to get last week from her mother's hairdresser.

There was no way to get all those coins into that purse, not even if she were sober. Jason had handed her a brown paper bag, damn him. How the hell was she supposed to cart that around? She began stuffing the bills inside her clothes, and threw the silver into the built-in paper-towel disposal can. There was only about fifteen dollars' worth. She wasn't going to run away till next week, anyway.

"Cathy!" She heard Ira's voice arguing with her mother, and something heavy, metallic, clattering. "M-mother?" she called weakly.

"My God," Mai said.

"I'm all right, Mother, I was just . . . throwing up." She scrambled off the floor and poured the rest of the champagne into the toilet. What could she do with the bottle? Never mind. "I'll be . . . right out." Suddenly she did feel sick. Shouldn't have taken those pills.

She stumbled toward the door, little white hexagons whirling dizzily under her feet, gasping huge breaths, storing them deep because the air was turning thick and black. Tiny gold pin-dots were already piercing the dark; the door must be straight ahead but it was shrouded now, vanishing. And in her ears the mosquito whine, the warning siren. Fumbling, twisting, simple thumb-turn lock, but it slid away and she couldn't see it. No, wait—there!

They heard it snap and pulled the door open as Cathy hurtled, vomiting, against her mother's silken apricot blur. Mai

cried out sharply, springing back, tugging her folds of threatened silk, and Cathy went down face first, teeth striking tile.

"Oh, my God!" But there was no time even to look at her.
The two of them gathered her up, folding her limply against
them, quick, the whole . . . unfortunate mess sealed, shielded
. . . as they rushed out. Out. Blood trickling like a thin stream
of curses from her mouth.

Bob Landau had danced a self-conscious waltz with his ex-
wife, an affectionate foxtrot with his daughter, and arm's-
length merengues with two of his ex-sisters-in-law. He was
saving Elly deliberately for last. There had been considerable
agonizing in the family councils over whether he should be
invited at all, but it was finally decided that of course he had
to be, on the grounds that unlike virtually all the other previous
Lowen consorts, whose rare postmarital communications were
almost exclusively through checkbooks and attorneys, Landau
was still unquestionably part of the family. How much and
what sort of part was not really pertinent, much less discuss-
able.

Predictably, it was Elly who suggested that Jill would just be
so devastated if her father were pointedly left out of such a
momentous family event, especially since Alison so pointedly
included him at the drop of any other occasion. And even more
especially since, having her old daddy present—tacitly, volun-
tarily, relinquishing his post to the new one, with dancing and
champagne—might even give her an exciting way to look at it.
Sort of like watching the Changing of the Guard at Bucking-
ham Palace.

If any of them had bothered to study Jill's tight little face
as she stiffly danced with both fathers—catching grim pictures
of herself in slabs of mirror, head bent forward at such an
awkward angle, her bunchy taffeta skirt pulled crookedly up on

the side where he, whichever one it was, held her—they might have decided that perhaps it had been a ghastly mistake after all. Elly had been wrong before, and it was faintly possible that this time she hadn't even believed herself. That she had just wanted—had perhaps just needed—*her* two men on hand, as usual. On the one hand, Ralph, her stolid rock, with his minimal demands; on the other, Landau, her brotherly lover-in-law. That in fact she could not possibly float through life, let alone Alison's wedding, except on the pungent crosscurrent, behind the comforting screen, of their commingled cigar smoke.

She was dancing with Chad when Landau cut in. "I have to talk to you," he said. She was annoyed by the urgency, which Chad couldn't have missed.

"My God, can't it wait, Bob? This is hardly—"

"No, it can't. It *has* waited." He tried to steer her toward one of the alcoves, but she resisted.

"You know, you're getting as whiny as Ralph lately," she said crossly. "I really can't stand it. He's in a mood tonight too; I don't know why the two of you can't at least stagger your tantrums."

"Would that make you happier, dear?" he retorted, wishing he could handle her better sometimes. "I'll talk to Ralph about it first thing Monday. But now I still have to talk to *you*."

She studied him uneasily. Oh God, one of his intensity attacks. "Bob?" She pressed softly against him, applying herself like a temporary dressing to the hurt. "Why can't we talk tomorrow night? Or even earlier if you want; I'll call you in the morning?"

His jaw muscles moved; no answer. She touched lightly where the movement had been. "I just don't think we ought to sneak around . . . conferring? . . . in the middle of Alison's wedding. Darling?"

"I don't even know why I'm *at* Alison's wedding," he said. "I've never been so uncomfortable in my life."

"Oh, is that it?" Breathing relief, Elly almost forgave him. But of course that wasn't it.

"Elly—" he began, and then looked at her unhappily. "Your hair," he said. "Always bounces. Alison's, I don't think she ever allows it to do that. Just stays right there the way she leaves it, like a kid that's being punished, having to sit still in a corner."

"Darling," she said. But why did it always come out like that —quick and flat and impersonal, as if she were reading the salutation of somebody else's love letter.

"I want you to leave Ralph, Elly," he blurted. "Want you to divorce him and marry me."

She stopped dancing and stared at him, shocked. Another couple dancing near them stared too, wondering if he had committed some rudeness.

"Divorce Ralph?" she repeated, like a Berlitz student with a foreign phrasebook.

His rage exploded then. "What the hell is so shocking? That I'm sick of this?"

"For God's sake," she pleaded in a furious whisper, thrusting herself back in his arms as if they could go on dancing. But the music had stopped, and she had to rear back at once. Where was Ralph? she thought wildly, and then spotted him, safely distant, talking.

"Never occurred to you?" Bob persisted, but calmer now, at least not uncontrollable. Remembering to smile, she propelled him toward a corner. "Alison's leftover husband, Elly's leftover . . . what?" he was whimpering. "Jesus, as of today, even Jill —nobody knows why I'm still here!"

Elly abruptly came to, jolted by some familiar electrical charge. "Alison!" she cried. "It's Alison! I have to make up for

121

Alison leaving you! You need a . . . consolation prize! Because she—because this is—you feel rejected again!" She sounded like a triumphant detective naming the killer.

"You know goddamn well it has nothing to do with Alison!" He was not convincing.

"Of course not! That's why you can't go on like this another minute." Elly felt panic now, and lashed out the way a drowning swimmer resists the rescuer (Leave me alone! I don't *need* —). "Not once in ten years—twelve!—has he said one word about marrying me, and now suddenly it just *happens* to come up, a big emergency, in the middle of Alison's wedding?" she laughed. "You're crazy! I really think you're crazy."

"Oh God, Elly!" he begged now, gripping her shoulders.

"Let go of me," she said icily, and he did.

"But please listen to me. Please."

"All right."

"It comes up now because it's been coming up in my head —for years, only I guess not up high enough, to where I could admit it. Okay, so maybe this is a release, in a way—Alison . . . getting married. Maybe it makes me feel less, I don't know, disloyal. Because it means I no longer, I'm no longer *connected*. But that's not *why*; it's only why *now*. Wanting you, wanting — My God, Elly how could Alison have anything to do with that?"

"Ralph is looking for me," Elly murmured.

"Elly, answer me!"

"Ralph is *looking* for me, I said. I'll call you tomorrow." She was already walking away.

He didn't care any more; he followed her. Very controlled now, very evenly, he made his announcement. "I'll give you," he said, "a week to decide. One week."

She hesitated only once in the march across the big room. "And Jason?" she said. "I'm supposed to bring Jason to your

122

two-room apartment? Or do I send him to Alison as a wedding present?"

"One week," he answered. "You call me." And he stopped following her.

"You leaving, Bob?" Ralph Berliner called. "We'll see you tomorrow, right?"

"Alison?"

"I'll be right there, darling."

The room was being redone, but nothing was finished. Meanwhile, she'd had to move a guest bed in from Jill's room, and it looked ridiculous next to her chaste little cot—mismated.

Alison had locked the dressing-room door; she was trying on nightgowns. Ghastly to leave it till the last minute this way, but after all, she'd had no time, so she'd told the lingerie buyer to pick out three or four things with matching robes and send them home. The chiffon, she guessed, but now looked at my hair.

"Oh God, darling, you are lovely," Chad murmured when she finally reappeared. "Let me just look at you."

She quickly turned off the light; perhaps she hadn't heard him. "Why did you do that? I want to look at you," he said. "At my glorious bride."

She stood there in the dark, fussing with the bow on her robe. "I must have tied it wrong—look, this loop came out twice as big—"

"Never mind, angel, it's beautiful. Alison, it's perfect. Now come on to bed."

"Chad, I'm very tired. It was such an exhausting—"

"I know, poor love." He reached for her. "Come on, here—"

"Chad—"

"Alison. Darling." He stretched to kiss her, and since she couldn't very well stand there bending over him forever, she let him draw her gently down. Arranging herself beside him, she tried to think it wouldn't take very long; after all, he wasn't going to . . . he already *knew* she didn't . . . didn't like . . .

Chad was leaning over her, frowning. "Alison? What is it, darling? You're not going to go all tense on me now, are you? Ah, no, you *are* going to, after all. Look at you." The teasing reproach. "I'm surprised at you, such a big girl."

"No," she protested. "I told you, I'm just very tired."

"I could never hurt you, Alison. I promised you that, remember? I've kept all the promises about that."

"Yes, I know." She tried a brave little smile, but then realized he couldn't see it in the dark. She wanted to say I love you. "Chad . . ."

Slowly he began placing her, like . . . like a display mannequin. Arms like this, legs—oh, but not . . . I don't—and she quickly undid it all, closing herself tight like a day lily retreating from twilight.

"Alison," he commanded. "Darling, I want you to hold me." Obediently she reached up to clasp her arms around his neck, but he caught them and guided them down his body.

"No!" she cried sharply, horrified. He couldn't want her to touch his—no! "Alison, you are *not* going to be afraid. I simply won't have any wife of mine being afraid, is that clear?"

She couldn't tell whether he was really annoyed. She didn't want him to be annoyed. "I'm *not* afraid," she protested. "Don't be ridiculous, why would I be afraid. I simply don't want to—"

"—to make love to your husband? To consummate your marriage? What, darling, do you simply not want?"

"That isn't—"—she gestured vaguely—"isn't making love."

"Of course it is!" He laughed, but gently now, taking another tack. "Alison, look at me!" She shook her head.

"Why not, Alison?"

"I simply. Don't. Want to." But he was right; that didn't sound reasonable. After all. "Of course," she said, placating, "I'll do . . . the normal thing. I don't mean—"

"And what is that," he said coldly. "The normal?"

"I'll have . . . normal . . ." She felt her face growing hot. Oh God, *why* must I"—*in*tercourse with you." She flung the word at him—there, take it!—so that no part of it would remain in her mouth.

"Without touching or looking at my body because you simply. Don't. Want to." He parodied, but only by a fraction. "Without moving or turning. You will lie there cast in stone, and *permit*—if I'm careful not to"—And then he gripped her shoulders and placed his body over hers, like the lid of a hinged box, locking the contents in cold silence.

Recognizing it, she endured it.

"Normal . . . intercourse," he repeated coldly when it was over. "Keep tightly closed and store in a cool place."

"Chad?" she murmured, reaching for his hand, braving the discomfort, the thick wetness. Clumps of twisted chiffon slimy and cold under her body. She couldn't bear touching anything, not even to straighten out the nightgown. "I'm sorry you're . . . disappointed."

"I'm not disappointed, darling." His light tone was not reassuring. "No reason for my being disappointed, or for your being sorry."

"Displeased, then." If not disappointed, displeased. She wanted to make up; she really did. She wanted it not to matter.

"Not displeased, either," he replied evenly. "My own fault, I understand that. Not having a better sense of your—of you

—by now. But it doesn't *matter*, darling, don't worry." He laughed. "I'm not all that highly sexed, myself; it'll be all right."

Exactly what she wanted to hear, yet when he said it, she was not comforted. "Chad, don't blame—"

"I'm not blaming," he said wearily. "I understand. Really."

"I did tell you," she persisted, "that first night we talked . . . when you wanted—I did try to tell you—"

"Mmm. You felt—what was the word?—numb, like a hand or a foot asleep, but not dead. Wasn't that it?"

"Yes."

"So I promised to wake you gently—and didn't you say you hoped I would? You thought there might be something to it after all? That you wanted to try?"

"I did want to. I meant to—"

"Never mind, darling," he said again. "It doesn't matter a damn."

He turned away from her, and impulsively she put out her hand, just barely touching his naked back. It felt very warm, almost feverish. Startled, she pulled back at once. "Please, Chad," she whispered. "Don't let . . . I mean this isn't going to spoil things, is it? We can still have so much that's . . . more worthwhile."

She couldn't see his smile, and he remained still so long that she began to feel frightened. Had she made it worse somehow? At last he answered, heavily, as if from a distance, "Of course, darling. Of course." And it might be so, he thought. Better this way, really. That she should have this unassailable personal sanctity. The holy untouchability of a retarded child. Not numb, as it turns out—not dead either, but the awful tenderness of a self-treated wound. He sighed. Why did they always turn out to be some kind of self-treated wound. "Of course, darling," he murmured again in his sleep.

Six

"I SAW THAT,"

Ned Greenstone said, scowling at Ralph's fistful of the day's newspapers laden with the golden publicity harvest of Alison's store-bought wedding. Ralph's bright smile evaporated. "On the other hand, you might want to see *this.*" He pushed a stack of papers across his desk. "Better sit down, Ralphie."

Ralph sat, skimming. Columns of red unlucky numbers, page after page of them. He wet his lips nervously. "*She* won't even look at them," Ned shouted suddenly, knocking the papers out of his brother-in-law's hand. "They *depress* her!" Ralph stooped, trying to collect the sheets in order, as Ned shot out of his black leather chair like a bursting thundercloud. The empty chair, released from his massive bulk, continued to rock and spin behind him, as if it were afraid to be left alone at a time like this.

Ned stormed across the shaggy field of mustard carpeting that Alison had selected for him—it always reminded him of the last stages of diarrhea—and kicked the door shut with all his 200-pound strength. Three secretaries outside quit typing and covered their ears. "WHAT THE HELL," he yelled, before it slammed, "is she doing to move the goddamn *merchandise!* Not a goddamn thing, is what! Pictures and windows and picture goddamn windows. Goddamn it! I hurt my *foot* again." He rubbed it.

Ralph had picked up the reports and was tapping them neatly to square the edges, like a dealer with a giant pack of cards. "Does look pretty bad," he agreed timidly. "Worse than last year?"

Ned hobbled back to the desk. "Look at that! What the hell's happening to those dogs in the sweater department?"

Ralph swallowed. "We're taking another beating there, on the bare midriffs. I can't understand it; they looked so great in those ads, and the display was a beaut. Even the name—Belly Whoppers! The kids seemed to flip for it; pulled a load of kid traffic, the buyer said. Not just regular Lowen's kids, either. Crowds."

"So?"

"So." Ralph shrugged. "Kids don't pay forty bucks for five inches of fluffy angora, I guess. Twenty, maybe *twenty-five* bucks, not forty. Not even the regulars."

"Jesus," Ned said wearily.

"And the women—well, it looks like your typical Lowen lady ain't got a midriff worth baring. With a few notable exceptions."

"Outside of a ninety-pound weakling model and maybe your starving wife, Elly, *I* don't know one living American female whose midriff could sit down in one of those things without rolling over and playing dead." He sighed. "Better mark them down."

"We did," Ralph said.

"Further down."

"They're fifty percent off already, and we only advertised them three weeks ago."

Ned swiveled heavily, turning his back to Ralph, and stared out the window. Last Friday an old lady had cracked up in that sidewalk telephone booth directly below his office. "Gimme back my *dime!* Gimme back my *dime!"* That thin high wail, like a trained macaw, and banging the receiver rhythmically against the glass walls of the booth, like a caged baby rocking its head for comfort against the crib bars. When they loaded her into the ambulance she was still clutching the receiver, the cord trailing in its silver spiral case. She kept hugging it to her bony chest, again like a baby—only dead, with its umbilical cord still attached.

"Try putting them in the babies'—the children's department," Ned muttered to the window.

"What?"

"The goddamn sweaters, what else! The Belly Floppers!" He was yelling again.

"Ned, for Chrissakes, calm down. There's five girls scared out out of their pants out there. Between you and no Christmas bonus again we're gonna be fresh out of secretaries."

"That'll be a break, Ralphie. According to this report here, we can't afford secretaries." Ned reached into his top drawer for the Thermos bottle and poured a cup of milk to wash down his antacid tablets. "By Christmas, I have this sugarplum vision —you and Alison running the place as a Mom 'n' Pop drygoods emporium. Maybe little Pem Wittenberg will stay on, for old times' sake, just to lend a little faggoty flourish to the last window display. One single divine sticker—*Lost our Lease! Everything Must Go!*"

"You don't really believe that?" Ralph said, hoping Ned didn't really believe it.

Ned's lip curled, brimming with milk; he licked it carefully. "Of *course* not, Ralphie old brother. Don't you worry your little head." He picked up the financial reports, shoved them back in the drawer and belched. "Now I hate to rush you, but I got a fair amount of shit to get through this morning. Anything else on your mind? What's that?"

Ralph consulted his notes, which he'd been trying to roll into a ball and save for the next time. "Oh," he said. "The shoes."

"The shoes," Ned echoed, tapping a pencil. The point broke.

Ralph began reading rapidly. "Shoe department volume's dropped twenty percent since we moved it upstairs."

Ned was ominously calm. "Oh, ducky," he said. "What was that crap she had to make room for? Bamboo something? Chinese bamboo slivers for under-the-nail chic, wasn't it?"

Ralph snickered. "The Bambootique. Wicker and bamboo summerhouse things. Hostess gifts . . ."

"That's it—*hostess* gifts. Two months, and a gross of what? Coupla thousand bucks *maybe*, and shoes are off a mere twenty percent. Uh-huh." He took another antacid tablet.

"So you were right. Jesus, Ned, don't you get sick of just being right?"

"Yes, Ralphie, I do. I do get sick."

"Well, what about *suggesting* something."

"Let's see now." Ned stroked his blue chin with the broken

pencil. "I'd suggest . . . putting the goddamn shoes back on the main floor."

"Alison—"

"Okay then, what about just samples? Stick some new shoes in the handbag display. Stuff scarves in them, or stockings. Stuff a naked girl in and let her walk around the Bambootique —whassamatter with a summer *host* gift? Jesus, I don't *care*, just don't stand there and let Alison think of another goddamn knockout way to put us out of *business!*" He took a very deep breath. "How's that for suggesting?"

On the way out, Ralph threw his ball of notes at Ned's wastebasket. It missed. "Get my broker, Ginny!" Ned bellowed after him. He never used the intercom; pushbuttons irritated him. Besides, he enjoyed the sound of his voice striking terror in the hearts of office girls; there were so few pleasures left.

Somebody—Alison?—had left him a clipping this morning about an auction of famous gemstones, including the Cortes fire opal. He had to get Celine a birthday present; what the hell was her birthstone? Did she even believe in birthstones? What difference did that make? The Cortes opal would do just fine. He studied the clipping: one of the world's largest, ancient, legendary, Indians believed magical power, great evil, fiery heart, ancient temple destroyed by fire after its theft from statue's eye, Nazis captured from Dutch dealer, historic treasure lost for two decades, a slight chip . . . Ned smiled. A slight chip. Now how much could an old chipped opal go for?

The telephone buzzed. "George?" he barked. "What's my top bid for the world's most famous fire opal, assuming it's got an evil heart and a slightly busted face?" The broker's voice crackled in his ear. "Oh, come on, George," he wheedled, like a kid asking for ice cream money. "What about all that Microfax? And my Synchrolite's up seven—hah? . . . Okay, George. Don't yell in my ear, George. I can't stand yelling. . . . Okay, I won't. Sure I will, George. Didn't I say I won't?" He hung up.

"Well, George, will he or won't he?" Pembroke said coyly, tapping at the open door with his ringed index finger.

"He may, Pembroke, he just very well may. What's the bad word?"

"Shoes," said Pembroke.

"Ah, yes, I remember. Something about all God's chillun, or baby needs a new pair, right?"

"Alison doesn't want—"

"Alison doesn't want, my ass."

"Well, *that's* certainly true," said Pembroke. "However, she also doesn't want your scruffy old shoe samples lying around the main floor. She says it'll look as if we have customers whose feet hurt. People with corns shop at Macy's."

"Bullshit, tell her. Tell her bullshit, *nicely.*" Ned's cheeks were turning purple above the blue beard.

Pembroke shrugged. *"You* tell her bullshit nicely; she's *your* sister."

"In-law, Pembroke, in law only. Ginny!" he roared. "Get my sister. In-*law.*" Pembroke folded his arms, flashing a wristful of braided elephant's-hair bracelets. Ned noted them with distaste and swiveled abruptly toward the window, stretching the fat coil of telephone cord as far as it would go. "It's Ned, Alison. About your shoes. According to our figures . . . Yes, I know, but according . . . I said I *know* that, dear. but you'll have to—"

Pembroke unfolded his arms. The bracelets whispered conspiratorially.

"Alison, I don't care *how* you and Pembroke work it out . . . Yes, I do think it's that important . . . No, I don't, but I'm

132

sure . . . They don't *have* to be on the floor. Hang them from the ceiling! . . . Sure, amusing ceiling fixtures. Shoes hanging like mobiles, why not? All the different . . . uh, hah."

Pembroke's eyes rolled. *"Jamais,"* he said. *"Jamais."*

"Yes, I am kidding, dear . . . Surely. See you tonight. What time again? . . . Fine . . . No, seven-thirty's fine. I'll be barefoot, as a sign of things to come . . . What? No, I was just talking to Ginny." He slammed down the receiver and glowered at Pembroke. "No shoe samples on the main floor," he said. "Thanks anyway."

Cathy squinted at the brightness outside, and shifted the small, heavy suitcase to her other hand. The buckle of one sandal was already sinking its teeth into her instep; she debated briefly whether to go back and put stockings on. No, you can't, she decided, and stepped off the curb.

The first time she had ever been allowed to cross a street by herself—she was eleven years old—she had made it last fifteen minutes. Crossing diagonally, pausing after every step to inhale the danger of it like a drug, soaking in it like a hot bath, slowly marching all the way down the long street before touching the opposite sidewalk. And then again at the next intersection, so that it took over an hour to walk the five blocks to school, and she was late. Having survived each perilous black crossing like a tightrope walker dancing over a canyon, risking the whole of herself. Thinking I could be run over any *second,* I am walking where cars go, one could turn the corner just like that and not see me. I am alive but I could die this second; I have the power. They would find me dead and be sorry. They would say they really loved me, and if only I hadn't died they were going to prove it.

It was still a little like that: the exhilaration, the tingling surge of truly having control. What if I died this second. And wanting to, half wanting, and then deciding no, you can't, you'd better not, because what if you only got hurt and didn't die, and what if they were only angry and not sorry. We should never have let her cross by herself.

Sandy hadn't wanted to let her, either, even though they were married like grownups and she was pregnant. Playing mommy and daddy-to-be in their dollhouse of an eight-room apartment that her mother and Aunt Celine and the decorator did. All white and furry like the cuddly stuffed animals she still kept on her bed. And Sandy's black bathroom. Sandy was more scared of having a baby than she was. Scared of doing it wrong, of Cathy falling and hurting its head, or suffocating it. What did he care? What had he wanted it for? Maybe he felt guilty. Or maybe he felt proud of himself—look what I did! He was only seventeen. I'll take care of you, he said, and you take care of the baby. Nobody ever let her take care of herself.

She hadn't thought about saying goodbye to the baby. Or the new nurse, who looked like a small shiny black prune. About sixty, with gold-framed glasses that must have impressed Cathy's mother. The morning she arrived, the first thing she did was ask to see the carriage. Cathy had to take her down to the bike storage room where it lived like an exiled aristocrat in a cell full of social inferiors, holding its immense gleaming pale body high above its silver wheels, avoiding contact with the flashy tangle of two- and three-wheeled creatures huddled on the floor, their red and neon green paint flaking, their spokes caked with city dirt.

Mrs. Fossey inspected the carriage from top to bottom, raising and lowering the hood, running her fingers over the body. She asked Cathy if there was some reason it was pale blue. The baby won't eat any other color, Cathy said. If a black person can give a black look, Mrs. Fossey did so over her glittering spectacles. I'll see the infant now, she announced.

134

Cathy took her back upstairs. He's in there. She pointed, murmuring, I'm afraid he's pale blue too, though.

The next day when Cathy was in the kitchen boiling eggs, Mrs. Fossey called her from the nursery. Are you by chance boiling eggs, Mrs. Rossbach? Yes, Cathy confessed, wondering if one oughtn't to do that near the baby. I'll have one too, Mrs. Fossey declared.

Cathy went back to the kitchen and obediently dropped another egg in the pot. It cracked when it hit the bottom, leaking albumen. Good for you, Cathy said.

So she hadn't said goodbye to Mrs. Fossey.

She did write a note for her mother, which she had to drop off at Mai's apartment house first, asking the doorman to take it upstairs. "Dear Mother and Ira: Don't worry. I'll call you if I need you." Then she crossed that out. "Please don't worry. I'll call you tonight to tell you where I am." Then she crossed out "tonight" and wrote "soon." "Love, Cathy." No, just "Cathy."

She wasn't actually sure where she'd be tonight. She remembered her mother saying something about dinner at Aunt Alison's, so that's where they'd be. Which was what gave her the idea. She would have to think about it some more though, because he might say no. Somehow she had a hunch he wouldn't. She was going to ask Uncle Chad if she could stay in his old apartment, until. Just for a while, until. Uncle Chad seemed to understand her, sort of; the few times she'd seen him, before the wedding and since, they had looked at each other and sort of saluted with their eyes. Some kind of recognition, like passengers waiting for the same delayed flight in an airport. Both caught there by accident, but it can't be much longer now.

She had told Chad a little about Sandy once, that she really still wasn't sure why it broke up, or whether she still might want to fix it, or what her mother would say if she did. Uncle Chad seemed to understand a lot of things about this family. Which was why he didn't really belong. She wasn't sure, though, about asking him. What if he said okay, she could stay there, and then he told Aunt Alison? He might think he *had* to tell his own wife. And of course, Aunt Alison would go tell Cathy's mother right away, and they'd come and find her before she had a chance to . . . cross the street alone.

She walked ten blocks to her mother's house to leave the note, and then six blocks to the subway entrance. The suitcase was really heavy. She hesitated before going down the stairs. Nobody in her family used the subway. Not even her governess would, though Cathy had always begged. Dark and low and dirty, some other form of life. At least you could see where a bus was going. Standing on the corner now, she wasn't sure.

A pickup truck stopped in front of her, and the driver blew his horn. "Going downtown, miss?"

Not honey or baby. Was it the respectful "miss" that made her wonder if she was too dressed up? She'd been careful not to wear anything from Lowen's, not to look as if she *ever* did. To look like an ordinary girl. I'm even wearing sandals, she reminded herself. The driver was waiting politely.

"Yes," she said recklessly. "Thank you." He opened the door and she got in. He had an uninteresting mild round face and soft tan hair. Middle-aged—forty maybe. She had never ridden in a truck; it was bumpy, but the bumps seemed very far down, Like something bouncing just below street level.

Suddenly she felt him looking at her, and her stomach lurched. "How far you going?" he asked. The voice was vaguely foreign.

"Uh, downtown."

"Village?"

"Yes." Greenwich Village, he must mean. Or the *East*

136

Village? "Where are *you* going?" she said. That would decide it.

"I got stops to make all over," he said. What kind of truck was it? She hadn't even noticed. It was very hot in here. She opened the window and leaned her arm on the grimy sill.

"You live around here?" he asked.

"Yes, I used to."

"Whereabouts wazzat?"

"In the Seventies, off Lexington." Park Avenue was one block from Lexington, so that was even true. She smiled, pleased with herself.

"My name is Frank," he said. He pronounced it Frahnk.

"Ca-Caroline," she said, pleased again.

"Ca-Caroline." He chuckled. "You ever wear stockings on your legs, Ca-Caroline?"

"Sometimes." My legs, she thought. Oh, help.

"You like sheer ones, I bet. Sheer alla way up, huh?" She shrugged uncomfortably and looked out her window. Maybe he'd have to make a stop and she could get out. I have to go back, I forgot something. But the truck had picked up speed; traffic was very light and he was on a one-way avenue. "I like to buy you some sheer ones like that. Alla way up," he said, "Five-dollar nice ones."

She sat very still now, trying to press closer against the door, away from him. But his leg was touching hers; he was pushing it against her, not pushing hard but not letting her move either. She looked at his big hands on the wheel. Very big hands.

"You scared of me now," he said, smiling as if that made him happy.

He's crazy, she decided. "No," she said, "why should I be scared."

137

"Shouldn't," he said. "I don't hurt your pretty legs. I just kiss you there, inside." He touched her thigh lightly. "Just right there, inside."

"No," she said. "No, Frahnk." She gripped the door handle. The truck went faster, as if her hand on the door had activated his foot on the accelerator.

"Five-dollar nice stockings," he said. "Just if I kiss you there. I don't hurt you at all. I wouldn't."

"Please," she said, "I want—this is where I have to get off here."

"Can't get off here," he said, "can't stop here."

The truck sped into a tunnel, and she felt his hand on her lap, stroking her. She could hear him breathing in time with the movement of his hand. He was gathering her skirt under his fingers.

Her heavy suitcase was on the floor next to her. She could swing it at his head. The truck would crash into the wall of the tunnel and they would both be killed. Or maybe just he would, and she would be charged with murder. "I have a baby," she said aloud.

"Baby," he said, "I have four!" He was squeezing her leg now, and he'd moved the short skirt way up. "I have to kiss you there now, you have to let me."

"All right," she said. "If you stop the truck when we get out of the tunnel."

He looked at her sharply in the dim light. "You promise?"

"Yes," she said. "I want you to." I am alive and I could be raped and killed. I am walking where the cars go.

When they came out of the tunnel he kept going, endless blocks it seemed, but finally he stopped. She could get out now, wherever they were—Houston Street? A strange empty space, wide blank streets that led to places but weren't places themselves. She didn't move. He kissed her there, where he wanted to, bending his head, like a field animal digging a burrow. She felt it distantly, like the bumps under the truck. Suddenly she sensed that whatever this was, she could escape it right now—and perhaps in another minute not. "I have to go now," she heard herself saying at last; the voice sounded very calm. Startled, he sat up at once, fumbling in his pocket. She stared; was he going to kill her after all? The big hand came out finally, clutching a ragged five-dollar bill. She took it and scrambled out of the truck.

Running through the blank streets, she thought I am a whore. Her foot was bleeding where the sandal had rubbed away the skin. She stopped and took off both shoes. Then she remembered; her suitcase was still in the truck. All her drugs.

Chad hadn't visited his old apartment for weeks. Life with Alison had already taken on a peculiar weightless quality, like a simulated space journey. He seemed to be adrift beside her, performing intricate automatic maneuvers—gestures, rituals performed in special clothing, slow or perhaps very fast motions on desolate terrain that must be full of something to seem so empty. Painstakingly sorting tiny dull clues for survival, even temporary survival, in this rarefied unknown.

So the precious neglected *pied-à-terre* gathered stale air and unopened third-class mail, neatly stacked by the cleaning woman Chad still employed to dust and sift things once a week. He hadn't even told her he was married and living elsewhere.

He called the landlady to arrange for Cathy. My niece will be staying a few days. He had been so startled by the girl's small orphan voice pleading for political asylum that it didn't even occur to him to say no. She had called his office at five o'clock when he had been just about to leave; Alison wanted him home early. "Are you sure, Cathy?" was all he had said to dissuade her. And he had promised not to tell anyone. "But then promise you'll call them yourself," he had insisted. "They'll be frantic." She had hesitated, and then promised. "Tomorrow, though, I swear, Uncle Chad—only I can't tonight."

As soon as he hung up he realized what an idiotic mistake he'd made. No matter how Mai learned where her daughter had run to, even if he were to call her at once and tell her himself, she would never believe that he had nothing to do with it. Mai, of all people. He tried to think of every self-incriminating word he'd ever said to Cathy or about her. Trying to convince Mai, to convince any of them, that the girl was well, that she was healing herself, that all she needed was time and understanding and faith. Someone's faith, anyone's. His?

And Cathy, if he betrayed her now, what would she say to their suspicions? He was already hopelessly compromised, and the longer he harbored that poor child, the worse it would look, from any of their angles. No, clearly he had to get her out of there. It was hard to imagine when he had last been so stupid.

Half an hour later, still in his office, he had thought of the only way out. It took another ten agonizing minutes to think of the boy's name. Luckily, there was only one S. Rossbach in the telephone book, and it was the right one.

Alison was shouting into the phone when he got home—apparently to Mai, who apparently was hysterical. He stood uncertainly at the bedroom door, wishing fervently that he had no idea what the trouble was. The police, he gathered, had not been called. If they were brought in, there would be no way to avoid the papers.

He heard Mai cry something with the word "dead." Perhaps no one could really transmit anguish through a telephone, he reflected. If Mai felt it, the taut sound she made emerged thin and tempered, as if the emotion had been compressed to fit the wire and then processed—coated with some smooth protective metal, electroplated.

"Did you call the doctor?" Alison demanded. "Doesn't he have any idea if she . . . What did he say?"

"What do you think he said? I should keep in touch with him. If she calls him he'll certainly let me know. He wouldn't even come in from the beach."

"But doesn't he know whether she might be—"

"No, of course he doesn't. Suicidal? He doesn't *think* so. He *didn't* think so Thursday. What good is Thursday?"

"Well, it's something."

"It is not!" Mai shrilled again. "It's nothing!"

Chad went over to the bar and poured a double shot of Johnnie Walker. Seconds later Alison's voice pursued him. "Chad? *Chad!*" And she followed it. "What are you starting to drink now for? Do you have any idea what time it is?" She, of course, did not. "Did you hear what's happened to my sister Mai?"

"To your sister Mai?" he echoed blankly.

"Cathy. Ran away this afternoon—they have no idea where. Walked right out of her apartment and disappeared. Mai is beside herself—"

"I can imagine," Chad said, hoping he had the right tone —something between shock and sympathy, but calming. "I'm sure Cathy's all right, though."

"What do you mean you're sure?" Alison snapped. "The girl is *sick.*" She paused, watching him flinch at the word. "Do you know how many times she's tried to—"

"I know," he said quickly, "I know. I think she's conquering that now. I've told you I think she's finding her way out."

"She's what? What kind of nonsense—is that Christian Science? Do you have any idea what my sister—"

141

"Never mind, darling," Chad said, sighing. "What time are people coming?"

Alison was distracted at once. "Any minute—my God, aren't you dressed? You're not wearing that!"

"Of course—what's wrong with it?" He peered down at himself.

"Well," she said, gesturing—there was apparently everything wrong—"you look all—you look as if you'd just come from the office."

"I did," he said, smiling.

"I *know* you did," she retorted angrily, "I want you to *change*. People you don't know—"

"I'm sorry, darling." He kissed the back of her head lightly, propelling her back toward the bedroom. "Better go finish your face; I'm not changing."

She stood there briefly, poised between rage and the need to do as he said, while he went back to the bar for a refill. Frieda, black company uniform crinkling, was there filling the ice bucket. It was going to be a very stiff night.

"Chad? *Chad!*" His wife's imperious summons again.

Chad closed his eyes; Frieda had finished with the ice, but she hovered until she was sure he wasn't going to answer. Just for that, he saw no reason not to drain the glass again, right in front of her. Frieda was very definitely counting.

"I'm so sorry my sister Mai and Ira won't be here . . . their daughter, suddenly ill." Chad winced. "And this is Chad. Miles . . . Boehm. Mrs. Boehm—Diane."

"I've heard a great deal—"

"—And my sister Celine, the birthday girl—"Alison went on fluttering. "Her husband, Ned Greenstone, of course you know. Miles . . . Boehm. Diane."

At Alison's parties there were always certain names which

she seemed to savor, holding them in her mouth before parting with them. Introductions made like exquisite little triumphs, as if they were terribly imaginative hors d'oeuvres to be exclaimed over. Mmm, Alison! *The* Miles Boehm? A name to be relished, rolled in sesame seeds and sautéed lightly in safflower oil, so that one might serve it again, cleverly mixed with other names to whom this one tasted more exotic than, for instance, the name Alison Lowen.

It was Celine's birthday, but Miles Boehm was being served for Chad. Alison wanted her husband to be discovered by someone like this, someone who might do something exciting with him professionally, as long as he was being so stubborn about Lowen's, absolutely refusing to consider it. You'd think there was something to be ashamed of. She had even made Ira talk to him; with his background Chad could fit right into the publicity end of the business with Ira. They actually could use someone like Chad there, someone really attractive and bright. It's not even as if we would just be making room, she had pointed out. Isn't that right, Ira? While Chad sat there, stone-faced, guzzling his damn Scotch, not hearing a word they said. I *knew* he'd do that, she thought furiously. Is that all, darling, he'd asked, at the end, with that repulsive yes-dear look he sometimes put on. All blank and cheery, as if he was imitating Ira or Ralph . . .

"You know, Chad is really such a brilliant—am I forgiven for bragging, Mr. Boehm, since I'm still a bride?" And she blushed like one, disarmingly. Boehm, the founder and owner of the immense advertising agency, Boehm Associates, was mildly intrigued. Ira, who certainly must know, had introduced him to Alison; enormously powerful, he had said. Ira himself could be more helpful to Chad if he wanted to, Alison thought; he seemed to have thirty lunches a week with these promotion and advertising celebrities—on his Lowen's expense account. Ira had a lot on his mind, though; she forgave him guiltily. Besides, it irritated her more that Chad didn't push himself. Not that he was lazy; apparently he worked extremely hard. But considering his experience, his obvious talent, or whatever it was one needed in that field, the level and the salary were by no means—well, not even adequate, if one also considered who he was now. A more suitable title, at least. She had begun to feel embarrassed about the expressions people assumed while she explained him. In . . . promotion, it's a smallish agency, but he does—and their eyes would begin to glaze, so she would rush on—he handles only their largest special accounts.

In fact, he was, she realized, clearly a very middle-management type in a field whose middle was notoriously over-managed. He was an interchangeable accessory, a name that no one remembered the taste of, a Mr. Alison Lowen, and without some extraordinary turn of the wheel, he would remain precisely that.

Overhearing patches of his wifes' running panegyric—she'd been cornering poor Boehm, on and off, for hours—Chad groaned. Like an insufferable mother, he thought, tugging all the wrong strings to get her son into a better school. "You must forgive my adorable helpmate, Mr. Boehm," he cut in at last, unable to ignore it any longer. "Promotion is one of the few areas of life Alison is somewhat naïve about."

Alison's eyes blazed. "It so happens," she retorted, "that I know a great *deal* about promotion. The store—after all, we do *plenty* of promotion, and not a bad job, either, I'm told." She added this lowering her eyes, so it wouldn't seem . . . well, she wasn't advertising her*self*, after all.

"So you do, darling," Chad agreed pleasantly. "I clean forgot. She knows more than you'd ever have guessed, Mr. Boehm. May I get you another of those?"

"It's Miles," said Boehm. "Scotch and water. Thanks." There was no way to tell what he thought.

Alison caught the edge of Chad's departing sleeve and leaned toward him. "Haven't you had enough?" she demanded, scarcely bothering to whisper it.

"Of certain things, dearest, most definitely," he replied smoothly. "Whereas not nearly enough of others." Deftly stacking Boehm's glass inside his own to free a hand, he took hers from his arm, raised it gently to his lips and returned it. Miles Boehm's hooded eyes peered at them curiously. An established owl recording the habits of flightier species. Alison had an uneasy sense of Chad's mocking her. It was always like being pelted with snowflakes: feeling the cold sting, reaching up to examine the source, finding nothing on one's face but what seemed to be startled tears.

She thought he had behaved shockingly all night, but there was no easy way to reproach him. "Darling, can't we afford reasonable ashtrays?" he'd asked her, jokingly, she supposed, when someone broke a tiny, fragile porcelain shell, stubbing out a cigarette. And then at the buffet table: "These are perfectly lovely little knives, darling, but are you quite sure they're not spoons? I mean, unless this is curried Pablum we're serving." And she was sure he hadn't eaten a bite; there was a full plate abandoned on one of the snack tables. It must have been his; he never liked eating off snack tables, but still.

"Chad, aren't you eating this divine food?" Alison had heard Diane Boehm ask him.

"I'm not big enough to cut my own meat," he replied, smiling michievously so that one should assume that was a joke too—of some sort.

At ten past eleven Ned Greenstone whispered something to Alison and disappeared into the bedroom, bounding like a playful black bear. Alison switched on the television set for the late news and Celine was escorted to a chair in front of the screen. "What—?" "You'll see."

Ned reappeared bearing a small black suede box, and kissed his wife. "Don't open till I say go," he said, beaming. The newscaster was still discussing war and hunger, so no one had to pay attention yet.

"Today at New York's famed Winfield Bates Gallery—"

"Sh!"

Ned gripped Celine's shoulder as if she might abscond with the box and ruin his moment. *Now!*

"—fascinating legend sold by international auction. The Cortes fire opal, believed—"

Trembling, Celine opened the box. The jewel lay there like a huge burnt tear, mud-colored against the black velvet, with only glints of the flame. But when she lifted it to the light the orange tongues leaped in it like dancers. Alison gasped.

"—another chapter in its colorful history . . . sold by secret bid to New York retailer Edmund Greenstone, whose wife is a member of the Lowen Department Store dynasty. Mr. Greenstone, vice-president of the New York branch of Lowen's, bought the gem as a birthday gift for his wife Celine, a former screen actress, whose sister Alison is president of Lowen's New York. The gallery declined to disclose the price paid for the historic opal, but it was believed to be close to a million dollars, the highest ever paid for a semi-precious stone."

"Oh, Ned, you shouldn't have!" someone shouted, and in Alison's creamy-beige living room, the historic legend took its rightful place. Celine dissolved in happy tears, and Ned swelled with conquest. He hadn't paid anything like a million; thanks to the chip, the closest bid against him was $550,000, from Cartier.

"Mr. Greenstone," the newscaster went on, "was notified at his office late today that he had acquired the famous opal. CBS asked if he were superstitious." (There was a brief close-up of Ned, needing a shave, growling "Not at these prices!") "His wife, Greenstone added, did not yet know about the purchase; he planned to give it to her at a surprise party this evening. CBS wishes Celine a happy birthday, and good luck as the new owner of an ancient jewel once thought capable of destroying the world."

"You ought to have a portrait done wearing it," Alison remarked.

"Unless she plans to just walk around clutching it in her fist that way," added Mai. She and Ira had arrived just in time, having finally seen no point in just sitting home worrying about Cathy. Ira had thoughtfully left Alison's number on his telephone-answering machine, and Mai left it with the psychiatrist and the maid.

"What *are* you going to do with the opal, Celine?" Elly asked.

"Not another ring, I hope," Alison put in quickly.

"Such a lovely fire is meant to warm the face; I would think a pendant," said Diane Boehm.

"By the way, *are* you superstitious?" said Chad.

"Like I said, not at these prices," Ned answered for her, "and not about jewelry, regardless."

Everyone laughed and began to drift back toward the bar as Alison switched off the television set. "That's not a bad idea you had, about the photographic possibilities," Boehm said to Chad. "Were you thinking of it for any particular magazine?"

Well—actually, Chad had not been thinking of it at all. He

was almost sure he hadn't said anything about photographs. Though somebody had—Alison; a portrait, she had said. Well, what difference; Boehm was apparently mellow.

"Because if not," Boehm was saying, "we might have some ideas. Mutually interesting—that is, if you—"

"Oh, I'm sure we could get together on . . . something," Chad said vaguely. "Though I doubt—I think she's a little camera shy, Celine is."

Boehm's hooded eyes opened slightly. "A former actress?"

"Like Garbo, in some respects." Chad smiled, thinking, Not the best respects, God knows, but some.

"I see." Boehm frowned. "Well, let me give you my card, Chad. We should have lunch in any case. Will you call me tomorrow?"

Chad nodded, pocketing the card. "My wife will be delighted."

"I beg your pardon?"

"Alison," he said, smiling again, "delights in my having lunch."

The Boehms left almost immediately, and Chad moved back to the bar, musing. What could Boehm want with Celine and her silly opal, anyway? Must represent some photographer who needs *Vogue* credits. Though Boehm didn't ordinarily bother with—Wait, wasn't there something he'd heard? One more double to clear the passages. Photographer. Of course! An Italian aristocrat, prince or duke. Vermicelli? Did sensational nude portraits with a Polaroid camera, of all things. Socially registered ladies. To the manner porn. He'd seen one magazine series—some bare-ass contessa peeing on a barn floor. Very artistic, but the police had confiscated the magazine when it hit newsstands in Rome. Several serious art critics defended him. Of course. But did Boehm represent him here? Somehow, Chad thought, not yet.

"Celine?" he called. "I've decided."

"You have?" She giggled.

Chad grinned mischievously. "You have to have a nude Polaroid portrait done by Edouard Vermicelli. Vermicini, it is. Wearing the opal wherever he says. Like a Roman candle."

The idea was greeted with predictable howls, until Chad noticed Celine's bewilderment. She looked as if she might burst into tears. "I thought he was serious!" she whimpered, turning to Alison. "Now I can't tell if he is or not!"

"How should I know," Alison said curtly. "I don't think he's being funny. But then I don't think he's been funny all night."

Chad drew his wife toward him with an elaborate hug. "Only half serious," he said carefully. "Though it was Miles Boehm's idea, in a way, and I doubt if a fella who looks like that ever means to be funny."

"Miles Boehm?" Alison cried sharply. "I don't believe it. Really?"

Chad shrugged, and then Ira cut in. "Well, *I* think," he began importantly, rocking slightly forward, *en pointe,* "I mean, if Celine really wanted something like that, there's no reason why we couldn't arrange it directly. I have a contact in Rome, *I* could"—he caught Alison's frown out of the corner of his eye—"I could put *Chad* here in touch first thing tomorrow. Besides, it would save Ned here a commission, right? I mean old Ned's spent enough for one birthday, hey?"

"Vermicini's never appeared in an American magazine," Celine said wistfully. "If—oh, it really would be kind of exciting, wouldn't it, if—"

Chad gazed mistily at the circle of rapt faces. When he was this drunk, he felt almost painfully tender toward them all— and at the same time, playful. The burned child doesn't necessarily shun the fire; next time maybe he'll know how to control it. In a few months he had learned enough about the Lowens to sense how thoroughly he could despise them. Just as he could despise himself for having needed to be one of them, once he overcame the need, which he still had, for some perverse reason he would never quite understand. Had Freud dabbled at all in Christian Science, he might have called it a passing-on wish.

"Ned?" Celine said, curling affectionately into her husband's lap. "What do you think?"

Ned had been feeling acutely uncomfortable. "Nude," he said doubtfully. "I don't see why it has to be nude."

"Because that's what Vermicini does," Celine snapped, suddenly realizing how intensely she wanted to do it. Every fashion magazine clamoring. Princesses. Princi*pessas.*

"How much does he charge?" Ned asked.

"A thousand dollars a shot, I think." Chad yawned. "Minimum of two."

"One with the opal on the left tit, and one on the right? In a magazine? Ce*line?*" Ned looked at his wife, his living bargain of a semi-precious stone, and sighed. Gently, raggedly, he said again, "Celine?"

She raised her chin. To be a starlet again, after all this time. Not just one of the Lowens, a sister of—but Celina Lowen as The Girl.

Chad watched, fascinated. What made them so impossible to dismiss, he decided, was that they still weren't bored, any of them. They were still so unsure of themselves, still trying on their power as if Papa had withheld permission to wear it except on special occasions. His lifetime had been spent aging the money, breaking it in so that they could all think of it as old wealth. And perhaps they did, but still only as *his* old wealth. All the world charged to Papa and sent home on approval.

Celine got up from Ned's lap and perched on the arm of his

chair. "Don't say no," she pleaded. "We wouldn't have to publish it—I mean if you don't like it. Though I understand they *are* considered works of art. Some of the best critics think they're magnificent—I just saw one in *Europa.* A Contessa something, and she was—really something. Anyway if . . . we could just hang it in the bedroom—I mean, nobody says we have to—expose it."

Ned grunted.

"Well, anyway," Ira said, getting up. "Let me know, Ned. Looks like she needs to do something baroque to live up to that historic legend."

Celine squealed excitedly, holding the jewel up to the light again. "You know," she said, turning it to kindle the sparks, "I *am* beginning to feel superstitious."

Seven

THERE WAS NO REASON
to flinch every time the telephone rang. Elly knew Bob Landau wouldn't call; he had clearly said that she was to call him. Yet she would stare, shivering, at the instrument, fat and smug in its black silence, like some dangerous animal raised in captivity, fed and petted but not really tame. She had turned the bell off so that it didn't even ring in the bedroom now, but the extensions three or four rooms away jangled like distant raw nerves. She felt her teeth ache at the sound.

He had said to call with her decision, and since there was none she could make . . . For days, Ralph could not stop asking what she and Bob could have quarreled about. He was hurt and angry that neither of them would explain and let him repair it. He had even called Landau himself, badgering him like a nagging wife—was the lease signed for the summer house, had he sent in his club dues, why the hell didn't he just come over tonight and have dinner and hash it all out, whatever it was. Whatever could it be, and how could it be anything to rupture a friendship like theirs. Elly had implored her husband to stop, and when he accused her of being unfeeling, she had said what was necessary. Bob is in love with me, she explained, in a prim schoolteacher voice so it wouldn't sound so inane. He asked me to leave you and marry him. So you see—and she spread her hands eloquently.

Stunned, Ralph knew she had taken the wise, the only possible course. For some reason it made him even angrier, like a child whose parents have done what they thought was best for him.

Still, it was certain now that Landau would not call. Which made this terror completely senseless. She was out, no matter who it was—out, she would tell the maids shrilly. She could not even talk to her sisters. She was ill; she felt cold. The bleeding had stopped, yet now she felt it always brimming, a full unsteady vessel on the brink of overflowing. She walked stiffly, with measured steps, but she could still feel it welling up from some stagnant underground pool.

And awake or in drugged sleep she would wait for the silence to shatter, for a call to come from someone she had failed, someone who must hate her or want something of her that she no longer had. From Sarah Saxon, whom she had loved and taught to love and then ceased to love. As if an ocean could be impetuous, reversing its tides and leaving its parched creatures there in the sand.

Sarah's last unloved face began to haunt her. Thin and

sallow, so that Elly could not see how she could ever have thought it was golden. But it must have been golden first, and then changed. Even her eyes somehow became yellow and small, forever in tears, red-rimmed and with clotted lashes. Sarah Saxon shaking with frightened grief. Please don't leave me, Elly. I won't bother you, I promise. Only please don't leave me. Sobs racking the thin bent shoulders hunched in grief, but they had always been hunched, hadn't they? Don't cry, don't cry! Elly had commanded her, frightened and angry that she had to have such power. She could not bear to be responsible; how could Sarah Saxon have done this to her? What right did she have to love *me*, Elly had raged. I only wanted to love *her*.

In the end she could not even see the Sarah she had pursued with such relentless passion; the Sarah whose rural pride and awkward perfect dignity she had so coveted. The graceful arc of glossy black hair, the bowed shoulders covered with soft faded blue—why had it seemed so beautiful huddled over grimy books in a tiny pool of yellow light? Less than a year later Elly wanted to seize those shoulders and wrench them back. Stand up straight, can't you! And the hair, Prince Valiant's glorious silken cap, unraveled into limp dull strands. Her chin had broken out in spots. And the awful way she had cried, without wiping her nose. Wanting, begging for love one last time. And Elly, sickened with guilt and shame, had given her something terrible instead. I'm sorry; this is all I have right now. Making love as if it were something one could make, as if it were making do or making believe. Hating her own hands, hating the thin desperate clinging body that responded by heart to echoes of old movements, like a mechanical toy that she only wanted to discard. And she wasn't allowed to. So long as she could still bring it to life this way, so intensely not wanting to. But look, Mama, she had wanted to cry, it's broken. We have to throw it away. No, it isn't—see, it still works, look! No, no, it's no good any more; it's broken. Its working was an unbearable affront; it accused her. It made her admit the truth. I don't care if it still works, I hate it—*I don't want it any more.*

"Are we meeting Aunt Elly?" Jill asked her father in the restaurant.

"Not tonight."

"How come?"

"Because she's—they're busy." He wouldn't look at the child; he kept studying the menu, even though they had ordered.

"But they were busy *last* Friday."

Landau looked up finally, resigned. He had to talk to somebody, anyway. "What the hell do I do if nothing happens?" Dr. Kantrow had neglected to answer that. "Suppose she just ignores the whole thing? What if she thought I was drunk? What if she *pretends* she thought I was drunk? Why did you make me do this, you bastard!"

"But she *has* decided—to stay with her husband, Bob. I think you must accept that."

"But then, what have I got now?" Landau had shouted at him. Dr. Kantrow had just sat there screwing the top back on his Thermos bottle. "But you were prepared. You agreed that this was possible. That her need was probably to feel safe. For Elly, two half-husbands are safer than one who demands a whole life. The kind of woman who can only be shared, because there is not enough. She will undoubtedly seek someone else to take your place in her marriage." Kantrow looked as if everything had worked out just fine.

Landau had left his office in a state of semi-shock. What have I done to my life? Like some heathen moron coming to pray to this stone god. I am unhappy. Ah, then you must give up your land, your sheep and your prized goat. I have done what you said. Good. But now I am unhappier. Of course! That will teach you to pray to a stone god.

"Jilly," he said, "I guess we won't meet them on Friday night any more."

"Ever?" Her eyes were already full.

"Don't cry, Jilly. She's still your aunt; you can see her any time. Do you want dessert?" Her entire hamburger was still on the plate; she'd mashed it up and pushed the pieces neatly under the vegetables.

"But Friday nights were the only time I liked. Because she didn't act like Aunt Elly then. Like my mother's sister. It was the only time she belonged to *me.*"

"I'm sorry, Jilly. I can't help it." He waved the menu at her.

"But what about the *summer?*" she persisted. "Aren't we still going to be with them in the *summer?*"

"I don't know," her father said uncomfortably, twisting around to find the waiter and avoid looking at her. "Maybe you'll go to camp this summer. Maybe I'll go somewhere, on a trip somewhere. I'm not taking any house."

"But *why?*" Now she was really crying.

Landau's anger exploded. "Because I *can't.* I can't take a house every year. I can't *this* year. Because I *can't,* and that's that."

"I don't want to go to camp!" she wailed.

People were looking at them. "Maybe a ranch then," he said, patting her hand.

"No. I don't want to go anyplace. Nobody cares what I want, nobody ever cares."

"Jill, listen to me," he said sternly. "Stop crying, first of all. Stop it!"

Jill choked on the sobs, but the tears continued to stream.

"Aunt Elly and I . . . Elly and I—"He looked down at his

plate. "I asked her to marry me. To divorce Uncle Ralph and marry me."

"You *did?*" She brushed at the tears to stare at him in astonishment.

"Yes, and she won't. Doesn't want to."

"Why *not?*"

"Because she'd rather stay with him, I guess."

Jill didn't hear him. "But she could be really my mother then!" she exclaimed.

"Yes, but she doesn't *want* to, Jill. So I can't be their friend any more."

"I don't understand! Why can't it just be like it was, then?"

"Because it can't," he said wearily.

"Your feelings are just hurt," she said. "You can make up." He shook his head. "If you love somebody," she went on, "you don't stop."

"You do if you have to," Landau said.

"Then it isn't love if it stops."

"How about some vanilla ice cream?"

She shrugged. The waiter came and went.

"I stopped loving your mother, for instance," he said.

"That doesn't count," she said vehemently.

"Why not?"

"Because you said my mother didn't want it anyway." Suddenly, for the first time, Jill wondered if her mother had refused it for a good reason. Maybe she had *known* he would stop.

"She never belonged to me, your mother," Landau said, half to himself. "Not even when I made her have the baby."

Jill squirmed; he was frightening her. But he was hardly aware of the child now. "She didn't want," he mumbled, "any physical part of me."

Was that why? Jill thought. Was her mother afraid? Alison

would never tell her, and she knew she would never ask. "When she had me," Jill asked her father, "what did she say? When I was born?"

Landau frowned vaguely at her, as if he were surprised to find her still sitting across the table. "I wasn't there when you were born," he answered. "I was at Elly's. Your mother didn't even want to be with me then. To see my own child. Some kind of revenge, I suppose, because I forced her to have it. But I thought it would make her love us both."

Jill swallowed to make her throat stop hurting. Could love be like Santa and Tinker Bell and star wishes, all the things she'd rather have than what there was? In the movies when something was terrible you could cover your face and peer through your fingers; it wasn't so bad if you only saw it in little pieces, and you knew your fingers could shut it out—all of it if you had to. Once there was this movie about war, and an old poor mother was knitting a big sweater for her son; it was very cold where he was fighting. And she didn't know how big to make it, because he wrote that he'd grown so tall. And then soldiers burst into her house. Here is your son! And they had this tiny little box. They put it in her hands and laughed, and she looked at the tiny box and then at the big sweater. It had taken Jill several minutes to understand, and then she began screaming. She couldn't stop and they had to carry her screaming out of the theater, her father and Aunt Elly. My God, someone had shouted, who would bring a child to such a movie?

Who would bring a child to such a movie? Jill tried now to picture what her mother had done when she was born. A nurse carrying this small lumpy blanket. No, thank you, none for me, and her mother turning away. But the nurse insisting, smiling; I'm sorry, you must take this; it was ordered for you. Finally her mother, wearing a pink bed jacket with marabou feathers, saying, Well, just leave it, then. Yawning. Maybe my husband wants it for something.

Her father was finishing his ice cream; Jill's was melting sorrowfully, edging up the sides of the dish. Landau looked at her and smiled; there was a tiny fleck of vanilla in the corner of his mouth. "I guess you and me, we'll just have to run away somewhere, the two of us. Jilly, you're the only girl I got now."

Cathy had not intended to see Sandy Rossbach until later, maybe tomorrow or the next day, after sorting things out, after sleeping. But now, with no pills, and still seeing the truck driver's colorless eyes, it was just as well he had appeared like this. She needed something; maybe he would get her something. When she heard his voice, just like that—he had pushed Chad's door buzzer five flights down: Hey, Cath? It's me—she was somehow not surprised. How did you know I was here? she asked, just to be polite, when he had climbed to her secret tower. I didn't know, he said, grinning at her. This is just my regular night for ringing doorbells on this block. Trick or treat. High on something, she thought.

Chad had left a case of Scotch in the apartment, and she had been trying to drink it straight, holding her nose and shuddering. Good girl, she would tell herself every time she finished a glass. Tomorrow you can go have your hair done, and Lance would give her lots of nice bottles filled with goodies that slid down with water. Nice Lance. Though Mother thinks I need more height at the sides, or did she say at the crown? Anyway, it needs something. Otherwise she thinks I should try Emil's at Antoine, or Antoine at Emil's. But I doubt if either of those would give me nice bottles.

She had been lying on Chad's unmade bed, on the raw mattress with loose buttons, wondering if this was what it was like in a Bowery flophouse. Only the room would smell awful, and there would be insects. And probably no women there; women always had their own unmade beds. She let the darkness fold around her, tucking her in like blankets, so when the buzzer rang, she'd been asleep for perhaps four hours.

Sandy had promised Chad he would come for her and take her someplace else. "This is Cathy's uncle. Chad Batchelder. I'm calling to ask you if you'll do me . . . do Cathy a favor. She's just left home and I think she needs not to be alone."

"Did she tell you to call me?" Sandy asked.

"No. But I think she'd be glad."

"Uncle who, did you say?"

"Chad. We've never met—I'm a new one. But I hope we will, soon. Uh, Cathy's told me—"

"Where's she at?" Sandy asked.

"I'll give you the address if you—this is the favor—if you promise to take her somewhere else tonight. She can't—it's just not the best place for her to be, where she is now."

"Did you"—Sandy's voice had a suspicious edge—"did you put her there?"

"No," Chad said smoothly. "She called me to ask if she could go, and I said okay, because she needed to. But it would be a bad mistake for her to stay." He paused, but Sandy didn't pick it up. "Sandy?"

"Yeah, I'm listening." Still suspicious.

"Just ask her to call her mother from—wherever she is. Will you?"

"What if she won't go with me?"

"I think she will, Sandy. I think you can work it so she will. Okay?"

"Hey, little wife," he said to her now. They had not seen each other in four months. Sandy looked different, Cathy realized. Older. But maybe it was just his eyes.

"You want to come home with me awhile? You want to ride in my new car? It's a Porsche."

"I have to stay here," she said, climbing back on the bed. "I have to sleep some more."

"You can't stay here, baby.," Sandy looked around curiously. "It's nice, but your uncle says no."

"Chad?" She sat up and peered at him. They hadn't turned on the lights. "Not true—he said I could. Stay." And she curled up again, squeezing her eyes shut against him.

"Maybe your mother's coming," Sandy said. "Maybe he told her where to come get you."

Cathy stiffened. "No. He wouldn't do that." But she was frightened.

Sandy smiled slyly in the darkness. "Okay," he said lightly, starting for the door. "So long, then."

"Wait," she called. "Sandy?"

"Yeah?"

"Okay," she said, groping for her sandals. "I'm coming."

It was raining hard when they reached the front door. "You wait here," he said. "The car's at the end of the block; I'll just back up."

She nodded obediently. Pressed against the glass door, watching him break the lines of slanting silver, running. It was steamy in the vestibule, and she wanted to go out. She wanted to be wet, soaked to the skin, shivering. You can't go out in the rain; you'll catch cold.

Still groggy, closing her eyes, she lifted her face to it. There was no sign of the car, and she began walking slowly in the direction he had gone. It was probably black; a Porsche, he said.

Seconds later she heard it, but she was already halfway up the block; he would pass right by her. She darted off the curb to call him, and her sandal struck an empty can that rolled under her foot. When she fell, the car skidded to a stop, barely grazing her; she had landed face up between the tire and the rear fender. Instinctively Sandy's foot pressed the accelerator to ease the car forward, to free whatever had fallen. Dazed, she had just lifted her head, so that when he moved, the sharp lower edge of the fender struck her face, tearing it like soft cloth.

When he got out to look, she was lying quite still, blood and rain soaking her long hair. He had no idea what to do. Get back in the car and drive away; I was never here. But the uncle would know. Police? Hospital? But he was stoned and they would think . . . Cathy stirred, making a faint sound. He raced to the lighted phone booth on the opposite corner.

"I'd like to—Mr. Batchelder, please. Sandy Rossbach."

"Uncle Chad? Cathy fell in the street," he began carefully, though he knew his voice was high and strange. "Outside your house; a car hit her." Then he began to sob. "She's all bleeding. Somebody better come."

White and shaken, Chad told Alison to call Mai at once. "I have no idea why the boy would call us," he said. "Except he couldn't very well call Mai, could he? She's not speaking to him."

"But, Ali love, I can't begin to fathom it." Pembroke laughed, sending pale ripples through his transparent blue silk shirt. "Unless they think I'm your secret weapon."

Lord & Taylor had offered him a vice-presidency at seventy-five hundred a year more than his Lowen's salary. Alison had burst into Ned's office with a stricken look. A discount house opening next door, he thought wildly, or else another elegant customer sauntering out in a stolen mink. "Is that all!" he exclaimed when she told him, barely restraining his glee, let alone relief. "Well, I *know* how you feel, Alison, but after all. In fact, it may be for the best—I mean—"

Alison didn't care what he meant. She sat stiffly in one of his tweedy chairs and made her announcement: "If we can't match the increase, and you'll have to prove to me that we can't, I want him made a vice-president with whatever financial—whatever we can manage. Even if you and Ralph have to take pay cuts."

"For Chrissakes, Alison," Ned exploded. "I can get you eight faggot display men up here in half an hour, every one of them a genius on the level of Pembroke Wittenberg. Not to mention available for five thousand less than we're paying him *now.*"

"You're very resourceful," she said coldly, "but then why wouldn't Lord & Taylor be chasing them, do you suppose?"

"Because they're just faggots, dear, not *Lowen's* faggots. Of course Pem is one of a kind." Ned took a deep ragged breath. "He's the only one that's got our label pasted on his—" But he caught Alison's baleful look in time. "There isn't a nickel's worth of raise for anybody," he said instead, "and you know it. Not a nickel."

"I'd like to see the last report. You might have missed one."

Ned escorted her to the door, closed it gently behind her, waited until the click of her heels disappeared into carpet again, and then kicked the door hard enough to remind him of her all day.

She rang at once for Pembroke, with no clear idea of what she could or could not promise him. Money was a painful embarrassment anyway; after twelve years she still gave Frieda her weekly check in a sealed envelope, and if Chad did nothing else for her, at least he handled tips. As for larger financial matters, she tried to maintain an enormous balance in the checking account so that she wouldn't have to keep score, as she called it. Nevertheless she had to call the broker constantly to cash in something right away; I don't understand how this could have happened, but I'm overdrawn.

"Sit down, Pem," she said, wishing there were something on her desk to look preoccupied with. It wasn't a desk any more; now she had an old English hunt table, a narrow curved sliver of rich wood, without drawers, behind which she had to sit very carefully, keeping her shoes on and her knees together because her whole body was visible from anywhere in the room. Furthermore, there was no space on top for papers. Only the telephone, a small vase of anemones, the parrot-green memo pad that said ALL, and a little antique bronze high-button shoe to hold two or three pencils. With *four* pencils it tipped over.

"Pem, you know I—we couldn't bear to lose you."

"Darling, I should be *flayed* for making you worry so. You're all frown lines. Quick, do this!" He grimaced in a facial isometric. She imitated it perfectly, knitting her eyebrows into a deep scowl, then making them spring wide apart into a caricature of surprise. "Four, five, six," Pem counted. "All right."

She put everything back. "Better," he said, nodding and folding his arms, which made the shirt sleeves billow sensuously.

"I don't know quite what to do," Alison said, beginning to frown again, but quickly dispelling it. "Ned's been scolding me for weeks about losses and overstock—you know what gloomy pictures he paints." Pembroke said nothing, so she rushed on. "We've had to cancel bonuses again; he says all belts have to be tightened. The lean and hungry look—except for Ned himself, of course."

Pembroke smiled and touched his own belt, caressing the spectacular gold buckle, two ornate unicorn heads with crossed horns and flowing tangled manes.

"Well," Alison said, with a vague fluttery gesture, "he says we simply can't match the Lord & Taylor salary offer." She glanced at him quickly; he went on pensively stroking his gold unicorns. "But how would it be if we made you . . . my special assistant. A new post! I haven't even thought it out myself yet —creative director, the title doesn't matter, does it? We could pick one together. And then I would personally"—she noticed his fingers had stopped moving, so she plunged gaily on—"I would sign some of my own personal stock over to you. As a sort of bonus. We'd have to check the current value. I don't even know what it's worth this minute, or how we'd arrange the, uh, payments, but whatever number of shares equaled about ten thousand dollars, which would—"

"Ali, darling, I'm suffused!" Pembroke clapped his hands. "Look—goosepimples! Can you bear them with this shirt? Of course I'll stay, I wouldn't dream of going, and you are simply angelic." He had calculated quickly; nothing had been said about a contract, so he could always go next year, with the stock and a bigger name; they'd publicize him now, naturally, which would—

"You'll have more of a voice in store policy," she was saying, "and we—you and I—can go on having as much elegant fun with this place as—"

"As Ned says we can afford!" he finished for her, and leaned impulsively across the hunt table to kiss her forehead. "Mmm! But promise me, darling, one teeny thing more," he said, with his most serious expression.

"Teeny?" she said hesitantly.

"You must let me be here when you announce it to *them*. Ned and Ralph. I couldn't bear to miss *les visages!*"

"But it was your father's *rule!*" Ralph wailed. "The number of outsiders and at what level. I mean, even in Chicago, where they've only got one second cousin, no one from outside ever—"

"My father never let go of talent," Alison replied tersely. "He also said there were several things thicker than blood—among them, brains."

Ned turned wordlessly and walked out. Within five minutes he had put in a call to Jerome T. Alswang, a real estate developer who had recently acquired several choice parcels of block-front in the mid-Fifties along the west side of Fifth Avenue. "And when you get him," Ned growled at his secretary, "no other calls until I yell." He shot a malevolent glance around the corridor. "And I do intend to yell." Aiming his good foot at the door, he remembered the other one just in time to limit this one to a barely satisfying slam.

"Jerry? Ned Greenstone of Lowen's . . . Right. I've only got a minute—about that proposal . . . right, some months ago. We weren't interested at all at that time. However . . . No, not exactly, but I think we could talk some more. I'll need to contact some of the other major stockholders, put some figures together . . . Yes, appreciate that if you would . . . Oh, just one other thing. My sister-in-law. Firmly opposed, you do remember . . . Right . . . We'd have to work around . . . Exactly . . . How about a week from Thursday? . . . Good, Jerry, looking forward."

In a single motion, Ned cradled the receiver and extracted his antacid tablets from the drawer. Swiveling toward the window, chewing thoughtfully, he considered the next moves. He'd need a sixty percent majority vote to close the store and sell the building to Alswang, who would undoubtedly demolish it. Ned personally—Celine and Ned—would clear perhaps five million, and he could then transfer to Lowen's Westchester,

166

which encompassed five thriving branches; the manager was due for retirement next spring.

Alison would clear five million too, of course, but she would hardly notice that. Well, she could always go play with Newark or any of the Nassau County shops. Not that she would; San Francisco, maybe. But that was her problem. He swung back to the desk and began jotting down names and figures. Alison owned twenty percent, Mai another twenty. Mai would definitely vote with Alison. Ralph and Elly, another twenty; he could count on that. An elderly uncle, long retired, in Palm Beach, had another ten percent, and two cousins, one living in Spain, the other with asthma on some cattle ranch in Arizona, split the rest. Someone would have to get to them all.

He grinned suddenly, picturing a forlorn Alison wandering the main floor of Bonwit Teller like a lost child. Tugging at the floor manager's sleeve. There's been a mistake! She stamps her foot. *My* store was right over there! Somebody took it.

Ned sighed, pushing the pill bottle back in the drawer. "Ginny!" he bellowed. "Get me—"

"How would you like it if we took next week off and went someplace beautiful?" Chad said expansively over the top of the *Times* travel section. "To celebrate my new job?" Miles Boehm had hired him, thanks to the nicely publicized coup involving Celine and the Vermicini portraits, and he was now Vermicini's U.S. representative, with a fifteen percent commission on all U.S. sales.

"You know I can't get away now," Alison said, irritated. "Would you undo this for me?" She held out a braceleted arm.

"What if," said Chad, working on the clasp, "I said we're taking next week off, darling, now get inside and pack. In a voice of firm masculine authority?" He unhooked the bracelet and handed it to her.

"I'd say you were drunker, earlier, than usual."

"That was a very unpleasant response," he said mildly, "so I'll ignore it and give you another chance. What if I said—"

"Chad, I'm very tired and we're very late. I promised to stop at the hospital to see Mai for a minute—she's been there with Cathy night and day, it's been a nightmare. Joking with you, if that's what this is, I just can't waste the time. And if by some chance you're serious, I've already said I can't get away right now. So please let's drop it."

Chad settled back in his chair, silent for a few charged seconds. "What if," he began slowly, "I said, quite seriously, that I'm going away for a week, and you can come if you like —or not." He tossed an envelope at her—plane tickets—and went over to the bar for a drink.

Alison was standing in the same spot when he returned. He ignored her and went back to his chair, retrieving the paper. He had a Beethoven symphony on the stereo. Too loud, as usual, she reflected.

"How dare you?" she asked, but her voice was unsteady.

"Not very easily, darling," he sighed, "but I do my best. Actually, I thought you might have been pleased. Oh, and by the way, I'm not going out tonight." He smiled. "I'm very tired too."

Alison started uncertainly toward the bedroom and then paused at the door, weighing the significance of what had happened between them just now. Finally she went in to change.

Half an hour later she was back, again at the doorway. He was still reading, his thin ankles still crossed, feet naked in the embroidered slippers he always wore. Only the music had advanced to another movement. "Chad?" she ventured.

"Yes, darling?" He looked up pleasantly at her, as if she'd just come home. She wondered if he could have forgotten the whole episode. The airline tickets were still on the floor. "Are you coming?" she said.

"No, darling, I told you. Have fun." He blew her a kiss and disappeared behind the paper.

At midnight when she returned, he was gone. At first startled, then frightened, she found herself searching for him, and then for some indication of how long he'd gone for. Opening drawers and closets to see what was missing. He slept in the den now, though the new twin beds had long since arrived. Frieda religiously turned them down every night and changed all the sheets every four days, knowing perfectly well that his had never been used. She also persisted in laying out his pajamas, robe and slippers in there, and carrying them all back from the den in the morning, to be hung in Alison's closet, just in case.

Alison was in his bathroom counting the toothbrushes when he walked in. She didn't see him, so he stood there a minute watching her. He kept three brushes, rotating them meticulously, using a fresh one after each meal. All three were in place. She was astonished at her own sigh of relief.

"Out of toothpaste?" Chad said then.

She almost screamed. "I was—where have you been?"

"Out," he replied. "Did you have fun?"

"Out where? Not visiting a sick friend. I didn't think Christian Scientists had sick friends."

"Darling, would you mind terribly leaving my room now?" he said wearily.

"Chad, I . . . came in to say I'd go with you. Next week. To ——I didn't even look at the tickets."

169

"Mexico," he said, sitting on the daybed to untie his shoes. He didn't bother looking up.

"Unless you don't want me to any more."

"No, of course not," he said, "I'm delighted. Good night, darling."

The Vermicini portraits were breathtaking. He had somehow warmed Celine's puffy blondeness with the opal's liquid flame, so that she looked lit from within, like a delicate sun, and the stone seemed only a vivid reflection. One of the two poses showed the jewel nested in the hollow of her throat, her chin raised and slightly turned. The long slender neck, arched like the stalk of a white plant with this fantastic golden drop of nectar at its root, and her face, a pink and gold haze behind shaggy petals of amber hair. One scarcely noticed the nude torso at all.

In the second pose she held the jewel tenderly in one cupped hand, or rather, it rested on the hand, like an injured bird or an offering. It shone between her breasts, so that if one held the two portraits one above the other, it seemed as if the opal had fallen straight down, of its own weight, to where it now lay, and that if there were later portraits, each would show it cascading progressively downward along her body, on some fateful journey. In this one Celine's head was bowed, and she appeared to gaze reverently at the jewel, in the attitude of a pagan madonna. Again the entire torso was nude, and here the angle of the body seemed to echo the sinuous curve of the tear-shaped stone, one the magnified image of the other. There was no doubt that the photographer was an artist.

Chad had promised Celine that the transparencies would be shown in strict privacy to only three carefully selected magazine editors, but before the third martini had arrived on their

NECESSARY OBJECTS

lunch tables, half the editors in town—newspaper and television, as well as magazine—knew all, or at least enough, about a bunch of obscene Polaroid shots of some New York society broad—what's her name, one of the Lowen girls—whose family had once blown the whistle on her career as a movie star.

By the following morning Celine had received a dozen requests to see the pictures, to be interviewed and photographed with or without them, and to appear on TV talk shows to discuss why she had posed for them. Everyone had called, Ned observed wryly, except the *Ladies Home Journal* and *Art News*, and Celine was still in bewildered tears over a columnist's syndicated exclusive in last night's *Post:*

Lost Star Shines A-Nude
In Prized Gem's
Reflected Glory
Remember Celina Lowen as The Girl? And whatever happened to her? One of those meteoric heavenly bodies that used to flash overnight and fade by morning in Hollywood's own evaporated Milky Way. This one was a *nova riche*, Celestial Celina, née Celine, a million-heiress (Lowen's Department Stores), a nebulous but nubile mini-talent who radiated just enough to catch a director's eye. Now—can it really be 18 years later?— she is better known as Mrs. Edmund (Ned) Greenstone, one of those 14-K. fashion-plated East Side bodies with chic parties and gold-plated Lowen's charge-a-plates.

All these years "Celina" has been just plain Celine, kid sister of lady store president Alison Lowen, and wife of a successful, ruthless retailing dynamo (who works for her sister).

But today, like Halley's Comet, Celina Lowen burst into lights again. This time, ladies and gents, she's appearing in the nude. Shedding her society-lady image, along with every stitch of her filmy Lowen's lingerie, Celine can be seen with the naked eye cavorting through a series of shocking-pink color photos snapped by a controversial Italian portrait photographer. The only thing she has on is a million-dollar fire opal, a recent birthday-suit present from her husband. Other portraits by the self-proclaimed camera artist who took these were recently seized in

171

Europe as pornography. The photographer and the magazine that published his masterpieces still face trial on obscenity charges in Rome.

Now how does a thing like that happen? Sit tight and we'll tell you. It all started when this doting husband couldn't think what to give his picture-pretty blond wife for her thirty-sixth birthday. Thirty-six! Half the summers gone! How about a fire opal, Mr. Greenstone? somebody said. A gem with the warmth of all summers locked forever in its red-gold heart. He decided to get her the most gorgeous fire opal in the world—the fabled Cortes. A flurry of secret bids, intrigue, suspense, an international auction, a retailing king's ransom, and presto! Ned Greenstone gives his Queen Celine the only thing she really wanted to wear: the Cortes opal.

This stone, you see, had quite a past, just like Celine. Both idolized by a worshipful public, both lost, both forgotten. The stone had been spirited away from Indian shrines and Continental treasure chests. The woman had vanished from the temples of Hollywood just days after her secret marriage to a brilliant young movie director, Jay Harvey Martin. The marriage was quietly annulled, and to this day, Celine has never made another picture. Maybe she just hadn't found the right costume.

Miniature slides of her newest releases were being hustled around news and magazine offices today—the hottest shots in town. The rumor factories indicate they may be issued for general release soon, probably with an X rating. *Stagshow Magazine* has reportedly offered five figures for one of Celine's, for a forthcoming centerfold.

P.S. When sister Alison remarried recently, one reporter at the wedding asked Celine if she had ever missed being a star. There was the slightest twinkle in her big brown eyes when she said, "In a constellation like the Lowens', we take turns." As of now, it looks like Celine's turn.

Celine spent half the morning calling Mai, Alison, Ira, and finally Chad for reassurance. What could she say to people? What *should* she say? What should she do about all these reporters? Was it true about *Stagshow Magazine?* She'd rather die. Wouldn't she? Shouldn't she?

"Well, first let's calm down," Chad suggested cheerfully, like a nurse with an obstreperous patient. "I guess it's going to take some careful handling, but you'll do it just fine. Lowen girls are known for careful handling, aren't they?" And Alison

172

observed that in any case it was too late to *undo* it. "You know there's no way to make news without attracting attention; *you* ought to know that better than any of us," she reminded Celine. Maybe if she got used to thinking of herself as a serious art patron, Ira thought. Nothing undignified about that, after all. Think about Goya and Manet and *their* models. Had she heard about the note in *Variety*, by the way? Had she seen the item in *Women's Wear?*

No, of course she hadn't. What did *they* say? She called Chad again and held her breath.

"Just that the portraits exist," he said casually. "And that *Vogue* is interested in publishing them."

"They are?" Celine cried. "You didn't even tell me!"

"How could I tell you?" Chad scolded her. "You were all ready to burn the pictures!"

"Now listen," Celine said. "Are you listening?"

He was. "Ira said to direct all these calls to you, at your office. That I shouldn't talk to anybody, they have to call my agent. That's you, all right?"

"All right," he said.

"And if I go out," she went on, "I'll tell the maid. I'll give her your number right now. And then you decide who and what and how I should be interviewed. All right?"

Almost inaudibly: "All right, Celine."

The first Chad-approved interviewer was a thin, serious-faced woman with dead hair and hard-bitten fingernails. She carried a large tape recorder which she kept apologizing about; this was the first time she had used it, and she was never quite sure it was on. Excuse me, oh, excuse me, and she'd peer into it. And would you mind saying that again? The photographer who came with her, a tall young black, wore a black suit, tie and shirt—an entirely black person except for his shoes, which were a blazing yellow, as if he had burst open at the bottom. He didn't say a word. They both seemed terribly uncomfortable, which made it twice as hard for Celine to be open, casual and confident, which everyone agreed was the right image. The woman kept getting up to inspect things, and then Celine would have to go over and answer questions about whatever it was, and then the photographer would follow them, stalking them in his silent, screaming yellow shoes, and then the woman would suddenly dash back to the tape recorder to see if it was still on.

Her first question was how much had the portraits cost, and Celine replied simply and straightforwardly, "Two thousand dollars." Then the woman had admired the living-room drapes. "That looks like very expensive fabric," she said. "I think it was seventy-five dollars a yard," Celine recalled, openly and casually. And so on: the furniture, a piece of marble sculpture ("A Barkan, isn't it? His work is very valuable now; I read somewhere it's tripled in value in the past few years." "Yes, it has," said Celine, "we paid fifteen thousand dollars for that in 1960").

The woman seemed to think Celine had been on the best-dressed list. "That was my sister, Alison," Celine said. Oh, of course, and what had Alison thought of the portraits? "She thinks they're very interesting." Did she think, the reporter wondered, wetting her lips and peering into her tape recorder, that the rest of her family might feel at all embarrassed? "No," Celine said confidently, "I don't."

What about her husband? "Oh, Ned—well, he was somewhat uneasy before the pictures were made," Celine admitted, "but now that he's seen them he's thrilled."

The story ran the next day; it was brutal. A feature on the women's page, with an eight-column streamer headline across the top. "The High Cost of Posing Naked; Socialite Reveals

174

All." Celine came through as vulgar, crass and incredibly stupid. " 'The material in those drapes cost seventy-five dollars a yard,' she confided breathlessly." " 'That scupture is a Barkan; we paid fifteen thousand dollars for it.' Mrs. Greenstone took pains to note that the sculptor's work had tripled in value since they acquired the work."

Also: "The former actress was not wearing the famous Cortes opal, which she explained was out being set, but was making do with a knuckle-crushing diamond ring."

Also: "As for her family's reactions to the life-size nude portraits, Mrs. Greenstone described them as follows: Her sister Alison, the president of Lowen's Fifth Avenue, who has been listed as one of America's best-dressed women, apparently damned the photographs with the classic faint-praise putdown: 'very interesting.' (Perhaps Miss Lowen will have more to say if her sister is nominated for this year's best *undressed*.) As for her husband, who, she confessed, had been uneasy at the mere idea of his wife posing nude, he was now "thrilled" by the results. Not a cheap thrill either, Mrs. Greenstone made clear; each click of the shutter had set him back one thousand dollars."

"My God, Celine," Alison telephoned to say. Then her voice rose sharply: "How in heaven's name—" Celine hung up, shaking.

Chad phoned later from his office. "I should have been with you," he said. "Celine darling, I'm so sorry."

"I don't think it would have mattered," she replied. "I think they did what they came to do. But I don't want any more. I think we'd better cancel *Vogue.*"

Chad hesitated. There was so much more at stake now than Celine's ego: Vermicini's American market, Chad's own professional reputation, the Boehm agency. He had to admit

175

he was surprised at all the venom. It was essentially a cheap story, except for Celine's flimsy society image; with nude photos of any other ex-actress, you couldn't buy a line on page 94, much less a scathing attack. Interesting. "It's up to you," he said finally.

"*I* think it would be a mistake," Alison said firmly when Celine called to ask her advice. "It's like admitting you had something to be ashamed of."

Celine called Chad back and began to cry. "Don't do that," Chad said gently. "The pictures are beautiful, and you know you've a right to be proud of them."

"But—" she said, and went on weeping.

"But," he said, "that *is* what it's about, really. After that, one deals with other people's poison arrows the best one can."

She was only half listening, but she believed him. Interviewers were only other people. She thought of her sisters, of other women, of herself, greeting each other in restaurants. That quick penetrating glance. Searching each other's faces for tiny signs that the other has aged just a little since the last time, that something enviable had begun to desert them. It never mattered whether you found what you were looking for, or failed to find it; you looked away with disappointment, either way. Because the other looked better than you'd hoped? Or than you'd remembered? No, it wasn't that, she didn't think. Whatever that other face showed was somehow frightening; that was it. You shrank from the small mean triumph because of what it told you about yourself. And because it said next—you're next. Elly had told her about suddenly discovering one day three delicate lines across her forehead, and racing to the mirror to disprove them. For months afterward she had seen nothing else in the mirror but those lines until they were etched in her mind's eye like a shocking news photo of a war atrocity. And finally, Elly had said, I accepted the fact of them. But not graciously.

Celine sighed. "Chad? I guess I'll stick."

"All right," he said, sighing too. Whatever she decided, he now had the uneasy feeling they would all regret it.

They tried television, and at first Celine seemed safer there. "What made you decide to pose for nude photos?" "I didn't think of them that way. My husband and I commissioned the artist to do two portraits. We believe they are fine works of art."

"Did you know that similar photos by this same, uh, artist, have been seized in Europe as pornographic? That the artist faces *obscenity* charges?"

"Yes, I know. Lots of artists, throughout history, have been attacked that way—Goya, Manet. Even artists who painted apples with angles instead of curves. They were all condemned as obscene."

"Well, this artist of yours certainly didn't do any angles instead of curves, ha ha, did he?"

"How was I?" Celine asked Chad anxiously after that one. His was the only opinion she valued now. "You were absolutely Celine," he said safely.

The next one wasn't quite so high-toned. "Would you commission similar portraits of your husband?" the grinning host demanded.

"No, I don't think so."

"Why not?"

"I don't know, really. I suppose I don't think of my husband as an ideal model for that sort of portrait." (Laughter.)

"How about another man, then? What would you think if, say, I posed, just in my new Audemars Piguet watch?" (Laughter.)

"I'd have to reserve judgment until I saw the portraits."

"Offhand, though?" he persisted. "Offhand would you say such a picture might be considered obscene?"

"Offhand I guess it would depend on your expression. If it was the one you're wearing now, I'd say yes." (Laughter.)

By the end of the week Celine was a personality, something between a celebrity and a cheap story. It was not an achievement she could feel. Surprisingly, Ned had borne up very well. Not altogether surprisingly; it was his wife, but it was also merchandising.

"Maybe the opal's unlucky after all," Celine said to him one morning at breakfast. "I almost wish you hadn't bought it."

"Nonsense," he said, kissing the top of her head goodbye. "You need a thicker skin. What happened to that tough Hollywood hide?"

She smiled wearily. "Don't you remember? Papa didn't let me stay there long enough to tan it."

She was offered a spot as a regular performer on a daytime television panel show. "You see?" Ned said cheerily. "No," she replied. "I don't."

And on the phone with Chad—her fourth call to him that day—she said thoughtfully, "It's not like Hollywood at all, is it?"

"Neither was Hollywood," he answered. "Though they both still have the same effect on the mind. Hallucinogens. Very dangerous unless you know what you're doing."

"And do you always know what *you're* doing," she asked softly, "when something is very dangerous?"

"No," he answered quickly, pretending not to understand. "I hardly ever know until it's too late." Ignorance, he reminded himself ruefully after she hung up, is no excuse. Especially ignorance of Lowen-laws.

Eight

THE BANDAGES

still covered two-thirds of Cathy's face, including her left eye.
The surgeons would not yet hazard a guess about the extent of
permanent scarring. She had graduated from intravenous feeding to a liquid diet, sipped through straws. But no talking,
laughing, crying, yawning or sneezing. Like the Queen of Eng-
land, she thought—though the Queen probably never needed
to do any of those things after they told her she must absolutely
not.

There was a pad and a red pencil next to the bed, but Cathy
had not written anything. No comment at this time.

Mai had arranged for the psychiatrist to come to the hospital for her regular sessions, and he would sit next to the bed, waiting. Finally, on his fourth visit, Cathy picked up the pad and pencil and drew him a picture, a girl's face divided by a jagged red line. He looked at it for about a minute and then drew a question mark underneath. Cathy put the pad back on the table and closed her eyes, one free and one under the bandage. After a while the hour ended. "I'll see you on Tuesday, Cathy," he said.

Cathy thought about how when they wanted to show the Invisible Man as a normal person they wrapped his invisible head in bandages and explained that he had been in an accident, so he wouldn't frighten people. Then when he was in danger he could just unwrap his head and there would be nobody there.

She was alone in a white room; wasn't there a white room like this before? She remembered curved bars outside the window, in the shape of a half-crown. A protective railing to keep a small child from falling out. But they were only on the second floor. A duplex maisonette. She had been frightened of kidnappers; she thought they could just pull themselves up, hanging onto those curved bars the way she did on the playground jungle gym. There must have been a big kidnapping case in the news; grownups must have been talking about it. She would lie there staring at the bars outside the window, knowing they were coming for her because she did not belong here. She knew they would come as soon as she fell asleep, while the nurse and the housekeeper were laughing far away in the kitchen.

Then one night the nurse and the housekeeper had both come in to say good night, with their coats on. Both were going out; they were leaving her alone. She lay there crying into the pillow because tonight the kidnappers would come and there would be nobody home even to scream when she was being

180

taken. Any minute these white-gloved hands would appear on the bars. And then she screamed, Help, oh, help. And someone was coming at once—footsteps. God, please, who could it be? Someone must have come up in the elevator, carrying a big rough sack that he said was something he had to deliver there in the middle of the night when nobody was home, and the elevator man had opened the door for him.

Her bedroom door burst open then and the yellow hall light streamed in, filled with strange faces. Help, oh, help. What *is* it, Cathy? She must be dreaming. Who was that, some strange lady who found out my name? Who are you? said Cathy. The woman laughed in a funny way, embarrassed. It's Mommy. See? I'm right here. You had a bad dream. Over her shoulder the Mommy said, It's all right, go on downstairs, everyone, I'll be right back. The other faces making noises went away saying poor little thing.

I don't understand, Cathy whimpered. How come you're here? Everybody went out. The Mommy laughed again, and it still sounded funny. I didn't go out. What made you scream? I saw the kidnapper coming, Cathy said. Out the window. Climbing up the bars. I saw his gloves.

The Mommy looked out the window. You were imagining, she said. Nobody can climb in. (They could, though; it was easy. That's how kidnappers always.) Anyway, never mind, the Mommy said, I'll be right here, go back to sleep. She patted Cathy's hand, and hers felt cool and light. You could feel the small bones in it, right through the skin. Cathy's hand didn't have any bones in it, she was sure. All fat. The Mommy left the door open so Cathy would feel safe, but the stripe of yellow light made strange shadows and changed the room. The kidnapper would probably rather come now, when the Mommy was there with company instead of the nurse and the housekeeper. The Mommy wouldn't scream in front of the company when they took Cathy away. Who was she, anyway? Why had the nurse and the housekeeper gone out? They never both went out, and they knew the Mommy wouldn't stop a kidnapper. Then all of a sudden Cathy realized she was *already* kidnapped. That was why she was here. But why had this Mommy, witch Mommy, this one, taken her from her real family? What was she going to do to her?

Mai stood quietly at the edge of her hospital bed. "Cathy?" she said to the fluttering visible eyelid. "It's Mommy. See? I'm right here." And her long cool fingery bones stroked Cathy's small fat hand.

Buxton Academy, courtesy of Horace T. Ambruster, headmaster, finally expelled Jason. His negative and disruptive influence on other students had finally reached a point. . . .

Several latest episodes were cited in a long letter inviting Elly to confer, if she felt it would be desirable, with either the school psychologist or Jason's faculty advisor, or both—in addition, of course, to the undersigned. Several latest episodes involving . . . presence of a quantity of illicit narcotic drugs, which alone constituted grounds for immediate dismissal according to school policy . . . Then the matter of the school's annual theatrical production, for which Jason had volunteered to contribute the musical score and lyrics. A brilliant musical score, quite astonishing, in fact, but Jason had been asked to revise the lyrics, which contained a great deal of highly objectionable language. Jason had refused to comply with this order, and at the last minute, with flagrant disregard for his fellow students, both those in the production and those for whom it was the year's major entertainment event—with *complete* flagrant disregard, Jason had destroyed the score, forcing the faculty to cancel the production for the first time in the history of Buxton Academy.

And finally a most unfortunate incident, a most serious problem, the nature of which fell into an area of personal behavior that could not be appropriately discussed in this letter. Jason and two other boys had been referred at once to the school psychologist, and his findings would of course be made available to any therapist whom Jason's parents might wish to consult about this problem.

Needless to say, we sincerely regret . . . painful decision, especially considering the great generosity Jason's parents had displayed toward the school, indicating their commitment to the standards of excellence for which Buxton strove and would continue to strive . . .

"There's no place left to send him," Elly announced at dinner that night. She had asked Alison and Chad over to participate in the crisis. Since her own recent trouble, she couldn't bear dealing with one more crisis alone. Meaning alone with Ralph. Not that she thought Alison would be a comfort, at least not in the usual sense. One could feel comfortable with Alison only if one drew solace from her superb ability to ignore other people's acute discomforts. There were times when that helped a great deal. For Elly, though, there was still something else. Being with Alison and Chad brought back something of the distant past—specifically, the period in which Bob Landau had first discovered how delightfully different she was from Alison. Chad, of course, was very different from Bob Landau, but still. Alison, after all, was the constant; Alison, who never saw or felt anything more unpleasant than lack of chic. At least, one assumed she never did.

"Why not keep the boy home, then?" Chad asked. "Some kind of serious musical training, if that's—"

Elly shook her head. "New York is still no place for a little boy. An only child."

"For heaven's sake, Elly, he's fifteen!" said Alison. "Look at Jill—New York hasn't eaten *her* alive."

"The point is, what do we *do* with him in New York," Ralph said.

Alison had a marvelous idea. "Chad, doesn't Miles Boehm —didn't Ira tell me that Miles Boehm represents Lewisohn?"

"Eli Lewisohn?" said Ralph. "The composer?"

Chad nodded. "I've met him."

"Well, why couldn't you arrange for *Jason* to meet him? Maybe Jason could even play for him. Shouldn't someone like that be the person to advise—"

"Well," said Chad uncertainly.

"He could at least tell us if the kid's really a genius," Ralph said. "If he is, maybe he never belonged in a regular school in the first place. Maybe they don't know what to do with a musical genius."

"God knows I don't," said Elly. She had told them about everything in Ambruster's letter, except the last part about the unfortunate area of behavior which couldn't be discussed. She had no intention of consulting the school psychologist about it, or any other therapist.

Jason arrived very early the next morning, before ten A.M. Elly was still in bed when he came in.

"Hello, Mother." He stood there with his dirty hair and his duffel bag, shifting his feet on the fluffy rug.

"Hello, Jason," she said.

"This is my last week's l—— dirty clothes," he went on, indicating the duffel bag. "They said there was—I wouldn't have time to send it out."

She sighed. "Take it in the kitchen."

"Take it to the kitchen," Jason amended, but only to himself, and turned to go.

"Jason?" But when he turned back, she couldn't think of anything. He was tall, and his curly brown hair needed washing, and his round puppy-brown eyes never showed the whites, and he was a boy, and she didn't know how to talk to anyone like that. "I want to talk to you," she said, and then reached hastily for the telephone, a lifeline. "But I have some calls to make first." She began dialing before he left the room, then put the receiver down. If Ralph were here, she could make him talk to the boy. Or his father; she could call Ted and insist that he—after all, a father's job, discipline.

She lifted the receiver again and dialed Chad's office number. "I'm sorry to bother you at work, I know how busy—"

It was all right; in fact, he had planned to call her. He had already spoken to Eli Lewisohn about auditioning Jason. Lewisohn would be delighted.

"Oh, that's wonderful. I was calling because I just happened to think, if you were free for lunch, by any chance, Jason just got in—I thought if you were free I'd bring him to meet you. Just, I thought, if you were going to arrange with Lewisohn, you should probably have a talk with Jason first. So you could tell—"

Chad said he'd be happy to take them to lunch.

Elly flew breathlessly into Jason's room in her nightgown, with the assurance of a mother who now had something definite to say. "We're meeting Uncle Chad for lunch." Jason looked blank. "Chad, Aunt Alison's husband. He's going to arrange an audition for you with Eli Lewisohn. He needs to get some idea about your musical—about your thoughts about . . . what you want to study. In music. Now I want you to get cleaned up, you're filthy, a shower—and wash your hair."

"Mother? What did Am—— the headmaster tell you about—"

She gestured, brushing it away. "We'll talk about that later.

When Ralph is here. And I haven't even spoken to your father—"

"Mother?"

"Jason, I have to get dressed. What is it?"

"It's . . . I don't w—— I can't play for Eli Lewisohn."

That frightened her. "Well, you're going to!" she shrieked, her small white face bruised with anger. "You're just going to, do you hear me?"

He stared at her. She was so tiny! He was almost a head taller. What if he hit her. What if he even just cursed at her. God . . . d-damn you, Mother, I won't play for Eli Lewisohn; you can't m-make me. Once he *had* cursed at her and she slapped his face. A silly weak slap, like a little kid. But her face, her brown eyes turning solid black, had really scared him. She'd *meant* that slap so hard. He still hated her, but not so helplessly any more. He didn't know what had changed, but suddenly it was she who seemed helpless.

Chad talked easily about music—jazz, Schoenberg and whether orchestral backgrounds really worked with rock solos. Since he didn't seem to want to talk at all about Jason, Jason relaxed and talked easily back, which pleased Elly at first and then began to irritate her. By the middle of lunch they were arguing raptly about tonality or atonality, and Jason wasn't stuttering at all, and she had finished her sliced tomato and there was nothing to do but sit there smiling emptily over her empty plate. Chad finally noticed. "Jason," he said, "have you ever accompanied your mother at one of her dance concerts?" They both looked bewildered. "Don't tell me he's never seen you dance at a party, Elly? She's pure tonality, your mother."

"He's joking," Elly said uncomfortably. Jason squirmed in his seat.

Chad thought he'd better move on to something else. "Did your mother mention Eli Lewisohn?"

"Yes, I did," said Elly. "Jason said he wouldn't play for him."

"Sure I will," Jason said, just to embarrass her. "All I said was I didn't see the p—— I didn't understand what for."

"I asked him to hear you," said Chad. "Your mother wanted some professional advice about your training."

"Advice? I'll bet. She wants—I know what she wants, some famous name to tell her I'm a genius."

"Jason, that's enough," said Elly sharply, but he went on.

"And if he says I am, then it's okay that I got exp—— kicked out of four different schools. Only what if he says I'm not— then what?"

"Then it will still be okay," said Chad, looking at Elly. "I don't think Eli Lewisohn's parents knew what to do about him and school either. He quit at twelve, and they couldn't even afford piano lessons." He paused, sipping the watery remains of his Scotch.

Jason was about to ask what Lewisohn did, but Elly got there first. "What did the parents do?"

Chad smiled. "They put him to work in their tailor shop, pressing pants. He told me that the only reason he began practicing piano with such dedication was that it was the only time he could sit down. I guess you have to play a pants presser standing up."

Jason laughed, a cracking middle-teen-aged laugh. Atonal. Elly realized she had never heard him make that sound, but then Jason rarely laughed in her presence. "You really ought to come hear Jason yourself, Chad," she said. "Before he plays for Lewisohn."

"Jason doesn't have to audition for me."

"But he'd like to—wouldn't you, Jase?"

The boy shrugged. "Sure, okay," he said.

"Matter of fact, I'd like to play something for Jason," Chad said. "My vintage 78 records. I've got all these scratchy Benny Goodmans that nobody I know will sit still for. They drive Alison up the wall."

"I really would like—" Jason began.

"I know what let's do!" exclaimed Elly, taking charge like a camp counselor. "Why doesn't Chad . . . and Alison . . . come have dinner with us tonight—can you? And bring some records, and Jason can play for you, and then we could all—"

Chad laughed. "Poor Ralph would be bored senseless, wouldn't he? Not to mention Alison—I once tried forcing an evening of jazz and pops on her. Just once."

"Oh, but it would be such fun," Elly persisted. "Ralph won't mind, he can go watch his TV. And Alison—well, we'll think of something."

Chad looked doubtfully at Jason, but the boy was attacking his apple pie. Tuned out. Grownups planning fun for him. "It's Jason's first night home, Elly. I don't think—"

Jason looked up apprehensively. "Oh, don't worry about *that!*" Elly cried. "We were only going to have a miserable depressing talk about school, weren't we?" She winked at her son; he stared back blankly. "And we can do that tomorrow! You'll give us a perfect excuse."

"Jason?" said Chad.

"Sure. Okay."

Alison did not of course feel up to it; she phoned Elly to explain how exhausted, and besides, she'd promised Mai she would stop in briefly at the hospital. Poor Mai. So Chad would come by himself, if they'd forgive her, and he'd bring those old records of his, and Alison would adore to hear Jason some other time soon.

All evening Elly floated like a Washington hostess, high on her own distinguished guest list, tossing her burnished hair, bubbling and splashing pale gold laughter like the champagne. And dancing. Drifting in a loose cloud of a silver robe that clung and shifted like blowing cobwebs. She moved to Chad's precious old records as if they were his own rhythm, as if she were some vibrant new arrangement of something he loved. A silvery responsive chord. A pretty girl, like a melody.

Even Ralph stayed, neglecting his TV, which he usually watched like an anxious governess, as if it might get into trouble the minute his back was turned. Tonight there was something better on, the spectacular shadow play of Elly's small taut body beating like wings inside its sheer silver cage. Her feet were bare, or rather, she wore narrow thongs of silver metal that had no soles, that had no sensible function at all except to make her tiny naked feet flash like sudden jewels. For an evening of musical virtuosity, she had composed a superbly classic self.

Jason huddled near the stereo, fiddling with dials to improve the sound. His mother might have been dancing somewhere else, reviving some other era of golden oldies.

Finally, breathless, she sank onto a sofa, wisps of silver drifting like mist. They listened to one more record, and then it was Jason's turn. He played Prokofiev for them, his technical skill gleaming like the piano's reflection of Elly's white flowers in a crystal bowl. Then a Gershwin concerto with throwaway Oscar Levantine precision, a poet expressing passionate indifference.

And last, a song of his own: "Crosswalk." Singing and talking it in a tired voice, the song subsiding into speech and then back into song. It was a dramatic story, about a retarded little boy whose dog learns how to cross with the green light, so the boy's parents let them take walks together. One night there is a snowstorm, sudden and fierce, and a massive power failure. Streetlights go out, but the boy and dog stand patiently at the corner, snow swirling around them, waiting for a green light that never comes. In the morning they are found, frozen to death.

As Jason played, Chad felt a startled rush of excitement; whatever Eli Lewisohn thought, the boy's talent was extraordinary. Chad had not expected it, and what, if anything, needed to be done to or with such a youngster at this point, he had no idea. Probably not much beyond letting him grow. Broadway musicals, film scoring, Jason might well move in such directions, possibly even now. Chad glanced at Elly: did she hear it? Probably not, he decided.

When it was over, he told Jason what he thought, quietly in a corner away from Elly and Ralph. He offered to help if he could—any way that Jason might think he could. "Thank you," said Jason, "I appreciate." Chad thought he saw tears in his eyes, but perhaps not. The boy said good night almost at once, waving it from the doorway to his mother and Ralph.

"And I should do likewise," Chad said, "I think we're all played out. I enjoyed the whole thing shamefully."

"I'm glad," Elly said, "and we'll let you go only if you promise to come do it again."

"Of course."

She kissed him good night with only the merest fraction of warmth past sisterly, and Ralph shook his hand, beaming. He left the records; in the elevator he admitted to himself that he meant to.

*   *   *

Elly made love to Ralph that night. She told him how sorry she was that it had been so long. Since she felt . . . really well enough. The bleeding, and the unhappy business with Bob Landau. She promised that things would be better now. And when Ralph fell happily asleep, turning his back to her, she tucked her own hands inside herself and thought about Chad and having a new brotherly lover-in-law.

The appointment with Eli Lewisohn was arranged for the following week. But Jason needed Chad to coach him, Elly said. Jason wondered if you were free . . . Or to Alison: Jason wondered if Chad could just stop in briefly; he wanted to play a new song for him and get his advice on the lyrics, in case he thought he should polish it for the audition.

After the third or fourth time it was understood that Chad would stop in every night for . . . rehearsal. Alison was working late, anyway, or she had promised Mai. Or Alison was . . .

And to some extent Jason did need Chad; no one else was listening. Ralph was closeted with his TV, and Elly hovered like a stage mother or a bird of prey. When Chad came, she would leave them mercifully alone, just peering in every so often to apologize for disturbing them.

But of course when Chad was leaving, she would want to talk to him alone for just a minute. "About Jason. I'm too worried, I know, but I can't help it." And what did Chad really think? What did he really think Lewisohn would think?

You must know it doesn't matter, Chad told her. That Jason doesn't need anyone's endorsement. Lewisohn might not even be the right kind of person to consult. After all, a traditionalist. Even if he had a reputation for being "with-it." Jason was wild; his academic training had been solid, as far as it went, but he had already traveled so far away from—

"But isn't that wrong? Isn't he too young to just . . . Doesn't he need more academic—shouldn't he be exposed—"

"I don't know, Elly," Chad sighed. "Maybe Lewisohn knows."

The next night she opened some champagne, and they talked about Mozart. Eleven years old and adapting other composers' works into something more or less original—but not too original. Something that would impress grown-up audiences, but not challenge them. At fifteen Jason was hardly Mozart, but on the other hand, Chad pointed out, he was already an original, and there was probably no going back from there.

"You've grown very fond of him, haven't you?" Elly asked him.

"He's a good kid. And I like his style."

"He hates me, has he told you?" she said casually, refilling their glasses.

Chad sipped, weighing his answer. "Don't you also hate him?"

"Of course not," she said quickly. "He's my child."

Chad shook his head, frowning. "Such a threadbare old answer, Elly—not like you. Why do you suppose every child admits it so easily? Sure, I hate my folks—don't you? But every parent still denies it so vehemently, so guiltily. 'Of course I don't hate him; he's mine.' "

She smiled. "But I really don't hate Jason. I just don't see much point in my having been his mother." She paused. "Or anyone's."

"Do you see the point of Jason?" he asked.

She didn't know. Unless he really was a genius. In that case she supposed—but clearly, she was bored now. She refilled their glasses again—just one more—and abruptly changed the subject. "Chad, do you like being a Lowen?"

"No," he admitted. "Though I can't imagine another family —institution?—I'd ever have felt so compelled to join."

"Have felt," she murmured.

"What?"

"You said ever *have* felt. As if you were looking back on it. On us."

"I always look back. It's always too dark to see in front."

She sat quietly for a minute, playing with the stem of her glass. "Are you sleeping with Celine?" she asked suddenly.

"No," he replied, not missing a beat.

"Not yet?" she amended, smiling. "I just wondered. You've been so close lately, your promotion work for her—I just wondered."

"No," he said decisively.

"What about us?" she said, turning to look straight into his silver-blue eyes. She smiled to take the intensity out of it. "Could you and I become lovers, do you think?"

"No," he said lightly.

"Not yet," she corrected. And smiled again. "In some Oriental countries, I've read, it's not customary to say a flat no to such a question. On the theory that no is either an arrogant assumption, or terribly pessimistic. If you ask a ninety-year-old peasant squatting in his Indonesian hut whether he has ever flown a jet to New York, he will say not yet."

"Perhaps he's only being polite," Chad said, "not to hurt your New York feelings. Asians have odd politenesses. In Tokyo people wear masks when they have colds. It's their way of apologizing for being in poor health in your presence. But they'll kill you trying to beat you onto the subway, in their apologetic masks. I really must go home, Elly, Alison will—"

"Will she?"

"Well, she won't attack me with a rolling pin, no."

"No, I didn't think she would."

"You mean not yet?"

When Ralph came out of his den as she was walking him to the door, Chad felt a vaguely guilty interior lurch. "You leaving, Chad?" he said cheerfully. "Didn't get a chance—I get so wrapped up in these old movies."

"That's all right, Ralph," Chad said uncomfortably. "I'm not really company, after all."

The three of them stood awkwardly waiting for the elevator. "Well, good night," Chad said, feeling like a kid in a car being searched by a policeman's flashlight. When Elly kissed him, he almost pushed her away, but then decided that would probably look worse. As the elevator doors closed, they both called, "See you tomorrow, right?"

"Hello, darling," he said cheerfully, depositing a light kiss on Alison's fragrant night-creamed cheek. She was sitting up in bed wearing a blue-lace bed jacket over a blue nightgown. A blue robe was folded at the edge of the bed. It struck him that she wore a complete matched ensemble for every activity of the day.

As he went to the closet to retrieve his pajamas and slippers, she looked up from her magazine. "Did you know," she said in a low neutral tone, as if she might be reading it, "that Elly was Bob Landau's mistress?"

Chad calmly took his clothes off the hook. Alison was not, he realized, reading it. "No," he said, "was she?" He groped for his slippers.

"Yes," she went on evenly. "In fact, it all started when Bob and I were practically newlyweds. Fourteen years ago, it must be."

He stood there holding his clothes. "Really?" He trusted she was not grading his responses.

"I understand," she went on, "*Jill* told me, actually, that they've just broken up. If that's the correct term, when one of them is married."

"Jill told you?" he said, looking for a place to sit down. He was so not at home in this room. Finally he perched on the other bed—"his" bed, still holding the clothes.

"Yes," said Alison. "Her father told her all about it. Instead of a bedtime story."

"Well, but what did he tell her? I'm sure not that—"

She shrugged and began turning pages. Maybe it was in *Vogue,* after all, and she was going to read him the rest aloud. "I gather just that he asked Elly to get a divorce and marry him. And that she isn't going to."

"Was Jill upset?" he said.

Alison went on looking at the magazine; the whole conversation seemed to hang on whatever she was looking for. "Yes," she said finally, stopping at "People Are Talking About." "Jill's very fond of Elly. You know, I think this is the first time Jill's ever told me anything important. Ordinarily she'd tell Elly first. And even now, I doubt that she'd have mentioned it to me except that she's so upset about the summer." She paused, but he chose to sit this one out. "The summer," she repeated. "Bob's decided not to rent a house near Elly's. He told Jill she'd probably have to go to camp, and she doesn't want to."

"Well," Chad said helplessly, wishing it were not so clear where all of this was leading. And why the measured pace? She was behaving in a most un-Alisonian way. He couldn't recall ever having been so unsure of her mood. "We'll have to think of something more appealing than camp," he said awkwardly.

"Yes, we will," she said, looking up again. "You've been over there every night this week. I just realized."

She had caught him off guard. "Realized what?" he stammered, wondering if he looked as foolish as he must sound.

She smiled indulgently. "Elly must need company."

"Are you making some obscure sinister point?" he demanded, trying for righteous indignation.

"No—just a simple obvious point, I thought."

"That I might turn into Bob Landau?"

"Well," said Alison, "you do have a head start from where you're sitting."

Chad got up angrily, dropping a slipper. "I find this—"

"—an offensive discussion?" she offered.

"Which you initiated, for some reason."

"I must have a reason, mustn't I?" she said, frowning, and closed the magazine at last. "It's just that I think I'd rather you and Elly"—her voice faltered, and she started over from the middle, as though she'd lost her place—"that I'd rather you took your dirty linen someplace else for washing."

He retrieved the slipper and started for the door. "I'll try to remember," he said icily. "Was that all?"

"Yes."

"Good night, then."

As soon as his door closed, she crumpled, folding like a blue-lace handkerchief against the satin pillow. *Vogue* slid glossily to the floor. The model on its cover kept her marvelous coral smile trained on Alison as she wept into the pillow, beating it with silent helpless fists. Not for the world would she have let Chad see this. Tears and anger veiled in blue lace and white satin, like one's body, with *Vogue* smiling assent. Sacred profanities.

196

Nine

CATHY HAD FINALLY

written something on the note pad. "How is Uncle Chad? Would he come to see me?" Alison said that of course he would. But he refused. Hospitals, condolence calls, funerals— he would not go to any of those, ever. Hadn't he made that clear?

"But Cathy *asked* for you," Alison persisted. "It's the first time the child has asked for anything since . . . I don't see what your religion has to do with it—this is a *child.*"

"I know you don't see, darling," he said. "It's part of your charm, the way you close your eyes." His usual light tone, his smile.

Alison never quite knew how insulting he meant to be, so she would smile back, following him into the den, gathering righteous anger about something else. "I'm not asking you to sacrifice your—principles, if that's what you call them. But to visit a child, your own family—she's having another operation Monday! How do you expect me to explain to Mai? Your indifference!"

"Darling, I don't expect you to explain anything about me to anyone. How could I possibly?" He sank into his chair with a book, hopefully signifying an end to it.

She hesitated. Then: "Have you any idea how it *looks*—" but his withering glance stopped that one. Finally, despairingly: "I *promised* you'd come; I promised *Mai.*"

"I'm sorry," he said coldly. "You had no right to promise me to Mai."

Childish, rude, selfish stubbornness. Deliberately doing this to embarrass me, that's all it is. She retreated to the bedroom to change. Her hands were trembling as she struggled with the lipstick brush. Damn him. And nothing sounded plausible. Uncle Chad is sorry, dear, he just doesn't visit anyone who's sick or hurt. He doesn't believe in anyone being sick or hurt. No, I don't understand either, but I'm sure that even if *I* were sick or hurt he wouldn't come to see me. Quite sure. Can you imagine me saying such a thing to that child covered with those bandages?

She punished her angry face with contradictory rosy shadows; it was impossible to glower until the mascara dried. If I could think of a serviceable lie, even. If he could be sick himself, or called out of town. But then why couldn't he come tomorrow, or the day after? Because. He doesn't give a damn about the child, or the family, or what anyone thinks, or—well, isn't that it?—me. What *I* want, what *I* care about. Cathy's face would heal itself perfectly if only we understood the real problem. It's not torn flesh at all, it's Error! Well, God knows it was somebody's error. Sandy Rossbach's. Mai's, for not keeping the girl locked up—out of error's way. There's something to that, anyway.

She was making final fretful adjustments in the hall mirror when Chad's door opened. "Wait a minute," he said. "Can she read?"

"Who?"

"Cathy— I mean, are her eyes covered?"

"One is," Alison replied coldly.

"I've written her a note." He handed her an envelope and closed his door.

Mai wanted to do something about Sandy Rossbach. She had been deliberating for days, locked in her private jury room, plotting, ever since the doctors admitted that even after the graft and the plastic surgery, Cathy wasn't going to look the same. That it would still be . . . noticeable. Mai had once known a girl in school whose face was burned by scalding soup. Afterward she had carried pictures of herself, thrusting them at other children. See, I used to be just as pretty as you when I smiled. I want the boy prosecuted, Mai decided finally. I want to charge him with vehicular assault, maybe even kidnapping. Who knows where Cathy was going with him? Or whether she wanted to. The psychiatrist would have to testify—

"What's the point?" Alison asked. And Ira reminded her about the newspapers. What's the point?

The point, she told them very calmly, was that Sandy Rossbach should be locked up. That he was dangerous; that he would go on being a menace to Cathy so long as he was allowed to walk around. Or rather, drive around in a ten-thousand-dollar sports car. So far, no matter how he's hurt her, all he's had to do is say he's sorry and go back outside to play. A baby, a nervous breakdown, now this— The point is to punish *him* for once, instead of Cathy. Instead of me.

Sandy had come to the hospital every day since the accident, and every day Mai had left instructions that he was not to be admitted to the room. When he brought things—candy, flowers, a book—she would collect them at the desk and distribute them at once to the nurses. Now that she had made up her mind to seek some more drastic revenge, Ira thought someone ought to at least talk to the boy.

Sandy usually appeared around four o'clock. At three forty-five Ira went downstairs and posted himself at the main entrance near the elevator. The boy walked right past him. "Hello, Sandy," Ira said.

"Uh. Oh, hi." The boy studied him intently, until he came to the shoes. "Mr. Wolf!"

Ira smiled. "Cathy still can't have any visitors, but I'd like to talk to you a minute. If you wouldn't mind?"

Sandy was mystified; he had exchanged perhaps a dozen uneasy words with this dapper little man who was Cathy's stepfather, and he hadn't seen him once since the divorce.

Ira was steering him nervously into the cafeteria. "I want to thank you, first of all," he said. "I appreciate this, your taking the time. Would you like something?"

"No, thanks," Sandy said uncomfortably.

Ira's buffed nails drummed on the table until the waitress came. "Two coffees and a plate of"—he looked despairingly at the pastry selections under their greasy plastic domes—"assorted doughnuts." An expense-account snack, even under the circumstances. Neither of them touched any of it, but Ira didn't speak until it was all set out. Protocol. Business entertainment.

"Cathy's mother," he began, "right now she's very upset. You can understand, I know you are too. That's why I thought I should tell you."

Sandy's dark face paled slightly as Ira outlined his wife's unhappy thinking. "Maybe she doesn't even mean it—I don't know," Ira said, folding and unfolding his paper napkin. "Maybe she's so upset she doesn't even know what she's saying. I told her already how I feel; I said what's the point hurting someone else too. This is enough hurt. It was an accident, we all know that, these terrible things happen. But she feels . . . you understand, she's at a loss what to do."

Sandy smiled wryly at that, imagining Mai at a loss.

"Maybe when it's all over," Ira went on, "when the bandages are off, and it's only a little scar, maybe she'll calm down then and get over it. But right now—" He looked at Sandy helplessly. "It's very hard to be Cathy's mother right now."

Sandy felt sorry for him. Poor little guy, married to that— but that wasn't Sandy's problem. "Tell your wife," he said slowly, "she's picking on the wrong guy. Tell her Cathy wouldn't be in here at all if her uncle hadn't kicked her out that night."

Ira's pale eyes blinked. Like a rabbit hearing a strange noise. Should he run away or stay and finish the carrot?

"Her uncle," Sandy repeated. His sullen handsome face looked menacing. Ira pressed back against his chair. "Called me and told me to get her out of his house." Sandy went on. "I never even heard of the guy. I didn't know where Cathy was, I didn't even know she'd left home. So if your wife wants to go crucify sombody, tell her—"

"Uncle?" Ira quavered.

"Uncle Chad. Mr. Batchelder."

Ira swallowed and put down his napkin. "You better stay here, Sandy. I think my wife . . . I think I should bring her down and you tell her. Just a minute, I'll bring her right down. Otherwise—" He stopped to summon the waitress: "Just leave everything, miss, we're not finished. I'll be right back—" And he fled.

When they came down, Ira darted out of the elevator first, terrified that Sandy might have left and that he would have to tell Mai himself. "Tell her," Ira panted, "tell her what you—"

Sandy told. "I don't know how long Cathy was up there in his apartment before he called me. Or why he called me. Like I said, I never even heard of any Uncle Chad." He shrugged. "Maybe she got to be too much for him, or he panicked. Worried about his wife finding out. I don't know—all I know is I went over there to help Cathy. And the accident, like I told you before, she just slipped and fell running behind my car. She'd been drinking a lot. Not with me. There were empty bottles all over the place when I got there." He paused. "She was . . . when I got there she was lying on the bed."

Mai didn't say a word until he finished. Then, hoarsely: "I don't believe you." Although she did, totally.

"Okay," Sandy retorted. "But then why do you think I called him when it happened? Go ahead and explain that! When I never even met any Uncle Chad."

Ira kept looking from one to the other, like a new zookeeper caught in the cage at feeding time. Sandy stared at Mai with his black olive eyes in that golden olive face that no one over thirty would ever trust. She glared back at him, a silent exchange of pure hatred. Then she rose and left the two of them sitting there with the cold coffee and the flies buzzing around the greasy doughnuts. "Well," said Ira. "I guess— Check, please, miss. I mean, if you're sure you don't want any more—"

*   *   *

With her hand on the doorknob to Cathy's room, Mai hesitated. "It's all right, Mrs. Wolf, you may go in," said a nurse brightly. Mai entered. "Cathy, darling," she said to the solitary brown eye, and smiled encouragingly. "Do you remember the night of the accident?" The bandaged head did not move; the eye showed no flicker of reaction. "Do you remember where you were just before?" Mai put the pencil in her daughter's hand. "Hmm?"

"Running," Cathy wrote, "away."

"Yes, darling," Mai said carefully. "But where?"

"In. the street," Cathy wrote, and dropped the pencil.

Mai bit her lip. She wanted to shake it out of her.

Cathy's eye closed. Uncle Chad! thought Mai. I should have guessed.

In the taxi going home from the hospital, Mai asked her husband casually, "If Chad lost his job with Miles Boehm, what do you think he'd do?"

"Go work for some other agency," Ira guessed. "Why?"

"What if no other agency would hire him? What if he were blacklisted?"

"Why would he be blacklisted?"

Mai breathed an exasperated sigh. "I was asking a rhetorical question. You don't answer a rhetorical question with another rhetorical question."

"I'm sorry, dear," Ira said. "What was it again?"

"What would Chad do if he were blacklisted by every agency in town?"

"I don't know, dear. One of the networks, maybe, or free-lance? You can't really blacklist anyone on Madison Avenue. Every company that can afford a typist has some kind of PR department."

"But he's an alcoholic," Mai said.

Ira laughed. "That whole Boehm agency is an unofficial A.A. chapter."

"He's a pervert, then," she said.

Ira didn't answer that.

"Alison would probably insist on giving him a job at Lowen's," she mused. "A vice-president, pun intended."

Ira shook his head. "Lowen's can't afford him. any more. If she hired him, it would be over Ned's dead body, I guess."

"Dead bodies," said Mai, "don't seem to bother Christian Scientists. Did you see the letter he sent Cathy? Alison brought it while you were with—"—she still balked at Sandy's name—"while you were downstairs."

He held the letter near the cab window and squinted.

Dearest Cathy:
     I want so much to help lift this awful shadow, and restore the light to your sweet face. All of us who love you must help you to free your mind. I pray that even those who love you imperfectly—and may thereby have caused this mortal sadness—may now come to understand. You too must believe that you can be free—healed and whole again. Once your thoughts are beyond pain, the wound itself and all its traces must vanish. You will have found the way. My thoughts are with you, and my love. Faithfully,
     Chad

"Well," said Ira uncertainly, "that's nothing. I guess it's Christian Science."

Mai didn't say another word until they were home. Upstairs in their yellow living room, she sat at her Chinese writing table and crossed her long legs. "I want you to start tomorrow," she announced. "I want you to call Miles Boehm and get him fired."

"Oh, Mai, don't start that again," he pleaded. "What good will it do."

"You want me to just forget what's he's done? Is that it?"

She didn't look angry, only startled. Her delicate brows lifted like drawn wings in flight; Chinese calligraphy. The perfect glossy lips slightly parted in a carved half-smile, like that of a white jade figurine.

Ira knew she would look just like that if she were about to kill him. "All right," he said meekly. "I'll call Boehm. Though why you think he'd care—"

"Oh, he'll care," said Mai, turning toward her desk. She opened the center drawer with a gold key and took out her large checkbook in its gold-brocade cover. "Didn't you say he's managing the Republican fund-raising campaign?" Ira nodded mutely behind her back. "You can just"—she went on firmly, writing—"fill in the amount after you've had lunch. I have no idea what a little favor like that might run to . . . on Madison Avenue." She folded the check and tucked it into his breast pocket, like a show hanky. Then she smiled. "Men are supposed to be better at haggling over the price."

Ned and Celine flew to Nassau for a four-day weekend, ostensibly for a rest, but primarily so that Ned could talk to the retired uncle who owned ten percent of the Lowen's Fifth Avenue stock. Isaac Heller was an uncle by marriage to Amos Lowen's sister-in-law, Sophy. He had lost Sophy fifteen years ago and promptly remarried an English lady twenty-five years his junior, enormously wealthy in her own right and the mother of three daughters. He had once been known as Uncle Ike, but now it was Uncle Zack. With Rowena and the girls, he divided his time between homes in London, Acapulco, Nassau, Greece and the yacht at Cap d'Antibes. It had taken Ned six weeks to track him down. The Greenstones were invited over for cocktails, and then they'd all go have dinner out—someplace gay; Rowena simply wasn't up to a party. "Over" for cocktails was meant quite literally. The house was on a private island separated from the Nassau mainland by a channel. Guests drove to the point opposite and rang a little bell, and the butler would row across to fetch them. The house was a pastel stucco San Simeon, filled to its pink brim with the treasures of a long, far-flung and incredibly self-indulged life.

One of the daughters, Hilary, took them on a breathless tour of the house and grounds. "I get so tired of pecking and unpecking," she said. "I shouldn't mind so much if only I didn't leave things in all the wrong countries . . . Deddy's just bought me a house in London, though, did you know? I shall be able to race under my own colors now. Deddy and Mum only come to London for the racing; it's the only time they're allowed, poor things."

Ned and Celine traded facial question marks behind her back, but she went blithely on. "So then I shan't come to Nassau any more, unless I want. There now, you've seen the lot, come have a punch."

"Nassau's such a nuisance, don't you find," another daughter asked Celine. This one was Mavis. "It's only fun when the Royal Family come," she added. "Not the scruffy parties, I don't mean, but people at least try. And when they leave, there are all the funny cars and things that have been made up for the visit, and poor Deddy simply can't resist. You'll see the Sunbeam later. Deddy bought that after Prince Philip used it. Of course, he only used it once."

"Oh, tell about the gadgets!" cried Valerie, the third one.

"I was," said Mavis crossly." It's got all sorts of super gadgets, electric wine poppers and built-in color telly . . ."

Uncle Zack finally sent the girls upstairs to change, so that he and Rowena could get in a word about their tax problems. That took close to two hours and eight rum punches, after which Uncle Zack rang for the man to come row them all to the mainland.

He hoped they liked this funny old inn; Nassau cuisine was not the most haute, he apologized. "Deddy and Mum just et here for the first time Sunday," said Mavis. "It was so nice, for Nassau, that Deddy couldn't resist."

"You mean you own it?" said Ned.

Uncle Zack nodded sheepishly.

"He will do that," said Hilary, giggling. "Poor Deddy. What else can he, though."

During dinner, Ned kept trying vainly to talk store business, but between the wine and food and brandies and the girls and Uncle Zack's tax stories, there wasn't much room. The tax business was enormously complicated; they juggled all their travel schedules, their purchases, and their whims and changes of mind or venue to float between the Scylla and Charybdis of British and U.S. tax regulations.

After the third brandy the three girls left the table to powder their super noses. Ned peered at Uncle Zack through his blue veil of Cuban cigar smoke and asked how he'd feel about the New York store being sold. It would only mean, he explained with some embarrassment, a profit of about 2.5 million for Uncle Zack personally, but—

"Good God," Uncle Zack exclaimed. "I'm sorry, dear boy, but it's quite impossible. Our American tax attorney wouldn't hear of it."

Rowena sighed. "You've no idea," she confided, "what it takes to keep a good tax attorney these days." Celine laughed; it was exactly the way people talked about their cook.

Even with the two cousins, plus Ralph and Elly, Ned knew that without this ten percent uncle voting with him, there would be no sale. He decided to try again tomorrow, when hopefully he'd feel more like a businessman and less like a rum punching bag.

*   *   *

On the return flight, Ned hardly spoke. Celine thought he might still be hung over. Uncle Zack, it had turned out, started punching every day at breakfast and didn't stop until the following dawn. Poor Deddy, as Hilary would say. What else can he? But Ned had stayed with him, matching him punch for punch, while Celine obediently trailed the girls all over the island on super shopping sprees. For once, Celine, the career customer, was hopelessly outclassed. Ned had worked feverishly on Uncle Zack's behalf, trying to work out tax loopholes into which 2.5 million dollars could safely be tucked. Late the night before, they had even called the tax attorney in Florida, rousing him from a sound sleep. Within three minutes (Uncle Zack kept a timer near the telephone), the attorney had plugged every loophole; there was simply no way for Uncle Zack to rake in another 2.5 million this year. Ned was flying home to Alison and Pembroke across an ocean of red ink. Poor Neddy, as Mavis would say. What else can he, though.

Jason took one look at Eli Lewisohn and knew it was going to be really bad news, well rehearsed though he was, and resigned finally to placating his mother. The man was another Horace T. Ambruster: big and florid, with that same wavy, oxidized hair that was either yellowing white or whitening yellow, but had probably once been red. Like Ambruster, he had even probably once been called Red. The same kind of craggy face and glinty slate-colored eyes. And he lumbered. If he hadn't been so big, you'd say he shuffled. But the worst thing was the forced puerile humor; he was full of dumb, youth-oriented jokes about dirty rock lyrics, which he laughed at to show how groovy he was. Getting a whole new sex education at sixty-five, he said. If it was hard to imagine him as a musical colossus, it was impossible to think of him as a twelve-year-old pants-pressing genius.

208

Jason was halfway through the Bartok—Chad had said he managed miraculously to civilize Bartok without taming him —when he decided, fuck it. He wasn't even going to try playing safe; he wanted to shock Lewisohn right out of his legendary pressed pants—Lewisohn and Ambruster both. Chad had warned him that Lewisohn hated scatology. Copulation yes, coprology no. So as soon as he finished establishing his technical credentials—he could already see the old man nodding imperceptible approval—Jason would treat him to his personal favorite of all the songs they'd refused to permit in the Buxton Academy annual theatrical production: *Duty Bound.* ("Mother wanted me to make it; make it all, make it big, make it now . . ." and in the end, when the narrator does make it, Mother flushes it all away. "She said, 'Son, everything you made today was—' ")

Watching Lewisohn's stony face turn more and more florid under his tarnished hair, Jason began to enjoy himself. By the time he reached the part where the lyrics described in precise and agonizing detail exactly what it is the hero makes, he felt he had given the performance of his life.

Lewisohn looked like a sunstroke victim, all crimson splotches and winces of pain. "Thank you for hearing me, sir," Jason said the instant his hands left the keys. A slight respectful bow. "It was a great privilege just meeting you." And he raced out of the room before the great old man could speak, in case he was thinking of it.

Elly and Chad were waiting on a small velvet-padded bench outside the studio. "How was—" they both started to ask at once. Jason shook his head sorrowfully and sat next to Chad. Worried frowns flew past him. After a minute or so, Lewisohn stuck his head out and called them in. The splotches had faded somewhat, Jason noticed, but he still looked extremely sore.

"First let me say that the boy does have unmistakable talent," Lewisohn said, grimacing at them. Elly was about to exclaim delightedly, but Chad squeezed her arm. "However," Lewisohn went on, lumbering toward the window so that his back was half turned to them, "in my opinion he is a severely disturbed young person." His words flowed smoothly, an adept legato. "Without some radical change I cannot imagine his making a real contribution to the field of music. I have no advice, I regret to say. Perhaps psychotherapy before pursuing further musical training. That is, of course, an amateur opinion." He sighed deeply. "The talent of course is there, as I said. But he has no present use for such a gift except as"—he made a vague, contemptuous gesture—"a toy. A destructive toy weapon."

He turned back toward them, thrusting his head forward like a charging bull. "In this boy's hands, music is distorted into barbaric clangor. A cry not for help, but for punishment. Like the crude scrawls that wretched murderers used to leave near their victims. In Jason's case, one would make out the scrawl to read 'Stop Me Before I Play More.'" Another tremulous sigh. "Now you must excuse me."

"Thank you, Mr. Lewisohn," Chad murmured, in that awed tone of the privileged reporter chosen to end the presidential press conference.

"Mr. Batchelder," said Lewisohn, inclining his head. "I'm sorry not have been more helpful."

Outside Elly flew at her son. "What did you do in there, for God's sake!"

"Elly, please," Chad whispered urgently, stepping between them.

By the time they reached the street, she had burst into violent tears. She could have pounded the boy with her fists, or clawed him. "Please," said Chad again, and then turned to

210

Jason with a wry smile. "I assume Mr. Lewisohn didn't appreciate your program?"

"Yeah," said Jason, grinning. "I guess."

Elly stared at them in horror. Wrenching free of Chad's restraining arm, she lashed at Jason, delivering a single backhanded slap with all her fragile strength across his stunned face. A sharp stab of pain shot through her hand, and she gasped. Before either of them moved, she was running toward a taxi. Jason began to cry.

Chad said gently, "You must have known how much that meant to her."

"Sure," he said, sniffling. "I knew."

"She didn't quite deserve this, did she?"

Jason shrugged, brushing his eyes with his sleeve, like a small boy.

Chad sighed. "I kind of hoped you could play it straight all the way. What happened?"

"I couldn't stand him," Jason said. "I couldn't st——I hated the whole thing."

"I figured," said Chad. "But what do you think happens now?"

"Now? Not much. I go home and get a lot of words in my ear. No music, just words. And they decide to send me someplace else. Maybe . . . she could probably still get me into some military school that's broke. She could donate a couple of thousand machine guns, or a tank."

"You ready to go home now?"

"And face the words?" Jason grinned. "Could we take a walk first?"

They walked to Central Park and through the zoo, and around the sailboat pond, mostly in silence. Once, while they were watching two boys reaching perilously far over the side to retrieve a three-masted schooner, Jason murmured something. "What?" said Chad. "I just said thanks," Jason replied.

There were dark streaks and two or three stars in the sky when Chad suggested that maybe it was time to get it over with. "Okay," said Jason. "Sure."

"Elly? I've brought your wandering minstrel home. Sorry we took so long, we were walking." Chad's light tone, aimed at relieving the tension, fell heavily.

"Go in your room please, Jason," she said, not looking at him.

"*To* your room," he muttered, going.

Chad glanced briefly at Elly's swollen eyes, and then at the hand that had slapped Jason. She was holding it stiffly at her side; he could tell that it still hurt. "I don't know why it was so important," she said tiredly. "It was just one thing that could have gone right with him."

"I know, and I'm sorry," he said.

But that made her flare up at him. "I don't understand you! Sympathizing with him! More than sympathizing; you were making a joke of it—as if he hadn't done something really destructive. Lewisohn even used the word destructive."

Chad started to interrupt, but she cut him off. "It doesn't *matter* what he did. Just that he deliberately alienated . . . a man like Lewisohn. Who could have done so much, could have *helped* him."

Chad shook his head. "Elly, he doesn't *want* that help. That's all the boy was saying, with whatever silly thing he did. Doesn't want it, and maybe—just maybe, doesn't need it."

"Don't tell me what he needs," she retorted. "He's my child."

"Yes, I remember," Chad sighed. "But I think he'd rather

212

be his own man, Elly. And I don't—I can't honestly blame
him."

"Good night, Chad," she said quietly. "Thank you for—
everything."

She looked so vulnerable, suddenly, gathering her autonomy,
that Chad could have kissed her. He felt a surge of tenderness,
but perhaps it was only for Jason; he could have kissed her for
having mothered Jason, in spite of herself. And as she stiffened,
backing away, perhaps sensing it, he knew that there would
never be anything tender between them.

Pembroke invited Ned into his newly decorated office for
the unveiling. Lowen's freshly crowned creative director had
celebrated by moving out most of the furniture and stringing
up an enormous handwoven rope hammock. "Mayan," he said.
"They give birth in them, I mean if only *my* mother had
thought of it." Fastened to the ceiling at both ends, the hammock swooped in a great diagonal U across the room. It would
hold eight in sublime comfort, Pem assured Ned, for confer-
ences. The only possible hitch was their suit buttons. Ned
looked bewildered. "Buttons catch in the *loops*," Pem explained. "Well, everyone would simply have to unbutton,
wouldn't they?" Ned forced a painful smile.

Besides the hammock, he had stationed exotic potted plants
in every corner and all along the sealed window wall. Vines and
tendrils snarling at each other for bits of filtered sun. God
knows what they really are, Ned thought darkly, surveying all
thos bristling pistils and stamens rearing their crimson heads
like so many obscene gestures. "Very nice, Pem," he said,
backing out.

All morning Ned had been popping antacids by the handful.
One of the new computers in the billing department had gone

berserk, possibly from the strain of replacing five elderly book-keepers, and a hundred thousand dollars' worth of credit had been erroneously issued to delinquent charge-account customers before anyone caught it. The mailroom lay buried under six-inch drifts of monthly statements that would have to be redone on somebody's overtime.

There was a call for him, Ginny said; his sister-in-law was on hold. "Yes, Alison, now what," he growled at the phone.

"It's not Alison; it's Mai."

"Mai?"

She had met a very interesting man at a party last night.

"How nice," he murmured, gnashing. "And I've got a hundred thousand dollars' of credit somewhere on the mailroom floor. What else is new?"

"Jerome Alswang, his name was."

"Alswang?" Ned echoed, groping for the antacid bottle.

"I haven't got time for you to be coy, Ned," Mai said crisply. "I just called to say you could count on my vote. I was sure you hadn't expected to. By the way, did you know that Chad was looking for a job?"

"What?" Ned stopped chewing, "What?"

"*Chad.* Looking for a job, I said. Not in public relations. Alison mentioned they were thinking of something at Lowen's for him. Something high-salaried and powerful, I'd imagine. I told her I thought it would be a terrible mistake. Don't you, Ned?"

"Uh. Yes, Mai, I'm listening," he said. "I'm sorry—Chad, you said, at Lowen's?"

"Yes. Well. That was why it was so nice to meet your Mr. Alswang, I thought. I mean it gives . . . everyone a choice. Better for Alison's marriage, and the store too, don't you agree. Not to, not to have Chad—"

Ned had finally recovered enought to interrupt. Had Alison by any chance been at the party? he wondered.

Mai laughed. "No, darling—and I didn't mention Mr. Alswang to her. I didn't think you'd want me to. Did you?"

"Uh, no," Ned said. "No, I didn't."

"Well, then," she said.

There was a mutually embarrassed pause. "Well, then," she said again. "I just wanted to let you know." and she hung up.

"Sixty percent?" he said into the dead phone. He was still dazed. "Without Uncle Zack!"

Ten

I

T WAS INEVITABLE
that as soon as he had mastered enough English to appear on
American television, Edouard Vermicini would be prime-
time's favorite new guest. Absolutely everyone wanted to hear
him discuss—or preferably dissect—Social Lionesses I Have
Shot. It was Chad's last assignment at Boehm Associates to
arrange his appearances, followed by a one-man show of his
most controversial works at a New York gallery. General cutting back, Boehm had apologized. Two major accounts lost in
less than a month, and much as he hated to lose a new man

with such promise, he had to consider seniority at a time like this.

Vermicini's Italian charm proved as instantly controversial as his work. He assailed his critics with delightful rancor, reading their disparaging reviews aloud to his TV hosts and audiences with a perplexed look and a Mastroianni accent. "This one with the title *Push Pull, Click-Click,* I do not understand even the headline. This push-pull critic," Vermicini sighed, "dismisses Vermicini's work. 'A decadent status symbol among those of the jet set who are slowing down due to age or other boring conditions. Regardless of who has planted your silicone, or who is lifting your chin,'" he read, smiling broadly, "'if you have not been "taken" nude by Vermicini, you have not yet arrived.' That is very funny, no?" Vermicini and the TV host laughed heartily.

The photographer went on to say that he hoped to work with much younger subjects in the United States. The host winked understandingly. Vermicini worried that the young women here might have some difficulty with his so-high fees, and he sighed. But there was only so much one could achieve in color with the body of a woman beyond, shall one say, the certain age. So far he had only photographed one American, to be sure, and she was beyond the certain age. Very beautiful, but beyond.

She was also, unfortunately, very identifiable. Celine called Chad at midnight, crushed beyond tears. How could the man say those things? How could Chad have let him? Celine darling, I had no idea. It was horrible; he knew how she must feel. There was no excuse. One could only hope nobody was paying attention. Hardly anyone ever did, he assured her, hoping he was right.

The worst possible people had been very attentive, as it

turned out, among them *Vogue*. Chad was notified the next morning that the magazine had regretfully decided not to run Celine's portraits. They were sure he would be pleased to know, however, that they were instead commissioning Vermicini to do an exclusive series for them, with young socialites as his subjects. Chad would of course collect his share of the fifteen percent commission on these, Miles Boehm informed him magnanimously, even though the payment would be coming through long after he'd left the agency.

All he had to do now was tell Celine. Sorry for not quite putting your name back in lights. Which you only half expected. And for not quite taking you anywhere else either. Somewhere you did fully expect. If not a star, if not The Girl, then at least The Principessa. Reintroducing Celina Lowen as . . .

Well, I did get you two pretty pictures, didn't I, each worth about fifty thousand unkind words? And you did get a fire opal. Whereas I got fired. If it were only eighteen years ago, he thought, I could say well, that's show business, Celine baby. What do I say now? Well, that's middle age, Celine—baby?

He went over to her apartment to tell her; he could at least not do it on the phone. A maid asked him to wait in the living room. He could hear Celine arguing with another maid somewhere. Scolding. Why had the maid removed the price tag? Now Bloomingdale's wouldn't take it back. "Haven't I told you a million times—" she was saying in her most incensed tone. Celine couldn't really shout; the breathy starlet voice grew reedy and uncertain up there. The only certainty, Chad would bet, was that the maid would never pay any attention to it. Anger made Celine very nervous; she seemed comfortable only when acting sweet, even though no one ever took her seriously. Even in restaurants, hers was always the order the waiter forgot.

After he had broken the news, she wept against his jacket, but when she finally stopped, she did not move, not even to dry her tears. He sat there holding her until he realized that she seemed to want something more of him. Something to help her believe that she had not lost her last chance, that she might still star in some key role, in some minor drama, a family picture. There probably was something he could do that would have consoled her, but he could not think of it just then. After a while he gently disengaged himself. And that would be what she would not forgive him for.

Cathy could go home at the end of the week, the doctors said. Mai wondered suddenly, Whose home? The girl was still heavily bandaged, though both eyes were now uncovered and the skin directly beneath the endangered eye had healed well. The eyes, like coals of lignite above the silent white mask, now seemed much larger and more watchful, seeing too much and revealing nothing, like the eyes of women in purdah.

Cathy was still very weak, and the liquid diet, sipped through a straw, had to continue. She must also remain in bed; speech and movement were hazardous to the still-healing tissues. Neither Mai nor Ira had quite faced what it would mean to have her stay with them, bedridden and requiring full-time nursing care. And what about the baby and *his* nurse? They could be left in Cathy's apartment, but then Mai would have to be running back and forth. If she took them all in, the cleaning woman would certainly quit, and possibly Ira too. Chaos littering the Ming yellow chinoiserie, and they only had six rooms. Perhaps it would be best to put Cathy back in her own apartment, with nurses around the clock? Mai sat beside her daughter, weighing alternatives.

Seventeen years ago she had given birth to this child. She had wanted a spinal anesthetic; she had a horror of being put to sleep like an injured animal. She had watched Cathy's birth in a mirror. The sea of blood, hers and Cathy's, and the small crimson body swaddled in live wet cellophane, the body all creased as if it had been left too long in water. Mai and her sisters had once watched a pet cat deliver her babies, five of them. Watched her calmly eating the cellophane packages, releasing each child in its wet fur coat, delicately consuming the silver cord, like a single strand of crystal spaghetti. Mai still remembered the expression on the mother cat's face: smug serenity, as in post-coital sleep; absolute assurance that each motion of her body, each stroke of her tongue over their bodies, like a rough towel, was right and necessary. A natural law unto herself. But one of the kittens, Mai remembered, had not acted like the others; there was something wrong with it. As soon as the mother noticed, she would have nothing further to do with that baby; she would not nurse it or clean its fur. She moved her other babies far away from it, and within two days the kitten died. It had never moved from the corner where its mother had left it to die. Mai had cried, she remembered— why can't *we* save the kitten? But her father would not permit her to feed it milk with a spoon or touch it. God, he said, would care for it; its mother understood that. A natural law unto herself. The maternal instinct.

Cathy stirred in her hospital bed; above her silent white mask, the unreadable eyes turned slowly toward her mother's face. Startled, Mai looked quickly away.

At first Chad seemed to carry off unemployment with his usual unruffled style. He had spared Alison his continued revulsion for the idea of going to work at Lowen's in any exalted capacity whatever. She had suggested it, to her credit, hesitantly this time, and with more than her usual sensitivity for his—or anyone's—discomfort. She'd said only that perhaps he might want to reconsider the idea now, that *she* had thought about it, and that she still thought it would be wonderful. That they really needed him. He thanked her and said he still didn't really think it was for him, but it was nice that she wanted him. He couldn't resist adding that, and for once she caught the irony and blushed.

Chad truly believed he would land on his feet; he had been in this silly business far too long, and had landed that way too many times. At first nothing suggested that there might be something special about this time.

But after a few weeks he could not bear the mornings. Jill up and gone to school by eight, Alison and her endless dressing ritual. In the past they'd had breakfast together, she still in bed and he fully dressed for work, sipping his coffee from an unsteady antique tray table which Frieda set up for him front of Alison's chaise longue. Now he was often still in a robe and slippers when she was rushing off, tossing him embarrassed smiles or annoying little requests. Would he mind calling So-and-so about the tickets for tonight; she'd been so busy she'd forgotten. Or would he tell Frieda what he wanted for dinner; she hadn't had time to think. Of course, darling, he would answer, both tacitly acknowledging that he had ample time.

Frieda endlessly picked up things around him. Frieda constantly excused herself for disturbing him. And he would make calls, and wait endlessly to be called back. No one refused to see him; everyone was terribly friendly and almost insultingly solicitous. How about lunch one day next week, or they would be in touch as soon as they got back from wherever, just in case anything opened up. Though right now it looked, to tell the truth, unlikely.

Finally Chad rented a place, one of those offices for the self-unemployed in one of those midtown skyscrapers with subdivided crawl spaces on the less desirable floors. Fifteen tiny cubicles in a row, occupied by a rapidly changing population of losers, and one receptionist for the sake of appearances, in case anyone ever had a visitor. She charged each of them by the week. "Mr. Batchelder's office," she would say in a normal secretarial lilt, and would pause the acceptable number of seconds before saying "No, I'm sorry, Mr. Batchelder isn't in just now," or, "I'll see if he is free, may I ask who—"

He had lunches and took walks. It was a matter of pride that he still paid the basic household bills, the maintenance on the apartment, the grocer, the butcher and the liquor store. It was a formality, of course, but it mattered, and in a way it mattered to Alison too. If he skipped lunch when no one with an expense account was buying, if he had his midday double Scotches at the office—three, lately—instead of putting them on the check, he could forestall, for a little while longer, the moment of having to say, Darling, would you mind paying the maintenance this month, and I'm afraid the grocer as well. Oh, and the liquor bill. The inevitable moment when it would have to be generally known and privately faced that he was now living off his wife.

There was no doubt in Alison's mind that something was going on between Elly and Chad. All of a sudden, after that maddening business of his rushing over there to be with her night after night, after the awful scene they had over it—all of a sudden he had simply stopped going. He never even mentioned her name any more. Nor had Elly called him, to announce in her transparent voice that Jason wanted him. Obviously they were seeing each other some other way now.

She didn't believe for a minute that his peculiar behavior lately had anything to do with his job crisis. That was just one more thing he wouldn't discuss with her. If she dared mention something—anything—about it, he would growl some mono-

222

syllable and retreat behind a book or a paper. He had never brought up the subject of Lowen's again. If he was desperate to work, she had certainly opened that door as graciously as she could. Obviously it had to be Elly. Everyone in the world must know about it, just as everyone had always known about Elly and Bob Landau. Alison couldn't let it all happen again. The humiliation.

Chad had mentioned the Eli Lewisohn debacle. It never occurred to him that she did not believe he had been seriously working with Jason, and that after the Lewisohn audition, there was no reason for him to go on advising the boy.

So Alison attached no importance to his report of how things had gone that day. How stupid, she told herself, they must think she was. The last time—she had known the last time too. About Landau. She simply hadn't said anything, that was all. She hadn't chosen to behave like some character in a bad play, to reduce herself to their level. So Bob Landau had left her, and the relationship—the affair—between her sister and her husband had gone on for years. Openly, even in front of Jill. Not again, she thought defiantly. She would confront Elly if necessary; she would shame her.

They had lunch, just the two of them, and Alison demanded to know what was going on. In fact, she already *knew* what was going on, so Elly needn't try any evasive answers.

Elly was all indignation and brimming tears. How could Alison possibly imagine. Alison could not imagine that she wasn't lying.

"All I wanted was the simple truth," she said bitterly. "I would have understood—at least I would have tried. Didn't I prove that with Bob Landau? Have I ever said a word of reproach? Not a word in all these years. Have I? And this is my reward. Again."

        *   *   *

Clutching her tattered innocence, Elly appealed to Mai. When they were small, Mai had always settled the quarrels. Tell her I didn't do anything, she won't believe me. And just as when they were small, Mai found a way not only to end the hostilities, but to reap a profit from them herself. Elly's tears and revelations were interesting, if only because they might be useful. Because they were welcome signs—symptoms that Chad and Alison were already suffering from terminal marriage. She promised Elly that she would do what she could to help.

"Alison, you can't be that naïve. Chad and Elly? You really thought that? I would never have mentioned it otherwise, but since . . . well, I'm surprised it didn't cross your mind that the attraction really was Jason."

"What do you mean?"

"Nothing. Just what I said." The implication merely shimmered there. Then Mai asked casually if Alison by any chance knew why Jason had been expelled from Buxton?

Alison tried to remember. Yes, hadn't Elly mentioned—marijuana? And then something else about a play at the school. Jason had refused to perform, wasn't that it? Anyway, what difference did it make?

Well, Mai happened to know that there was one other reason: that Jason was homosexual. He had been . . . involved with several others. No, of course *Elly* hadn't mentioned that. Some close friends of Mai and Ira's—the Kirklands, Alison knew them, didn't she?—well, the Kirklands had a son at Buxton.

Mai circled slowly over Alison's head; only midway through their next long lunch would she pounce. "If you and Chad were happy, darling," she began softly, "you wouldn't be so troubled about what he might be up to . . . elsewhere. Am I wrong?"

224

Alison had no answer.

"Alison?" Mai went on, even more softly. "I care very much."

And Alison believed her. How could she not believe, when with all her own heartbreaking problems, Mai had tears in her eyes? Just over Alison's unhappiness. It was wonderful that they were still so close. This was what sisters were for.

The day Mai announced her defection—Ned still only dimly understood that she would vote to sell Lowen's rather than let her sister give Chad Batchelder a job there—he had called Jerome Alswang to reopen negotiations. Less than a week before, he had told the developer that the project was dead—unless somebody sank Uncle Zack's floating island, or burned up his racing stable, or got Rowena to sue for more alimony than Lowen's was worth. Short of inventing the year's most indisputable tax loss, Ned had been ten impossible percent shy of the majority vote he needed to close the store. Now he had been handed Mai, thinly disguised as a fairy godmother.

Alswang had to be out of town for several days, but he was flying back ahead of schedule to put some new figures together for the meeting. Ned and Ralph were expected at his office at ten A.M. on Monday. On Sunday afternoon, however, Ralph suffered a heart attack on the ninth hole of a golf course near Purchase. Near Purchase—only Ned would ever appreciate the irony. Ralph's last ball, blasted out of a sandtrap, was still spinning toward the green, blurred by a nimbus of flying sand, when he collapsed. It was the most spectacular shot he had made all day. An easy eight-inch putt and he would have had a birdie on one of the toughest holes in Westchester County. He never regained consciousness, and eight hours later he was dead.

Ned and Ralph had agreed from the beginning that there

was nothing to be gained by discussing the Alswang offer with Elly. When the appropriate time came, they reasoned, she would go along with them simply because in her situation it made supreme financial sense. The store was losing money, and Ralph's future association with the Lowen empire—the future of the empire itself, for that matter—no longer rested on this foundering Fifth Avenue flagship. Like Ned, he would sail better without Alison's flamboyant hand steering his course, and whatever else Elly felt about her husband, she would certainly trust his judgment if he could show her how a stubborn sister on a sinking flagship imperiled her own personal fleet.

But with Ralph dead, the key to Elly was gone. Ned was astute enough never to bank on logic alone with any of his sisters-in-law. Besides—or perhaps in the first place—Elly disliked him. She had once said that of all the men any of them ever married, Ned was the only one who took after their father: icy and strong, ruthless and brutal. Conquering, but no hero. If she had ever been given a choice, Ned had no doubt that she would have voted against Amos Lowen. He thought of Ralph, and of Jason, and of Jason's father, and then he smiled ruefully. In a way, Elly was spending her whole life voting against Amos Lowen.

So on Monday, the morning after Ralph Berliner died, the morning Ned and Ralph were to have made their daring break for freedom, Ned greeted his heavy, miserable, stubbly face in his shaving mirror. "Amos, old man," he said aloud, "no sale."

Every day now Cathy would write to her mother. She wrote long letters with the red pencil on her writing pad. The nurse would prop her up and she would scribble furiously, hour after hour, as if there were some urgent deadline that had to be met. So that when Mai came to see her, to sit uncomfortably at the side of her bed offering books and magazines and more or fewer pillows, there would be a long letter for her. Something interesting to read while waiting, like at the hairdresser.

"Do you remember," Cathy wrote, "what you gave me for my twelfth birthday? I was trying to remember. It was right after you decided I didn't need a governess any more, so you sent Nanny away, the last Nanny, the one who used to put pepper on my tongue when I wouldn't eat the fat. You didn't actually give me the present; you left it for me in the kitchen. I found it on the table the maid set out with the cereal and my orange plastic bowl. I sat there by myself opening the big box. It had blue paper and a white satin bow, and the card said 'Happy Birthday to a Big Girl from Mommy.' Only I can't remember what it was."

Another day she wrote: "Sex criminals in Germany are allowed to volunteer for castration now. Sandy told me. It's like surrendering unlicensed weapons. Do you know if they give any scofflaw amnesty period? In the public library when people have these very overdue library books, sometimes they just keep the book for twenty years because every day is another nickel and they can never pay the fine. So they wait until this amnesty period and then they can go to the library and return it and they don't get punished.

"So if they work it that way with the sex criminals, a molester could just do all his molestering—is it molestering like hamstering? I always forget—and then when his conscience bothers him, even fifty years later, he could bring in his old organs and they'd take them, no questions asked . . .

The longest letter, and the one Cathy knew would upset Mai the most, was the one about joining the WACs.

"The only time," Cathy wrote, "I ever took a bath without your telling me. It was such a nice idea, I wanted to have the uniform and be all packed and everything, before I told you. I was going to surprise everybody, right in the middle of some dinner party you had. I would just appear in this uniform, I thought, carrying the baby in the duffel bag, and you'd all look up, and I'd yell Surprise!

"Anyway, I went where they gave the physical, some crumbly old building near Times Square. A shooting gallery and a karate parlor and physicals for girls. It all smelled of popcorn and urine. You'd think what Uncle Sam Wants You for is something besides military duty. There were hundreds of nervous pimply girls, they had pimples all over, which showed because everyone had to wear a little angel robe—you know, like a poncho from an old torn sheet. Freshly laundered, though, Mother, *very clean*, you could still see creases from the ironing. But they didn't close at the sides, not even on the skinny girls. Aunt Alison wouldn't have them in stock, I don't think, even for junior resort wear.

"You had to be very careful not to bump into anybody because of the urine. That was where it came from, the smell, all these girls carrying full bottles of it with no tops. Filing slowly past the typing pool like in a slow-motion sack race, because you couldn't spill your specimen. And the typists in there were all men with big red ears who never looked up. GI Joe dolls. You could tell they had orders not to look up.

"Then in the other room we lined up against the wall to wait for the doctors. A whole platoon of them with shiny rubber-tipped arms that they held straight up like fixed bayonets. Or maybe toilet plungers, because they were really all plumbers coming to check the valves. It's funny how nobody was supposed to be embarrassed in that room, only silent. All these wax museum figures playing doctor.

"They made us bend over and grasp our ankles, please. Doctor would see us now. Hold your buttocks further apart, please. *Further.* All these insane orders. Organizing search parties with flashlights—what were they looking for, for God's sake? Hundreds of us bent over like grazing cows. I wanted everybody's tail to twitch, just once, and flick off the buzzing insects. Nobody twitched, though. Silent buttocks looming like big puddings. Someday somebody will bite one.

"Or else laugh. Nobody did that. If anyone laughed, I bet there would be a stampede of the cows. Nobody can stand like that holding her ankles if people laugh. Though you could in a theater. Or in a sanitarium. Because that would change the whole thing. I mean, in a sanitarium there wouldn't be *real* girls' bare behinds in the air at all, or sweaty spectacled men peering gravely up them. It would be all imaginary.

"Now what if the men were naked, and the girls dressed? Would anybody laugh then? Did you ever think about that, Mother? But now this way, as long as it is this way, with the girls naked and the men in those white priests' collars with their rubber rosaries dangling around their necks—this way, there's obviously no doubt it must be a serious investigation. Into.

"Oh, and I almost forgot the pelvic! All those rubbery arms lost at sea. Disappearing inside dark underwater caves, many of them never before explored. If you squint, all those doctors look like amputees, or Peeping Toms imprisoned in the stocks. But I could tell a lot of the girls were really scared; they would gasp, and some of them actually screamed. All the eyes looking up from the examining tables were wide open, and all the eyes looking down at the tables were closing behind foggy glasses. A few girls cried—it was all such a shame. Or else they were hurt—you couldn't really tell, there were so many girls there. And the doctors had to work fast, which hurts more. I figured out that if they did it slowly, I mean if they were careful, or gentle, then maybe some of the girls would have misunderstood. Ahem, this isn't for fun, young lady. It hurts me as much as it does you. And his face had to be this closed-eye mask. I don't think the regulations even permit any reassuring smiles. Smiles could be interpreted as indicating the doctor likes to . . . imagine getting paid to do *that.* Wow. Like being a movie critic.

"I guess they've never been authorized to enjoy it, even if they're not in the army. It's like a law, see, there's nothing to enjoy. That's why they look so grim, until you stand up and put your clothes back on.

"There was a girl lying on the next table who asked the doctor if this was what an intercourse felt like. He made some noise that was authorized instead of a laugh. 'Not,' he said, in this gruff voice, 'exactly.' I laughed though, because I knew why it was different. Sex isn't supposed to hurt, and a pelvic *is.* Not a lot, but just enough so you know not to enjoy it either. I mean since *he* isn't allowed to.

"And also it's probably the best way to toughen a girl up for the army. Just in case she gets captured; you never know what kind of instruments they'd use to torture a WAC. The enemy, I mean. Maybe the enemy uses the same instruments as our side? After all, how many kinds of instruments are there? Maybe all the enemy does is a routine pelvic. 1. It hurts. 2. It doesn't show bruises.

"Imagine being captured and bringing your own torture chamber.

"On the other hand, a pelvic could be a violation of the Geneva Convention. Is there any place to look that up? If it's a violation, you have to notify them in scarlet letters. On the meter, when their time has expired. *Violation* is a silent red automatic duly authorized scream . . .

"Anyway, one of those wet gloved arms disappeared inside me, too. And he said relax. There, only a few seconds. There.

He was just reaching for the womb. Man's reach must exceed his grasp, or what's a woman for. I guess they have to check if you're pregnant. Conduct unbecoming a WAC. Why was he in there so long, though? Maybe his arm was too short. They should have longer arms available for these things. Maybe I didn't bring any womb; I couldn't remember when I had it last. Do you think they ever found anything valuable inside an enlisted WAC? A smuggler could certainly stash *something*. Uncut heroin, the largest shipment ever seized? Jewelry might travel better, though. There it is, the Star of India, twinkling murkily through the alkaline secretions. Is alkaline safe for highly polished surfaces?

"When he got his arm out, he said, 'Just one more thing, miss.' Loyalty oath. Oh, I *swear* that the above statements are true. Because guilty of falsifying is punishable. Not less than the maximum penalty. Supreme penalty? No, just the maximum is all. Whew. So I swore and pledged allegiance to the flag of. I held my angel robe with one hand and my urine specimen in the other.

"Just think, Mother, I was supposed to report for boot training six weeks ago! Aren't you surprised? Hi, Mom, guess what! And Aunt Alison would have asked, 'What is she all *gotten up* for?' 'I'm not gotten up,' I was going to say. 'I'm uniformed. Uncle Sam wanted me, even if you didn't. So now I am a private.' Do not enter without knocking. 'How do you like my uniform? I thought I'd have it shortened instead of buying a new transitional double-knit cocktail ensemble.' 'Well, maybe we could have it picked up just a little at the shoulders.'

"I failed to report though, didn't I? Do you think I'm AWOL? Mother? Do you think I'll always be AWOL? Wouldn't it jar you if I grew up to be the first WAC ever shot for desertion?"

She would put the girl away, Mai thought, frozen in horror

next to the bed; she would send her to some institution. Or *she* would go away, move to Europe, and let the child stay here alone, with *her* child, and set up a trust with lawyers and executors to pay for the care. She would—

But she knew she would not. What was permissible, what was natural law for a cat whose child did not look or act right would not be permissible for her. She couldn't have eaten the cord or the cellophane package in which Cathy had been securely wrapped at birth; someone else took care of that. From the first minute someone else was supposed to take care of that. And now that it was not even a child, now that it was whatever it was—how could she be responsible? The child itself—that was what frightened her so. The child itself would forever hold Mai responsible.

Eleven

I THINK MY EYES

are my best feature, Elly used to say to Sarah Saxon. Don't you?
Sarah would study her gravely, scrutinizing each feature in turn
with a hard, appraising frown. Elly would begin to squirm; she
hated being looked at too closely, even then. Finally Sarah
would make her decision. No, they're nice, your eyes, she
would say, but they're not your best feature. She never said
what was. Later Elly asked Millicent the same question, and
Millicent would just smile and touch Elly's mouth, tracing the
lips slowly with her finger, as if she were drawing them on. Elly
could still remember her knees trembling with excitement

when Millicent did that. Sometimes she closed her eyes and touched her own mouth that way, remembering.

The week after Ralph died, just as other distraught women take to their beds, Elly took to her mirror. She would sit huddled in her dressing room, watching herself cry, monitoring the changes in her reflection, pausing to correct them. Examining and repairing and re-examining. Look at that, it's not going away, that puffiness. As if the face in the glass were a somewhat unstable friend whom she was obliged to stay with during a difficult time. Left by itself, in distress, there was no telling what such a friend might do. Elly would stiffen with sudden alarm: that line, the little one on the left right here, wasn't there before, or I would have noticed it. Unless it's the light. Wait—no, I can still see it.

The female face is a caricature of her body, Elly had read somewhere. A cartoon set of signals for the male, a coded map, with the mouth painted red just under the cheeks so that he would have no trouble recognizing the real one. Elly thought this was wrong; it must be the other way around—the body was the caricature, the grotesque distortion. The breasts were swollen sleepless eyes—on some women wall-eyes, peering stupidly in opposite directions. Or blank, frightened stares, straight ahead. Eyes that would droop, that were blind and mute, that would never change or betray an emotion or be mistaken for mirrors of any soul. The navel resembled a nose that needed fixing, or sometimes one that had been botched. And then the mouth in its perpetual pout of discontent—the only time that mouth had any other expression was when it yawned over the arrival of a baby.

Yes, the body was definitely the caricature, the mocking insult. One's only defense was to try to erase it, or at least make it extremely small and cover it carefully. Discipline it, punish it; if it is hardly noticeable, no one will notice the resemblance to me.

In the opinion of her masseuse, the same Baroness who attended Alison, what Elly needed now was available only at a small clinic near Gstaad, Switzerland. The Baroness herself knew the directress of this clinic—had in fact once been privileged to visit there and see her miraculous hands at work, molding flesh into works of surpassing art. Indeed, a sculptor was how the Baroness described her, one who released beautiful forms from wads of imprisoning human clay.

The Baroness spoke as she worked, in brief, zealous gusts, pausing when her fingers seized and crushed pieces of Elly's body, resuming when she relinquished them, hastily pushing the bruised fragments back where she had found them, smoothing away the traces of her assault. Elly still bit her lip to keep from crying each time the Baroness forced her attentions on the abdomen.

"The massage of Madame Macher," the Baroness was saying reverently, "is the most profound in Europe."

"Does it hurt as much as yours?" Elly gasped.

"Ah, far more," said the Baroness, sighing. "One does one's best," she added modestly, "but Madame Macher . . ." Another pause, as the Baroness flexed her hands, shook them briskly and stretched them out flat, like gloves to be dried. She would use them on edge now, like chopping blades, beating a rapid, rhythmic tattoo on Elly's quailing midsection. "Madame Macher," she began again, surveying the next target area, "is *nonpareil.* It is not, however, the pain by which one judges; it is the profundity. In Gstaad, Madam Macher insists that the masseuse penetrate beyond the tissue." She lifted a pinch of thigh, gingerly, as if it were something to be carried swiftly to the wastebasket. "Beyond the tissue," she repeated, "to the cellular *essence.*" Certain key words were pronounced in French, in the accepted tradition of the American beauty subculture. One's hair was, if possible, *coiffé,* one patronized the *hautest couture,* one did what one could about the *derrière.* Thus, the masseuse nonpareil must reach the *es-sahns* of the cell.

Elly nodded eagerly. "And besides the massage—?"

"Besides the massage," murmured the Baroness, "there is the Process."

She was working on Elly's abdomen, and for the first time Elly scarcely felt it. "Process?"

The Baroness nodded. "You have not heard of it?"

Elly had not. The Baroness could describe it only in very general terms. So much was of course secret. Aromatic oils; preservatives, which also shrank the fatty portions of the cells. The absorption of these substances hastened by encasing the body—

"You mean taping?" Elly cried. "Taping is done here—"

"Not taping," the Baroness retorted angrily. "The Process is nothing whatever like taping! A tourniquet of bandages applied to the body! The Process is based on classic techniques which Madame Macher learned in Egypt. Where even the dead retain physical beauty for a thousand years."

Elly's eyes widened. Mummification? she thought. My God. But she would not interrupt again.

"The body is encased in treated cloths. There are macerating salt baths. No drying of the skin is permitted; one is condensed, but one does not shrink. The oils, heated salts, dry sand —you will turn now, please, Mrs. Berliner." Elly obeyed. "Before one is prepared," the Baroness went on, "one is analyzed for the proper balance—ba-*lahnce*—of warmth, moisture and liquid."

Elly stiffened under the rain of blows. "You must relax, Mrs. Berliner."

"How long—" Elly began.

"Just a few more minutes."

"No, I mean the Process."

"Ah. One rests for several weeks."

"Like that? Being macerated in hot salt?"

"Of course," the Baroness replied. "The length of time depending on the needs of one's body. In Egypt the process took seventy days."

"But they were dead!"

"Yes," said the Baroness. "Madame Macher's adaptation has taken that into account."

"Can you read? Can you walk?"

One might read, but not walk. One's face was attended to, and one's hair. There were in fact exercises for the hair. When one's time was up, one was unwrapped and bathed in other solutions. Occasionally a paste— She stopped pounding; the massage was concluded.

Elly sat up. The Baroness, stretching her fingers, smiled. "And then one emerges." An eloquent shrug. *One emerges.* Elly picked up the fingertip towel with which one scrupulously covered one's private parts during the Baroness's ministrations. Holding it discreetly, like a violet figleaf, she jumped down from the table. "Madame Ma——What was it?"

"Ma-cher," said the Baroness, and spelled it. "You are interested?" Elly nodded. "Then I must write at once to recommend you. One cannot simply go—one *applies.* Madame Macher is extremely careful in the selection of patients. The Duchess of Sittingbourne was refused, and Princess Shushtar, and last year she even turned down a cousin of Queen Juliana. Their bodies were not"—the Baroness shrugged—"not suitable."

Elly looked forlorn, like a girl with a canceled date for New Year's Eve. "What if she won't take me?"

The Baroness smiled reassurance. "She will take you."

The question of Jason's school had not been settled, but in the meantime he would be leaving for camp in a week. He detested camp, but what choice was there? Ted, his father, had already gone to Europe, leaving her with the boy at a time like this.

The Baroness wrote to Madame Macher on Elly's behalf, apologizing for the lateness of the application, particularly at this time of year, but assuring Madame that Elly was eminently suitable for the Process, having been under the Baroness' own care for nearly a year.

The application was promptly accepted, provided payment of the requisite $1,750 deposit was received within five days. One regretted this urgency, but space at the clinic was in such demand. Elly would not have been considered for admission until the winter, but an exception was being made because the recommendation had come from Baroness von der Nordestern, for whom Madame Macher had the highest personal regard.

Jason was dispatched to Camp Quogoneck, where he was certainly not going to be forced into any intense athletic competition, "Uncle Merv" Tafel, the director, assured Elly. No, ma'am; in fact, it ran directly counter to camp policy to force a boy who didn't want to compete. As for Jason's musical bent, far from being neglected, that would be more than nurtured at Camp Quogoneck, which, if Uncle Merv had to say so, modestly prided itself on producing the well-rounded youngster who took an avid interest in other cultural activities besides sports. This year they were especially fortunate in having found

238

a really topnotch music counselor—actually, Uncle Hi would be in charge of the entire arts and crafts program, but he would be placing special emphasis on music activities. Yes, ma'am, Uncle Merv felt sure that Jason would really take to Quogoneck. They'd had a lot of experience with his kind of youngster, believe me, and the parents were always amazed what they could do with them in one summer.

Within a day or two of their arrival, the faces of the patients at the Macher Clinic acquired the fragile translucence of permanent convalescents. Elly noticed that the ambulatory ones, those who were still in the first intensive massage and analysis phase, also walked alike—the slow, excruciatingly careful pace of women in the corridor of a hospital maternity ward, exchanging wan smiles as they shuffled painfully past one another in their clumsy fur slippers.

Madame Macher herself was a magnificent woman, possibly in her mid-forties, who wore a white doctor's coat open over black dancer's leotards, a costume offering explicit testimony as to the condition of her body. She not only had the superb form, but also the air of a prima ballerina *assoluta*—imperious, but having earned, rather than inherited, the right to be.

The clinic itself, a self-contained little cluster of three round, interconnected white buildings, nestled in the lush Swiss landscape like fresh eggs in a green salad. They housed laboratories, a complex of salons, sleeping quarters, a kitchen and Mme. Macher's private apartment. When the Process began, patients were transported from one area to another in wheelchairs, covered to the neck with sheets of heavy black rubber, like those used by x-ray technicians for protection against overexposure.

Once prepared, the patient moved into the salon, where she was immersed in a tub filled with the prescribed hot salt or sand solution. The tubs were enormous clear fiberglass bubbles, raised on pedestals and capable of being rotated by the press of a button on their base, so that the head of the occupant could be raised or lowered. One signaled the attendant when one wished to sleep or to sit up. If one wished privacy, curtained partitions could be rolled into position between one's own tub and everyone else's. Mme. Macher hoped eventually to replace the tubs with newer designs that would permit patients to raise or lower themselves.

During the Process, one's diet was severely restricted to liquid and paste mixtures, so that bodily wastes were liquefied and eliminated through fitted tubes that ran from the patient's single garment, a sort of rubberized bikini diaper, through the wet sand or salt and out through the bottom of the tub into a chemical disposal system.

The attendants, wholesome Swiss blondes dressed in white leotards, with tape measures dangling around their necks like tribal ornaments, glided gracefully among the tubs carrying books, magazines or steaming tea kettles freshly filled with brownish liquids prepared in vats in the preparation rooms. At regular intervals the heat and moisture ba-lahnce in each tub had to be checked by hand and adjusted by adding more liquid or raising the individual thermostat.

Several times a day Mme. Macher would make the rounds herself, examining charts and inspecting the ba-lahnce. Thrusting her graceful hand deep into the tub, as one tests the bath water, she would nod or, occasionally, frown, snapping her fingers at an attendant and crying " *Vite, vite!*" until the necessary adjustment was made. As scalding liquid seeped through the densely packed salt or sand, streaming inward over limbs and into bodily orifices, patients would grasp or grimace, but no one ever cried aloud. However, one *was* expected to cry during the massage phase. One cried only when kneaded. If the pain was not sufficiently intense, the masseuse could not be reaching the es-sahns of the cell. Likewise, one had to be tightly packed in one's salt or sand solution; if one could hardly breathe, if one had headache and pounding in the ears, one could rest assured that one was deriving the maximum benefit.

Patients soon found that they could not read or write easily in the tubs, even though their forearms and hands remained free. Most would doze off between the attendants' visits. There were occasional lessons—instructions in exercise of the hair through scalp movement, instructions in smiling without moving the cheek muscles, or moving the cheek muscles without smiling, for toning the face. Shampooing and vigorous brushing of the hair upside down from the roots, treatments of the facial skin, meals, dozing, discussions of one's body and the progress of one's Process. One soon lost track of the days.

Elly was happier at the Macher Clinic than she had been in years. At the end of her third week a letter arrived from the headmaster of Knickerbocker Military Institute, accepting Jason as a transfer student for the fall term. She wrote to Jason at once, a long affectionate, chatty letter full of her own doings, or rather, the clinic's doings unto her. She hoped he was having fun at camp, despite his misgivings, that he was making friends and participating in some of the normal activities for a boy of fifteen. The games—he must recognize that these things were important too. Even the greatest musician cannot function without a healthy body.

Five days later there was a telegram from Merv Tafel, the director of Camp Quogoneck. "Regret unfortunate canoeing accident today. Await your instructions Jason, please call camp at once. Sincerely." No details were given, not even whether the child was alive. Fifteen words; they could have left out the sincerely.

Uncle Merv had worked out with his wife and the head counselor what to say. They were worried sick that the camp might be held responsible. If the child had actually drowned, what kind of an excuse would it be that his canoe just happened to be lagging so far behind the others, that they lost sight of him for a few minutes, and . . . Thank God the counselor and the other kids had at least discovered him before it was too late. Even so, it looked pretty bad from a legal standpoint.

On the other hand, Jason had deliberately lied about his swimming ability to qualify for this two-day canoe trip, and apparently Uncle Rafe, the swimming counselor, had slipped up somewhere in giving him the test. The kid hadn't been swimming all summer, or they would have found out long before, but they gave those tests the first week, and he was already in the infirmary with his asthma, so somebody just took his word for it that he was an advanced swimmer; after all, he'd spent the last eight summers in other camps. The point was that if the kid really was trying to commit suicide, the scandal could hurt worse than a lawsuit. What about that youngster who was so miserable at Quogoneck that he tried to drown himself? What do they do to kids up there?

Uncle Merv decided to stick with the straight accident. Maybe the kid's mother didn't even know he couldn't swim a stroke; most of these mothers barely knew their kid's name. And to think how relieved they'd been when Jason signed up for the canoe trip; it was the first activity he had shown any interest in since he arrived. Until then he had sat in his bunk moping, or checking into the infirmary every other day. Asthma and hay fever in July; he said he always got it that early.

Even the music. His mother had said he was such a musical hotshot, but he never once went near Uncle Hi for arts and crafts. Sure, he'd asked if he could use the piano by himself in the main lodge after lights out every night; well, that's strictly against camp rules. Lights out is lights out, and oddball or no oddball, the kid had to hit the sack, Merv told him, at nine o'clock like everybody else.

So when he suddenly signed up for the big canoe trip, they thought maybe something had broken through. Maybe he was tired of being an oddball, getting his bed frenched every day and frogs stuck in his shoes. The only kid in the tent who talked to him was Howie Schupack, the bed-wetter, so they'd thought that maybe, with the summer half gone, Jason had decided to try and shape up.

During rest hour, the day before the canoe trip, Jason had written a letter to an uncle of his, Mr. Chad Batchelder, but he didn't have the address. The uncle wasn't listed in the camp office, so they sent it to the kid's mother in Switzerland with a note asking her to mail it. It was the only letter Jason had written to anybody. The telegram, of course, got there first.

After Elly called Uncle Merv and determined that Jason had in fact not quite drowned, and was now in the infirmary, Mme. Macher brought a chair to sit beside her and try to help her decide what to do. Two sets of curtained partitions were stationed around them, and Mme. Macher, who rarely spent more than a few minutes in the Processing salon, ordered tea and gelatin for them and told the attendants she was not to be disturbed. She spoke very gently to Elly, and her own cool amber eyes were full. One of her children, she confided, had died in an automobile accident at the age of five. The question was whether Elly must fly home at once and take Jason out of that camp, or leave him there for the rest of the summer, despite what had happened. Madame felt that Elly would be wise to stay at the clinic and leave the boy where he was for a few more weeks; it would be such a shame to waste all of the Process that Elly had so far undergone; it was not, after all, a matter of the boy being *ill*.

Elly wanted to stay, of course, but it seemed so . . . heartless, did it not? After Ralph's death, and the boy barely escaping such a tragic fate. It seemed very wrong to—well, just ignore him. For the sake of, in a sense, her own personal vanity? One *could* look at it that way, couldn't one? She gazed imploringly at Madame.

Certainly not, Madame retorted. It would seem a far greater wrong, in her opinion, for Elly to ignore herself, considering her recent tragedy of the loss of her husband and the attendant shock to her emotional system. Very wrong indeed. Irresponsible.

Still Elly hesitated.

"In any case," Madame added firmly, "you could not possibly leave immediately. Ten days at the very earliest. The clinic could not sanction such a risk to your *physical health*. If you were to be removed from the salt solution at this point, you would be *gravely* ill. So it is out of the question. Perhaps in ten or twelve days, depending on how your son . . ."

"You are very kind, Madame," Elly murmured.

"Please call me Marie-Ange."

For some reason Elly burst into tears then, for the first time since the telegram arrived. Perhaps it was because until that moment she had felt so alone, insulated within her solitary bubble of salt, and within her strangeness. Except for her wealth, she was very different from the other patients, most of whom were much older women—Europeans—and seriously overweight. Elly had checked into the clinic weighing her usual ninety-six pounds.

Marie-Ange took a soft handkerchief from a pocket of her doctor's coat and gently dried Elly's tears. "I hate," sobbed Elly, "I hate to cry."

Marie-Ange nodded with perfect understanding. "The skin," she said. "Still, the *lavage* restores the clarity of the eyes,

244

so one must not condemn it entirely. One must consider the ba-lahnce." They both smiled. "Would you like to rest now?" Elly shook her head. "But you must go; I understand."

"Not at all," said Marie-Angie. "I shall just arrange." She rolled a partition away and snapped her fingers for the attendant. "Not to disturb for another twenty minutes, and to bring"—she turned to Elly—"more tea?" Elly nodded. She held out the handkerchief, and Marie-Ange, reaching for it, touched her hand briefly, perhaps by mistake. "Have you never been to Switzerland before?" she asked.

"Once," said Elly. "I went to St. Moritz and tried to ski."

"You did not enjoy it, then?"

Elly sighed. "I was, as usual, a casualty. On the third day. An arm, an ankle, and something to the knee cartilage which has never properly healed. Until then I enjoyed it."

"You were very young?"

"Twenty. I don't remember the skiing at all, only the rescue. The ski patrol untangled me from my tree and stretched me out on a sled. A toboggan, I guess. Anyway, they tied me up and sent me hurtling down head-first. With a man on skis straddling me, holding the rope of my sled. I've never felt so . . . so utterly powerless—that is, until you put me in this." She indicated her salt-bubble prison, and Marie Ange laughed.

"Between the two—imprisonments," she asked when the tea had come, "which has been worse?"

"Being rescued by the ski patrol," Elly replied gravely, "was absolutely the worst experience I have ever had." She sipped her tea thoughtfully. "I was broken in about nine places, and freezing, and scared. But the worst thing was having to lie there staring up at my rescuer. All I could see was the straining crotch of those black ski pants stretched over my body. I never saw his face. There was pain shooting through my arms and legs, and I knew that if the rope slipped out of his hand, I would die. I would slide at some breakneck speed—assuming my neck wasn't already broken—straight down into blurry white hell. And then halfway down I began to laugh. I began to recite, 'He is the master of my fate, he is the captain of my soul. He is a black guard in a white world.' A white world of death framed by this black wishbone of a strange man's outstretched legs. He is my rescuer. And I thought how appropriate, after all." Elly sighed, suddenly embarrassed. "I haven't the faintest idea why I began all that."

"I have," said Marie-Ange. She stood up to go. "You must rest now. And tomorrow," she added quietly, "we shall arrange for everything." A pause. "You will stay, will you not?"

Elly nodded. "Yes, Marie-Ange."

Jason's letter to Chad arrived the same day as Uncle Merv's long explanation and profound expression of regret about this unfortunate occurrence, the first such incident in Quogoneck's history (thirty-two years of happy boys' happiest summers). It went without saying, of course, how deeply appreciative they were that Mrs. Berliner's confidence in the camp remained unshaken, and that Jason would be remaining for the rest of what Uncle Merv personally guaranteed would be a wonderful summer for him, in spite of everything . . .

Elly opened Jason's letter to Chad. The message was very brief:

Dear Chad,
    The music is good but the words are all shit now, Eli Lewisohn notwithstanding. Please tell my mother not to feel bad about Knickerbocker Military Institute, since it could only be worse than Camp Quogoneck. P.S. I hope you're having a nice summer. Love, Jason.

Elly read it twice and decided not to worry about something that didn't even make sense.

When she emerged at last from her saline cocoon, like Lot's wife in reverse, Elly felt sure that she had made the right decision. According to Uncle Merv, while Jason had not become an all-around Quogonecker, at least he was managing to stay out of the infirmary. He was coming along fine in arts and crafts, and she would be pleased to hear, they knew, that they had changed the camp rules just so Jase could keep up with his piano practice.

And Elly herself felt physically reborn, as if her entire past life had been gently sloughed away, like one more salt-worn layer of exhausted skin. Her face now seemed smooth and lustrous, almost luminous, she thought; her body had never felt so taut and supple. One had emerged, as the Baroness said; one had been superbly Processed. But for what? It was preposterous to think of staying any longer. The cost was really outrageous, and one could not endure another week of profound massage.

After the unwrapping, Elly had returned to the sleeping quarters for the final phase of treatment, a matter of special cleansing baths and light exercise. One was being groomed for the return to another life. There was a large package on her bed. A present. She picked it up and held it for a long time before opening it. She did not want a going-away gift from anyone, least of all from Marie-Ange.

Finally she began to remove the wrapping gently, as the attendants had removed hers. There was a card inside: "For Elly, with the fond and perhaps not foolish wish that she may wear these at home, thinking of—Marie-Ange." Elly glanced at the gift with a cry of startled delight, and flew down the corridor, carrying the package and its trailing ribbons, through the courtyard to Marie-Ange's small apartment. It was too early for her to be in, but the door was usually unlocked.

Trembling, Elly slipped inside and removed her clinic robe to try on Marie-Ange's gift: a black dancer's leotard and a white doctor's coat, to be worn open, offering explicit testimony to the magnificent condition of one's body. When Marie-Ange came in, she found Elly staring at herself in the mirrored bedroom wall.

At herself, or this person who might be herself, or who might have been, at some other time. Behind her, Marie-Ange smiled at this new mirror image of her own mirror image.

Later, lying sleepless in the firm, supple arms of Marie-Ange, Elly would try to blur the memory of that reflection, for when Marie-Ange stepped into the room, just before they embraced for the first time, Elly had noticed . . . something, wasn't it the same, yes, that ugly little line, a crease, still on the left side, and it seemed a fraction—but how *could* it be?—deeper. Perhaps not, she told herself, turning toward Madame's dazzling smile, perhaps it was just the light.

Twelve

NED SEEMED ANGRY all the time now, shouting at everyone, at Celine, at the servants; they could all hear him shouting before his key turned in the front door. His thundering voice frightened Celine more than anything except being alone or not being allowed to have nice things. Whatever it was that so enraged Ned now, she sensed it was nothing she had done, but it didn't help. He had come home rumbling and erupting, striking with his voice if not his hands, every night since right after Ralph died. Celine had begun to stiffen when she heard his footsteps. He never hit her, of course. But still she would tense, and her amber eyes would cloud with a strange impassive dullness while his voice crashed around her. She would sit motionless during his tirades, like an old refugee crouched in safety on the hill, watching her village burn.

What was wrong of course was that without Ralph, or someone, to run interference for him at the store, Ned now had to deal constantly and directly with Alison, and with Pembroke, who seemed to be turning into a dangerous clipped poodle. The sale of Lowen's had been Ned's single chicken, counted so carefully at the very instant of hatching. Within a few months, had luck not been so viciously against him, the store might have been neatly razed, surgically excised from Fifth Avenue like a gray limestone wart. Demolished; that quick, painless, highly profitable death. Instead, the building stood there mocking him, while Alison and Pem ran the business slowly into the ground. They had begun to confer in whispers, closing their office doors to keep their idiocies secret from him —children plotting behind teacher's back. Later they would tell him blandly, when the orders were in or the bills arrived on his desk. Oh, yes, that was something Pem and I decided on; she thought Pem had mentioned it to him, or Pem was sure *she* had. Anyway, just take care of it, will you, Ned, thanks.

A dozen times a day he would walk past Ralph's empty office, cursing the darkness. There was no longer enough antacid in the world.

One night after closing time, Ned had walked into that dark office and sat down to think. Maybe just another Ralph Berliner, just a warm body to prop up between him and them, to deflect some of it, or absorb some. A scout could talk to Alison, smile at Pembroke, and report back carefully to Ned. Someone to keep everyone at arm's length, or whatever the optimum distance was between throats. The right sort of liaison man, impervious to the charms, if any, of either Alison or Pem, could at least avert some disasters. and help brace him for the others. If the luck was ever going to change, Lowen's could still be afloat. Another straw drifting downstream, another Jerome T. Alswang, a shift in Uncle Zack's fortunes. Something might break besides Ned's spirit, his health, his balls.

A buffer. But who?

For days Ned pondered it. It need not even necessarily be someone who knew merchandising, he decided. All the man had to do was know who Ned was, and remember to tell him everything. He was still pondering it in the bathtub several nights later, when he heard his wife's voice, heard her rustling packages, sighing her weary storewide-clearance shopper's sigh. "Celine!" he yelled. "My God, why not?"

He loomed up out of the tub to peer into the bedroom; there she was piling her boxes on the bed, like a hunter unloading the day's kill. Celine, he thought excitedly. Introducing Celina Lowen as the Girl Reporter. My liaison man, my under-the-counter spy! She's always been such a good listener.

Grabbing a towel, he dashed out to hug her, pressing his damp, hairy bulk against her new squirrel-belly fur coat. He even kissed her, ignoring her squirming, her "Ned, please!" A huge, bristling kiss. Then he released her, whirled around and whacked the pile of boxes off her bed. "Listen to me, Celine!" he shouted. "Are you listening?" She nodded, eyes widening with fear. He scowled at her so that she didn't dare begin brushing up the wet spots on her fur. "You're going to start earning your *keep!* Is that clear?" She nodded, again mutely, thinking that he was finally insane; he was finally going to kill her. He started laughing then, shaking in his brown bath towel with the gold monogram, the NG vibrating across his stomach.

Finally he subsided into heavy sighs, took off the towel and began drying himself, slapping his shoulders vigorously while he told her what he had decided. Though not exactly. He told her about this dream he had for her, about how it had bothered him, knowing she wanted to do something creative, knowing how disappointed she had been over the business with the portraits and publicity, and how he wanted her to be happy. Smoothly, effortlessly, he merchandised his idea. She would come to work at Lowen's; she could start some kind of special department, something fun—imports, knickknacks, he didn't know what. But mainly she could help them, him and Alison, run the whole store. Now that poor Ralph . . . they needed her. Alison would have to approve, of course, he hadn't even discussed it with Alison yet, but he was sure she'd see how helpful Celine could be. There were, he knew, areas, where Alison's taste and Celine's were not exactly . . . but they could work that out. Alison didn't always sneer at Celine's ideas, did she? Of course not; for instance, she liked—well, he'd think of some examples.

The more he talked, the more convinced Ned was that he had found the way to save them all. Amos, he thought, would have been proud. Alison would certainly let her sister have some little toy that she herself didn't want to play with right now. She'd find all kinds of chores, he was sure. Celine could amuse herself between crises, going on shopping sprees for her department, or whatever they gave her. Her nonsense, all those endless things in boxes. And she wouldn't even have to carry them home. Go talk to Pembroke, he would tell her, when he sensed the naughty children were plotting something; see what Alison's up to. Let me know what their thinking is on . . .

She would even be good at it. She was nervous and insufferably silly in her own way, in her own excesses, but he could control that. Selling Alison was going to be trickier; she would hardly consider Celine a brilliant executive asset. On the other hand, he reasoned, the last thing Alison would ever want was a brilliant executive asset. Look at the way she treated him, for

252

instance. The important thing was that Alison would talk to Celine; she could boss Celine; she always had. And with Celine on the premises, she would never have to talk to Ned any more. That alone ought to be worth something. In fact, it ought to be worth almost everything.

Chad and Alison saw very little of each other now. Small unavoidable encounters, like tenants with similar hours meeting in the elevator, nodding hello. Or dull, unpleasant little business exchanges: We're supposed to have dinner at the Palmers' tonight; I assume you're not going. Shall I call? What do you want to do about these tickets we ordered?

They no longer had to discuss bills, of course; Alison paid them all. It was really nothing more than a slow wearing away of surfaces, and it was relatively painless.

Chad had taken to spending afternoons in a Christian Science Reading Room, rather than returning after lunch to his dismal office. The cellblock. He would soon have to give that up too; it no longer served any purpose, least of all, pride. He would have to give up several things. At least he had managed to keep the drinking to less than a pint a day; not bad, considering.

He had written to Jason once, after the accident, and to Elly to say how glad he was that the boy was all right. Neither of them had replied. Elly had never bothered to send him Jason's note. He knew from Alison's terse communiqués that Cathy was back in her own apartment, with nurses and lighter bandages, and that Mai hardly left the girl except to go home for dinner with Ira, and to sleep, and of course to leave the room when the psychiatrist banished her. Chad still had no inkling of Mai's hand in his professional downfall, though by now he knew there must have been someone's hand.

From overheard fragments of Alison's telephone calls, Chad

had gathered that Celine was about to become another Lowen's executive. On an impulse one day, he sent her flowers: "Good luck from your former press agent, to a star who doesn't need one." Like Elly, Celine did not choose to acknowledge the gesture. He didn't blame either of them. Still, he recognized these little slights for what they were: invisible reweaving. It was time, he reflected dispassionately, to settle accounts. He went to his old apartment to see what needed doing. He had had to let the cleaning woman go, and the place smelled of neglect. Dusty letters. In a few weeks an old friend from Wichita would be in town, and Chad had heard he was opening a small New York office. He had already written the man, in case there might be a job—anything at all. The friend had emphasized how extremely small an office it would be—not really anything that would interest Chad. He was almost embarrassed. But he would be in town shortly, and perhaps they could have lunch.

That night Chad and Alison and Jill were having dinner together for the first time in weeks. Alison was going out afterward, to a gallery opening. Frieda had been cooking furiously since early morning, as if a royal feast had been decreed.

Frieda, Chad had noticed lately, was forever mending his shirts now, shining his shoes, paying frenzied attention to every detail of his wardrobe, like an anxious mother whose son is leaving for college. Not so much to prepare him, he realized, as to prepare herself, or to suggest that maybe he should not go after all. For who would take care of him out there? Hence, he supposed, the royal feast. The empty-nest syndrome.

He had resolved to display his most exemplary behavior this evening, even to take pains with his clothes, to put himself together in a way that would please Alison. To make charming, affectionate jokes about Frieda's fragrant kitchen, her epic

254

dinner, her flaming anxious face when she stood over him, asking "Is it all right? Too rare?" when he hadn't yet lifted a fork. Above all, he had resolved not to upset Jill.

But from the fruit cocktail on, he failed. Alison objected to his tie; it was too formal with that knit blazer. He offered a caustic apology, tore off the tie at once and hung it ceremoniously over one of the big brass dining-room doorknobs. Alison's eyes blazed at him across the full gleaming expanse of mahogany table, but she said nothing until Frieda and the new maid, Margit, came in to serve the soup. "Would you take Mr. Batchelder's tie into the bedroom, please," she said stiffly. "It's there, on the doorknob."

"Take it into *my* room, Frieda, if you don't mind," he said. And the moment she left with it, he took off the knit blazer too, hanging it across the back of his chair. "You don't mind, do you, darling," he said, watching her anger flicker through the candlelight. "It's terribly warm for chicken soup." Frieda returned, but Alison could not send her scurrying back with the jacket. Chad smiled, rolled up his sleeves and opened his collar.

Jill studied them both guardedly over her steaming silver spoon. She rarely ate dinner with them. During school she was always fed early on a tray served in her room. Then they had sent her to a new six-week "Western adventure" camp—a ranch in western Connecticut. She had been home only a few days, but she had felt the tension instantly and already suspected its source. Sitting there alone halfway between them, at a table that could seat twenty-four, she decided to concentrate on not sweating. A girl at the ranch had told her how. I will not sweat, I am cold, my fingers are numb and turning blue . . .

"Jill darling," Alison was saying, "you haven't told us a thing about camp. Aunt Celine asked me today, and I didn't even know what to say."

Jill swallowed a scalding spoonful of soup, and her eyes swam with defensive tears. "It was nice," she blurted through the mouthful of pain. "I had a horse named Catullus." She paused to pour a sip of water on the blaze. "Catullus," she said again, reciting as if in Sunday School. "They let you pick your horse and name him and take care of him all summer."

Chad wanted to know what color Catullus was. "Very black," Jill said. "The color of hopeless unrequited passion."

"What else did you do," said Alison, stifling a yawn.

Jill resumed the recitation. "We went swimming, and on hayrides. Rodeos, trail-blazing, campfires. Corn-eating contests."

"Mmm," said Alison, "sounds like fun. What time is it, Chad? I'm supposed to be there at nine, and I'm not dressed."

"You have plenty of time, darling," Chad replied, without checking his watch. "How many ears?" he asked Jill.

"I had nine," she answered. "The winner had twelve."

"Ears?" said Alison.

"Corn," said Chad. "Eating. Contest. In camp."

"Mmm. Are you sure I can't talk you into coming to this opening?" she said. "It's very interesting work, this man's work."

"I'm sure," said Chad. "What man is it?"

"I forget his name. Balder—something."

"Dash or snatch, I imagine," he murmured.

Jill giggled into her water goblet.

"Mmm?" said Alison.

"I said it sounds very interesting, his work."

Jill hiccuped loudly, trying to muffle another giggle.

"Drink some water," Alison commanded, frowning at her. "You don't just go on eating if you have hiccups." She pressed the floor buzzer, and before her foot left it Frieda had staggered in with another heaping platter of meat and vegetables,

Yorkshire pudding, horseradish sauce and fresh sprigs of decorative parsley. Even the platter looked as if she had just polished it again.

Chad groaned. "Oh, Frieda, no more for me. It was superb, it was monumental, but I couldn't."

Paying no attention, Frieda slid another piece of beef onto his plate. "Just this one little piece more wouldn't hurt. I'll be insulted."

"I'm sorry, Frieda," he said firmly. "You must all begin to pay attention when a fellow has had enough." He folded the damask napkin and stood up. "Excuse me, everyone." He left the dining room and headed straight to the bar closet, leaving his discarded jacket shrugging its shoulders over the back of the chair.

"How do you like that," Frieda muttered. "After I knock myself out . . . Here," she said, loading another piece onto Jill's plate.

"I don't want any more either."

"You'll have this one little— I don't need that from you," Frieda retorted. Then she set the platter down and went out to the bar to reclaim Chad. "I made you a peach pie," she announced in a menacing tone, loud enough so that there would be witnesses if it came to a duel. "The first peach pie I made the entire summer, up to now the peaches have been too hard, they had no taste. You're going to dare and tell me you don't want any dessert?"

"No, Frieda," he said resignedly. "I'm not going to dare." He followed her meekly back to the table, carrying his drink.

Alison's baleful look did not quite shatter the glass. "Chad," she began, conveying her softest disapproval, "I have asked you not to—"

"Oh dear," he said, "I forgot." And drained the glass, depositing it carefully on Frieda's silver tray. "There, darling, I am not swilling my liquor at the table." He held up both empty hands. "I would have spared you, but Frieda insisted I come right back and have dessert. Didn't you, Frieda?"

Frieda cleared dishes noisily, covering her silence.

"I don't care for any dessert," Jill announced.

"Hmp." Frieda flounced angrily into the kitchen and sent Margit back to finish the clearing. Seconds later, though, she was back, armed with her pie, eyes darting from one end of the table to the other. *Nobody leaves.* She set it down in front of Alison, and with a final warning look, bent her head to begin cutting three enormous slices. "There's practically nothing in it but peaches and butter. How often do I even bother to bake any more? Nobody eats pies. A peach pie, you pay twelve-fifty in Greenberg's and it wouldn't have a drop of butter."

They ate, forcing down silent sweet mouthfuls while she stood there glowering triumph, defying each of them, any of them, to taste the bitterness of their life together while coating their tongues with her ambrosia. They would eat, and then they would know how to live.

Finally Alison's fork descended. Her plate was empty. Frieda was ready, though: "You'll have . . . just this one bite more. Look, it's only the *crumbs.* "

"No!" Alison cried, quickly pushing back the chair. "Chad? Did you decide to come with me?"

"No!" he replied, precisely echoing her.

Startled, she stood uncertainly for a minute. "Well, I'd better collect myself . . . if you're sure." She made her escape, and Frieda retreated sullenly to her kitchen, carrying the rejected remains.

"Why do you do that?" Jill murmured, only half audibly.

"What?" said Chad.

"You know. My mother is no match for you."

He laughed. A short, bitter sound. Mocking himself, not Alison.

"She's really not, I'm serious," Jill persisted. "Half the time she practically doesn't understand what you even mean. Whether you're kidding."

"I don't kid any more, Jill," he sighed. "Your mother understands that, I assure you."

"Well, whatever it is. Matching wits. The way you make jokes over her head and they're always on her and she never even hears them."

"That's true," he conceded. "But imagine how miserable we'd both be if she *wanted* to hear them."

Jill pushed herself back from the table. "I think it's mean," she said.

He caught her hand as she passed him. "Jill." His face was very serious. "Let's go inside and talk, okay?"

She hesitated. "Okay. But wait." She went back and switched their dessert plates, leaving the larger hunk of unfinished pie in front of him.

"Frieda's wrath," he said lightly, "shall be my everlasting penance."

It was well after nine when Alison dashed past the doorway of his den, calling anxiously, "Am I very late, Chad? *Chad?*"

"Just a little late, darling," he responded cheerfully, settling even further into his chair. "Have fun."

Jill, who had been summoned to help assemble her mother's costume, reappeared. "Now, what would you like to listen to?" he asked.

"Anything. Something quiet and sad."

"The color of hopeless unrequited love? Sinatra as Catullus?"

"Unrequited *passion,*" she said. He fiddled with the stereo knobs and she sat down quietly.

When the records began, Chad lit his pipe and sipped his Scotch, slipped his feet out of shoes and into the embroidered slippers, letting the silence deepen.

"Are you very unhappy with my mother?" Jill asked softly.

"Very," he said, but with his wry smile. "And she with me, I assume."

"I wish," said Jill, "it had never happened. I wish you had listened to me. I *told* you."

"Yes, you did," he said. "But I *did* listen, Jill. To what you said, and even to what you felt but didn't say. I listened to all of that. You wanted it, you know, more than either of us."

"I want everything more than she does," Jill said solemnly. "That's probably the curse of being an unwanted child."

"One of them, anyway," he agreed.

"Yes, one. Chad—"

"'Mmm?" He watched her struggle with it.

"Don't," she said, "Don't tell me how you failed her. Or anything." She looked down unhappily, her voice trailing off. "I don't—I don't want any more fathers to tell me."

"I wasn't going to," he said gently. But of course he would have.

She got up to go cry in her own room, and he didn't say anything to stop her, so at the door she turned, walked slowly back and leaned over his chair to kiss him. Chad moaned, a low agonized growl like a hurt animal, and reached for her, drawing her down. She sat very still on the chair with him, like a small girl waiting to be told.

He began to caress her, touching her body as if it were something fragile, some centuries-old sacred object covered with dust or tradition, and he a priest entrusted with this awesome power, this right to perform the holy ceremony, this laying on of hands. He could be my father, she thought. Is my father. Was.

"Your mother," he was murmuring against her hair, chanting it against her throat, "your mother does not want."

Jill shivered. Whose sacrificial victim am I. Upon whom will the gods smile as a result. I am the apology, she thought then. I apologize on behalf of my mother. Not her fault but mine. My fault, my fault. I wanted him to make her be all right. To cure *me*. My own selfish self.

And it had failed. Not he, but Jill. My fault, this broken father. Another broken father. You're the only girl I have left, Jilly.

"Oh, sweet, oh Jesus, sweet . . ." he was chanting. "Here, this. Take . . . this." The invocation, the symbol, the penance, the repentance, the body and blood, extreme unction. "Hold . . . me just a little . . . sweet time. Here—oh, yes."

"Like . . . this?" she whispered.

"Yes, yes—Ah."

She did as she was told. Taking all his holy orders, and he was pleased. Appeased. He kissed her tenderly good night, her Father whose will had been done.

She went to her room, thinking, God bless my mommy and make me a good girl. Make me a whole woman forever and ever. I don't want to be cold. Amen. But she was shivering and she was sure what it was from. She was sure this was how you got frigid.

Alison was still asleep when Chad left the following morning. Jill was awake but still in bed. He opened her door a crack, enough for her to see him all dressed, carrying two suitcases. He held a finger to his silent lips, then tiptoed into the room and pressed the same finger gently to her mouth. That was all.

She waited for a few minutes after she heard the elevator

closing distantly, and then got out of bed and padded in her white fur slippers to her mother's room. Blinking in the dark —even at ten A.M. Alison's room was midnight—she said softly, "Mother, Chad's gone."

Alison sat up, groping for her bed jacket. "Gone?" she echoed. Bewildered? Frightened? Jill could not tell.

"Yes," she answered, feeling the rush of her own tears. Was that what her mother felt?

Alison peered through the darkness at her daughter's stricken face, and stretched out her hand. A ghostly white arm reaching awkwardly from the dark satin bed like the arm of someone drowning. Jill moved closer and took it. "Mother," she said, looking everywhere but toward the bed, "I'm so sorry." I am not apologizing, she thought; I am only sorry.

"Don't cry, darling," said her mother. She had no idea whether Jill was crying.

The telephone rang then, and Alison sprang to life. "Celine? Yes, darling, I'm up. I'll be . . . late, though." She lowered her voice, as befitted the news. "Chad . . . left this morning . . . Yes, I guess it was. I'm . . . all right. I know it's your first day, Celine, but don't worry . . . As soon as I can. Tell everyone. Tell Pembroke . . . As soon as I can." She hung up and switched on the bedside lamp. Tear-streaked, Jill watched her intently.

"Darling—" Alison tried to think of something. "Would you like to . . . to meet me downtown for lunch?"

Jill shook her head. "I . . . you'll be busy. And I have"—she thought quickly—"a date with some friends. From, uh, camp."

Frieda was straightening up Chad's den while Jill lay sprawled on the floor, turning magazine pages. "I suppose she'll do over the room now," Frieda shouted over the roar of the vacuum cleaner. "Make it more cheerful-looking, I suppose."

"Mmm," said Jill.

"I never thought he'd leave," Frieda went on, shaking her head. "So much to put up with, with her, but yet I never thought."

"Too much," Jill agreed.

"Hah?"

"To put up with."

The vacuum cleaner struck something metallic under Chad's chair; Frieda stopped to pick it up. A barrette. "That's mine!" Jill exclaimed, scrambling across the floor to retrieve it. "I must have dropped it."

Frieda's hazel eyes widened, then narrowed thoughfully, but she went on vacuuming. After a minute she said again, "I guess she'll do it over." Jill didn't look up. "To tell you the truth," she went on, "I never cared for such a dark color. I understand he picked the color."

"I like it," said Jill defensively, sliding the barrette into her hair. The color of hopeless.

"Well," said Frieda, nodding. "She'll probably do it over a little more cheerful now. Not so dark. Something light." She switched off the vacuum cleaner. "You know, I'm sorry though. Such a nice man, all in all."

"Very nice," said Jill.

"I don't mean that your father isn't nice," Frieda said quickly. "I don't mean that at all. I always said your father—"

"My father," said Jill, in a funny, tight voice. "My father . . ." and the voice broke; she couldn't help it. Right in front of Frieda: big, hurting childish sobs.

"Tsk! You see that?" Frieda exclaimed irately. "It's still the child that ends up suffering." She put her arms around Jill, clucking and muttering. "Though it's still worse to lose the *real* father, especially for a girl."

Jill went on sobbing against the pillowy bosom. "He'd come back tomorrow, Mr. Landau, I guarantee you, if she'd learn how to give in a little. A woman that's supposed to be so smart in business, and still can't get along with a man. Can you explain it to me, a stupid little poor woman, that never had a college education, why I should know more than your mother?"

Jill couldn't explain it to her, so Frieda droned on, absently patting the dark head bobbing violently against her clean pink daytime uniform. ". . . So if I were you I'd tell her when she comes home tonight, only don't say *I* said so, you'll just tell her, in a nice quiet way, you don't mean to be fresh but if she isn't too nervous to listen, you'll say, Mother, or Mommy, I would like very much if you and Dad would make up together. In your own words, I wouldn't tell you how to express it, it's not even my business. But that you're very sorry about Mr. Batchelder, he was a nice man, you have nothing to say bad against him, but he's still not your father. And as long as she wasn't so happy with this man, you'd like her to try and make up with your father. If you really want to be smart, that's what I'd tell her if I were you."

Jill's tears had stopped, but there seemed no compelling reason to extricate herself from Frieda's soft, heavy cushion of an embrace. The voice pelted her with its endless silly message, an old folk song set to Muzak; a white sound machine, smelling faintly floury. It did its soothing job, pouring light, steady, dumb noise into all the empty corners of lonely, frightening contemporary structures—broken homes, psychiatrists' waiting rooms, express elevators. Only one phrase lodged in her mind . . . *worse to lose the real father, especially for a girl.* Jill meant to ask her why, but Frieda never broke vocal stride, not even to breathe, so she tried to figure out why by herself. Maybe if the real father goes away, then no other man ever has to stay with you, either, like when the Supreme Court establishes a precedent. The historic case of Landau, Batchelder

264

et.al.,v. Jill Lowen Landau, a very minor female. Clearly establishing that the sins of the mother are visited upon the daughter, whether she likes it or not.

Even Chad had warned her, all those months ago. There was only one cure for it, he said, and that was too risky for most people. Learning to believe in love, and then—hadn't he told her?—saying yes, please, when someone offers it. And the risk was that there might not be any such thing.

She wished there had been time to ask him one more question before he left: whether he thought the Lowens were afraid to take the risk . . . or whether maybe they *had* taken it, each of them at least once, and lost.

Well, maybe someday she would figure it out for herself. With her swollen face still pressed against Frieda, Jill made a solemn promise, half in honor of Chad. When I grow up, she vowed, I will not be a Lowen girl. Even if there really is no such thing as love.

By the time she arrived at the store, Alison had one of her classic stomach aches. As a child she used to get them every time the piano teacher said she had finished with a piece and it was time to begin a new one. But *why,* she would cry. I know this one, this one is hard enough. I only want to play this one. And her stomach would cry out too. Why can't I just stay right here.

They had to decide on the Halloween theme this morning, and she had told them absolutely no orange. She was sick of orange for Halloween; it was tacky. Indeed, Halloween was tacky.

"But nothing else looks *Octobral,*" Pembroke complained. "And if anyone strews one more golden russet leaf in here," he swore, "I'm going to start playing with matches."

Alison stretched out painfully, flattening the ache against

the glass conference table. If I die, she thought, it will happen here, like this, on this frozen crystal slab. Pristinely alone.

Aloud she moaned, "Black. Drape everything black and let's call it a night."

Celine giggled nervously, and then raised a timid hand.

"Unless you have to go powder your nose, Celine darling," Pem said acidly, "speak up."

"Apples. I was just thinking about apples," Celine squeaked. "Wasn't it Halloween when we bobbed for apples?"

Alison didn't bother to roll over. "Red," she sighed doubtfully.

"Apples, though," Pembroke mused, thoughtfully tapping his unicorn belt buckle. "Black velvet, and comfort Alison with apples. *Rouge et noir.* Place your bets, ladies."

"A black ceiling," said Celine, gesturing, "with apples hanging?"

"They're only three dollars a bushel," Ned offered helpfully. Celine, he thought, was doing fine, if she'd only calm down.

"All right," sighed Alison. "I can't think straight. We'd hang them on thin silver chains, I suppose."

"Oh, black strings!" cried Celine. "And a wind machine, so they'd float. I mean bob!"

Strings, Ned calculated, were approximately one tenth the cost of thin silver chains. And the wind machine could be rented . . . First morning on the job and look at her go. My poor little rich girl selling apples in the great Lowen's depression. For once, we could even use the leftovers. Waste not, want not. Now is that a display of genius, I ask you? He did not, however, say one word aloud, but when the meeting ended, he squeezed his wife's arm on the way out.

"You'll do," he whispered, and pinched her bottom for good measure. "Possibly we may live through the week."

*   *   *

Alison was in exactly the same position when Celine and Pembroke returned some twenty minutes later.

"We just wanted . . ." Celine said. "Are you all right? To show you this. About the new department? Alison?"

"I hear you," Alison said, lifting her head imperceptibly with tremendous effort.

"Pem and I have already collected a few things, as you suggested. But we can show you those later. Anyway—" She held out a large cardboard paste-up for a possible ad.

Alison stuck out a hand and slid it under the table; it was easier to study it through the glass than to sit up. INTRODUCING . . . it read. "Naturally," murmured Alison. INTRODUCING . . . Les Objets! A new department bursting with surprises for incurable shoppers (aren't we all?) Les Ornaments, Les Bibelots, Les Choses. All the absolute must-haves . . ." "That's fine," said Alison, letting it fall gently to the carpet. "All the absolute must-haves . . ."

As her sister bent to retrieve it, Alison groaned, and Celine suddenly remembered about Chad. "Darling," she said solicitously, "wouldn't you like to lie down, or go home, or something?"

"I'm tired," said Alison in a flat voice. "I'm tired of things. Of Les Choses."

"Nonsense," Pembroke said. He began to rub the back of her neck, his elephant's-hair bracelets whispering softly against her ear. She closed her eyes. "Don't worry," Pem said to Celine, "she'll be all right."

"Nonsense," said Alison, imitating his voice. "I'm tired of nonsense too. And objets, I'm sick to death of objets."

"Oh," said Celine, feeling hurt now. "Well, we can think some more about the name."

"I suppose so," said Alison. "Pembroke?"

"Pem's here, Ali darling," he said, still rubbing.

"Pembroke," she sighed, "there's really no point in thinking any more about the name. Is there?"

"I suppose not," he said. Then he motioned to Celine to leave them alone for a while, and after a few minutes, he leaned close to her ear and whispered again, "Pem's here, Ali."

She had fallen asleep, so that when the phone rang, he pounced on it, catlike, with a fiercely protective *"Sssh!"* And then giggled apologetically. "I mean, Miss Lowen's office. Who's calling her, please?"

It was Mai. "Well, Alison is resting, dear," he announced firmly, like an attending doctor. "Shall I give her a message for you?"

Mai hesitated. "Well. Does she know Elly is back from Switzerland? . . . *Elly*, yes. Flew in last night, so we're all meeting for lunch. I guess Celine didn't have a chance to tell Alison? . . . I wasn't sure myself until just now that I could arrange to leave my daughter . . . still very ill, I suppose you know that. But with Elly just home, it seemed . . . Anyway, if Alison felt up to it, we thought she might join us . . . But if not, I'm sure Elly will understand . . . " Mai hesitated once more, before adding how much *good* it would do Alison, she thought, for all of them to get together . . . at a time like this . . .

Pembroke doubted that Alison could stomach . . . uh, that Alison's stomach could handle one of those lunches today, he cooed. But he'd certainly tell her.

"Elly darling! You look marvelous! Doesn't she look marvelous?"

"And I love what they did to her hair. I think."

"Face is a little thinner, though. I'm not sure I like Elly's face so thin. Maybe it's the make-up—all that white around the nose and mouth. Never covers lines anyway, I don't think."

"Never mind *me*," Elly protested, fleeing behind her compact mirror and wiping furiously. "I want to hear about everyone else. Isn't Alison coming?"

"Well, you know about Chad. She's apparently prostrate in her office, and Pembroke's got custody of the stomach ache."

"Poor darling. Not that I'm surprised. Just this morning, it happened?"

Celine told about the meeting, with poor Alison stretched out on the table like an accident victim.

"Well," sighed Elly, "she's right to try and work anyway. One has to try something. Unless one tries absolutely nothing, like I did. She tries on her belly, I try on my back." She shrugged.

"It must have been heavenly, though, the rest," said Celine.

"Mmm, yes, for a while. Until you want to die from the damn *purity* of it. Made me think about that Japanese beef that's supposed to be the tenderest in the world, you know? Because they keep the animal trussed up between two trees for his whole life, so that he can't ever move a single muscle. And after every meal someone comes by and massages all the right places, so the fat gets perfectly marbled. His whole *life*. That's what I thought of, lying there. Being perfectly *marbled*. Why are we still discussing *me*, though— I'm up to *here* with me! How is—how is Cathy?"

"Oh, much better," said Mai quickly, though not with her usual conviction. Her smile tightened as she spoke, as if this might be her last show of force. As she recited her catechism of Cathy's progress, the others nodded at the familiar passages. "The doctor thinks—"

"Which doctor?" asked Elly. "The face doctor or the head doctor?"

"Oh, both," said Mai. "They're *both* very . . . hopeful."

"That's wonderful, darling," Elly murmured. "That sounds really wonderful."

"Starting this new department," Celine cut in brightly, "in the store. I started to tell you before. My first day. And the newspapers, I mean everyone's been so excited about it, they're coming to interview me this afternoon, the *Times* and *Women's Wear*. Both. And to photograph some of the things I've been—we've been collecting. Mmm? Oh, this?" Elly had seized her elaborately gesturing hand and was examining the chunky gold bracelet. "Yes, Ned surprised me with it this morning. Sort of a send-off to celebrate my new"—she smiled, modest but triumphant— *"career."*

Mai covered a tiny yawn, and Elly said, "Mmm. But nobody's really told me what *happened* with Chad."

"Well, nothing happened," said Mai. "I mean, no *one* thing."

"I hate to say it, but I could see it months ago," Elly replied. "Not just the drinking, I don't mean."

"Well, a man who's flunked the course that many times . . ."

"And Jill?" said Elly. "Is Jill very upset?"

Celine thought Alison had said Jill was taking it very well, considering.

"Wrong kind of man for Alison. I sensed it right away," said Mai.

"Did you?" Elly murmured.

Celine nodded. "Weak. Alison needs a forceful man."

"Like Ned, you mean?" Mai laughed. "Only Celine needs anything *that* forceful."

"And only Mai needs the opposite extreme," Celine countered.

"I myself," said Elly, "need another Bloody Mary. Not too spicy."

"And another man or two on the side," Mai observed.

"What's wrong with that?" flared Elly. "Anything wrong with that?"

No one replied. Abruptly, they all retreated to their salads, as if their appetites had been restored.

Finally Celine thought of a safe topic. "You know, I wouldn't be surprised if Alison wound up with someone like Pembroke."

"What a revolting thing to say," Elly exclaimed.

"Why?" Celine looked genuinely puzzled. "I mean, wouldn't *you* consider a Pembroke in Alison's position?"

"No, she wouldn't," Mai said shortly. "Elly wouldn't be in Alison's position." Elly began to smile gratefully, until Mai finished her thought. "Unless Alison were already in it with a Pembroke."

Celine giggled. "Why do you suppose we're all being so disagreeable today?"

"Maybe because Chad's gone," said Mai. She had meant to be flippant; why had it come out sounding . . . rueful?

Celine began repairing her make-up, moving the brushes and crayons slowly, the stones in her bracelet casting desultory flashes as she worked.

Elly sighed and fished a cigarette out of her gold case. "That's pretty. Is it new?" Mai asked. Celine's lipbrush paused in midstroke, as if the completion of that perfect upper curve hung on the reply.

"What, this?" said Elly wearily, snapping the case shut. She glanced at her sallow reflection in it, and shook her head. "No, of course not." She sighed. "Nothing is new."

Kimberly Ann Elliott
Richard B. Freeman

CAN LABOR
STANDARDS
IMPROVE UNDER
GLOBALIZATION?

INSTITUTE FOR INTERNATIONAL ECONOMICS
Washington, DC
June 2003

Kimberly Ann Elliott is a research fellow at the Institute for International Economics and has a joint appointment with the Center for Global Development. Her previous books include *Corruption and the Global Economy* (1997), *Reciprocity and Retaliation in US Trade Policy* (1994), *Measuring the Costs of Protection in the United States* (1994), *Economic Sanctions Reconsidered* (2d ed., 1990, and 3d ed., forthcoming), and *Auction Quotas and United States Trade Policy* (1987). She served on the National Academies Committee on Monitoring International Labor Standards in 2002–03 and, in 1999, as chair of the Task Force on Civil Society of the State Department Advisory Committee on International Economic Policy.

Richard B. Freeman is Ascherman Professor of Economics at Harvard University, co-director of the Labor and Worklife Forum at the Harvard Law School, and director of the Labor Studies Program at the National Bureau of Economic Research (NBER). He is also co-director of the Centre for Economic Performance at the London School of Economics (LSE) and visiting professor at LSE. He has published over 300 articles on a wide range of topics including the job market for scientists and engineers, the growth and decline of unions, and the effects of immigration and trade on inequality. Some of his books include *What Do Unions Do?* (1984), *When Public Sector Workers Unionize* (1988), *Labour Markets in Action* (1989), *Immigration, Trade and the Labor Market* (1991), *Working Under Different Rules* (1994), *What Do Workers Want?* (1999), and *What Do Unions Do to the European Welfare States?* (2001).

INSTITUTE FOR INTERNATIONAL ECONOMICS
1750 Massachusetts Avenue, NW
Washington, DC 20036-1903
(202) 328-9000   FAX: (202) 659-3225
www.iie.com

C. Fred Bergsten, *Director*
Valerie Norville, *Director of Publications and Web Development*
Brett Kitchen, *Director of Marketing and Foreign Rights*

Typesetting by Sandra F. Watts
Printing by Kirby Lithographic Company, Inc.
Cover photo: Andy Sacks/Photographer's Choice

Printed in the United States of America
05 04 03   5 4 3 2 1

Library of Congress Cataloging-in-Publication Data

Elliott, Kimberly Ann, 1960–
Can labor standards improve under globalization? / Kimberly Elliott, Richard Freeman.
    p. cm.
Includes bibliographical references and index.
ISBN 0-88132-332-2
1. International labor activities. 2. Labor laws and legislation, International. 3. Labor laws and legislation—Developing countries. 4. Globalization—Moral and ethical aspects. 5. Environmental policy. 6. Child labor. 7. Sweatshops. 8. Wages. 9. Industrial safety. I. Freeman, Richard B. (Richard Barry), 1943– II. Title.

HD6476.E44 2003
331.2—dc21   2003041703

Contents

v

Preface

The Institute has conducted extensive research on trade policy throughout its history. Over the last decade or so, we have extended that work beyond the traditional dimensions of the issue to consider the relationships between trade and the growing number of social issues that have come to be associated with trade in the public debate. The most relevant of those issues include overall foreign policy, as addressed in our extensive work on economic sanctions; corruption, as in Kimberly Ann Elliott's *Corruption and the Global Economy* (1997); the environment, as in Daniel C. Esty's *Greening the GATT: Trade, Environment and the Future* (1994); and especially labor, including international labor standards.

Trade, of course, has a considerable impact on workers in both exporting and importing countries. The Institute has studied those effects extensively, most recently in Dani Rodrik's *Has Globalization Gone Too Far?* (1997); William R. Cline's *Trade and Income Distribution* (1997); Kenneth F. Scheve and Matthew J. Slaughter's *Globalization and the Perceptions of American Workers* (2001); Lori Kletzer's *Job Loss from Imports: Measuring the Costs* (2001); and Robert E. Baldwin's *The Decline of US Unions and the Role of Trade* (2003). The benefits of globalization to workers (and others) has been assessed in Howard Lewis III and J. David Richardson's *Why Global Commitment Really Matters!* (2001) and Richardson and Karin Rindal's *Why Exports Matter More!* (1996). We considered US policy on trade and international labor standards in *The New Politics of American Trade: Trade, Labor, and the Environment* by I. M. Destler and Peter J. Balint (1999).

We are delighted that Richard B. Freeman, one of the world's leading labor economists, has now joined our own Kimberly Ann Elliott to develop this comprehensive analysis of the relationship between globalization and international labor standards. They address the key questions concerning the topic, as listed in the first paragraph of their introductory chapter, and offer answers to each. The study then proposes a set of policy changes, at both the national and international levels, that would simultaneously improve the prospects for workers in developing countries and strengthen the global trading system. The authors conclude that there is a market for labor standards that will enable globalization and labor standards to be complementary rather than competing ways to raise living standards around the world and that the two should thus proceed together over the coming years. We hope their work will contribute to resolving this highly contentious issue in a manner that will be satisfactory to the respective supporters of international labor standards and of globalization.

The Institute for International Economics is a private nonprofit institution for the study and discussion of international economic policy. Its purpose is to analyze important issues in that area and to develop and communicate practical new approaches for dealing with them. The Institute is completely nonpartisan.

The Institute is funded largely by philanthropic foundations. Major institutional grants are now being received from the William M. Keck, Jr. Foundation and the Starr Foundation. A number of other foundations and private corporations contribute to the highly diversified financial resources of the Institute. The Ford Foundation provided generous support for this study. The Andrew W. Mellon Foundation is also supporting this and our other work on globalization. About 31 percent of the Institute's resources in our latest fiscal year were provided by contributors outside the United States, including about 18 percent from Japan.

The Board of Directors bears overall responsibilities for the Institute and gives general guidance and approval to its research program, including the identification of topics that are likely to become important over the medium run (one to three years), and which should be addressed by the Institute. The Director, working closely with the staff and outside Advisory Committee, is responsible for the development of particular projects and makes the final decision to publish an individual study.

The Institute hopes that its studies and other activities will contribute to building a stronger foundation for international economic policy around the world. We invite readers of these publications to let us know how they think we can best accomplish this objective.

C. FRED BERGSTEN
Director
June 2003

Acknowledgments

We would like to thank participants in seminars organized by the National Bureau of Economic Research in April 1999 and August 2000 for their comments on an earlier version of what became chapters 2 and 3. We are particularly grateful to Charles Kernaghan, Archon Fung, Mark Levinson, and Thomas Kohler for serving as discussants of our paper at these seminars, and to Elaine Bernard, Joseph Altonji, and Larry Hunter for sending us comments and advice. We are also grateful to participants in a study group organized by the Institute for International Economics in November 2002 that examined the entire manuscript.

Judy Gearhart, Eileen Kaufman, and Shawn MacDonald helped us with the details of the monitoring programs overseen by Social Accountability International and the Fair Labor Organization, respectively. Numerous people at the International Labor Organization (ILO) offered comments on various iterations of the ILO chapter, as well as insights into the evolution of the organization in recent years. We are especially grateful, however, to Tony Freeman and Mary Covington of the Washington branch office, who were particularly generous with their time.

Gary Burtless, Steve Charnovitz, Mac Destler, Lori Kletzer, Tom Palley, and Bob Senser read the entire manuscript and provided very helpful comments. We are grateful to Fred Bergsten for institutional support and for commenting on various pieces of the manuscript at various times. We would particularly like to acknowledge the contributions of Dave Richardson who read numerous drafts, engaged in ongoing discussions of the project, and always had thoughtful, and thought-provoking, things to say about it.

We are grateful to Peter Siu, James Griffith, and Sumaira Chowdhury for research assistance and to Valerie Norville, Marla Banov, Madona Devasahayam, and Katie Sweetman for skillfully seeing it through the publication process.

This book has been a long time in gestation, and many more people than we can acknowledge here contributed to it. For those who are not named, we hope you know that we are extremely grateful for all your help. As always, any errors that remain are ours alone.

KIMBERLY ANN ELLIOTT
RICHARD B. FREEMAN
June 2003

Introduction

Can the enforcement of global labor standards improve the lives of workers in less developed countries (LDCs)? Do antisweatshop campaigns in advanced countries raise labor standards in LDCs, as their advocates claim? Or are they protectionism in disguise that will harm workers in those countries, as their critics claim? Do company codes of conduct improve working conditions in their overseas and outsourced operations, or are they a sham? Should labor standards be part of trade agreements, with the World Trade Organization (WTO) imposing trade sanctions on countries that violate those standards? What role should the International Labor Organization (ILO) play in protecting the rights of workers in countries with low labor standards? What steps can individuals, international agencies, governments, companies, activists, and unions take to improve working conditions, spread the benefits of trade, and empower workers in poor countries?

This volume addresses these questions. The questions are controversial ones that have elicited a vituperative debate as economic globalization has accelerated during the past decade. Globalization enthusiasts believe trade and investment are the best levers for helping workers in poor countries. They see the activists who favor raising labor standards in LDCs as at best naive or at worst as closet protectionists who seek to close markets in advanced countries to LDCs. Critics of globalization see the enthusiasts as callous to all rights but those of capital. They deny the charges of protectionism and reject the fears of enthusiasts and of many LDC governments that higher labor standards will cost jobs and slow economic growth in LDCs.

1

In this volume, we argue that the globalization versus labor standards debate poses the problem incorrectly. Free trade and labor standards are complementary rather than competing ways to improve welfare. Globalization enthusiasts are right that increased trade can contribute to growth and that the jobs created by global engagement are generally better than those in agriculture or the informal sector. But the enthusiasts downplay the increased income inequality within some countries produced by globalization and the possibilities for directly improving conditions for workers in LDCs without risking economic growth. Workers' rights advocates are right that global labor standards can spread the benefits of globalization more broadly and discourage the worst abuses of workers. But they undervalue the need to increase access to global markets for products from LDCs, which will shift workers from agriculture to more productive jobs.

In our analysis, increasing trade with LDCs naturally highlights these countries' labor conditions and thus creates consumer pressures in advanced countries for higher standards. Higher standards, in turn, reduce pressure for protectionism in rich countries and increase support for free trade.

Thus, in our view, the world economy will function more effectively if the implementation of labor standards is improved, as standards advocates insist, and if market access for LDC products is improved, as globalization enthusiasts insist, as long as these products meet minimum global standards. One way to do this is through corporate codes of conduct that inform consumers about workplace conditions and allow them to choose products made with higher standards. Another way to improve standards is to provide more resources to LDC governments to enable them to enforce their own labor codes. Yet another way is to enhance the ILO's resources to help these governments enforce standards. Ensuring that globalization and labor standards are complementary goals also means responding to the market distortions created when governments—by law or by looking the other way—repress standards with the goal of increasing exports or attracting foreign investment.

Because the intended beneficiaries of global labor standards are workers in LDCs, one might expect this book to be the story of their struggle to raise conditions at their workplace to acceptable global norms. In advanced countries, workers and labor unions are in the forefront of struggles to improve working conditions, either through collective bargaining or legal enactment and enforcement. But the actors that appear most often in these pages are activists, consumers, and firms from advanced countries, along with government officials, economic researchers, and international institutions. Unions based in advanced countries play a prominent role in the debate over globalization and labor standards, but workers in poor countries are rarely heard from.

The reason for this gap is that many LDCs, particularly those with less democratic governments, do not provide the legal protections necessary for freedom of association and collective bargaining. If workers in poor countries had a greater opportunity to protect their own interests and voice their concerns, there would be less need for activists from advanced countries to intervene on their behalf.

Globalization and Labor: From Abolition to the Antisweatshop Movement

Global integration, human rights, and international activism have been intertwined for centuries. The first transnational advocacy coalition was born in 1787 with the creation of the London Abolition Committee, which quickly linked up with groups in Philadelphia and New York and throughout the British Empire.[1] The abolitionists' initial target was the international trade in slaves, which had burgeoned along with the trade in sugar, tobacco, and cotton grown on the plantations of the new colonies in the Americas. In just 20 years, the antislavery movement succeeded in ending direct US and British involvement in the international slave trade, and 20 years after that, in 1838, Britain abolished slavery throughout the empire.

It took another quarter of a century and a civil war to end slavery in the United States. Even so, the Nobel laureate economic historian Robert Fogel concluded that

> it is remarkable how rapidly, by historical standards, the institution of slavery gave way before the abolitionist onslaught. . . . Within the span of little more than a century, a system that had stood above criticism for 3,000 years was outlawed everywhere in the Western world. (Fogel 1989, 204-05)

But the Civil War did not end all forms of forced labor.[2] A combination of laws criminalizing vagrancy and employer exploitation of worker illiteracy meant that sharecropping and other bonded labor often turned into virtual slavery for recently freed African Americans in the South. In the American West, employers imported Chinese and Indian laborers to work in the mines and on railroads under conditions that often differed little from slavery. But the end of the 19th century also saw the rise in the United States of Progressive Party demands for national regulation of corporations (then known as "trusts") and improved working conditions in the growing manufacturing sector.

---

1. For a broad history of global labor regulation, see Braithwaite and Drahos (2000, 223–24); on transnational advocacy movements, see Keck and Sikkink (1998).

2. Braithwaite and Drahos (2000, 225); Foner (1988, 406–09).

At the same time in Europe, activists pushed to supplement national labor reforms with international agreements to coordinate social policy, such as working hours, so that international trade would not undermine any single country's efforts to improve conditions. The ILO's roots may be found in this largely European movement. In the first international agreement on working conditions, reformers succeeded in convincing many countries to ban the production of white phosphorous matches because of the effects of their manufacturing process on workers' health (Lorenz 2001, 39–50).

In the aftermath of World War I, there was a major push for global labor standards. The world leaders who gathered at Versailles to plan the postwar world were horrified by the losses from that conflict and created a collective security system—the League of Nations—that they hoped would prevent it from ever happening again. But they also feared that the social pressure associated with globalization and industrialization could provide an opening in their countries for the communist ideology that had triumphed in Russia. To address these concerns, they created the ILO, asserting in the preamble to its Constitution that "universal and lasting peace can be established only if it is based upon social justice." Moreover, the ILO's founders believed that an *international* organization was needed because, as the preamble continues,

> the failure of any nation to adopt humane conditions of labor is an obstacle in the way of other nations which desire to improve conditions in their own countries.

This belief reverberates among labor standards advocates today who fear that globalization will bring a race to the bottom, whereby low labor standards in one country pressure other countries to lower their standards.

Similar convictions were reflected in the efforts to build an international system to promote peace and prosperity after World War II. Even before the end of the war, in 1944, the ILO's annual conference met in Philadelphia and reaffirmed the organization's goals, stressing in particular freedom of association and the right of workers to organize unions and engage in collective bargaining. In addition, negotiators working on the charter of the planned International Trade Organization stated in Article 7 that

> the Members recognize that unfair labor conditions, particularly in production for export, create difficulties in international trade, and accordingly, each Member shall take whatever action may be appropriate and feasible to eliminate such conditions within its territory.[3]

The major advanced countries were concerned, however, about other provisions in the International Trade Organization and it never came into being. Instead, they developed the more limited General Agreement on Tariffs and Trade as a framework for liberalizing trade (Aaronson

---

3. Quoted in Charnovitz (1987, 566).

1996, chapter 6). This agreement had only one reference to labor, Article XX(e), which allows countries to restrict the import of goods produced using prison labor.

As prosperity spread and trade revived in the 1950s and 1960s, mainly among advanced countries, pressures for global standards faded but never totally disappeared. In 1950, the US House of Representatives approved a bill (HR 7797) stating that trade between advanced and less developed countries "can be promoted through agreements . . . to establish fair labor standards of wages and working conditions"; but it did not become law (Charnovitz 1987, 567).

In 1974, well before debates over social clauses in trade agreements became heated, the Trade Act that authorized US participation in the Tokyo Round of multilateral trade negotiations included a provision directing the president to seek "the adoption of international fair standards and of public petition and confrontation procedures in the GATT" (Elliott 2000c, 126, n. 8). As with many attempts to link trade and labor over the years, however, this one was more symbolic than real. A decade later, the US Congress made the link real when it included conditions on workers' rights in the Generalized System of Preferences, which grants duty-free access to eligible LDC exports to the US market.

In the final decades of the 20th century, trade increased greatly between the United States and LDCs. As manufacturing moved to emerging markets, an increasing proportion of manufactured imports into the United States and other advanced countries came from LDCs. In 2002, China surpassed Japan as the single largest source of imports to the United States outside North America.

With consumers purchasing more goods from LDCs with low labor standards and with workers in manufacturing facing competition from low-wage exporters, the issue of workers' rights in LDCs moved to the center of debates over globalization and global economic governance. At WTO meetings, thousands demonstrated for a social clause in trade agreements. From street protests to seminar rooms, advocates of global labor standards debated free trade advocates on the role labor standards should play in the process of globalization—creating the subject matter for this book.

Plan of the Book

Chapter 1 lays out key issues in the debate on globalization versus standards. It surveys evidence that globalization by itself is not a panacea for underdevelopment and that LDCs can improve their labor standards without endangering their comparative advantage in labor-intensive products.

Chapter 2 presents a core theme of this book: that consumers demand labor standards much as they demand other aspects of goods and services and that this demand creates a "market for standards" that has the same legitimacy as markets for other goods and services desired by consumers. It shows how increasing the supply of standards can shift the benefits of trade in favor of labor and also increase support for free trade.

Chapter 3 examines the role of the activist groups that campaign for labor rights and that monitor corporate compliance with labor standards. The behavior of these groups shows that they seek to improve conditions in LDCs, not to close markets to them. They have induced corporations to develop codes of conduct for their suppliers, not to flee LDCs.

Chapters 4 and 5 turn to how international agencies address labor standards. Chapter 4 reviews the approaches used in bilateral and regional trade negotiations to overcome the trade-labor impasse. It argues that the WTO should address egregious violations of core labor standards that are intended to increase exports or attract foreign investment, but otherwise should not be involved with labor standards. Chapter 5 turns to the ILO's role in promoting and overseeing global labor standards. The desire of many governments and the business community to deflect pressure from the WTO to enforce labor standards has directed attention to strengthening the ILO's ability to serve as the international community's voice on labor standards.

Chapter 6 looks at several examples of the evolving links between globalization and labor standards in LDCs. It examines situations in which trade brought attention to the problem of labor standards, and in which pressures to meet global labor standards brought local and international stakeholders together to improve conditions for workers: child laborers producing Bangladeshi garments, Pakistani soccer balls, and West African cocoa; and Cambodian apparel workers. This chapter also assesses the challenge of improving conditions for workers in China, which, given its size and recent accession to the WTO, is becoming a leading economic and political force in these debates.

Chapter 7 gives a scorecard on the campaign to raise labor standards and offers recommendations for improving labor standards in LDCs. To answer our title question: Yes, labor standards can improve under globalization. Individuals, governments, and international agencies can take steps to improve labor standards and increase the benefits of trade for workers while still promoting growth in LDCs.

1

Globalization Versus Labor Standards?

Hey hey, ho ho, globalization has got to go!
—Protesters in Prague, Fall 2000

I know what they are against but have no sense of what they are for.
—Trevor Manual, South African finance minister, Prague, Fall 2000

Seattle, 1999. Prague, 2000. Quebec, 2001. Washington, 2002. Dark-suited officials watch as helmeted police confront young, colorful protesters chanting opposition to globalization, the International Monetary Fund, the World Trade Organization, and the World Bank. The protesters demand global protection for workers and the environment equivalent to that provided for investors and intellectual property owners. Meanwhile, behind closed doors, policymakers discuss the need for multilateral trade agreements monitored by little-known international organizations run by "faceless bureaucrats." Labor and other human rights are fine, in their view, but should not get in the way of promoting growth through free trade and markets.

The battle between the proponents of a global economy with rules to guarantee free trade, capital mobility, and intellectual property rights and the proponents of global standards to protect labor and the environment has replaced the struggle between communism and capitalism over the best way to deliver the benefits of economic development to people around the globe.[1]

More than the substance, the styles and approaches of the contestants on the front lines are in stark contrast. The critics of economic globalization

---

1. On the debate over how to reconcile trade and environmental goals, see Esty (1994).

mount campaigns against companies whose suppliers abuse workers and "take trade to the streets" in protests against neoliberal economic agreements and institutions (Aaronson 2001). The nongovernmental organizations, trade unions, and human rights activists that support them have few resources and no authority to make policies. The only way they can make their case is through public opinion and political pressure. They are guerrillas in the public arena.

The policymakers that promote globalization, by contrast, have government, international, and corporate resources behind them. They have the authority to develop trade policies and to administer the structural adjustment and financial stabilization programs that they view as in the world's interests. They are powerful figures in the global economy, with billions of dollars to leverage their policy prescriptions.

Given the relative resources of the two parties, the battle over labor standards should be no contest. Not only do globalization enthusiasts in government and international economic institutions administer laws and policies, they can also force countries to take their orthodox economic medicine or face severe financial strictures. By contrast, the advocates of labor standards and critics of the current form of globalization have only moral suasion to carry their message to the public and street protests to force those in power to listen to their complaints.

But what looks like a one-sided contest has in fact been more even. The advocates of standards helped to derail negotiations on a Multilateral Agreement on Investment in 1998 and to stall the planned launch of a new round of trade negotiations in Seattle a year later. By refusing to go away and let officials make decisions behind closed doors, standards advocates have rearranged the agenda for the discussion of globalization. All of a sudden, the World Bank is talking about inclusion and local "ownership" of the programs it funds. All of a sudden, the International Monetary Fund is stressing that one of its main goals is poverty alleviation. If nothing else, the advocates of standards have forced international economic officialdom to pay attention to the effects of its policies on poor people in less developed countries (LDCs).

The activists have also impelled multinational corporations to develop codes of conduct and to accept some social responsibility for their actions. The activists have inspired consumers to ask for fair trade coffee and to worry about the labor conditions behind the production of their favored brands of sneakers and clothing. And spurred by activist pressure, 175 members of the International Labor Organization (ILO) agreed in 1998 on four "fundamental principles and rights at work" that all countries, regardless of their level of development, should respect and promote:

- freedom from forced labor;

- nondiscrimination in the workplace;

- the effective abolition of child labor; and

- freedom of association and the right to organize and bargain collectively.

But despite agreement on these core labor standards by virtually every country in the world, the battle over whether and how to implement these and other labor standards in LDCs continues. Many LDC governments and firms fear that aggressive promotion of global labor standards and activist attention to such issues as living wages and working conditions beyond the core standards will reduce their competitiveness. Globalization enthusiasts believe that increased trade and foreign investment are the best means of promoting growth and welfare in LDCs and regard demands for trade sanctions to enforce standards as protectionism in disguise. They believe that growth will naturally lead to improvements in working conditions and, along with most LDC governments, they want measures to promote labor standards to remain outside trade agreements.

The advocates of global labor standards argue the opposite. They claim that without standards, globalization disproportionately benefits capital, increases income inequality, and creates a race to the bottom for workers worldwide. They fear that standard IMF stabilization policies and World Bank structural adjustment programs do more harm than good, in part because labor does not have a seat at the table when the experts hammer out the programs. They view parallel tracks for trade and labor standards as equivalent to the separate-but-equal farce of Jim Crow days in the US South. They want labor standards grafted onto trade agreements with the same sanctions to enforce these standards that apply to commercial disputes.

Evaluating the Debate

From the arguments of the two sides, it would appear that enforceable labor standards and trade are polar opposites, fire and ice, that cannot be fruitfully combined. It is either the chanting protester or the dark-suited minister of finance or trade. We reject this dichotomization of the debate. Rather than being polar opposites, globalization and labor standards are complementary ways to raise living standards in LDCs. They are intrinsically related not by some artificial grafting but by the way globalization works. The appropriate metaphor is that of Siamese twins who share vital organs and cannot be separated. One may be stronger than the other, but neither can advance without the other; and the effort to separate them endangers both.

We regard it as natural for the expansion of trade to result in more attention to working conditions in LDCs and to create a demand in advanced countries for improved and enforceable global labor standards. As long as consumers care about the workplace conditions underlying the items they consume and look askance at products made under poor conditions, increased trade with LDCs will arouse concern about labor conditions in LDCs and create pressures to improve them. Contrary to the fears of globalization enthusiasts, improvements in labor standards in LDCs can increase the benefits of free trade to workers in these countries and expand the constituency for improved market access for the goods these countries produce.

The key to this virtuous circle is consumers' willingness to pay higher prices for goods demonstrably made under better working conditions. Activist groups play a critical role as intermediaries in this circle—by informing consumers about labor standards and engaging their moral sentiments, and by pressuring the world trading community to give a greater share of the benefits of trade to LDC workers.

It is also natural that increased trade with low-wage LDCs, and increased international capital mobility, should concern workers and trade unions in advanced countries. Low-wage workers in advanced countries lose relative to high-wage workers and capital when trade and capital flows increase between their country and LDCs. This is what standard trade theory leads economists to expect, and the evidence supports this expectation.[2] Thus it is not surprising that apparel workers in North Carolina are upset by imports produced by underage girls or migrant laborers in LDCs who work in abysmal conditions unprotected by their own country's labor laws. Nor is it surprising that union negotiators, when faced with threats to relocate production to countries where union organizers are routinely beat up or fired, do not look favorably on trade without labor standards.

In addition to responding to these concerns, those seeking to hew to the line of unfettered globalization face two challenges. First, enthusiasts have undermined the case for globalization by overselling the benefits and glossing over the weaknesses of free trade and capital mobility. Because a good number of countries have followed IMF and World Bank rules without experiencing miraculous growth while others have succeeded by following interventionist policies that run counter to IMF and Bank prescriptions, it is unconvincing to argue that orthodox economic policies and globalization are the only ways for countries to develop.[3]

---

2. Cline (1997) provides a comprehensive review of the literature on the impact of trade on wages and inequality in advanced countries and, like most analysts, concludes that the impact has been modest. Kletzer (2001) provides a detailed analysis of the costs of job loss in import-competing sectors.

3. Orthodox policies advocated by international financial institutions typically include the privatization of state-owned enterprises, trade liberalization, reduced subsidies for consumption goods such as food and energy, increased flexibility in labor markets, and

Second, the negotiation of enforceable international rules to protect intellectual property owners and foreign investors, but not the owners of labor, makes the imbalance in global governance too blatant to ignore. If capital needs international protection from potentially corrupt and rapacious government officials, surely so does labor.

Contrary to arguments by opponents of standards, moreover, raising labor standards in LDCs does not mean imposing advanced country rules on recalcitrant countries. The problem of low standards in LDCs is not that these countries fail to care about the well-being of their workers. Most LDCs have laws mandating decent labor conditions. And most of these countries also have signed ILO conventions that commit them to global labor standards.[4] Except under authoritarian regimes, which repress independent unions for political reasons, the problem of low standards often stems from a lack of capacity to enforce labor codes. The ministries that are supposed to monitor labor laws are weak bureaucracies with limited resources. Instead, the best enforcers of standards are likely to be workers themselves, operating through a collective organization; but unions are also generally weak in LDCs, outside a few limited sectors.

Labor standards are a way to balance the interests of workers and capital within countries and in the world economic system. This balance, in turn, is an essential element in building public support for continued globalization. It is also possible to improve the implementation of global labor standards without imposing "Northern" values on LDCs or undermining their comparative advantage. The first step in doing so is to distinguish between standards that can be applied universally and those that must vary with income level.

Core Standards and Cash Standards

The ILO declaration on fundamental principles has largely ended the debate about whether there are universal labor standards other than a ban on forced labor. The four core standards in the ILO declaration pertain to the rules that govern labor market transactions. They are comparable to the rules that protect property rights and freedom of transactions in product markets, which most economists view as necessary for market economies to operate efficiently. And just as universal property

---

public budget surpluses. When countries face debt repayment or balance of trade problems, these policies are designed to shift resources to traded goods sectors. For example, the South African Growth, Employment, and Redistribution (GEAR) program did all these orthodox things—but has thus far failed to deliver improvements in income per capita.

4. On average, 149 of the ILO's 175 members have ratified each of the eight core conventions, and 86 have ratified all of them.

rights and freedom of market transactions do not imply identical laws or market institutions among countries, universal core labor standards do not imply uniformity in the details of protections or in implementing institutions.

There is little controversy over two of the four core standards. First, prohibiting forced labor has not been controversial since the US Civil War. And second, prohibiting discrimination based on gender, race, ethnicity, or religion has had no adverse effects on the United States or other economies and has potentially improved economic performance by increasing the pool of workers and skills for jobs throughout economies.

The third, however, if it meant universally applying an immediate ban on child labor, would be more problematic, because working children usually come from the poorest families and often work because economic circumstances force them to do so. But there is broad agreement on the goal of eventually eliminating child labor, and a consensus has formed around the ILO approach of targeting the "worst forms" of child labor. ILO Convention 182, adopted in 1999, defines the forms of child labor that should be eliminated immediately: forced labor, labor in illicit activities, such as prostitution and drug trafficking, and "work . . . likely to harm the health, safety or morals of children."[5]

The fourth core standard, freedom of association and the right to collective bargaining, is the most controversial. It lies at the heart of the debate over more vigorous enforcement, because the freedom to form unions and negotiate with employers increases the power of workers relative to that of the state or businesses. But by giving workers a mechanism for raising and negotiating solutions to workplace problems, this freedom actually becomes the foundation for addressing all other labor standards. This is particularly true in LDCs, whose governments often lack the resources to enforce their own labor codes.

Moreover, giving developing-country workers a "voice at work" can reassure consumers and reputation-conscious foreign investors that conditions are minimally acceptable. And implementing this fourth standard offers a defense against demands from activists in advanced countries for excessive living wages or expensive working conditions that could reduce LDC competitiveness. If local workers and employers freely negotiate wages and working conditions, that agreement should take precedence over any outside claims about appropriate levels of pay and conditions.

Some analysts, though not opposing freedom of association in principle, regard unions in LDCs as elitist, corrupt, rent-seeking institutions

---

5. Convention 182 is being ratified at the fastest pace in ILO history, with 135 ratifications in just four years, and it may become the first universally ratified convention in ILO history. By contrast, as of the end of 2002, 123 of 175 members had ratified Convention 138 (setting a minimum age for work), the lowest rate of any of the core conventions.

that will reduce the country's growth prospects, and thus they oppose unions in practice. In some LDCs, unions fit that image. But these also are usually countries where politicians, policymakers, and firms are also elitist, corrupt, and rent seeking. In such countries, the solution for unions, as for other actors, is the same: exposure to competition and democratic reforms to ensure that they are accountable, in this case to their members.

In other LDCs, unions are a force for democracy and the protection of property rights. For instance, since the late 1990s, Zimbabwe's trade unions have been the main opponents of Robert Mugabe's dictatorship and its land seizures. Unions were also a leading force in the campaign against apartheid in South Africa. The Solidarity trade union was a major force in toppling the communist leadership of Poland in the 1980s. Because transparency, democratic accountability, and competition are central goals of globalization enthusiasts, their goals and those of labor standards proponents are consistent and mutually supportive.

Going beyond the four ILO core labor standards, a wide array of other standards are of concern to activists and consumers around the world. These protections and benefits are called *cash standards* because they mandate particular outcomes—such as minimum wages, working hours, and health and safety conditions—that directly affect labor costs, and thus also potentially affect trade competitiveness. The level of these cash standards depends on the level of economic development, because rich countries can afford higher minimum wages, shorter working hours, and greater investment in workplace safety.

Yet differentiating core and cash standards is far from sharp. Some analysts argue that cash standards such as health and safety conditions should be included in core standards because poor health and safety can threaten workers' lives.[6] In fact, some improvements in health and safety— such as unlocking exit doors, installing fire extinguishers and fans, and providing clean water—might cost a firm less in the short run than, for instance, eliminating discrimination or child labor.

However imperfect the distinction, core standards are currently at the center of the debate over enforcing labor standards at the global level and including them in trade agreements. Proponents view these standards as the basic framework of rules for labor market transactions in the global economy and believe that better compliance with them, especially freedom of association and bargaining rights, will lead to improvements in other standards. Still, because consumers and some activists feel strongly about some cash standards—particularly whether workers receive decent wages and work in conditions that do not threaten their health and safety—these standards are often included in corporate codes of conduct. For the foreseeable future, this division between international agreements

---

6. For more on the debate over which labor standards should be in the core, see, e.g., Freeman (1996), OECD (1996), Fields (1995), and Portes (1994).

that focus on core standards and unofficial codes that include some cash standards is likely to continue.

Do Globalization and Growth Make Labor Standards Unnecessary?

Granting the existence of a broad, rhetorical commitment to the legitimacy of the core labor standards, the debate continues over how much effort to put into implementing labor standards and, in particular, whether to link them to trade. Globalization enthusiasts believe that increased trade and foreign investment will produce economic growth benefiting the bulk of the population in poor countries and eventually leading to improvements in working conditions. Standards advocates, by contrast, believe that globalization by itself will leave many workers behind and may cause a "race to the bottom" as countries compete by repressing unions and failing to improve or enforce labor laws. The rhetoric on both sides is heated, but the issues are factual. Does globalization increase growth rates in poor countries? Are its benefits spread broadly among the populace?

There is little question that growth reduces poverty. In cross-sectional comparisons, the absolute level of poverty is invariably inversely related to GDP per capita, which is indicative of the long-run impact of growth on poverty. Statistical analyses show that countries with faster growth rates typically have more rapid declines in poverty than those with slower growth rates (Dollar and Kraay 2002). This has been true even in countries where inequality has increased, such as China and India (Bhalla 2002).

If the evidence also showed that proglobalization policies systematically produced growth, globalization enthusiasts would have a strong case. But the evidence that openness to trade and investment, without other economic and political reforms, can raise growth rates is hotly debated. In general, removing trade barriers improves the allocation of resources in a country, lowering prices for consumers and raising living standards. The improvement in static efficiency resulting from increased trade is a one-shot spur to output, rather than raising the growth of output per capita. Trade affects the rate of growth only if it increases the growth rate of labor or human capital or other capital or encourages technological innovations that increase productivity.[7]

---

7. Cooper (2001, 8) lists five ways in which globalization can increase economic growth: by raising national saving rates and thereby investment; by reducing the price of investment goods, which allows a given level of national savings to finance additional investment; by encouraging increased flows of productive foreign investment on a sustained basis; by encouraging people to upgrade their skills; or by allowing for technological or knowledge spillovers from foreign producers to domestic producers. But even these

Because data do show that trade is positively correlated with economic growth, many trade economists have tried to demonstrate empirically that trade and growth are causally linked.[8] It has proven difficult, however, to find robust and compelling evidence that the linkage is causal, or that it results from free trade policies. Studies showing positive links between various measures of trade policy openness and growth have been subjected to extensive scrutiny and have been shown to be sensitive to the particular openness measure chosen.[9] For instance, in examining several openness indicators, Yanikkaya (forthcoming) finds trade barriers to be positively related to growth, particularly for LDCs, although those countries appear to benefit from trade with the United States. And when researchers doing cross-country analyses vary the other explanatory variables, in particular adding proxies for institutional quality, the connection between trade and growth invariably weakens.[10]

In the face of weak cross-country evidence, many globalization enthusiasts cite China and India as the two star performers demonstrating a positive relationship among globalization, growth, and poverty reduction. But Rodrik (2000) notes that growth in both China and India accelerated before those countries opened their markets to imports and foreign investment. In addition, the contribution of openness versus industrial policies in the success of the "East Asian miracle" economies remains the subject of debate. Initially, the World Bank put forth Hong Kong, Singapore, South Korea, and Taiwan as economies that relied on global markets for their success. But independent researchers, such as Alice Amsden (1989) and Robert Wade (1990), have documented the trade and industrial policy interventions that Korea and Taiwan (as well as Japan earlier) had used in achieving their growth spurt—some of which would be difficult to replicate under current international trade rules.[11]

More damaging to the globalization and growth story are situations in which today's globalization success turns into tomorrow's economic

---

give only a one-time boost to the rate of growth. Srinivasan and Bhagwati (1999) note that different assumptions in other growth models allow for other dynamic links between trade and growth. Empirical evidence of these theoretical effects has been elusive, however.

8. Among others, see Frankel and Romer (1999) and Dollar and Kraay (2001).

9. Levine and Renelt (1992) find that a variety of openness measures are weakly and nonrobustly related to growth. Harrison (1996) similarly finds that some measures of trade are positively related to growth but others are not. Rodriguez and Rodrik (2001) summarize and critically evaluate several analyses linking trade policy measures of openness to growth.

10. Rodrik, Subramanian, and Trebbi (2002, 1) argue that the quality of institutions "trumps everything else" in explaining variations in income levels around the world.

11. For a summary and skeptical assessment of industrial policies in the region, see Noland and Pack (2003).

basket case. For example, in the late 1990s, Argentina was a poster country for globalization, lauded by the IMF for opening its capital and goods markets and maintaining macroeconomic stability. Two years later, Argentina could not pay its debts and suffered a major economic crisis.

Along with questioning whether globalization contributes to growth in general, critics also question whether its benefits are broadly shared. Trade theory predicts that low-skilled workers in labor-abundant LDCs will gain from trade while highly skilled workers will lose, thereby reducing inequality. But the facts are often otherwise. Dollar and Kraay (2001) report that, on average, in 23 globalizing countries poor people gained proportionately from growth. But their detailed results show that inequality (as measured by Gini coefficients) rose in 10 of those countries, in 4 it barely changed, and in 9 it fell. Two of the most prominent globalizers in recent years, Chile and China, were among those with large increases in inequality.[12]

Detailed case studies of the links among trade, foreign investment, and inequality in several Latin American countries other than Chile also show that inequality increased as they reduced trade barriers and opened to foreign investment.[13] Some analysts argue that outsourcing could be responsible, because the low-skill activities that moved out of higher-wage advanced countries required *relatively* highly skilled workers in LDCs where they relocated (Bardhan 2000, 8–9; Feenstra and Hanson 2001). At the same time, inequality has fallen in South Korea and remained low in Taiwan, both of which markedly increased their trade as they grew.

The safest generalization from this research is that the impact of trade on growth and inequality depends on country-specific institutions and conditions. Latin American countries were highly unequal before they undertook liberalization, whereas the East Asian economies had relatively narrow income distributions, in part because of earlier land reforms and investments in education. Globalization does not trump local factors and the institutional and policy environment in which globalization takes place. This opens the door for labor standards to serve as a market-strengthening institution that can address inequality and help to resolve conflicts that might otherwise impede growth.

---

12. The Gini coefficient, which is a measure of income inequality that goes from 0 for perfect equality to 1 for maximum inequality, increased from 0.46 in 1971 to 0.58 in Chile and from 0.32 in 1980 to 0.403 in 1998 in China (Rodrik 1999, 14; Dollar and Kraay 2001, table 4).

13. See Harrison and Hanson (1999), Hanson (2003), Revenga (1995), and Robertson (2000) on Mexico; Robbins (1994) on Chile; Robbins and Gindling (1999) on Costa Rica; and Green, Dickerson, and Arbache (2000) on Brazil.

Do Labor Standards Undermine Comparative Advantage?

Although it is rarely acknowledged, globalization enthusiasts and their activist critics do have something in common. The flip side of labor activists' concerns about a race to the bottom is the concern of developing-country governments and globalization enthusiasts that higher labor standards could reduce growth by threatening the trade prospects of poor countries. The enthusiasts fear that raising standards to global levels would also raise costs so high that they would destroy the comparative advantage of many LDCs in the global marketplace.[14] The evidence suggests that both sets of concerns are exaggerated. Globalization with low standards is not stimulating a race to the bottom for workers worldwide, and universal core labor standards would not be so costly as to undermine less developed countries' comparative advantage in low-wage exports.

The first point that needs to be emphasized is that promoting global core standards does *not* mean forcing LDCs to adopt advanced-country standards. Nor does it imply uniform systems of industrial relations. The application of core labor standards differs widely among advanced countries, and the ILO conventions defining the core standards allow for broad flexibility in implementation. Second, cash standards cannot be uniform across countries, but many of them could be raised at relatively low cost, as many multinational corporations are finding as they implement codes of conduct in factories around the world. In addition to corporate codes, governments could realize significant benefits from better enforcement of their national labor standards, especially in the areas of health and safety. Let us first consider each ILO core standard.

Forced labor and child labor increase the supply of labor and could be used to increase low-wage exports, but both are uncommon in export industries (ILO 2001, 2002). Thus, taking action against them would have little impact on international comparative advantage. Taking children out of factories and enrolling them in schools could even increase productivity in the longer run by building human capital. Enforcing this standard would also remove the danger of a consumer backlash against companies or countries caught engaging in forced or child labor practices even sporadically.

The effects on trade of discrimination and repression of unions are conditional and depend on the sectors and environment in which they occur; they are also more common than child and forced labor in many parts of the world. In theory, discrimination alters trade, depending on the relative intensity of discrimination in traded goods compared with other sectors. If firms in an export sector discriminate against a particular

---

14. For a review of the literature on these issues, see Brown (2000).

group of workers, this reduces the labor supply to that sector, which should lower production and exports (Maskus 1997). In this case, a reduction of discrimination would increase exports and trade.[15] By contrast, discrimination concentrated in the nontraded goods sector increases the supply of labor to traded goods and thus increases trade, so adhering to nondiscrimination would reduce trade.

In many LDCs, discrimination discourages female employment outside of sectors requiring less-skilled work in low-wage industries, such as clothing, footwear, and toys. In Bangladesh, for example, young women are overrepresented in sewing jobs and underrepresented in jobs requiring more skills in apparel factories and in all other sectors of the economy. Manufacturers reportedly prefer to employ women in sewing jobs because they are more docile, less likely to join unions, and more likely to accept low wages, in part due to discrimination in other sectors (Paul-Majumder and Begum 2000). The result is a large supply of female workers in that sector, which lowers prices and increases production and exports of clothing relative to what would happen otherwise. In short, discrimination outside the export sector benefits the consumers of export goods at the expense of disadvantaged groups.[16]

A similar analysis could be done of the impact of unions on trade, depending on the sectors in which they are strongest. More important, the effects of unions on unit labor costs also depend on whether or not productivity increases enough to offset increased wages (Freeman and Medoff 1984). Although the effects of unions are indeterminate a priori, governments and employers fight hard to keep workers from forming independent unions in much of the world. In some countries, such as China, the motivation is political, to prevent any challenge to the government's hold on power.

In other countries, the motivation is the economic fear that unions will raise costs and reduce production in low-wage, low-productivity activities. For instance, Bangladeshi government officials, employers, and foreign investors have long resisted US and ILO pressure to allow unions into its export processing zones (EPZs), for fear that this would deter investment and lower exports. Pakistan also restricts union rights in EPZs, and Malaysia discourages unions in its foreign-investor-dominated electronics sector. Even in the absence of formal government restrictions, unionization rates might be low in EPZs because wages and working

---

15. If import-competing firms discriminate, this will give imported products an advantage, and imports will increase, which in turn may require increases in exports to keep the trade account balanced.

16. Dollar and Gatti (2000) and Klasen (2000) provide empirical evidence on the links between gender discrimination and growth, income inequality, and development. The case studies and a summary of the report, *Engendering Development*, are available at the World Bank's Web site, www.worldbank.org/gender/prr/index.htm (May 7, 2003).

conditions are generally better than in alternative jobs.[17] But by denying labor organizers access to EPZs and by blacklisting workers who seek to organize unions, governments and employers do not allow workers to choose whether to unionize—a violation of the freedom of association.[18]

Looking beyond the core standards, many of the cash standards that unions or activists want to raise would not be so costly as to threaten comparative advantage. Consider the following list of common complaints about working conditions in LDCs:

- dark, crowded, hot, noisy workplaces;

- no emergency exits or fire extinguishers;

- inadequate or no time to go the toilet;

- no canteen or place to eat;

- abusive supervisors who strike young workers;

- below-minimum-wage payments;

- an absence of written contracts;

- compulsory overtime;

- sexual or other harassment of workers; and

- late or short wage payments.[19]

How expensive would it be to remedy some of these problems? Providing emergency exits or lights in a workplace or fire extinguishers or giving workers security from sexual or other harassment or the right to go to the toilet should be relatively inexpensive. And such improvements might induce greater effort from workers, offsetting at least part of their modest cost.

Other standards, however, can have a considerable cost for the producer. Nike spent millions making its Indonesian factory safe from chemical fumes. But spread over thousands or hundreds of thousands of items, increases in the unit cost and the price of the final product are likely to be modest. Improvements that a firm publicizes widely, moreover, could

---

17. An International Labor Office (1998a) survey found that unionization rates in EPZs were often lower than in the rest of economy; see also US Department of Labor (1989–90).

18. The ILO points to the spread of wildcat strikes and other evidence of labor unrest as evidence that a worker demand for more or better representation exists in the EPZs. If lower unionization in EPZs were simply a matter of worker preference, the governments and employers would not have to enact policies that make union organization more difficult than in the rest of the economy.

19. For specific examples, see Varley (1998, chapter 4) and Chan (2001).

give it a marketing advantage with consumers concerned about workplace conditions in the products they consume. To meet the requirements of codes of conduct, firms should raise the standards that are least expensive to implement before moving on to more expensive ones.

However, a firm's cost-benefit calculations cannot be determinative. Violations of labor standards, be they national or global, or breaking laws on minimum wages or hours worked, might add to one firm's profits but could reduce national productivity. Child labor and forced labor can lead to lower costs and increased output and exports of low-skill, low-wage goods in the short run. But they will reduce the human capital of future workers and could spur a consumer backlash. A firm whose bad safety conditions cause injuries to workers may be able to replace the injured workers without bearing any of the cost. But the injuries are an adverse spillover to the rest of society, which will pay for the injuries through reduced productivity, higher health expenses, and the nonmonetary misery of the workers and their families. A study on gender equality by the World Bank (2001) argues that, though discrimination may boost labor-intensive exports, its negative effects on national well-being impede development overall.

Researchers have tried to detect potentially adverse effects of higher labor standards on economic outcomes through cross-country studies of the type often used by globalization enthusiasts to measure the effects of trade on growth. These studies suffer from many of the same weaknesses that afflict the trade and growth studies, including poor measures of the key explanatory variable (standards compliance, in this case) and the possibility that important explanatory variables have been omitted.

The greatest barrier to empirical analysis of the effects of labor standards is the absence of comparable cross-country information on compliance. The usual measure is the number of (core or total) ILO conventions that a country has ratified. Because countries with relatively high standards, such as the United States, may adopt only a few conventions, whereas others may adopt many conventions but not implement them, the ILO conventions are a weak measure of standards compliance.

Some studies use an index developed by the OECD (2000) that purports to measure compliance with the freedom of association standard. However, this index is inherently subjective and covers only 76 countries, nearly half of them advanced. There are no measures of discrimination across countries, though it would be possible to develop rough proxies for gender discrimination for some countries. But even if there were ideal measures of standards, the wide range of other (potentially more important) economic and social differences among countries would make it hard to pin down the adverse effects of standards—if any existed.

With these caveats noted, these studies have some interesting results. In general, the studies find no link or positive association between the level of labor standards and economic growth and no consistent relation with labor costs; none of them supports the allegation that foreign direct investment seeks out countries with low standards or that the aggregate exports by such countries are higher.[20] Some do find a link between relatively lower standards and exports of low-wage textiles and apparel, but these results are not robust and may suffer from problems of multicollinearity and omitted variables.[21]

Finally, the World Bank, which has traditionally viewed unions ambivalently at best, published a survey of more than 1,000 studies of the economic effects of unions that concluded there is "little systematic difference in economic performance between countries that enforce [freedom of association and the right to organize and bargain collectively] and countries that do not" (Aidt and Tzannatos 2002, 4). The survey shows that what unions do varies, depending on local institutional and legal arrangements and the competitive environment in which they operate.[22] When product markets are competitive, as is likely with free trade, unions have limited scope for raising wages. When product markets are monopolized and there is little transparency or accountability, unions will often behave as firms do in such an environment, lobbying, pressuring, fighting to retain monopoly rents for themselves. The union, or firm, is simply responding rationally to the incentives it faces, and the real problem lies in the noncompetitive market structure. In general, however,

---

20. Two OECD studies (1996, 2000) using the index of compliance with freedom of association (FOA) and bargaining rights found no link with economic growth, real wages, trade, or investment. Kucera (2001, 33), who developed his own measures of compliance with the core standards, also reports no "solid evidence" showing a link with labor costs or foreign direct investment. Flanagan (2002) comes to similar conclusions looking both at links between economic outcomes and standards at a point in time and links between outcomes and changes in standards over time, but he uses as his measure of compliance the more questionable number of convention ratifications. Rodrik (1996) and Morici and Schulz (2001) use measures of child labor and the OECD FOA index, respectively, and find no link between compliance and foreign direct investment, though they do find a correlation between low standards and low labor costs.

21. Rodrik (1996) found that that more child labor was associated with higher exports of textiles and apparel in a sample of low-income countries. But Morici and Schulz (2001), using a similar model, found that the measure of child labor was no longer statistically significant when they added the OECD FOA index, which suggested that a suppression of union rights was associated with greater apparel and textile exports. In addition, when the measure of freedom of association was added, the measure of labor costs was no longer statistically significant. Finally, using basically the same data and model, we found that a measure of gender discrimination was statistically significantly linked to textile and apparel exports but that the significance of the coefficient on the union rights variable depended on the sample used and that child labor was still an insignificant factor.

22. See the World Bank's *World Development Report 1995: The Challenge of Development*, as well as Aidt and Tzannatos (2002). The evidence from these studies, as well as from the ILO, underscores the fact that adherence to core labor standards, and freedom of association in particular, does not imply harmonization to one particular model. See also Freeman (1993).

the Bank study finds that estimates of the economywide welfare losses from union wage premiums are quite small and that a high density of unionization reduces earnings inequality (Aidt and Tzannatos 2002, 7–8, 11).[23]

But the short-run cost of enforcing standards is not the only issue facing LDCs today. The coming phaseout of textile and apparel quotas in 2005 will make it more difficult for many small, low-productivity countries to compete only on price. In the new, post-quota environment, they may find that good labor conditions can be a marketing tool, both to consumers and to multinational firms that want to protect their brand names from scandal and their operations from instability.

Catch-22: Protecting International Capital and Intellectual Property but Not Labor

There was only one catch and that was Catch-22, which specified that a concern for one's safety in the face of dangers that were real and immediate was the process of a rational mind. [Army Pilot] Orr was crazy and could be grounded. All he had to do was ask; and as soon as he did, he would no longer be crazy and would have to fly more missions. Orr would be crazy to fly more missions and sane if he didn't, but if he was sane he had to fly them. If he flew them he was crazy and didn't have to, but if he didn't want to he was sane and had to.

—Joseph Heller, *Catch-22*

For many people, a global economic system that provides international protection for capital and for intellectual property but not for labor is a Joseph Heller *Catch-22* world. Capital is internationally mobile and can escape predatory governments and unfair legal systems. Most labor is immobile, limited by immigration rules, and cannot readily escape predatory governments and unfair legal systems. Because capital can exit to take care of itself, why not rely on market forces to protect capital? Because labor cannot exit to gain its rights, should not the global community seek stronger, enforceable international standards for labor rights? Instead, the thrust of global economic policy has been to develop rules to protect international capital because local governments and laws may be untrustworthy, leaving immobile workers to rely on the same governments whose laws foreign investors seek to avoid through international agreements.

To a trade economist, however, this state of affairs is perfectly logical. The benefits of improved labor standards primarily accrue to workers in

---

23. The debate over the potential costs of raising global labor standards has echoes in national policy debates. When the United States passed antidiscrimination legislation and developed affirmative action policies, some feared this would raise costs and lower efficiency. The evidence, again, is to the contrary (Holzer and Neumark 2003).

their country, with few international spillovers.[24] Agreements to promote increased flows of trade and investment, conversely, improve both national and global economic welfare. Relying solely on the exit option as protection for foreign investors results in suboptimal levels of investment compared with a situation in which governments agree to constrain themselves vis-à-vis foreign investors.

International investment agreements can also overcome what is known as the "obsolescing bargain." In this scenario, multinational firms underinvest in some countries because, even if the government initially welcomes them, the firm fears, perhaps because of past experience, that the government will change its policies in the future and render its investment unprofitable. Similarly, firms that rely heavily on intellectual property will not export to or invest in countries that provide inadequate protection against theft. This truncated market could also impede innovation.

This view of the world clearly has merit, but it ignores some important real-world problems. First, it ignores how capital mobility affects relative bargaining leverage. Bronfenbrenner (2000) documents how employers use the threat to move abroad to blunt union-organizing campaigns in the United States. And, as has been noted, some small, poor LDCs restrict unions' rights or fail to enforce labor laws for fear of losing foreign investment. This suggests a need for some rules to balance the rights of workers with those of investors. In addition, the broad arguments in favor of rules to protect foreign investment and intellectual property do not provide guidance on the details, and many observers (including some globalization enthusiasts) view the evolution of these rules in practice as troubling. Two agreements in particular—those protecting investors in North America and intellectual property globally—trigger concerns.

Many critics believe that the North American Free Trade Agreement (NAFTA) goes well beyond what is needed to overcome the obsolescing-bargain problem. Under NAFTA's Chapter 11, multinational corporations that believe a local, state, or national government in another member country has lowered the value of their investment in a way that constitutes a "taking" of their property can sue for compensation. The definition of a taking under the agreement is much broader than physical expropriation or nationalization of property, and many of the cases have challenged environmental regulations that appear legitimate to most observers.[25]

---

24. Potential spillovers with respect to the environment are more obvious and more common, and the need for more balance in global governance with respect to the environment is discussed in detail in Esty (1994).

25. A number of these cases remained under review as of early 2003. But even if ultimately rejected, they clearly raise the cost to governments of regulating business, and some have argued that Chapter 11 has led to a "regulatory chill" in NAFTA member countries (Deere and Esty 2002; see also International Institute for Sustainable Development and World Wildlife Fund 2001).

An additional concern is that these Chapter 11 grievances are heard by international experts, who determine culpability behind closed doors and decide what compensation is appropriate with little public input (Barenberg and Evans 2002). By contrast, under NAFTA's side agreement on labor, complaints about freedom of association in trade sectors can trigger an investigation and ministerial consultations, but there is no provision for an independent expert committee to resolve an issue or for any sanction if a complaint is verified.[26] To many, NAFTA's investment protections go too far and its labor protections do not go far enough.

The development of the Uruguay Round of multilateral trade negotiations' Agreement on Trade-Related Aspects of Intellectual Property Rights (TRIPS) further underscores the inconsistencies in how global governance treats labor and other inputs. At the Uruguay Round, US negotiators and TRIPS supporters cast the international protection of intellectual property rights as a rights-based or moral issue, the problem being theft and piracy. US supporters of TRIPS insisted on putting the new rules in the World Trade Organization, even though the World Intellectual Property Organization (WIPO) exists to promote the harmonization of intellectual property policies.

The argument was that the WIPO was weak, so effective enforcement required the use of trade sanctions under the World Trade Organization. Proponents of TRIPS wanted to replace a patchwork of inadequate national laws and practices related to intellectual property with high-level protection based on international standards and to enforce the new rules with trade sanctions. Replace the phrase "intellectual property" with "labor rights," and we have the argument for labor standards: to replace a patchwork of inadequate national laws and practices relating to labor rights with high-level protection based on international standards and to enforce the new rules with trade sanctions.

The problem, again, is not the issue of protection for intellectual property rights in trade agreements, per se, but the specifics of the TRIPS agreement and whether it opens the door for labor standards. Analysis of the likely *net* global welfare benefits of the TRIPS agreement as negotiated is ambiguous.[27] There is a danger that the agreement will result in poor countries—which have little innovative activity to protect—transferring billions of dollars in royalties, license fees, and high prices to

---

26. Although the agreement provides for monetary fines for violations of child labor standards or of the country's minimum-wage or health and safety laws, no complaint to date has come close to this stage.

27. Economic analysis supports the need to give temporary monopolies in the form of patents or copyrights to inventors and creators to give them incentives to innovate, but the optimal level of such protection is the subject of much debate. Renegotiation of the terms to allow poor countries to import generic drugs to treat HIV/AIDS and to address other health problems was ongoing at the time of writing.

multinational corporations in rich countries (Maskus 2000a, 184). Thus, there is an argument for including in international trade rules a narrow agreement targeting egregious trade-related violations of intellectual property rights, but not necessarily for the broad agreement with detailed, uniform rules that resulted.

Similar reasoning applies to protecting labor in trade agreements. The argument here is that "new issues" should be included in trade agreements when they improve markets and only to the extent necessary to address market distortions. Maskus (2000b) argues that the inclusion of intellectual property protection, but not labor standards, in trade agreements is legitimate because the former are more trade related than the latter.

But the choice is not all or nothing. The world would be better off if Uruguay Round negotiators had approved a narrower, more balanced TRIPS agreement. It would also be better off, in our view, if Doha Round negotiators accepted the need for a narrow agreement targeting egregious, trade-related violations of labor standards, as we recommend in chapter 4.

Implementing Labor Standards and Globalization

Contrary to the protest chant that serves as one of the two epigraphs at the start of this chapter, globalization is not going away. And contrary to the finance minister's puzzlement expressed in the other epigraph, concerns about labor standards in a more integrated global economy are real and substantive. As researchers have carefully examined the connections among trade, growth, and inequality, empirical support for the claim that economic globalization is the cure for underdevelopment has eroded. And the fear that acceding to core labor standards will cost poor countries their comparative advantage also does not stand up to empirical analysis.

Encouraging more effective implementation of the ILO's core labor standards through corporate codes of conduct, ILO technical assistance, and narrow World Trade Organization rules would help to spread the benefits of globalization more broadly. It would also eliminate any competitive advantage for firms that perceive a cost advantage in repressing labor standards and threaten or bribe officials not to enforce them.

Finally, activists and consumers will not wait for better labor standards to trickle down after decades of growth while the world trading community applies global standards to business and intellectual property rights. Globalization means that consumers and workers in rich countries will scrutinize the labor standards in countries producing consumer goods, such as apparel and footwear. Globalization versus labor standards? No, globalization *and* labor standards.

2

The Market for Labor Standards

Not to sound Pollyannish, but I believe there is a basic decency in the American people that these companies don't understand. We have to try to tap this decency. When we do that, we get a tremendous response.
—Charles Kernaghan (*New York Times*, June 18, 1996, B4)

Brand image, the source of so much corporate wealth, is also, it turns out, the corporate Achilles' heel.
—Naomi Klein (1999, 343)

The role of sweatshops in economic development burst onto the international agenda in the 1990s because activists in advanced countries roused consumer concerns about working conditions and threatened to block trade agreements that did not address their issues. Fearing that consumers might reject products made under poor conditions, major corporations such as Levi Strauss, Reebok, Liz Claiborne, and later Nike decided to address the labor standards problem. They developed codes of conduct for their subcontractors and monitoring programs to verify compliance with those codes. The US Department of Labor initiated a No Sweat program and promoted the multistakeholder Fair Labor Association initiative to improve standards. College students organized the United Students Against Sweatshops to pressure university administrators to set standards for firms making products licensed to bear college logos. The United Nations created the Global Compact to encourage businesses to promote respect for human rights, labor rights, and the environment. And the OECD updated its Guidelines for Multinational Corporations.

Does this surge of concern about labor standards in less developed countries (LDCs) derive from nefarious protectionist interests seeking to reduce imports, as LDC governments and globalization enthusiasts fear? Or does it reflect a genuine desire to help workers in poor countries, as the standards advocates claim? If the latter, why are activists so important in rousing consumer concerns? What determines the response of firms to activist pressure?

Here we examine these questions from the perspective of the economic analysis of markets. Without gainsaying the insights and value of other approaches to studying the labor standards and antisweatshop movement, we treat the demand for standards in the same way as economists treat demand for any other good—as something that consumers want and are willing to pay for. Similarly, we treat the supply of standards as economists treat the supply of any product—as something that producers provide when they can make a profit from it. In our analysis, low standards reflect not moral deficiencies but rational business decision making when the costs of improving standards exceed the benefits. High standards in this analysis reflect normal business behavior when consumers, activists, or governments make it more profitable to produce under good working conditions.[1]

Consumer Demand for Labor Standards

The starting point for a market-based analysis of labor standards is that people care about the workplace conditions associated with the goods they purchase. If consumers were indifferent to those conditions, firms would ignore activist complaints about poor standards. Antisweatshop activists would be found at the Speakers' Corner in London's Hyde Park, next to someone warning about the end of the world, rather than leading a worldwide campaign to which brand-name multinational firms respond.

What gives the antisweatshop movement power is that consumers care not only about the physical attributes of goods and services but also about the workplace conditions associated with them. Consumers are willing to pay higher prices for goods produced under decent conditions because they feel better about consuming such products. This willingness to pay more creates a financial margin for improving conditions or increasing wages in LDCs.

Because economists prize consumer sovereignty over almost everything else, the claim that consumers care about standards has great weight among economists in the debate on standards and globalization. If consumers want improved working conditions for the goods they buy,

---

1. This analysis also downplays "social responsibility" as a motivation for firm behavior, though we recognize that some owners and managers choose to emphasize personal values with respect to labor conditions and social issues in their business operations. But even socially conscious businesses have to make a profit or go out of business.

the most devoted global enthusiast cannot readily dismiss this demand. After all, it is the job of markets to deliver the products that people want. Globalization enthusiasts also cannot complain about activist campaigns that inform consumers about working conditions any more than they can complain about advertising campaigns that inform consumers about the quality or price of products.

Treating standards as part of the product parallels Adam Smith's and Alfred Marshall's analyses of compensating differentials in the labor market. In *Wealth of Nations,* Smith noted that the "agreeableness or disagreeableness of the employments themselves" affects wages. In *Principles of Economics,* Marshall differentiated between the bricklayer who cares whether he works in a palace or in a sewer and the seller of bricks who does not care whether his bricks pave the palace or sewer. The bricklayer's concern creates compensating wage differentials in the job market: higher pay for sewer work.[2] Modern economic analysis of consumer behavior also recognizes that diverse factors define consumer products (Lancaster 1979), of which the working conditions that produced the product can readily be one.

The evidence that consumers want decent working conditions associated with the goods that they consume and are willing to pay for this comes in four forms:

- surveys of consumer preferences;
- experiments that give individuals the option of behaving in their narrow interest or of taking account of the interest of others;
- the response of shareholders and share prices to allegations that firms produce goods under poor conditions; and
- corporate responses to antisweatshop campaigns.

Survey Evidence

Suppose you are offered two identical T-shirts with your favorite logo. One was made in good conditions in a less developed country. The other was made in a firetrap building by workers paid near starvation wages. Which T-shirt would you buy . . . when the T-shirts cost the same? When the shirt made under good conditions costs a bit more? When it costs much more?

---

2. The theory takes as given the options facing a worker, which in some cases may be very limited—e.g., among caste workers in India. It does not predict that low-wage workers have better conditions than high-wage workers, but rather that given a choice, workers who want particular standards can obtain them by accepting lower wages than they could otherwise make (or conversely, that the firm that offers particularly onerous work has to pay more than if that work were less onerous).

Table 2.1 Findings from three surveys on the expressed consumer demand for labor standards

Survey sponsor and question	Period and measure		
	1995	1996	1999
Marymount University Center for Ethical Concerns			
Would avoid shopping at retailer that sold garments made in sweatshop (percent)	78	79	75
More inclined to shop at stores working to prevent sweatshops (percent)	66	63	65
Willing to pay $1 more for $20 garment guaranteed made under good conditions (percent)	84	83	86
Most responsible for preventing sweatshops (percent):			
Manufacturers	76	70	65
Retailers	7	10	11
Both	10	15	19
What would most help you avoid buying sweatshop clothes (percent):			
Fair labor label		56	
Sweatshop list		33	
University of Maryland Program on International Policy Attitudes			
Feel moral obligation to make effort to ensure that people in other countries producing goods we buy do not have to work in harsh or unsafe conditions (percent)			74
Willing to pay $25 for $20 garment that is certified not made in sweatshop (percent)			76
Find arguments for or against labor standards convincing (percent):			
Standards will eliminate jobs			37
Standards interfere with national sovereignty			41
Low standards give unfair advantage			74
Low standards are immoral			83
United States should not import products in violation of labor standards (percent):			
Products made by children (under force or without chance for school)			81
Made in unsafe and/or unhealthy places			77
Workers not allowed to unionize			42
Do not expect workers in foreign countries to make US wages, but expect countries to permit wages to rise by allowing unions and/or stopping child labor (percent)			82
Favor lowering barriers that limit clothing imports (percent):			
Without hearing about costs of protection			36
After hearing costs of protection			53

(table continues next page)

Surveys that ask questions of this form invariably find that the vast majority of Americans *report* that they would choose the garment made under better conditions, even if it cost a bit more. Table 2.1 summarizes the results from three surveys: one by Marymount University's Center

Table 2.1 *(Continued)*

Survey sponsor and question	Period and measure		
	1995	1996	1999
National Bureau of Economic Research[a]			
Sample A			
Consumers who say they care about the condition of workers who make the clothing they buy (percent):			
A lot			46
Somewhat			38
Only a little			8
Not at all or no response			8
Willing to pay more for an item if assured it was made under good working conditions (percent)			81
Additional amount willing to pay for $10 item (dollars)			2.80
Additional amount willing to pay for $100 item (dollars)			15
Sample B			
At same price would choose alternative to T-shirt that students say is made under poor conditions (percent)			84
Would not buy T-shirt made under poor conditions at all (percent)			65
Would buy T-shirt made under poor conditions at average discount of (dollars)			4.30
Would pay more for T-shirt if came with assurance it was made under good conditions (percent)			78
Average additional amount would pay, including as zeros those who did not offer to pay more or were inconsistent (dollars)			1.83

a. The two samples reflect different people being asked different sets of questions in order to ensure that responses were not dependent on the way the question was asked.

Sources: Marymount University Center for Ethical Concerns (1999); University of Maryland (2000); and for National Bureau of Economic Research survey, Elliott and Freeman (2003).

for Ethical Concerns; one by the University of Maryland's Program on International Policy Attitudes; and one by the National Bureau of Economic Research that was conducted under our direction.[3]

The Marymount surveys were conducted in 1995, 1996, and 1999. In each, three of four consumers said they would avoid stores if they knew the goods being sold had been produced under poor conditions; two of three said they would be more inclined to shop in stores that make an effort to avoid sweatshops. Eighty-five percent of respondents said they would pay $1 more for a $20 item if they could be assured that it had been made under good conditions.

---

3. This section draws heavily on Elliott and Freeman (2003).

The 1999 University of Maryland Program on International Policy Attitudes survey asked slightly different questions but obtained similar results. In this survey, roughly three out of four respondents said they felt a moral obligation to help workers faced with harsh conditions. A similar proportion said they would pay $5 more for a $20 garment if they knew that it had not been made in a sweatshop (University of Maryland 2000).[4]

The Program on International Policy Attitudes survey also asked about attitudes toward increasing LDC access to US markets in general. Nearly 90 percent of respondents said that "free trade is an important goal for the United States, but it should be balanced with other goals, such as protecting workers, the environment, and human rights," even if this slowed the growth of trade and the economy. Focusing on the apparel sector, where sweatshops abound, the survey asked whether respondents favored lower barriers to clothing imports. Without any information about the costs of protectionism or compensation for those who lose from free trade, only 36 percent favored lower tariffs. But when the survey told them about the economic costs of protectionism (which are almost invariably higher than people expect), the proportion favoring lower tariffs rose to just above 50 percent. Finally, when asked if government assistance for workers hurt by trade would affect their views, the proportion favoring reduced tariffs and greater access to world markets rose to two-thirds.[5]

The Program on International Policy Attitudes survey also tested arguments for and against making labor standards part of the trade agenda. Most respondents agreed with arguments for minimum standards—that harsh workplace conditions are immoral, and that labor standards eliminate unfair advantage through exploitation. By contrast, few were convinced by typical arguments against standards—that they reduce jobs in affected countries and impinge on national sovereignty. However, consumers differentiated among labor standards. Consumers in this survey were more concerned about child labor and job safety than about the right to unionize. More than four-fifths (82 percent) said they did not expect workers in foreign countries to earn US wages. An overwhelming 93 percent of respondents agreed that "countries that are part of international trade agreements should be required to maintain minimum standards for working conditions."

---

4. Comparing the surveys by Marymount and the Program on International Policy Attitudes, a higher premium on a $20 item, $5 versus $1, reduces the number of people who say they would buy the good made under decent conditions. In this range, moreover, the demand appears to be modestly inelastic. Revenues would rise with the increase in price from $21 to $25, but, because purchasers fall from 85 percent of persons to 75 percent, revenue would still be maximized at the $20 price.

5. For more analysis on public attitudes toward trade, see Scheve and Slaughter (2001).

The results of our National Bureau of Economic Research survey (Elliott and Freeman 2003) show that consumer concern about the working conditions associated with the goods they buy produces a downward sloping demand curve for standards.[6] We asked one set of respondents, Sample A, "how much more would you be willing to pay for items made under good working conditions" for items worth $10 and $100. We asked a second set of respondents, Sample B, if they would buy a $10 T-shirt made under poor conditions if its price were lowered to $9, and then $8, and then $7, and so on, always asking the higher price first. We also asked how much they would pay for the T-shirt if it were made under good conditions.

Most consumers said they were willing to pay modestly higher prices for higher standards but the proportion who said they would pay more was inversely related to the price differential. Among Sample A respondents, consumers said they were willing to pay, on average, 28 percent more for a $10 item and 15 percent more for a $100 item when the items were made under good standards (including as zeros consumers who said that they were unwilling to pay extra for the assurance) (table 2.1). In Sample B, large majorities (84 percent) said they would avoid a T-shirt "with a nice logo" if local students informed them it was made under poor conditions. Nearly two-thirds said they would not buy the T-shirt made under poor conditions at any price. The one-third who said they would buy it wanted a mean discount in the price of $4.30 or 43 percent of the $10 price.

The results from Sample B reveal a fundamental asymmetry in responses to information about good and bad working conditions. Consumers said they would pay an average of $1.83 to know a product was made under good conditions (including zeros for persons who said they would not pay the extra amount, or who refused to answer or were inconsistent in their responses to questions).[7] This is not even half of the discount consumers demanded to purchase a product made under bad conditions. The greater price response to information about bad conditions than to information about good conditions is consistent with prospect theory, which shows that people weigh potential losses more heavily than potential gains (Kahneman and Tversky 1979). The Marymount surveys also show this fundamental asymmetry.

Figure 2.1 shows that both survey designs confirm the asymmetry: a high elasticity of demand for products made under good conditions but

---

6. The survey of a small number of randomly chosen persons in the United States in fall 1999 was conducted by Springfield Telemarketing. A split sample design was used that posed different questions to different respondents to see whether responses varied with the wording or presentation of questions.

7. Due to a coding problem in the survey, this estimate may be too low. But if we had deleted these observations, our results would be qualitatively the same.

Figure 2.1 Estimated demand curves for labor standards

Sample A question:
What would you pay for an item if assured
that it was made under good conditions . . .

if the initial price was $10?

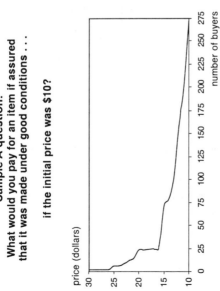

if the initial price was $100?

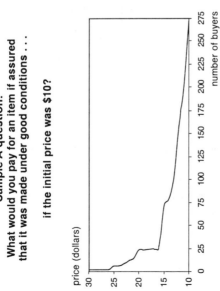

Sample B questions:
What would you pay for a $10 T-shirt if assured
that it was made under good conditions?

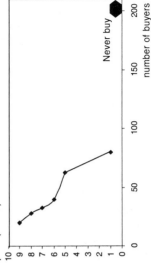

**What would you pay for a $10 T-shirt if informed
that it was made under bad conditions?**

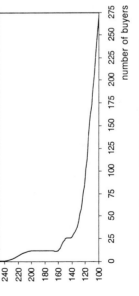

Source: NBER Survey, Elliott and Freeman (2003).

a low elasticity of demand for products made under bad conditions. The willingness to pay for items made under good conditions has an elasticity on the order of –3.0 to –5.0. Roughly 20 percent of consumers say that they are unwilling to pay anything extra, and the proportion who said they would buy the product made under better conditions falls sharply as its price rises. The loss in revenue is not recoverable from those willing to pay more. By contrast, roughly two out of three consumers say they would not buy the item made under bad conditions under any circumstance. Among the third who said they would buy the item at a discount, the proportion saying they would make the purchase rises only modestly as the price drops. This produces an inelastic demand for T-shirts produced under bad conditions (the estimated elasticity is just –0.29).

The implication is that firms can lose greatly if their product is identified as being made under bad conditions but they have only limited space to raise prices for products made under good conditions.[8] The varying responses to information about good and bad conditions helps explain, we argue later, the behavior of activists and firms in the market for standards.

Experimental Data: Do Consumers Act as They Say?

I still shop at those brand-name stores, but I feel really guilty about it.
—Founding member of a New York City high school Student Committee
Against Labor Exploitation (*Business Week*, September 11, 2000)

What people say on a survey may not accurately presage their behavior, so the survey evidence need not convince the skeptic. People rarely admit that they do not care about anything but themselves, even when this is their true feeling. To see if people actually sacrifice material interests for the sake of others, as they say on surveys, economists and psychologists undertake laboratory experiments. These experiments present subjects with a choice of acting in their narrow self-interest or sacrificing something for the well-being of others. The experiments demonstrate that in actual situations with real money at stake, people act as if fairness toward others is part of their utility function. Because what motivates the demand for standards is a willingness to pay more for the benefit of others, these results suggest that people in fact behave in ways consistent with their statements on surveys.

---

8. Because we did not specify the conditions under which the alternative product was made, this is an inference from responses to the two sets of questions. The design that would provide a test of this inference would be to ask consumers to compare a product known to be made under good conditions with one known to be made under bad conditions (at varying prices) and a product made under good conditions with one made under unknown conditions. Our analysis compared bad conditions with unknown conditions and good conditions with unknown conditions.

Table 2.2   Experimental evidence on willingness to sacrifice some personal gain for the well-being of others

Game	Predicted behavior of person only by himself or herself	Actual behavior in experiment
Prisoners' Dilemma	Always defect	Often cooperate
Ultimatum Game	Boss takes almost all	Boss usually offers 30 to 50 percent
	Workers accept crumbs	Workers reject highly uneven division of money; prefer smaller amount fairly shared
Dictators' Game	Dictator takes all	Most people give moderate amount to partner
Standards	People buy cheapest product	People pay more for product made under good conditions

Table 2.2 summarizes the findings from the major experiments in economics that underlie this conclusion. The most famous experimental game is the Prisoners' Dilemma. There are two players. If they cooperate, each gains some money; if one defects and the other cooperates, the defector gains more than from cooperating while the cooperator gets the lowest payout. If both players defect, each gets more than if he or she were the sole cooperator but less than if both cooperated or if one defected and the other cooperated. The rational response in a one-period game is to defect. But in fact, players frequently choose the cooperative strategy. It is a stretch from the Prisoners' Dilemma game to the standards problem, because "power" is equally divided between two players in this game, whereas demand for labor standards depends solely on the consumer who can choose the cheap product if he or she so desires. But the outcomes from Prisoners' Dilemma games show that people are more cooperative and less selfish than economic self-interest predicts.

The Ultimatum Game comes closer to the standards problem. It focuses on how individuals react to divisions of a given pie. Player one, the boss, divides a sum of money, say $100, between himself and player two, the worker. If the worker accepts the boss's offer, each gets the amount determined by the boss. If player two rejects the division, the entire amount disappears. If all that matters is the amount that each person gets, the boss will take $99.99 and offer the worker $0.01. Because both are better off, theory suggests that the worker should accept. But no one behaves that way in practice. In response to such a one-sided division of the money, people who play the worker's role will reject the offer, so that no one gets anything. Knowing this, most "bosses" offer workers a greater share of the pie. On average, bosses offer workers 30 to 40 percent of the money, with a modal amount of 50 percent. Workers reject almost all offers that give them less than 20 percent of the amount. In multiperiod versions of the game, where the pie shrinks over time, workers often accept second-period offers that give them smaller absolute amounts of money than they could have had in the first period, as long as the second-period distribution is more even. The "unfairness" of the boss taking the vast bulk of the funds affects behavior. The stretch to the standards problem is shorter.

The Dictators' Game fits our case even better. In this game, whatever the boss decides goes. Two players are selected and given envelopes. One envelope has $100 and the other has nothing. The player with the $100 envelope can keep the $100 and say too bad for you! Yet even in this case, people do not behave in a purely self-interested manner. Only about 20 percent of players keep all the money. Most people share some with their partners, albeit less than if their partner could veto their division. They typically take 60 to 80 percent of the money. In short, even under conditions that allow people to be completely selfish, most give some money to others.

Generous behavior is, of course, not limited to the laboratory. The majority of Americans contribute to charity and many volunteer time for charitable activities as well, often in response to appeals from activists (Freeman 1997). Both in experiments and in the social world, people behave as if they care for more than their own immediate pleasure. Thus, our presumption is that if people say they care about labor standards and that they are willing to pay a bit more for products made under good conditions and would shun products made under poor conditions, they are more likely to be telling the truth than deceiving the surveyor (or themselves).

Ultimately, however, we want direct evidence that consumers reject sweatshop products in favor of a more costly product made under good labor conditions. The ideal evidence would be a "standards experiment" that would offer consumers two identical products for sale, one purportedly made under good working conditions and the other made under bad conditions, at different prices. Instead of asking which item they would buy, the experiment would offer them an actual choice in a retail setting. The sign over one pile of T-shirts might say, Made Under Good Conditions Meeting World Labor Standards; the sign over the second would say, Made by Child Labor in Sleazo's Sweatshop, or more realistically, Made Under Unknown Conditions. Then we could observe how many consumers buy the Good Conditions T-shirt rather than the Child Labor T-shirt at different prices.

There have been a few studies examining consumer willingness to pay for better working conditions in a real-world setting, but they have not yielded definitive answers about the demand for standards. In one analysis, a University of Michigan team placed two stacks of identical socks next to each other in a store, with a sign stating that those in one stack had been made under good working conditions. The socks made under good conditions cost from zero to 40 percent more than the others, but to obtain many sales, both sets of socks had been priced at bargain rates. This study found that at the same price, half of the consumers chose the socks made under the unspecified conditions, which could imply that the average consumer paid no attention to the statements, or did not care about standards. When the price for the socks made under good conditions was increased relative to the price of the other product, the proportion of purchasers that chose the good-conditions socks fell to about a third, but many persons stuck with the socks made under good conditions even at the largest price differential.

The implication of this study is that there is a niche market for socks made under good conditions that could garner a quarter to a third of the sock market and generate enough additional revenue to improve wages and conditions for workers, but that those socks would not sweep the market. Yet because the socks were not visibly branded and were not associated with a campaign to sensitize consumers to the standards issue, the results may not carry over to other situations.[9]

In another case, Occidental University in Los Angeles created a "sweat-free" zone in one corner of the campus bookstore. The zone consisted of a single T-shirt design, produced by a unionized apparel factory in Pennsylvania. But the sweat-free T-shirt was not identical to the comparable non-sweat-free item. It was made of lighter-weight cotton, was available only in white, and sold for $2 less. Sales of the sweat-free T-shirt were double those of the traditional white T-shirt with the same logo, but this could be because the lower price, meant to compensate for the lighter-weight cotton, in fact did more than that.[10]

In the specialty coffee market, Starbucks sells coffee certified by Transfair USA. The Fair Trade Certified coffee comes from cooperatives where farmers earn a minimum price above the commodity market price. The fair trade beans are sold alongside other Starbucks coffees in its company-operated stores and online at a price of $11.45 a pound, which is not the highest-priced coffee sold by Starbucks, but higher than the $10 to $11 a pound charged for most of its other varieties. Starbucks Coffee occupies a premium market niche, with both prices and quality well above the average for the typical commodity coffee sold at the grocery store. It

---

9. The results have been described to us in a draft that is "for your reference" only, but with permission to cite here.

10. The heavier-weight T-shirt in a more popular gray color remained the top seller overall. This information is based on a private communication with the manager of the bookstore.

is also not clear how customers view the standards associated with uncertified coffee sold at Starbucks since the company paid an overall average price of $1.20 per pound in 2002, compared to an average commodity coffee price of 40 cents to 50 cents per pound (and a minimum fair trade price for nonorganic coffee of $1.26 per pound).[11]

Thus, the Starbucks experience is not an ideal experiment, but it does provide information on behavior. The 2002 Corporate Social Responsibility Annual Report from Starbucks (available at www.starbucks.com, p. 8) shows that purchases of Fair Trade Certified coffee increased sharply from 653,000 pounds in fiscal 2001, the first full year in which it was available, to 1.1 million pounds in fiscal 2002. However, Starbucks also reports that it sold less than half the total purchased in 2002. By contrast, Starbucks reports (p. 9) that it nearly tripled its purchases of Conservation [Shade Grown] Coffee, a result of the company's partnership with Conservation International to protect biodiversity globally, to 1.8 million pounds in 2002, "to meet increased consumer demand." Thus, like the socks, this suggests that higher-standards products can capture a niche market but are unlikely to sweep the field, even among "elite" consumers who are more likely to know about them and be able to afford to pay a price premium.

Still, responses of other retailers to the Starbucks initiative suggest that firms see enough demand for fair trade coffee to change their behavior. For instance, Borders announced in April 2001 that it would offer fair trade coffee at its in-store cafes, and Seattle's Best Coffee signed an agreement with Safeway to sell organic and fair trade coffees at 1,400 stores around the country. In April 2003, Dunkin' Donuts, the "largest coffee and baked goods chain in the world," announced that it would use Fair Trade Certified coffee for all espresso drinks (including cappuccino and latte) offered at its stores nationwide.[12]

As of fall 2002, Transfair USA reported that an estimated 160 importers and roasters, 10,000 retail outlets, and 200 college campuses were offering fair trade coffee. But these are still small numbers in the $18 billion coffee market.[13] In Europe, where fair trade products have been available for longer, the highest-profile fair trade coffees in the United Kingdom and the Netherlands have roughly 3 percent of the market.[14] Overall, the Fair Trade Federation estimates that worldwide fair trade

11. Starbucks Coffee, *Corporate Social Responsibility Annual Report 2002*, www.starbucks.com/aboutus/CSR_FY02_AR.pdf (May 8, 2003).

12. www.dunkindonuts.com/pressroom/press/pressrelease.jsp?id=78 (May 7, 2003).

13. "Fair Trade Update," Fall 2002, www.transfair.org/pdfs/Update_Fall2002.PDF (May 8, 2003); Associated Press, September 24, 2000, available on the Global Exchange Web site at www.globalexchange.org/economy/coffee/ap092400.html (September 26, 2000).

14. Tallontire, Rentsendorj, and Blowfield (2001, 13), www.maxhavelaar.nl.

sales were $400 million annually by the late 1990s, a mere 0.01 percent of total world trade.[15]

Shareholders and Stock Prices

If you owned shares of Nike or Starbucks or some other well-known firm and learned that the firm or its subcontractors were mistreating workers, what would you do? Would you congratulate management for possibly making a few extra cents for you? Or sell the shares because you find such practices offensive? Or sell the shares because you fear that consumers might shun the firm's products and reduce profits? Or demand at the annual shareholders' meeting that the company behave morally?

There is evidence that in the capital market, as in the consumer goods market, people are concerned about how companies treat workers and act on those concerns. In 1999, socially responsible investment funds, which invest in firms that meet some social standard, accounted for about 13 percent of the estimated $16.3 trillion under professional management in the United States.[16] At various times, shareholders have dumped shares in firms that engage in morally reprehensible business practices or have complained about those practices at shareholders' meetings. In the campaign against apartheid in South Africa, many groups divested shares of firms that did business in that country.

These policies or practices will affect investors' portfolios but may have little impact on share prices if enough investors are indifferent to the issues and happy to buy the shares. Antisweatshop campaigns, however, are designed to influence consumers, whose purchasing decisions will determine the profitability of the company. Even investors unconcerned about the social issues may decide to sell shares because they fear the campaign will affect profits, thereby reducing the stock price.

To see if campaigns have this effect, Rock (2003) identified 59 cases in which campaigners claimed that a firm or its contractors operated under poor labor conditions and where nothing else important to the firm occurred that might affect the share price and 12 cases (all Reebok) where the firm received good press for its efforts to improve working conditions. In roughly two-thirds of the cases of alleged poor labor conditions, share prices fell immediately after the campaign generated bad publicity. Nike, which faced a continual barrage of allegations of poor conditions, experienced a cumulative drop in its share price of 19 percent from 1996 through 2000 that was attributable to the bad publicity.

---

15. "Fair Trade Fact," available at www.fairtradefederation.com/ab_facts.html (May 8, 2003).

16. See www.socialfunds.com/page.cgi/article1.html (May 8, 2003).

Among all the firms examined, there was a 6 percent median drop in share values associated with an antisweatshop campaign. By contrast, the increase in Reebok shares due to good news was 2 to 3 percent. Using the data from this study, we estimate that the share price fell by 1 to 2 percent for each news item reporting sweatshop conditions or protests thereof, whereas the share price rose by less than 0.25 percent for each news item on good conditions. This is the same asymmetry to good and bad conditions found in our National Bureau of Economic Research survey.

More broadly, in a summary of 80 studies comparing the share price of a firm to its social performance, Margolis and Walsh (2001) report that more than half the studies found higher share prices for firms with better measured social performance. Only 5 percent of studies found lower share prices for the firms with better social performance, while the remainder showed no consistent pattern. Studies that analyzed the effect on share prices of anti-apartheid pressures or other human rights violations, however, found weaker results than did the studies looking at other aspects of corporate social performance, suggesting that investors viewed company performance in these areas as less important to them or as having less impact on profitability.[17]

Managers of firms that operate with poor labor standards also face pressures from shareholders at annual meetings. From the beginning of 2002 to mid-2002, shareholders, including major pension funds with substantial ownership stakes, had made 45 proposals to press management to be more attentive to global labor standards. The biggest pressure was at Unocal over its business in Burma, where forced labor was sufficiently common to induce the International Labor Organization to take punitive action against a member government for the first time in the organization's history (see chapter 5). At Unocal, shareholders voted one-third of the shares for a proposition that would have the company adopt a code of conduct that included the core standards of the International Labor Organization.[18] In many other firms, ranging from Sears to Home Depot

---

17. However, Margolis and Walsh (2001, 10–11) point out several weaknesses in the studies they review, including in the theory, research design, and quality of data used.

18. A more compelling reason for companies to become interested in "corporate social responsibility" strategies may be the threat of litigation under the Alien Tort Claims Act. In recent years, this 1789 law has been the basis for lawsuits by the International Labor Rights Fund against Unocal over the use of forced labor in Burma, Coca-Cola and Drummond (mining) Company for the murder and repression of union organizers at their operations in Colombia, Exxon Mobil for human rights abuses in Aceh, Indonesia, and Del Monte for repression of union organizing at banana plantations in Guatemala.

Cases have also been brought by others against Shell and Chevron for human rights abuses in Nigeria and against Rio Tinto related to its operations in Papua New Guinea. A Washington-based law firm has also filed a class action suit under the Alien Tort Claims Act on behalf of South Africans seeking reparations from 20 large banks and

to Colgate-Palmolive to Stride Rite and Delphi Automotive, substantial minorities of shareholders also supported global standards initiatives.

The Response of Firms

Allegations of sweatshop abuse generally arise in the labor-intensive, geographically mobile, and highly price-competitive apparel and footwear sectors. American multinational corporations in these sectors typically focus on product design and marketing, while contracting out most or all of the actual production. Because the firms that market apparel and shoes have high brand-name recognition and recognizable logos (e.g., Nike and Levi Strauss) and because the retailers that sell the products have a prominent market presence (e.g., Wal-Mart and the Gap), they are vulnerable to activist campaigns. Part of their product is the image the brand carries—the statement the product makes about the person consuming it (Klein 1999).

If activist charges stick to the product, they could reduce sales, particularly to teenagers and young adults whose demand for branded clothing and footwear may be especially faddish. Who wants to buy Nike shoes or Gap jeans if they say to the world that you are indifferent to young women or children slaving in a stifling factory for 12 hours a day? If it becomes gauche to wear a given label's apparel because it was made in a sweatshop, retailers could lose sales quickly.

Faced with a campaign charging that they sell or produce goods made under poor conditions, the first response of firms has been to deny the allegations. But because activist campaigns invariably rest on experiences to which workers or observers will attest, this defense rarely succeeds. Activists proclaim: This firm says its product was not made under harsh conditions? Here is Luisa, who works in the factory 12 hours a day with just 5 minutes to go the toilet and 5 minutes for lunch . . . all for 50 cents an hour. If the multinational manufacturer or retailer claims ignorance that its subcontractors operate under such conditions, they now know. And their previous ignorance shows that they must not have cared about conditions. If activists can uncover such poor working conditions, so could the firm if it tried.

In response to allegations of bad working conditions, firms have developed corporate codes of conduct. These codes specify that their factories and those of subcontractors will maintain good working conditions.

corporations for "aiding and abetting" the perpetuation of apartheid. International Labor Rights Fund Executive Director Terry Collingsworth believes that this latter case will not be successful unless plaintiffs can prove a direct connection between company actions and specific injuries under apartheid. See "The Alien Tort Claims Act: A Vital Tool for Preventing Corporations from Violating Fundamental Human Rights," at www.laborrights.org (February 12, 2003).

Levi Strauss adopted the first code addressing sweatshop issues in the early 1990s after allegations of abuse among its suppliers in Saipan. Wal-Mart followed after its products were linked to child labor in Bangladesh.

Nike initially rejected responsibility for conditions in its supplier factories but then took steps to improve conditions in order to blunt criticism from activists. By 2001, it had improved the conditions among its suppliers in Indonesia and provided information on conditions in other facilities on its Web site. Reebok avoided being tarred by the same brush as Nike by creating a human rights award to honor activists fighting for democracy and against child labor and other abuses.[19] Critics argued that Reebok had actually done little to upgrade working conditions among its suppliers; but if Reebok's stance was hypocritical, it worked. Activists have not targeted Reebok as they have Nike.

The growing number of corporations with corporate codes and the formation of multistakeholder groups to help firms deal with labor standards problems, such as the Fair Labor Association in the United States and the Ethical Trading Initiative in the United Kingdom, is prima facie evidence that firms believe that some consumers will shun their products if the consumers feel that the products are made under poor working conditions. In 2001, the OECD reported that 246 major firms have corporate codes. The Global Reporting Initiative states that more than 2,000 companies use its guidelines to report on their economic, environmental, and social policies and practices.

Simply developing a code, however, is not enough to assure consumers that a firm's products are made under decent conditions. Factory managers or subcontractors might post the code somewhere obscure in the factory (the boss's office) and proceed as they have in the past. Firms must monitor subcontractors to ensure that they pay attention to the corporate code. Some firms pay for independent monitoring by groups that specialize in assessing and improving labor standards, such as Verité, a small firm created by a former buyer of goods in China who was upset with labor standards in the factories where she placed orders. Many firms have hired PricewaterhouseCoopers to audit their subcontractors. A few firms have agreed to independent monitoring by nongovernmental organizations in LDCs. The Gap spent $10,000 annually for independent monitors at a single plant in El Salvador, plus additional management time for dispute resolution. It estimates that replicating this model throughout its supply chain would cost 4.5 percent of its total profit of $877 million in 2000 (*New York Times*, April 24, 2001, A1).

The pattern of corporate denial, admission of problems, the introduction of a corporate code, and eventually monitoring of the code is typical

---

19. Not surprisingly, there are consultants who help companies with "cause branding." Cone, Inc., of Boston points to the Reebok human rights award as one its "most impactful programs"; www.coneinc.com/pages/cause_brand.html (November 20, 2002).

Box 2.1   Excerpts from Timberland Statement on its Code of Conduct and Monitoring

We put together a Code of Conduct in 1994, because we believe that every-one we impact with our business deserves the right to a fair, safe and non-discriminatory workplace. . . .

In 1998, we started working with Verité, a nonprofit, non-governmental orga-nization (NGO) to audit factories making Timberland products. This included all footwear and apparel vendors, along with some licensees' facilities.

In 2000–2001, all facilities making Timberland products, including tanneries and major component suppliers, were audited. In 2000, audits of all footwear facilities were performed for health and safety issues, including air quality sampling, noise, and light measurements. In 2001, follow-up audits by Verité were per-formed on behalf of the vendor base. In addition, we have compliance moni-tors in Asia that visit factories every 8–12 weeks. These auditing efforts have helped improve worker conditions. . . . We work with factories to make changes by providing training and information. For example, in 2001, we organized Verité payroll training in 24 factories in China. This impacts about 6,000 workers. We choose to use local resources such as NGOs and government agencies, to provide training and programs that are more effective and can make lasting changes.

Source: Timberland Web site, www.timberland.com/cgi-bin/timberland/timberland/corporate/tim_about.jsp?c=global%20labor%20standards (May 8, 2003).

among the major firms that have faced allegations that their products are made under poor labor conditions or that recognized that they could face such allegations. Box 2.1 summarizes how the shoe firm Timberland moved from developing a corporate code in 1994, to employing Verité to monitor its subcontractors, to building training about labor standards into its moni-toring process. Because most shoes sold in the United States are produced in low-wage LDCs, where activists might readily find violations of labor standards, it is important for a brand-name firm such as Timberland to avoid becoming the target of an antisweatshop campaign.

Finally, some firms have responded to consumer complaints about labor conditions in subcontractors by dropping their business activities in ar-eas where labor standards abuses are severe. Pepsi withdrew from the Burmese market after protests against human rights abuses, including forced labor, threatened its share of the lucrative college market. Protest-ing students had convinced Harvard University to reverse a decision switching a $1 million vending contract from Coca-Cola to Pepsi because of Pepsi's Burmese operations. And Stanford University students had collected 2,000 signatures on a petition opposing a Pepsi-owned Taco Bell restaurant on campus over other labor standards issues (*Washington Post,* January 28, 1997, C2).

However, dropping out of a market to avoid charges of operating under poor working conditions can be difficult. In 1993, Levi Strauss announced that it was going to stop producing in China because the human rights situation there was unacceptable. But Levi Strauss never completed the withdrawal, and in April 1998 it reversed course and announced that it was expanding operations in China. The Chinese market and potential as an export platform are so large that few firms are likely to withdraw from China as some have done from Burma.

In sum, the ways firms respond to allegations of worker mistreatment show they believe that consumers will penalize them if they do not undertake corrective action. And consistent with survey findings that consumer demand for good and bad conditions is asymmetric, firms respond largely to negative publicity, improving conditions to avoid losing sales.

The Supply of Standards

In Alfred Marshall's famous analogy, economic markets are like scissors with the two blades, downward-sloping demand and upward-sloping supply. In the market for standards, the demand blade derives from consumers who want decent labor standards and are willing to pay for them; the supply blade derives from firms that improve standards because it is profitable for them to do so. Just as consumer behavior produces downward-sloping demand for standards, producer behavior produces an upward-sloping supply of standards.

Without an antisweatshop campaign that risks costing it money, we assume that a multinational firm cares nothing about labor standards and leaves decisions about working conditions to its contractors. The contractors will balance the costs of improved workplace conditions against the possible gains from higher productivity or workers' willingness to accept lower pay for better conditions. Because consumers have not been informed about conditions, the price the firm receives does not depend on the labor standards followed in producing the product.

An activist campaign changes the economic calculus facing the firm. It creates a new price schedule that depends on labor standards. By galvanizing consumers around working conditions, the campaign reduces the price the firm gets for producing under bad conditions and raises the price the firm gets from producing under good conditions. Given the asymmetry in consumer response, however, the campaign will produce a price curve that is kinked around the minimum level of standards that consumers would accept. Firms suffer large reductions in price for below-minimum standards but gain only modestly from above-minimum standards.

Given the new price schedule, the firm will change its labor standards depending on the cost of doing so. If the cost of improving standards is steep, it may decide against doing so, even though it will suffer price declines and a loss of sales because of its poor working conditions. The campaign will have failed in two ways. It will have failed to pressure the firm to raise standards; and it will have given the firm an incentive to fire workers, reduce their wages, or even to shut down, because it faces lowered profitability.

By contrast, if the cost of improving standards is modest, the firm will choose to raise standards. If consumers are willing to pay much more for the higher standards, the firm may even make more money by adopting high standards than it did before the campaign. The firm can advertise that it has improved standards and position its products differently in the market.[20]

That consumers are more willing to penalize firms for making products under poor conditions than to reward firms for making products made under good conditions explains why activists and firms battle so intensely over transparency and disclosure issues. Information about bad conditions can greatly reduce the price at which firms sell their products, whereas information about good conditions raises revenues only modestly. If consumers responded more to information about good conditions, activists and firms would have common ground on which to work. Instead, the kink in the price schedule facing firms means that information about standards becomes an important battleground in this market.[21]

Activists in the Market for Standards

In the simplest model of a market, consumers and firms interact to determine prices and outcomes. Consumers have perfect information about the attributes of products and buy from businesses that provide the quality with which they are comfortable. For instance, someone who wants super premium gas for their car pays a bit more than someone who

---

20. In the apparel industry, the move to "lean retailing" and the advantages of quickly responding to changes in consumer preferences, coupled with the tariff advantages of the North American Free Trade Agreement and other hemispheric trade preferences, have led US firms to source more production in Mexico, the Caribbean, and Central America (Weil 2000). Geographic closeness has also made it less costly for activists to uncover abuses and to bring workers from alleged sweatshops to the United States to buttress their allegations. This in turn increases their ability to alter the price schedule facing firms in favor of higher standards.

21. The battle over information became more intense in 2002–03 after a San Francisco man filed a consumer fraud case against Nike in California, claiming that Nike's claims regarding conditions in its factories were misleading. Nike claims that, if upheld, the case would have serious negative repercussions on code monitoring and transparency. Activist groups claim that legal recourse is necessary to prevent "blue-washing." The Supreme Court agreed to take the case and is expected to rule sometime in 2003. See *San Francisco Chronicle*, May 2, 2002, and www.nikebiz.com.

wants regular, and both are satisfied. There are no third parties seeking information about products, organizing consumers against some goods, and altering the price schedules facing firms.

The market for labor standards is different. The major reason is a lack of information about the working conditions associated with products. This information is costly to obtain and unavailable at the point of purchase. Firms will not publicize the information that consumers care about— possible poor working conditions in their factories or those of subcontractors. The incentive is to cover up or distort such information or, better yet, to play a "don't ask, don't know" game.[22] Consumers concerned primarily with using the product cannot be expected to invest in finding out about work conditions by themselves. Thus, the market for standards operates only because there are activist intermediaries who seek out information about workplace conditions and publicize those conditions to consumers.[23]

To rouse consumer interest, antisweatshop activists highlight the evils of low labor standards and stress how far current standards are from the minimum level activists seek. But simply arousing concern is not enough. In the long run, activists need firms that will respond to standards campaigns and will take the initiative to improve conditions. The market for standards is, after all, supposed to produce levels of standards above those that would exist if consumers did not care about working conditions. In addition, once firms respond to antisweatshop campaigns with codes of conduct and promises to do better, there is a further need for third-party groups, including nongovernmental organizations, to monitor how firms implement their promises and to provide this information to consumers as inexpensively as possible.

In the market for standards, the role of activists as intermediaries who verify information and provide it to final consumers is not unique. Financial markets also rely heavily on intermediaries who provide information about the conditions of firms or people. In financial markets, a borrower has no incentive to tell his or her financial problems to potential creditors; a company has no incentive to publicize bad news to the

---

22. Gathering information is costly for firms, as well as consumers, because of the long and widely dispersed supply chains that characterize many global industries today. Even those at the top of the chain often do not have complete information about conditions in their operations around the world. This creates another disincentive for firms to compete for market share by advertising how good they are to their workers because exposure of violations would cost them credibility with consumers. In addition, because activist groups have limited resources and must focus their muckraking efforts on a handful of market leaders, other firms have an incentive to keep their head down and try to avoid attracting the activists' attention.

23. As pointed out in Freeman (1994), if labor standards have a public goods aspect, then activists would still play a role in pressuring governments and international organizations to provide a minimum level of standards.

stock market. The firm will put as positive a spin on its situation as it can get away with. In turn, banks and other lenders and investors will discount the firm's own claims of creditworthiness and forecasts of future profitability.

In financial markets, given the high costs of acquiring credible information about a firm's true situation and prospects, agencies such as Moody's and Dun & Bradstreet rate creditworthiness and research analysts specialize in particular industries and firms. Antisweatshop activists dress differently and talk a different language than information brokers in financial markets, but they are the labor market counterparts of these Wall Street intermediaries.[24]

---

24. For a discussion of transparency and disclosure policies in other areas that have been used in lieu of or in addition to direct government regulation, including the role of intermediary groups, see Fung, Graham, and Weil (2002).

3

Vigilantes and Verifiers

Look, I don't have time to be some kind of major political activist every time I go to the mall. Just tell me what kind of shoes are okay to buy, okay?
—Teenage girl, Saint Mary's Secondary School,
Pickering, Ontario, Canada (Klein 1999, 399)

The market for labor standards requires activists who investigate labor conditions associated with products, agitate for better standards, and stimulate consumers to demand higher standards in the products they buy. We call these activists human rights *vigilantes*. They focus on the human rights of workers. They are vigilantes because they are self-appointed rather than the elected representatives of workers in less developed countries (LDCs) or of consumers in advanced countries. Examples of vigilante activists include Corporate Watch, Jeff Ballinger's Press for Change, and the National Labor Committee, all of which focus on digging up dirt on workplace abuses.

The market also needs activists of a different sort, to monitor standards in particular firms or countries and make that information available to firms and consumers. We call the groups who monitor compliance with standards human rights *verifiers*. Firms or other parties, including vigilantes, hire these groups to make plant visits and audit working conditions to determine whether firms are complying with codes of conduct. Examples of verifiers include social audit groups, such as Verité, and nongovernmental organizations (NGOs), such as Social Accountability International.

Although agitating and monitoring are not exclusive activities, there are differences between the two tasks and the groups that undertake them.[1] Vigilantes are more aggressive. Their job is to find human rights abuses and rouse consumer concerns about them. Verifiers are more conciliatory toward firms. Their job is to help a firm carry out its commitments to improve conditions. The market for labor standards needs both groups of activists to function well. Vigilantes keep consumers riled up with their exposés. Without them, most firms, governments, and international agencies would ignore demands for improved standards. Verifiers help firms respond positively by demonstrating improvements in working conditions. Without them, firms would be unable to convince anyone that they took their codes of conduct seriously. Both groups are needed to raise labor standards commensurate with consumer desires and the costs of improving standards.

The Work of Vigilantes: Antisweatshop Campaigns

Human rights vigilantes produce campaigns for labor standards that alert consumers to poor workplace conditions associated with branded products and then try to use that awareness to pressure corporations in their operations and among their suppliers. Vigilantes need entrepreneurial and political smarts to succeed with antisweatshop campaigns that necessarily involve a number of tasks (box 3.1). In the short run, they must uncover the facts about workplace conditions in overseas operations and present the facts to the public in a way that resonates with consumers and induces managers to improve conditions.

However, because even the most extensive antisweatshop campaign can affect only a small number of workers in export sectors, the vigilantes must also pressure governments and international institutions to take steps to improve working conditions more broadly in LDCs. The broadest and most lasting improvements will come if their campaigns enhance the ability of workers to form unions or to otherwise represent their own interests. What makes this activity difficult is that vigilantes have no official power to change anything. They must induce, cajole, or pressure consumers, managers, governments, and international agencies to take actions that those groups would otherwise not take.

The first step in the campaign—to obtain accurate, credible information about labor conditions in factories that produce brand-name goods—requires investigative reporting skills. Getting such information is difficult for both technical and political reasons. On the technical side, the chains

---

1. The International Labor Rights Fund is the most prominent group that plays both roles. It is behind many of the lawsuits against multinational corporations under the Alien Tort Claims Act; but it also helps train NGOs in Central America to gain accreditation to verify compliance with the Fair Labor Standards code. Also see Winston (2002), who characterizes the two styles as those of "confronters" and "engagers."

Box 3.1 Guide to an activist campaign

Task 1: Find out the truth about working conditions. You must make sure the information is accurate, because the firm will ridicule you mercilessly if it is not. The hard part is getting access to the workers. If you have good information, you will force the firm to catch up, because the odds are that the firm has gone out of its way not to see the real conditions.

Task 2: Find a symbol of the problem that resonates with consumers. Most consumers care a lot about children working long hours under abusive conditions. They care if a worker risks serious injury, illness, or even death to feed her family. They typically do not care about union rights and assume that adult males can take care of themselves. So find an exploited young worker with some presence and charisma.

Task 3: Keep the pressure on and use the firm's responses to advance the campaign. The firm will first deny that there are problems. Then it will announce a code of conduct for its subsidiaries that it will promise to monitor internally. Or it may ask its usual business auditor to verify code compliance. This is real progress, because the firm is now accountable. Even though their code of conduct may be designed as a fig leaf, you can force them to make it real. Remember, "Important social change nearly always begins in hypocrisy" (William Greider, *The Nation*, October 2, 2000). Also, try buying some shares and agitate at stockholders' meeting for the firm to live up to its own word. Remember, the firm has money, you do not.

Task 4: Leverage the campaign to pressure governments and international organizations to do more to raise labor standards generally. The firm will stress that it pays more and has better conditions than most employers in developing countries. That is right. If your target firm can improve conditions, so can many others. The goal is to improve conditions broadly, not just in a target firm. For this, you need help from governments and international institutions.

Source: Authors' analysis based on Keck and Sikkink (1998, 16–25), who identify four categories of tactics common to most transnational advocacy efforts: information politics, symbolic politics, accountability politics, and leverage politics.

---

that link manufacturers or retailers to workers in LDCs are often long and complicated, making it hard to know which goods are produced under what conditions in the global economy.

Consider the chain of production for apparel for the US retailer, J.C. Penney Company, Inc., in just *one country*. Figure 3.1 shows that J.C. Penney procures its infant and children's apparel in the Philippines from an importer that gets them from a contractor that relies on subcontractors and home-based production. Through its entire supply chain, J.C. Penney contracts with more than 2,000 suppliers in more than 80 countries, each of which may subcontract to many other producers. Another major US retailer, Nordstrom, has more than 50,000 contractors and subcontractors.

Figure 3.1 The chain of production for a typical US retailer

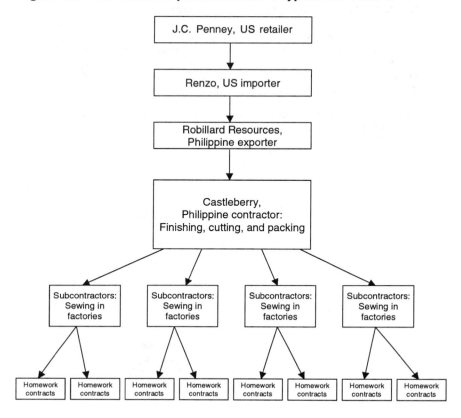

The National Labor Committee estimates that Wal-Mart has used 1,000 factories in China and that Disney products are made in 30,000 factories around the world.

On the political side, managers of export processing zones and authoritarian governments often try to prevent activists from uncovering information about poor working conditions. In some countries, firms have gated factories to keep workers in and union organizers or others concerned with workers out. In some countries, workers live in factory-run dormitories and eat in factory-run canteens under conditions that make it difficult for them to publicize or protest bad working conditions. Outsiders seeking to interview workers may be arrested, deported, or physically attacked. Workers who report bad conditions may be assaulted by company guards or fired and blacklisted by local firms.

The situation is especially difficult in countries with closed political systems, such as China. Although China's labor laws provide for reasonably good working conditions, the government does not permit independent unions. Neither the official All-China Federation of Trade Unions nor other government agencies have much power to enforce the laws. For activists to find out what is going on inside a single major supplying factory can take considerable resources. In 2001, the National Labor Committee successfully investigated a few Chinese factories, but no human rights group would have the resources to assess conditions in the 1,000 or so Wal-Mart suppliers in China, much less in the hundreds of thousands of suppliers for the US market as a whole.[2]

The second challenge facing activists is to package what they learn about working conditions in a way that resonates with consumers and generates enough publicity to put labor conditions on the public agenda. Human rights vigilantes do not have large public relations budgets. In a world plagued by catastrophes, wars, and multiple injustices, they compete for attention with other compelling issues as well as with the weekly entertainment, sports, and scandal reports. To obtain public attention, activists often personalize their message to consumers by telling the story of a particular worker or group of workers that become the symbol of exploitation. This is called giving the problem a "face." Where possible, they also highlight the closeness between the consumer and the product, as with logo clothing products for the college market or toys produced with child labor.

The type of abuse that consumers care most about also affects what activists can do. As chapter 2 showed, child labor and unsafe working conditions attract more sympathy from consumers than do restrictions on union activities. It is easier to rouse the public about Maria, the 13-year-old milliner who works 70 hours a week in Honduras, than about José, the union activist killed by a right-wing death squad in Colombia. In addition, consumers pay closer attention to conditions associated with some items, such as clothing, footwear, and coffee, than with others, such as pencils or punch-hole machines. Activists must pitch their campaigns to deal with these preferences.

The third challenge facing vigilante activists is to get firms to institute corrective policies. The typical firm response to a campaign highlighting labor standards problems is to announce a code of conduct to prevent such occurrences in the future. Activists usually must apply additional pressure to get the firm to specify how, if at all, it intends to monitor and enforce compliance with its code. When firms resist independent monitoring of compliance, activists must use the firm's own words to pressure it to follow with deeds—what Keck and Sikkink (1998) call "accountability politics." The typical antisweatshop campaign must generate several rounds of publicity and pressure to change behavior.

---

2. See www.nlcnet.org/china/1201/toysofmisery.pdf (May 8, 2003).

It is perhaps surprising that few activist groups try to answer the bottom-line question that the young woman from Ontario raised at the outset of this chapter: Which shoes are okay to buy? Activists are cautious about making lists of products to buy or to boycott, for two reasons. First, they fear that a campaign that reduces sales of items made under bad conditions will harm the very workers the campaigns want to help (so much for protectionism!).

Second, they fear that if they give a clean bill of health to a product, someone will find that somewhere in the world the firm or one of its subcontractors nevertheless abuses workers (highly likely given the long supply chains), which could reduce their credibility. With many competing activists in the antisweatshop movement, if group A declares Nike a "good employer" but group B finds that in some factory Nike has treated workers poorly, group A's standing in the movement and in the public eye will deteriorate, and resources will go to its rival B.

Still, some groups offer seals of approval for certain products, often by removing the intermediary and shortening supply chains. For example, Transfair USA certifies coffee and a few other "fair trade" products. A growing number of NGOs and commercial firms systematically monitor firm compliance with codes of conduct and give reports that the firm can cite to show that it is doing the right thing. But when Consumers Union expressed an interest in the 1990s in including an evaluation of labor standards in its product ratings, activist groups did not respond with a listing.

Such skittishness about giving consumers a positive alternative to sweatshop products is understandable given the informational burden involved, but it reduces the potential impact of campaigns. Without a widely accepted "good conditions or making improvements label" to apply to firms or products, antisweatshop campaigns will never be able to harness consumers' demands for better products on a large scale.

Global Antisweatshop Campaigners

Campaigns to improve conditions in low-wage, labor-intensive production, particularly in apparel sweatshops, have been around almost since the Industrial Revolution began. At the opening of the 20th century, poor working conditions in US sweatshops roused Progressives, particularly after the famous Triangle factory fire in New York in March 1911.[3] With the shift of the industry to LDCs and the acceleration of globalization in the 1980s and 1990s, antisweatshop campaigns became more transnational,

---

3. A total of 146 mostly young immigrant women were killed when a fire broke out in the factory and they could not escape because the doors were locked and pathways blocked. See www.ilr.cornell.edu/trianglefire/ (May 8, 2003).

with activists based largely in the United States and Europe targeting working conditions in poor LDCs.

To be sure, there has been a resurgence of sweatshops in the United States, fueled by the immigration of low-skilled workers from Mexico, Central America, and China, many of them illegal. But the vast majority of sweatshops are located in LDCs (Weil 2000; Duong 2000). In 2000, 85 percent of US consumption of footwear and more than 50 percent of apparel was imported.[4]

Campaigns to improve working conditions in LDCs necessarily differ from those in advanced countries. American and European activists cannot use courts or voting to pressure developing-country governments to improve conditions where the activists have no legal presence. Instead, the activists must harness consumers or shareholders in their own country to pressure multinational corporations to raise labor standards in overseas operations. They can also lobby advanced countries to negotiate to add labor standards to trade agreements.

The strategy of pressuring corporations in one's own country to help remedy problems in other places where the firm also operates has roots in the anti-apartheid movement. In the 1980s, the Reverend Leon Sullivan and other American activists developed a set of principles for companies operating in South Africa. The Sullivan principles required that firms initiate personnel policies—for example, training and promoting nonwhites—that they hoped would ultimately undermine the apartheid system. At the same time, these and other activist groups demanded that investors, including universities and pension funds, divest themselves of the stock of firms with South African investments.[5]

The end of apartheid in South Africa and the fading of the Cold War led many activists to shift their focus to other human rights issues, including labor standards in LDCs. Some antisweatshop activists—such as South African Auret van Heerden, the executive director of the Fair Labor Association—come from the anti-apartheid movement. Others trace their lineage to protests on human rights abuses and political repression by governments during the Cold War, particularly in Central America. For these groups, antisweatshop campaigns are a new phase in the fight for social justice.

Appendix A lists some of the key US-based groups, along with their Web site address and key characteristics.[6] To obtain this listing, we updated a 1999 directory of US antisweatshop organizations done by

---

4. US Department of Commerce, "Trade and Economy: Data and Analysis," available on the International Trade Administration Web site at www.ita.doc/td/industry/otea/usito98/tables_naics.htm (February 7, 2003).

5. For a detailed history of the anti-apartheid movement, see Massie (1997).

6. For a list of roughly 100 groups involved in the broader protests against globalization, see Elliott, Kar, and Richardson (forthcoming).

Global Exchange, removed groups that seemed to have disappeared, and added groups outside the clothing area (e.g., coffee farmers, rug makers). A more extensive search of the Web and activist networks would undoubtedly yield more groups. Slightly more than half of the groups in our list were formed in the 1990s, and nearly 80 percent have existed only since 1980. Most are small operations rather than mass membership organizations.

We classify the groups into four types: activist-left—those that are relatively more likely to play a vigilante role; "do-gooders"—those that are relatively more likely to engage with firms to verify compliance, or provide services, such as legal assistance, directly to workers; ethnically oriented groups; and religious groups—those associated with churches or with a faith-based orientation.

For example, we categorize the National Labor Committee, which grew out of the Central American peace protests, and United Students Against Sweatshops (USAS) as activist-left. We categorize groups such as Co-op America and Verité, which monitor conditions of subcontractors for firms, as apolitical "do-gooders." We categorize the Interfaith Center for Corporate Responsibility, which was a key actor in the efforts to reduce foreign investment in South Africa, and the New York State Labor-Religion Coalition as "faith-based." Because such groups vary across many dimensions, our classification is just one of many ways in which one might seek to organize the groups.

In some cases, the activist-left groups have been more aggressive than the other groups, but in other cases, they seem more attuned to the economic realities that limit what can be done for workers in poor countries. For instance, some of the groups we categorize as activist-left pressure factories to improve working conditions while accepting that wages will be low. By contrast, the Interfaith Center for Corporate Responsibility has argued that "a factory may be clean, well organized and monitored, but unless the workers are paid a sustainable living wage, it is still a sweatshop."[7] Faith-based and student groups are important for bringing "muscle" to the antisweatshop movement because they can enlist large numbers of people. Religious groups draw on their congregations, whereas USAS draws on college students.

Key Campaigns

Appendix B summarizes the major antisweatshop campaigns of the 1990s. The first substantial action was a preemptive one in 1992, when Levi Strauss adopted a code of conduct in response to allegations that its supplier factories in the US territory of Saipan underpaid workers and violated

---

7. This is quoted from an Interfaith Center for Corporate Responsibility press release issued upon the center's declining to endorse the Apparel Industry Partnership agreement.

labor laws (Varley 1998, 12). Shortly thereafter, a national television broadcast showed children in a Bangladesh factory sewing Wal-Mart label garments, leading Wal-Mart to develop its Standards for Vendor Partners. But in the spring of 1996, Wal-Mart found itself in bigger trouble when the National Labor Committee reported that clothing endorsed by television personality Kathie Lee Gifford and sold at Wal-Mart was made under exploitative conditions in Honduras.

The Kathie Lee Gifford exposé brought the sweatshop issue to national attention. The symbol for this campaign was 15-year-old Wendy Diaz, a Honduran orphan who had worked long hours for low wages at the plant since she was 13 to support herself and three younger brothers. Diaz's story struck a particular chord because the Gifford labels advertised the celebrity's commitment to children and pledged a share of the profits to children's causes. In tears, Gifford initially denied the allegations on her television show, then condemned the sweatshop practices and pledged to ensure that her clothing line was never again made under such conditions. After other Gifford-endorsed clothing was discovered being manufactured in a New York City sweatshop that had violated wage laws, US Secretary of Labor Robert Reich enlisted her in his No Sweat campaign to combat sweatshops in the United States (Chowdhury 1997). Reich had launched this campaign after investigators found illegal Thai immigrants sewing garments in slavelike conditions in El Monte, California, in August 1995.

At about the same time, Charles Kernaghan, the director of the National Labor Committee, and other activists pressured the Gap to allow independent monitoring by a local NGO at a contract facility in El Salvador. In 1997, US unions and the US-Guatemala Labor Education Project (now the US Labor Education in the Americas Project) pressed Phillips-Van Heusen, whose chief executive officer sat on the board of Human Rights Watch, to recognize a union at a joint-venture facility in Guatemala. This was the first time a union had been recognized in that country's apparel-for-export sector (Varley 1998, 12–13).

Student activism on the antisweatshop movement took off in the late 1990s in a sudden and sharp spurt of the type that often characterizes social movements (Freeman 1999). In 1995, the Union of Needletrades, Industrial, and Textile Employees (UNITE) hired a young college graduate, Ginny Coughlin, to coordinate its emerging antisweatshop activity on campuses. The AFL-CIO's first Union Summer in 1996 generated some student interest in the issue, but it was Coughlin who did the most to catalyze student antisweatshop activity.

In 1997, UNITE hired 11 summer interns, all of whom had been active in a campaign against Guess jeans in California, to work on antisweatshop activities. One intern, Tico Almeida, returned to Duke University in the fall and initiated an antisweatshop campaign there. When Duke agreed to student demands that the university require its licensees to produce items under decent working conditions and allow independent monitoring, the story was reported in the *New York Times* (March 8, 1998, A16).

By the spring of 1998, there was enough campus activity on antisweatshop issues nationwide to form USAS, whose major demand was that the Collegiate Licensing Company, the agent for 160 universities, implement stronger codes of conduct for its suppliers. In just two years, USAS had chapters on nearly 140 campuses, ranging from elite universities with a tradition of student protest to small liberal arts schools.

Initially, student activists demanded that firms disclose the location of their overseas operations, so that outside groups could assess the quality of workplace conditions. The firms refused to provide this information on the grounds that it was a trade secret. Yet because many factories produced items for different brands and any firm that wanted to find competitors' factories could do so relatively easily, the firms' claim had little credibility.

Persistence on the disclosure issue was rewarded in the fall of 1999, when several firms agreed to make this information public. Nike released a list of 41 plants that produced its licensed apparel for several universities (Duke, North Carolina, Georgetown, Michigan, and Arizona).[8] Once these firms agreed to list their plants, the door was open for pressure on others. In June 2000, under USAS pressure, more than 150 universities voted to require all their licensees to uniformly disclose plant locations.

The student activists were able to focus attention on sweatshops in a particularly powerful way because they are major consumers of college logo items and are geographically concentrated. They could easily identify the relevant consumers—fellow students—and mount protests at identifiable sites—college campuses—that would gain their attention. Other groups have to appeal to consumers in the broader marketplace, where it is harder to identify particular concerns and to focus on particular products.

The Work of the Verifiers:
Code Development and Monitoring

To stave off attacks that their products were made under poor working conditions, many firms with brand-name products adopted codes of conduct. An International Labor Office report (1998b) on corporate codes and social labels identified 200 codes of conduct, whereas the Investor Responsibility Research Center (Varley 1998) collected 121 codes from a survey of Standard & Poor's 500 companies and 80 retailers.

These initial codes varied widely in content. Most pledged to avoid child labor, but few dealt with freedom of association. Most of the codes did not specify how the firm would monitor and enforce compliance,

---

8. See www.nikebiz.com/labor/disclosure.shtml (January 1, 2001).

raising the danger that managers overseas would just post the code in their offices or send it to subcontractors and proceed to do business as usual. One leading activist derided these internal corporate codes as having "flunked the fox-in-the-chicken-coop test" (Compa 2001).

But the codes were not useless. Once firms accepted responsibility for conditions in supplier facilities, human rights vigilantes could pressure the firms to accept common standards and to allow independent external monitoring to verify their compliance. The result was a sudden growth of multistakeholder codes and monitoring schemes, some oriented toward human rights activists and others toward the business community.[9] To many vigilantes, independent verification meant hiring NGOs from relevant LDCs to undertake monitoring. To firms, however, independent monitoring meant hiring audit firms with which they regularly did business in other areas to make plant visits and report on compliance. For those firms that agreed with the activists on the need for some independent verification of compliance, controversy focused on the merits of the different schemes.

By the end of 2001, there were three codes with external monitoring and verification efforts: the Fair Labor Association (FLA), Worldwide Responsible Apparel Production (WRAP), and Social Accountability International (SAI). In addition, USAS developed the Workers' Rights Consortium (WRC) as an alternative to FLA for universities seeking to implement codes of conduct, using a very different model. Rather than undertaking systematic monitoring, WRC carries out ad hoc investigations of complaints, operating more like a grievance mechanism.

FLA grew out of the Apparel Industry Partnership, which US president Bill Clinton, US Secretary of Labor Robert Reich, Kathie Lee Gifford, and others launched at a press conference in August 1996, following the Wendy Diaz controversy. This initiative followed Reich's *domestically* focused No Sweat campaign (Chowdhury 1997). The Apparel Industry Partnership brought together apparel manufacturers and retailer-importers, unions, and NGOs to develop an industrywide code and monitoring mechanism to verify compliance globally. When the group released its draft code and principles for monitoring in April 1997, antisweatshop activists differed on its merits. UNITE president and Apparel Industry Partnership member Jay Mazur called the code "unprecedented . . . a step in the right direction." Activist Medea Benjamin of Global Exchange blasted it as a "lousy agreement," primarily because it did not include a living wage.[10]

---

9. All of these initiatives are constantly changing and adapting to new demands, so we encourage readers to visit their Web sites for updates: www.fairlabor.org, www.wrapapparel.org, www.sa-intl.org, www.workersrights.org, www.ethicaltrade.org, and www.cleanclothes.org. Another excellent source for information on codes of conduct is the Maquila Solidarity Network's "Codes Update," available at www.maquilasolidarity.org.

10. *NewsHour* transcript, April 14, 1997; see also Benjamin (1998).

In November 1998, the Apparel Industry Partnership unveiled plans to create FLA to oversee the implementation and monitoring of the code. At that point, UNITE, the Retail, Wholesale, and Department Store Union, the other union that belonged to Partnership, and the Interfaith Center for Corporate Responsibility left the group. They complained that the new FLA gave corporate board members too much influence; that the FLA code failed to require firms to pay a living wage; that FLA did not adequately address union rights in nondemocratic countries; and that it had a weak monitoring and verification mechanism. They left the group. Four years later, FLA's board still had no union representatives, though Lenore Miller, president emeritus of the Retail, Wholesale, and Department Store Union, served on FLA's NGO Advisory Council in a personal capacity.

Controversy and difficulty notwithstanding, FLA began, slowly, to do what it was created to do. By summer 2002, FLA had approved 12 companies for participation in its inspection system, up only slightly from the 10 original corporate members, including Nike, Reebok, Phillips-Van Heusen, Liz Claiborne, Adidas-Salomon, Eddie Bauer, GEAR For Sports, Patagonia, Polo Ralph Lauren, and two college licensees, Zephyr Graf-X, and Joy Athletic. Levi Strauss, saying it was frustrated by the slow pace of FLA's efforts, announced at the end of 2002 that it would withdraw from FLA. But at the same time, Nordstrom became the first major retailer to join. In addition, the more than 170 universities affiliated with FLA pressured nearly 1,000 suppliers of college logo apparel and other products, including class rings, yearbooks, plastic rugs, and other knickknacks, to apply for limited participation in FLA monitoring.[11] FLA also had accredited 11 monitoring groups operating in Latin America and Asia, including NGOs based in Guatemala, Thailand, and Bangladesh.[12]

In response to FLA, the American Apparel and Footwear Association developed its own code and certification system for individual manufacturing plants, the WRAP program, whereby retail "endorsers" were encouraged to purchase from certified suppliers. But WRAP has little credibility with NGOs and received little consumer or media attention. One activist group, the Maquila Solidarity Network, characterized it as

---

11. As a result of the influx of college-licensee applicants with diverse operations, FLA created four categories of participation: category A companies are fully participating, meaning that all or most of their product lines are covered (listed above in the text); category B companies have revenues over $50 million and have the same monitoring obligations as category As but submit for monitoring only those facilities that produce college-licensed products (16 companies, including Land's End, Josten's, Inc., and Russell Athletic); category C companies have under $50 million in revenues; and category D companies have under $1 million in revenues, are located in the United States, and have different monitoring obligations geared to their smaller size (www.fairlabor.org; November 4, 2002).

12. See www.fairlabor.org (August 21, 2002).

"generally considered to have the lowest code standards and the least thorough or transparent monitoring program."[13]

For example, whereas the FLA code (which many activists regard as inadequate) requires firms to pay workers the higher of the local legal minimum wage or the prevailing local wage and requires firms to give workers 1 day off in every 7, the WRAP code refers only to paying whatever minimum compensation local law requires and allows firms to suspend the 1 day off in 7 to meet urgent business needs.[14] Moreover, WRAP's Web site neither identifies the plants certified nor the links between them and retail endorsers of WRAP, which means that it gives consumers little guidance in making purchases.

In 1996, the Council on Economic Priorities, which for years had provided information on the social and environmental policies of companies, initiated a third monitoring initiative, the SA8000 standard. The council created an advisory board comprising NGOs, unions, and business representatives from around the world to develop a code that could be used globally and across all sectors (Leipziger 2002, 12).

The SA8000 standard is based on International Labor Organization (ILO) conventions. Its verification system is modeled on the ISO 9000 and ISO 14000 standards issued by the International Organization for Standardization,[15] which are written to be "auditable" and which emphasize the role of management systems in promoting product quality and better environmental practices, respectively. The Council on Economic Priorities also created a multistakeholder agency, SAI, to accredit auditors of the SA8000 standard. As of March 2003, this group had accredited 9 international certification agencies, which had in turn certified as in compliance with SA8000 more than 200 manufacturers or business service organizations with more than 135,000 employees in 32 industries in 35 countries. In addition, 10 retailer signatories, including Avon, Toys "R" Us, Dole Foods, and several European companies, agreed to encourage certification throughout their supply chains.

Although the SA8000 standard includes a strong provision on freedom of association that calls for companies to provide "parallel means" for worker representation when governments restrict this right, it has come under criticism for the application of its system in China. Firms in China, where nearly a fifth of SAI's certified facilities are located, cannot easily follow this provision because China prohibits independent organizing by workers. In addition, in 2000, an SAI-accredited auditor decertified two

---

13. "Memo: Codes Update," Number 9, November 2001; www.maquilasolidarity.org/resources/codes/memo9.htm (May 8, 2003).

14. See www.wrapapparel.org/index.cfm?page=principles (May 8, 2003).

15. International Organization for Standardization is a nongovernmental network of the national standards institutes of 146 countries. ISO provides technical and business standards for companies around the world; www.iso.ch/iso/en/isoonline.frontpage.

plants in China after confirming that there were problems, as alleged in a National Labor Committee report and in a third-party complaint from a Hong Kong–based NGO. The head of the Chinese office of the auditor in the case admitted, "Right now, in labour-intensive industries in southern China, the SA8000 standard cannot be enforced effectively. . . . The factories always find a way around the auditors."[16]

The last major code organization in the United States is that of WRC. As was mentioned above, USAS—viewing FLA as overly influenced by its corporate members—pressured universities to join WRC instead. By August 2002, more than 100 universities had done so, including some universities that were also affiliated with FLA, such as Brown University and the University of Michigan.

WRC did not invite business representatives to participate in its development. As a result, it has a stronger code than FLA, for example, calling for the payment of a living wage. More important, WRC adopted a radically different monitoring approach that rejects the notion that any auditor visiting a plant once or twice a year could verify that a single plant, much less a corporation with hundreds or thousands of suppliers, was "in compliance" with its code. Instead, WRC relies on a complaints-based system of investigating violations reported by workers or local NGOs. This places it in the position of a mediator that seeks to resolve problems that arise between workers and management—hardly the protectionist role that some critics of the organization feared it would play under the influence of its union allies.

In addition to these multistakeholder initiatives, NGOs and international organizations have responded to the demand for verification of labor standards by developing information-gathering and reporting capacities. Some NGOs have entered the social audit business in competition with the traditional accounting firms. For example, Verité is an NGO established in 1995 to independently monitor working conditions for firms through human rights inspections of supplier factories worldwide, particularly in China and Asia, where its founder has particular expertise. Verité was accredited under FLA, but reportedly decided to withdraw from that activity in 2002. It had also been seeking SAI accreditation, but like other NGOs, it has been frustrated by the technical requirements of that organization's management systems approach. Although paid by the companies that hire it, Verité claims it maintains its independence by diversifying its funding sources and by keeping its fee-for-service revenues to no more than 25 percent of total revenues.[17]

---

16. *BusinessWeek*, October 2, 2000; and "Codes Memo: Number 8," Maquila Solidarity Network, August 2001; www.maquilasolidarity.org/resources/codes/memo8.htm#a (May 8, 2003).

17. This goal is stated on the Web site (www.verite.org), but no budget documents are provided online to show whether or not it has been achieved in practice.

In Europe, the Ethical Trading Initiative, a collaboration between activists and companies with initial funding from the UK government, and the Clean Clothes Campaign, a pan-European initiative based on coalitions of consumer organizations, trade unions, human rights, and women's rights organizations, have focused primarily on information gathering and experimentation with pilot projects to identify best practices in monitoring and verification. The Clean Clothes Campaign's Dutch chapter developed a monitoring and verification mechanism called the Fair Wear Foundation, which it launched in the spring of 2002.

Other information-gathering and voluntary reporting initiatives include the Global Sullivan Principles and the UN Global Compact, which rely on broad principles rather than detailed commitments and which require companies to report annually on their progress in achieving these principles. Neither involves external monitoring or verification, however. The Global Reporting Initiative is still another effort to develop general principles to guide companies in meeting the growing demand for company reports on social and environmental issues in a more consistent and transparent fashion, but again without external verification.

In sum, the increased demand for standards initiated by the human rights vigilantes in the 1990s produced a supply response beyond what any activist could have possibly imagined: a plethora of codes and monitoring groups competing in the market for standards.

Competition among Codes—A Race to the Top?

Economists usually find virtue in competition. Competition pressures firms to produce what consumers want at the lowest price and creates diversity in products as different competitors fill niches in the market. But economists do recognize that in some cases, it is better to have a monopoly than competition—one national government, one set of laws, one air traffic control system, patents for new inventions.

When we began analyzing the market for standards, we thought that having a single labor code and monitoring organization would work better than having a group of competing codes and organizations. We feared bad standards would drive out good ones. Companies that failed to meet FLA, SA8000, or WRC standards would create their own organization and confuse consumers by claiming that yes, they too were improving conditions when in fact they were doing little. The proliferating number of codes and certification groups risked consumer confusion and frustration (Freeman 1998; Liubicic 1998). It also risks being costly for plants that have to implement different codes.

We were mostly wrong. So far, competition among monitoring agencies has improved the market for standards (Sabel, O'Rourke, and Fung 2000). To be credible with activists and consumers, firms have improved codes and given monitoring to independent groups rather than weakening standards. Competition has produced a new professionalism in the business of monitoring compliance with codes of conduct. Without competition from WRC, FLA might never have moved from being a fox-in-the-chicken-coop organization to a genuine verifier. Without FLA, WRC might never have been able to work with firms as effectively as it has in some cases.

Perhaps the right analogy for the competition among monitoring agencies is the market for guidebooks for restaurants (or the market for financial market analysts, discussed in chapter 2). There are many such guides, and though some may sell good reviews to restaurants rather than give honest reviews, competition has worked against dishonest reviews. Guidebooks build a reputation among consumers. Some specialize in "cheap eats." Others identify four-star restaurants. Those that provide bad information can lose market share. Those that provide good information can gain readers relative to their competitors.

The restaurant guide analogy falls short in one respect, however. Unlike a café owner, the factory owner bears the direct costs of verification. Some factories report "monitoring fatigue" from having to submit to often duplicative efforts. Some form of mutual recognition, at least among initiatives that have credibility, could be useful in reducing compliance costs for plants and information-gathering costs for consumers.

What Is in a Corporate Code?

Companies prefer that codes of conduct not be too demanding, because it is more likely that a subcontractor or their own plant will violate a strong code than a weak one. Activists want strong codes to prevent firms from labeling products as "sweat-free" when they make only superficial changes in their modes of operation. The most divisive issue in the content of codes has been whether to include a living wage—one that allows workers to have a minimally decent standard of living.

The idea of a living wage appears in the preamble of the ILO's constitution, dating to 1919, and it resonates with many people. But defining a living wage that fits a broad array of different circumstances around the world is difficult and controversial. Living standards depend on the number of workers in a family, the availability of public services in a community, and the goods and services that a society considers normal. One 1999 study by a group of Columbia University graduate students, for the National Labor Committee, calculated that a living wage in El Salvador would be three to four times the legal minimum wage in the country, in part because it included such things as health care and child care that many workers do not have even in the United States (Connor et al. 1999).

In response to these competing pressures, some groups have included a living wage in their code of conduct; others have not. The SA8000 code includes a living wage, with guidance on how to measure it in different countries. WRC includes a living wage as part of its code, but it has postponed implementing that provision pending research on how to measure living wages. In its first report responding to a complaint of code noncompliance by a Nike contractor in Mexico, WRC concluded that some wages were inadequate to meet basic needs but that "in the absence of a workable and recognized standard for calculating a living wage on a country-by-country basis, the WRC regards this conclusion as preliminary."[18] FLA and WRAP standards do not include a living wage nor do most private corporate codes.

The other difficult area in codes of conduct is freedom of association in countries where the state restricts this right. The biggest problem is China, which recognizes only the Communist Party–run All-China-Federation of Trade Unions and represses independent union organizing (*Washington Post*, October 15, 2002, A1). The easiest way to comply with a freedom-of-association standard would be to refuse to operate in China, but withdrawing from the Chinese market would not improve workers' rights in that country.

The FLA code calls on firms to "recognize and respect the right of employees to freedom of association and collective bargaining." But the FLA charter also has special country guidelines for such countries. These guidelines set as a principal FLA goal "to promote and encourage positive change in these countries so these standards become fully recognized, respected and enforced."[19] The charter calls on member companies to seek out suppliers that recognize these rights and that will not "seek the assistance of state authorities to prevent workers from exercising these rights." SA8000, by contrast, requires employers to "facilitate parallel means of association and bargaining" when local law restricts these rights. Reebok, Levi Strauss, and other companies are also experimenting in China with workers' rights training, health and safety committees, and other means of achieving this goal.

However, firms still risk having the authorities arrest workers or managers if they view these activities as a threat to their control. Such experimentation illustrates the value of engagement, and companies that are at least making an effort should have some space to make the best adjustments they can to the local situation.

Verification Procedures

To be more than pieces of paper, codes require a credible mechanism for verifying that firms or subcontractors are implementing them in good

---

18. See www.workersrights.org/report_kukdong_2.pdf (May 8, 2003).

19. FLA Charter Document, amended January 2003, p. 26, www.fairlabor.org/all/about/FLAcharter.PDF (May 8, 2003).

faith. In creating such mechanisms, several key questions need to be answered: Who does the monitoring, and what qualifications do they need? How often should plants be visited, and what proportion of a firm's supply chain needs to be covered to provide a reasonable picture of overall compliance? Who pays the auditor?

To operate compliance mechanisms, many multinationals have hired the accounting and auditing firms that they use for their financial audits, notably Ernst and Young and PricewaterhouseCoopers.[20] This gives the hiring firm some influence if not control over the compliance mechanism. By contrast, activists want NGOs from the relevant country or area to audit a firm's labor conditions. They argue that an NGO will be more independent than an accounting or auditing firm with a long-standing business relationship with the multinational and more likely to get workers to discuss potential code violation. However, because multinationals pay for most monitoring and because accounting and auditing firms have the resources to undertake monitoring quickly, accounting and auditing firms do the bulk of social auditing today.

Though these firms may be imperfect monitors, they do not simply whitewash their clients. This was made clear in 1997 by the different reports to Nike from Andrew Young, former US ambassador to the United Nations and former mayor of Atlanta, and from Ernst and Young. Andrew Young—with no experience in factory auditing, social or otherwise—undertook a whirlwind tour of factories for the firm and concluded that all was well. But just after his visit, the Transnational Resource and Action Center posted on its Corporate Watch Web site (www.corpwatch.org) a leaked Ernst and Young audit that concluded that Nike had violated a number of Vietnamese labor laws.

The major problem with the Ernst and Young report was that it was not a public document that allowed activists and consumers to see what it said and how it had been done. In a review of Nike audits, O'Rourke (2000) also identified problems in monitoring conducted by PricewaterhouseCoopers, particularly in the areas of freedom of association and health and safety, and concluded that the firm's methodology was biased toward management and that its auditors were inadequately trained.

FLA and SAI try to guard against these problems by requiring companies to use auditors that the organizations have certified. Both require monitors to consult with local NGOs and encourage NGOs to apply for accreditation. As of 2002, FLA had accredited local groups in Bangladesh, Guatemala, and Thailand to do monitoring for its members. FLA also accredits NGOs to monitor particular parts of its code without being

---

20. PricewaterhouseCoopers spun off the social auditing piece, creating an independent entity called Global Social Compliance, but there are still questions about its qualifications to do social audits. See O'Rourke (2000) and the Maquila Solidarity Network's "Codes Update" for December 2002–January 2003, 3.

expert in all of them. SAI, by contrast, had not accredited any NGO to monitor for it as of 2002, reportedly because its accreditation procedures are too complex and expensive for most NGOs to master.

Both FLA and SAI believe that the internal company changes stimulated by requirements for internal monitoring, reporting, and management systems will, in and of themselves, bring about meaningful changes in company operations. The analogy is with US civil rights legislation, which led firms to develop internal affirmative action and equal opportunity policies that led to far greater compliance with the laws than any external agency could have produced (Holzer and Neumark 2003).

WRC's approach is different. Arguing that even the best monitoring system cannot certify that even one factory is in compliance with a code 365 days a year, WRC rejected giving any type of "good housekeeping seal of approval" to companies. USAS and WRC also objected to audit plans that relied heavily on commercial audit firms and did not publicly disclose information because such plans left too much of the process under the control of corporations.

FLA—taking these criticisms as having some merit—responded in April 2002 by tightening its monitoring system. No longer will it allow member companies to present a list of factories, with a presumption that FLA would monitor those chosen enterprises. Instead, FLA staff will select factories itself, using a list of risk factors and a random sample model. It will also use a statistical model to determine the number of factories to be monitored in any year so that it can give reasonable assurances that compliance was maintained throughout the supply chain. In addition, FLA staff obtained the authority to audit companies' internal monitoring programs, which apply to 100 percent of supplier facilities, and to conduct field visits to observe the work of internal compliance staff if appropriate.

Finally, FLA rather than the member firm obtained the authority to select and pay the accredited independent monitors. Unfortunately, at about the same time these reforms were adopted, the US government cut back on its financial support for FLA. At least until other funding sources are found, FLA will have to cut back on the planned number of factory visits (Maquila Solidarity Network, "Codes Update," December 2002–January 2003, 3–4).

Disclosure and Transparency

Firms want to monitor compliance with their codes of conduct so that they can identify and alleviate problems before the public learns about them, which would risk losing some sales. Activists want access to information about poor working conditions so they can generate consumer interest and pressure firms to improve matters more quickly. There is thus an intrinsic conflict of interest between firms and activists over disclosing the results of audits. No firm wants to pay for a social audit that trashes it in public. No activist can give credence to a secret audit that it cannot independently verify.

Wrestling with these competing pressures, FLA adopted a proposal in 2001 from board member Michael Posner of the Lawyers' Committee for Human Rights to disclose more information about its audits. FLA agreed to publish factory-specific information on working conditions and remediation efforts in each independently monitored facility, withholding only the name and address of the facility. In addition, FLA agreed to prepare an annual report on the global compliance record of each member company. Responding to complaints that FLA would still be certifying companies as sweat-free on the basis of having independently monitored only a small proportion of factories, FLA executive director Auret van Heerden emphasized that FLA "will consider what form of recognition should be given to companies which achieve solid compliance records," but with no commitment on timing (FLA press release, February 4, 2002).

The WRC model—requiring complete disclosure of plant locations and information on conditions in them, backed by a system of local NGOs prepared to receive workers' complaints—is anathema to corporations. Nike, in particular, objected to the unwillingness of USAS to include corporations in the negotiation of WRC principles and what it called "gotcha monitoring."[21] Because Nike felt very strongly that the WRC approach was inimical to its interests, it ended its licensing agreements with Brown and the University of Michigan and cut off corporate contributions to its chief executive Phil Knight's alma mater, the University of Oregon, after these universities joined WRC.

Since then, both Nike and WRC have shown a willingness to compromise. In January 2001, Nike and the University of Michigan reached a seven-year licensing agreement that bound Nike to abide by the Collegiate Licensing Company's code of conduct, to provide annual "summary reports" on factory locations and enforcement of that code, and to conduct internal and external monitoring. Shortly thereafter, Nike cooperated with a WRC investigation team when the organization received its first complaint of alleged code violations at a Mexican factory (Kukdong) that supplied college-licensed apparel for Nike, as well as other apparel for Reebok. WRC investigators found that further remedial actions were needed, but WRC praised the companies and factory management for taking "significant constructive steps" to remedy the problems found in the investigation.[22]

Whatever the monitoring mechanism used, outside parties also need to "monitor the monitors" to be sure they are doing their job and to resolve conflicts over the validity of particular reports. One way to ensure this is

---

21. See www.nikebiz.com/media/n_uofo.shtml (September 1, 2000).

22. See www.workersrights.org/report_kukdong_2.pdf (May 8, 2003).

by publishing reports with the details of factory locations. Though competition among monitoring groups has produced greater transparency and disclosure in monitoring than seemed possible in the mid-1990s, such efforts still fall short of complete disclosure. Because WRC responds to complaints, it has taken the lead in disclosure and has won plaudits for its reports on factories in Indonesia and Mexico. But it has no way to get into factories to educate workers about their rights or about WRC grievance procedures.

FLA's decision to disclose factory-specific information on conditions is a step toward transparency, though it still keeps its list of facilities confidential. FLA's use of independent monitors has improved its verification procedures, but the organization has not adequately responded to criticisms of the auditing firms it has accredited. SAI publishes a list of certified facilities but keeps its audit reports confidential and also does not publish summaries. It has increased transparency, however, by deciding to publish information on the resolution of third-party complaints challenging plant certifications. WRAP remains the least transparent and the least credible, with the weakest code and no third-party complaint mechanism.

One suggestion for improving the credibility of monitoring, to which we will return below, is to have independent mediators work with activists and monitoring groups to help them resolve disagreements about factual matters and whether or not particular workplaces violate codes and how much they may have improved in an effort to meet codes (Zack 2003). A challenge facing all the monitoring groups is how to attract new corporate members and thereby expand their coverage.[23]

The Missing Element: The Voice of Developing-Country Workers

In the end the only ones who can stand up for workers' rights are workers themselves.
—Medea Benjamin[24]

If workers in LDCs could freely form trade unions or other independent organizations to improve working conditions, antisweatshop campaigns would operate much more effectively. Workers can provide the day-to-day scrutiny of facilities that no outside group can do—be it an NGO, government inspector, or top manager (Frost 2000; Bernard 1997). Workers are the best judges of the value of improved working conditions and of

---

23. For a broader and more detailed update on where the various monitoring efforts stand, see the year-end review in "Memo: Codes Update," no. 13, December 2002–January 2003 at www.maquilasolidarity.org.

24. *Human Rights Dialogue* (Carnegie Council on Ethics and International Affairs), series 2, no. 4 (Fall 2000): 7.

the wage that they can gain through bargaining—a wage that improves their living standard without risking loss of employment. Having activists in advanced countries intercede for workers is a second-best alternative to workers defending their own rights, negotiating with management on appropriate standards, and jointly monitoring implementation.

Unfortunately, antisweatshop campaigns to date have made little headway in empowering workers themselves. Corporations concerned with standards often leave union rights out of their internal codes of conduct (International Labor Office 1998b; Varley 1998). The WRC, FLA, and SA-8000 codes include respect for freedom of association and collective bargaining rights, but implementing these provisions is difficult. If there is one thing most businesses do not want, it is a strong union in their workplace because this shifts authority and revenues from owners to workers. The governments of many LDCs, including China, oppose freedom of association because unions are an independent source of power that could threaten the rule of a single party or narrow elite. These attitudes make unionization difficult to attain, even in countries that nominally accept the ILO's standard for freedom of association. At the same time, as we have seen in chapter 2, consumers are less concerned about the freedom to unionize than other issues, making it hard for activists to mount campaigns focused on organizing rights.

Campaigns in which unionism was a key issue, as with the Phillips-Van Heusen plant in Guatemala, have usually not been sustained for long.[25] Firms that accede to other demands often do not accept demands for organization. At the Gap's Mandarin supplier factory in El Salvador, the struggle began when management fired union organizers to prevent workers from forming a union. After the campaign publicized violations in the company's code of conduct, the Gap worked to improve conditions and even guaranteed a minimum number of orders, offsetting orders from elsewhere that had been lost because of negative publicity (Varley 1998, 302). The Gap arranged for independent monitoring, but there is still no union at that plant. If the results are sustained, however, the Kukdong case, which led to recognition of the first truly independent union in Mexico's maquila sector, could lead to a more hopeful conclusion.

Reaching out to and strengthening NGOs and workers' organizations in LDCs is important as well because antisweatshop campaigners need workers' groups in these countries as allies in the labor standards battle. In their analysis of transnational advocacy groups, Keck and Sikkink (1998) find that campaigns are far more likely to succeed when the outside activists have allies within the targeted country. For instance, vocal support for international economic sanctions by black leaders in South Africa,

---

25. The plant closed not long after the union was recognized because Phillips-Van Heusen cut orders from the plant, supposedly because of a drop in sales. Critics questioned why orders could not have been cut at a different, nonunionized facility (Varley 1998).

even though they were the ones expected to suffer the most economic pain, was an important factor in the success of the anti-apartheid campaign. Both USAS and WRC emphasize the need to engage and strengthen local workers' organizations and NGOs by providing financial and technical assistance, but they have limited resources for actually doing so.

Moreover, although USAS, WRC, and the National Labor Committee have close ties to trade unions, in general there are serious tensions between the vigilante groups and unions (Compa 2001). Antisweatshop NGOs in developing as well as in advanced countries are usually run by middle-class activists. They are accountable to consumers, funders, and other Western supporters but not to the workers whose well-being they seek to advance. Some trade unionists fear that the vigilantes' demands for corporate codes of conduct and independent monitoring create a weak substitute for unions. On the other side, the NGOs feel that they can accomplish something, whereas it is unrealistic to expect free and independent unions to operate in many countries of the developing world.

Just as determining "what workers want" is critical to improving labor laws and workplace governance in the United States and other advanced countries (Freeman and Rogers 1999), antisweatshop campaigners and multinationals seeking to improve conditions will be able to do so more effectively if they involve workers in LDCs and ask them what they want. For example, in a September 1998 workshop organized by the British-based NGO Labor Rights Network (the NGO representative to the Ethical Trading Initiative), representatives from LDCs stressed the importance of involving both local NGOs and unions in antisweatshop campaigns to ensure that campaigns address *local* priorities and interests. They agreed that while

> codes could be useful as a means of exerting leverage on management, the key issue was workers' own level of organisation and ability to carry out collective bargaining. . . . The ideal combination is for NGOs to play a supporting role by providing training and services and campaigning for the respect of trade union rights, and encouraging more traditional unions to take up previously unrepresented groups and gender issues.[26]

Labor Rights in China, a Hong Kong–based NGO, has proposed a monitoring model in which workers would be the principal monitors. This organization recommends that NGOs or other outside groups train workers on their rights and how to register complaints about violations (Jeffcott and Yanz n.d.). The role of external verifiers would be to investigate complaints and to cooperate with workers and management on remediation. Other Hong Kong–based labor rights groups are working with American

---

26. See the report by the Catholic Agency for Overseas Development at www.cafod.org.uk/policy/policyviews.htm (May 8, 2003).

health and safety experts in factories in southern China to train workers on health and safety issues and, in the process, to inform them about their basic rights. In a case that will be discussed further in chapter 6, Asia-based NGOs worked with Reebok in 2002 to organize secret-ballot elections for union leaders at two footwear factories in southern China.[27]

These efforts reflect a belief that workers themselves are the most effective and efficient monitors of working conditions. Using workers rather than outside firms to monitor conditions should also be less expensive for firms than hiring expensive auditors. Relying more heavily on workers to verify conditions could also be a mechanism for encouraging mutual-recognition agreements among the various external verification agencies, thereby reducing monitoring fatigue in plants with multiple buyers. In commenting on the election experiment in China, Reebok's director of human rights programs, Doug Cahn, echoed WRC concerns about external monitoring:

> We have inspections of factories, both announced and unannounced. But you just don't have the assurance that things will be the same the next day. Factories in China are incredibly sophisticated at finding ways to fool us. The best monitors are the workers themselves. (*Financial Times*, December 12, 2002, 14)

---

27. "Memo: Codes Update," no. 13, December 2002–January 2003; www.maquilasolidarity.org.

Labor Standards and Trade Agreements

The WTO does not recognize the link between trade and labor. . . . That is intellectually indefensible, and over time, it will weaken public support for global trade.
—US Trade Representative Charlene Barshefsky,
November 1999

Down the pike, global labor standards through international organizations like the WTO will make more sense than private efforts.
—Larry Graham, president, Chocolate Manufacturers Association,
November 2001

Labor rights activists want trade agreements and World Trade Organization (WTO) rules to include social clauses, with trade sanctions to enforce core labor standards, because they believe that globalization creates a race to the bottom in working conditions. Like the corporations that wanted to move enforcement of intellectual property rights to the WTO, many of these activists believe that the WTO is an extraordinarily powerful and effective agency—the "tough cop" who could enforce labor standards with the nightstick of sanctions. Make labor standards part of the international rules of trade, their argument goes, and countries will lose the incentive to repress standards. Burma will give up forced labor. Central America will clean up factories in its export processing zones. China will allow the creation of independent workers' associations. In the view of these activists, labor standards would improve and trade would still grow because the threat of sanctions would be so powerful that sanctions would never have to be implemented.

To globalization enthusiasts, however, the race to the bottom is a myth and the notion that the WTO should use trade sanctions to enforce global labor standards is anathema. Unions and import-competing firms in advanced countries would capture the process of enforcing standards for protectionist purposes. Less developed countries (LDCs) would lose market access, resulting in less trade, less growth, and worse working conditions. Even talking about a link between trade and labor rouses these enthusiasts' hackles. A WTO study group on trade and labor standards? Joint meetings of the WTO and International Labor Organization (ILO) to discuss cases in which egregious labor violations attract investment and spur trade? Never! The barbarians are at the door, seeking to sacrifice free trade to protect their high-wage jobs.

The evidence rejects both these views. Standards advocates exaggerate the WTO's power and the extent to which linking standards to trade can remedy labor standards violations. The worst conditions are typically outside the traded goods sector and cannot be directly influenced by manipulating trade flows. The threat of economic sanctions has worked modestly under some conditions, but it is not as all powerful as many think. And in its first decade, the WTO's vaunted dispute settlement system is under strain and in need of reform to handle politically sensitive, nontraditional issues arising from existing trade agreements.[1]

For their part, globalization enthusiasts ignore the fact that there are *trade-related* violations of core labor standards. They also exaggerate the likelihood that trade measures to address these violations would inevitably be abused for protectionist purposes. There may not be a generalized race to the bottom, but there are enough examples of countries that explicitly waive or ignore standards to attract foreign investment or to promote exports to be of concern. These cases logically fit under WTO rules because they distort flows of goods and capital. Moreover, experience with labor linkages in existing trade agreements and with the WTO dispute settlement system to date suggests that safeguards are possible to guard against protectionist abuse.

Thus, the WTO's role in enforcing trade-related labor standards should not turn on ideology but on pragmatic issues regarding the appropriate target of trade measures, the conditions under which such measures might be effective, and the ways in which policymakers can prevent protectionist abuses. Moreover, trade negotiators can no longer ignore labor issues. In August 2002, the US Congress approved "trade promotion authority," which includes labor standards as trade negotiating objectives and endorses "equivalent" dispute settlement procedures and remedies for labor and environmental as well as for commercial objectives. To do their job properly, policymakers must understand how trade measures

---

1. Both Charnovitz (2001) and Lawrence (forthcoming) are critical of the use of trade sanctions in the WTO dispute settlement system and propose alternatives, including monetary fines or compensation; for a broader analysis of problems in the system, see Barfield (2001).

can improve standards and the risks of protectionism implicit in their use. The US Generalized System of Preferences (GSP) and other trade agreements that incorporate labor standards provide the basis for such an understanding.

What Do Sanctions Do?

The GSP program provides duty-free market access for specified imports from eligible LDCs subject to certain conditions, including that countries have taken steps or are taking steps to ensure that workers have "internationally recognized" rights.[2] The US legal definition of these workers' rights, which was incorporated into the GSP legislation in 1984, differs in important respects from the subsequent ILO definition in its Declaration on Fundamental Principles and Rights at Work. The US list includes freedom of association and the right to organize and bargain collectively, and the need to end forced labor and child labor. But it ignores discrimination in employment and includes "acceptable conditions of work, including minimum wages, hours of work, and occupational health and safety."[3]

Officials determine what is covered under the GSP program in part via a petition process that allows private-sector groups, businesses, unions, and nongovernmental organizations to challenge the eligibility of either specific products or beneficiary countries. How the United States and foreign governments have responded to these petitions sheds light both on the utility of trade leverage in promoting workers' rights and on the risk that linking labor standards to trade will result in protectionism. To assess these two issues, we supplement evidence on the impact of GSP conditionality on workers' rights with evidence on the effectiveness of trade sanctions in other areas.[4]

GSP Conditionality on Workers' Rights

In the first decade after Congress added labor conditionality to the GSP program, more than 100 petitions were filed that challenged the adequacy of workers' rights in nearly 50 countries. Union organizations, usually ones belonging to the AFL-CIO, filed most of the petitions. The International

---

2. For the history and evolution of labor rights in the GSP program, as well as detailed discussion of several cases, see Compa and Vogt (2001).

3. Trade legislation in 2002 extended GSP and amended the definition to reference the ILO's new convention on the "worst forms" of child labor, but did not address the inconsistencies in the two lists.

4. For more details on the GSP program and the analysis summarized here, see appendix C and Elliott (2000d).

Labor Rights Fund, which had lobbied in the 1980s for adding this conditionality to GSP, also filed a substantial number of petitions. As of 1998, the interagency Trade Policy Staff Committee, which oversees the program, had accepted 47 of these petitions for review, had rejected 35, and had folded the remainder into previously initiated reviews (see table C.3 in appendix C).

Of the 47 petitions that the committee accepted for review, we exclude 15 cases because they either did not involve a trade threat or conditions changed for reasons clearly unrelated to GSP conditionality, for example a change in government (appendix C). The 32 remaining cases are almost evenly divided between successes (15), where conditions improved, and failures (17), where there was no discernible progress. The failures, in turn, are nearly evenly divided between those in which the government made no effort to improve workers' rights and those in which the government promised changes but did not implement them.

Table 4.1 summarizes the results and provides insight into what works and what does not in applying trade pressures to improve labor rights. The table shows relatively higher success rates when human rights groups are involved in the petition, perhaps suggesting that they bring greater legitimacy to the demands for improved workers' rights. The degree of democracy in a country also is associated with the success of petitions. Only 2 successful cases involved countries that Freedom House, which assesses political freedoms around the world, judged to be "not free." By contrast, among the 17 failures, 9 were in countries judged "not free," with Freedom House giving the worst possible ranking (a 7) to 3 of the 9. In addition, political conditions deteriorated in a third of the failures, while they improved in nearly a quarter of the successful cases.

Another factor that affects the probability of success is the category of workers' rights the petition emphasizes. The cases that failed to achieve improvements involved practices—forced and child labor—that are more likely to be rooted in political, institutional, and social conditions than issues such as minimum wages and safety. Union rights are politically sensitive in many countries, but our assessments provide no information on that issue because every petition included complaints about inadequate protection of freedom of association.

The data in table 4.1 also indicate that greater trade increases the leverage provided by GSP in determining outcomes. Target countries where the GSP petition succeeded in changing behavior sent 30 percent of their exports to the United States, as compared with 20 percent for target countries where the process did not change behavior. Similarly, countries where the trade pressures succeeded in changing behavior had a larger share of exports that received duty-free GSP treatment than countries where the trade pressures did not work.

Moreover, the data in table 4.1 suggest that the problem in countries that promised to improve workers' rights but failed to do so may have

Table 4.1 Cases of success and failure with workers' rights conditionality under the Generalized System of Preferences

Key characteristics	Little or no discernible change (9 cases)	Change not implemented or enforced (8 cases)	All failures (17 cases)	Change apparently due to US pressure (15 cases)
Petitioner type				
Union (usually AFL-CIO)	5	8	13	9
Union plus human rights groups	3	0	3	3
Human rights groups	1	0	1	3
Target respect for civil liberties				
Average Freedom House rating[a]	6	4	5	4
Number judged "not free"	4	0	4	2
Number judged "free"	0	1	1	1
Change in status[b]	3–	1+	3–, 1+	4+, 1–
Rights targeted in complaint[c]				
Forced labor	4	1	5	2
Child labor	1	4	5	2
Subminimum working conditions	3	5	8	7
Average target trade, size, and income[d]				
Total target country exports (billions of dollars in year of petition)	2	9	5	17
Percent of target exports going to United States	15	29	20	30
Duty-free GSP exports as percent of total target exports (1992)	8	19	14	19
Population of target (percent)	30	40	33	28
Per capita income in target (dollars)	873	1,267	1,045	2,754

a. Freedom House is a nongovernmental organization that ranks countries on two scales, one for political rights, such as the right to vote in free and open elections, and civil rights, such as freedom of association and the right to form unions. Each scale is measured from 1 to 7, with 1 or 2 indicating that a country is largely free and 6 or 7 indicating that it is not free.

b. A minus sign indicates that a country went from being free to only partly free or from partly free to not free. In the case of Peru, which was judged to have failed to implement promised changes, it moved from being almost not free (a score of 5) at the time of petition, to being almost free (a score of 3) in 1997, so it is included even though it did not change categories.

c. Either freedom of association or the right to organize and bargain collectively, and usually both, are cited in every petition.

d. These figures exclude Bahrain because it is an outlier in terms both of size and of wealth.

Source: Elliott (2000d).

been one of inadequate resources rather than lack of will. These countries look similar to the countries that improved workers' rights in their level of democracy and dependence on the US market for exports. The glaring difference between them and the countries in which the petitions produced improvements is that the countries that promised but failed to implement improvements are much poorer. They have an average per capita income of just under $1,300, compared with more than $2,700 for countries that did improve the protection of workers' rights.

Economic Sanctions for Foreign Policy Reasons and for Trade Reasons

Coercive trade sanctions, or the threat thereof, will change the behavior of a foreign government when that government *perceives* that the costs of the sanctions will be greater than the *perceived* costs of complying with the sanctioner's demands. Thus one reason that workers' rights conditionality works reasonably well in the GSP program is because the target countries are mostly small and poor, and they perceive that defying US demands will have higher costs than complying with them. The prevalence of "acceptable conditions of work" complaints among the successes suggests further that countries were able to satisfy US demands by tweaking minimum wages or technical standards in their labor codes, thereby keeping down the cost of compliance.

An analysis of sanctions imposed for foreign policy reasons and of trade threats in commercial disputes, summarized in table 4.2, tells a similar story about the determinants of success in using sanctions to alter behavior.[5] The upper half of the table shows that in cases involving unilateral US sanctions in the period 1985–94 (the period for which we have data for all three types), foreign policy sanctions were successful 20 percent of the time; that US trade threats under Section 301 of the Trade Act of 1974 were successful 61 percent of the time; and that GSP workers' rights cases were successful 47 percent of the time. The table's bottom panel shows that in foreign policy cases involving "modest goals"—such as releasing a political prisoner or reversing or compensating an investor in an expropriation case—sanctions contributed to at least partial success a third to half of the time. By contrast, demands involving "major"

---

5. Hufbauer, Schott, and Elliott (forthcoming) examine economic sanctions involving a broad range of foreign policy goals, and sanctioning countries and targets, ranging from World War I to the UN sanctions against the Taliban regime in Afghanistan in 1999. Bayard and Elliott (1994) and Elliott and Richardson (1997) examine the use of trade threats by the United States in commercial disputes from 1975 to 1994. The targets in these cases are typically larger and richer than in the foreign policy cases or GSP cases, with the European Union, Japan, South Korea, and Taiwan accounting for more than half the cases studied.

Table 4.2 Use and effectiveness of economic sanctions

Type of case or goal	Total number of cases	Number of successes	Success rate (percent)
Overall results:			
Foreign policy cases[a]			
All cases, 1914–99	185	63	34
All cases, 1985–94	54	18	33
Unilateral US cases	127	40	31
1945–69	19	12	63
1970–99	54	8	15
1985–94	15	3	20
US Section 301 cases			
All cases, 1975–94	87	45	52
Cases, 1985–94	62	38	61
Workers' rights and GSP			
All cases, 1985–94	32	15	47
Goals and categories of:			
Foreign policy cases, 1914–90			
Modest goals	51	17	33
Major goals	30	7	23
Adjusted modest goals[b]			~50
Adjusted major goals[b]			~20
Human rights cases, 1970–99	48	7	15
US Section 301 cases, 1975–94			
Border measures	25	19	76
Other market barriers	47	16	34
GSP workers' rights, 1985–94			
Forced or child labor	14	4	29
Subminimum working conditions	15	7	47

~ = approximately

GSP = Generalized System of Preferences

a. These results are preliminary and subject to change. The authors do not expect the basic story.

b. The original analysis probably does not adequately account for differences in the intensity of interest between the sender and target with respect to some of the goals defined as "modest." The adjustment shown here involves moving some human rights and nuclear nonproliferation cases from the modest to the major category. This issue will be revisited in more detail in the third edition of Hufbauer, Schott, and Elliott (forthcoming).

Sources: Hufbauer, Schott, and Elliott (2d ed., 1990, and 3d ed., forthcoming); Bayard and Elliott (1994); Elliott (2000d).

objectives—such as ending apartheid or inducing Iraq to withdraw from Kuwait—were successful less than a quarter of the time.

Another factor that may help explain the differences in success rates between cases with limited objectives and those with more ambitious goals is the greater ease of defining and observing compliance in the former case. When the objectives are limited, it is easier to judge outcomes: a political prisoner is or is not released; a tariff is or is not lowered. Within the universe of trade cases, US Section 301 investigations were more than twice as likely to result in some market opening if the barrier was tariffs or quotas than if the barrier was an agricultural subsidy, which the subsidizer could change in form without having the actual effect altered. The broader and more complex the issue, the more difficult to define and measure success—and the easier for a country to maintain the status quo.

Finally, compliance in cases involving regulatory issues often requires the target government to adopt costly measures to create or strengthen enforcement mechanisms. In such cases, as in half the failures in the GSP cases, trade threats may elicit promises to change but without the capacity to fulfill them.

In sum, our analysis shows that trade sanctions are not the deus ex machina in the enforcement of labor standards. Trade sanctions succeed in some situations and not in others. They are more likely to be effective when they directly target imports of particular goods produced under identifiably abusive conditions and where it is relatively easy to define the remediation measures. In the labor rights area, the weakness of administrative agencies enforcing labor codes is likely to be a major problem, so that countries promising improvements may be unable to deliver them. In these cases, threats of sanctions would presumably work best if they were coupled with technical and financial assistance to strengthen the relevant ministries and institutions seeking to protect workers.

The Danger of Protectionist Capture

The major worry of globalization enthusiasts is that including labor standards in the WTO and trade agreements, and authorizing trade sanctions to enforce them, would lead to protectionist abuse. Industries or unions would allege that there were labor standards violations in LDCs in order to deny them access to US or other advanced country markets. These fears are based on suspicions about the motives of proponents of a social clause, particularly unions, and on the experience with commercial antidumping rules, which have been diverted for protectionist purposes.

We reject these fears on four grounds. First, we demonstrate that antisweatshop activists and the international union movement have little direct protectionist motivation when promoting global labor standards. Second, we show that the petitions in the GSP workers' rights process and in other bilateral and regional trade agreements have not followed the rationale of protectionist intent. Third, we show that the US government has implemented trade-labor linkages in the GSP program in a nonprotectionist fashion, even under a pro-labor Democratic administration. Fourth, we note that international rules can be written to constrain the protectionist use of trade remedies by governments tempted in this direction.

Are Demands for a Social Clause Protectionist?

Opponents of labor standards in trade agreements recognize that some advocates of a social clause want only to improve working conditions for LDC workers. But they believe that these advocates are naive participants in an antisweatshop movement driven by protectionist labor unions. This attitude is reflected in the Third World Intellectuals' and NGOs' Statement Against Linkage and in the Academic Consortium on International Trade (ACIT), a group formed to oppose the antisweatshop movement on college campuses because they concluded that "much of the social activism in the United States regarding labor standards was motivated by protectionist considerations especially on the part of organized labor."[6]

These academics hold these views despite clear statements from major activist groups, such as Charles Kernaghan's National Labor Committee, that what they seek in campaigns (in this case regarding toy production in China)

> is *not* a boycott. We certainly do not want to hurt the U.S. toy industry or to take needed jobs out of China. What we are asking is that U.S. companies treat the three million toy workers in China—who produce 80 percent of the toys sold in the United States—as human beings and that their human and worker rights be respected. (www.nlcnet.org; emphasis in original)

ACIT is particularly uneasy about potential protectionist sentiment in the Workers' Rights Consortium (WRC), created by the United Students Against Sweatshops (USAS) to help enforce university codes, because these groups are linked to the Union of Needletrades, Industrial, and Textile Employees (UNITE). But WRC explicitly states that it would be a serious violation of its principles for a corporation to "cut and run" when confronted with problems of low labor standards (www.workersrights.org/key.asp). WRC also backed up its words with actions in the 2001 Kukdong

---

6. See www.columbia.edu/~jb38/twin_sal.pdf (April 13, 2001); www.fordschool.umich.edu/rsie/acit/documents/anti-sweatshopletterpage.html (March 26, 2003); and Brown, Deardorff, and Stern (forthcoming). Deardorff and Stern are on the ACIT steering committee.

case involving alleged code violations at a Korean-owned factory in Mexico that produced for Nike and Reebok. In this case, "WRC and many of our affiliate schools encouraged Nike to stay and work for change and that is the course the company chose" (www.workersrights.org/about_faq.asp). Though there may be some protectionist motivation in the quest for a social clause, it is not the ever present bogeyman that global enthusiasts believe it to be.

Union motivation for promoting a social clause stimulates the greatest suspicion, but it is not monolithic and not necessarily protectionist. The International Confederation of Free Trade Unions represents unions around the world, including unions in LDCs. These unions support policies that would give them greater leverage in negotiating with firms or their governments, but some worry that trade sanctions would cost them jobs. The confederation favors enforcement of international labor standards but does not want a mechanism that would harm some of its members, and its proposals for a social clause contain safeguards against protectionist abuse. One proposal calls for the ILO to review and monitor member states' compliance with the core conventions. It allows for a period of up to two years' consultation on how to rectify failure to comply with the core standards before referring the matter to the WTO for action. The WTO would then determine the appropriate action, with trade sanctions reserved as a last resort (International Confederation of Free Trade Unions 1999, 44–47).[7]

The observed implementation of the GSP program also contradicts fears that protectionist motivation underlies the desire for improved labor standards on the part of US unions.[8] The more than 100 petitions for improvements in workers' rights contrast with only 13 petitions to remove products from eligibility for competitive reasons, which would seem a more direct route to reducing access to the US market.[9] Unions, usually AFL-CIO members, submitted 73 percent of petitions accepted for review, and about half the petitions alleged violations of the "minimum conditions" of work, including lack of or inadequate minimum wages.

But the primary focus of petitions was the core rights of freedom of association and the right to organize and bargain collectively, which suggests this was the key motivation rather than reducing developing-country

---

7. The crucial difference between this proposal and a similar one that we make below is that we limit the WTO's enforcement role to *trade-related* violations of the core labor standards and leave broader enforcement of international standards with the ILO.

8. More detail on the GSP data set is given in appendix C.

9. The difference in activity levels is probably not due to a higher rejection rate for product removal petitions than for workers' rights petitions. The opposite is more likely, because a product petition will only be rejected if it has been submitted and denied in the previous three years. By contrast, the standards for accepting workers' rights petitions have been harshly criticized as nontransparent and overly stringent; see GAO (1994, 77).

competitiveness. In those same years, 246 petitions to *add* products to the eligible list were accepted for consideration, so that the overall pattern was for increased market access rather than reduced imports.

In addition, unions do not complain about the largest GSP-eligible exporters, which they might be expected to do if they had protectionist goals. On average, in the year the petition was filed, countries targeted in petitions involving unions exported 40 percent less than countries targeted in petitions with no union involvement ($2.4 billion vs. $4.1 billion). Moreover, only 3 of the top 10 beneficiary countries in 1998 had been subject to a workers' rights review, and the other 7 had never been the subject of a petition (see appendix C). If unions were seeking to reduce imports under the GSP, why would they spend resources on such small targets?

As for other groups advocating labor standards, far from trying to use the GSP to deny market access to LDCs, several workers' rights groups have suggested using partial GSP eligibility withdrawal as an alternative to complete suspension from the program, which they regard as too blunt. Bill Clinton's administration did this for the first time when it suspended Pakistan's eligibility for exports of hand-knitted and woven carpets, sporting goods, and surgical instruments—industries in which abusive child labor was found to be a problem (*International Trade Reporter*, November 8, 1995, 1853).

The reality is that, while globalization enthusiasts regard protectionism as so terrible that they expect protectionists to disguise it, protectionist unions or politicians usually do not hide their intent. They brag about it. Unions are not defensive about supporting protectionist activity if they believe it will protect their members' jobs.[10] And politicians want credit for saving their constituents' jobs from foreign competitors. In 2002, when George W. Bush's administration used tariffs to protect the steel industry, the policy was sold as protecting American jobs. It was a simple protectionist deal, supported by unions and firms in the sector, with no disguising of its intent.[11]

Protectionism in Action?

Whatever the motivation in pushing a social clause, there is little evidence that the United States has implemented existing trade-labor linkages in

10. See, for example, the comments by AFL-CIO economist Thea Lee at an Inter-American Dialogue conference in November 2002, www.iadialog.org/publications/program-reports/trade/ftaa_lee.pdf.

11. It has been noted by many observers in early 2002 that the Democratic President Clinton refused to provide import protection to the American steel industry, despite his close ties to labor, whereas the Republican President Bush did so. The rhetorically free trade Reagan administration bragged in the mid-1980s that it had imposed more trade protections than any administration since Herbert Hoover's (Baker 1987).

ways that sacrifice trade goals for labor standards. The Clinton administration favored organized labor's international agenda more than the Ronald Reagan or George H.W. Bush administrations. But none of these administrations implemented the GSP, the North American Free Trade Agreement (NAFTA) side agreement on labor, and other initiatives in ways that increased protectionism.

In dealing with GSP workers' rights petitions, the Clinton administration rejected 44 percent (8 of 18) of the labor conditionality petitions it received, similar to the 49 percent rate of rejection for the earlier George H.W. Bush administration (17 of 35), and a higher rate than the 32 percent of labor conditionality petitions rejected by the Reagan administration (11 of 34). The Clinton administration suspended the eligibility of beneficiary countries in 15 percent of cases, compared with 6 percent for Bush and 24 percent for Reagan (see appendix C).[12]

Overall, only 13 countries out of the 47 reviewed by any US administration have had their GSP eligibility terminated or suspended. Benefits were restored in 5 of these cases. Most of the cases—Burma, Chile, Liberia, Nicaragua, Romania, Sudan, and Syria—also involved foreign policy interests far beyond workers' rights, and the suspension of benefits cannot be attributed to protectionist pressures.

The countries that have lost GSP benefits as a result of inadequate protection of workers' rights tend to be smaller and poorer than the average beneficiary country. There is an even greater size and income gap between countries sanctioned and those that have never been the subject of a petition, much less a review. These facts may raise questions about the willingness of the US government to bear significant costs to promote labor standards, but they undermine the assertion that the primary motivation is to protect US workers. Globalization enthusiasts can sleep more soundly; their fears that protectionism lurks under the bed are exaggerated.

Labor Links in US Trade Agreements

US experience with bilateral and regional trade agreements that include labor issues, which are summarized in table 4.3, also leads us to reject the premise that such links inevitably lead to protectionist abuse. In the fall of 2001, the US Congress approved the US-Jordan Free Trade Agreement (FTA), with enforceable labor and environmental standards in the main body of the agreement as demanded by social clause advocates. In

---

12. In the summer of 2000, the Clinton administration revoked Belarus's eligibility because of inadequate protection of workers' rights. On the basis of preliminary information on other petitions investigated by the Clinton administration, this would raise the rate of suspensions only slightly, to 17 percent.

Table 4.3 Approaches to linking trade and labor standards

Approach	Pros	Cons
Social clause in trade agreements authorizing trade measures: • Against any violation of labor standards		Not appropriate because most labor violations are in nontraded sectors and trade experts are not competent to resolve labor standards disputes
• Against trade-related violations of labor standards	Market-improving	A political nonstarter for the foreseeable future
NAALC: Side agreement on labor	Provides mechanism for problems to be investigated and discussed; enforcement with fines possible for technical labor issues and child labor	Creates tiers for labor standards that are inconsistent with international consensus on core labor standards Provisions requiring only enforcement of national laws provide disincentive to raise standards
Canada-Chile FTA: Side agreement on labor	Similar to above	Same as above Relies on local judiciary to enforce, which could be problematic in other developing countries
US-Jordan FTA: Labor standards in main text	Treats trade-related labor standards violations equally with other potential distortions of trade and investment flows	Labor language so weak as to exert little upward pressure on labor standards Vague dispute settlement provisions risk abuse by leaving too much discretion to individual governments
US FTAs with Chile and Singapore: Labor standards in main text	Provides for "equivalent," though not identical, dispute settlement procedures Does not distinguish among the core labor standards	Excludes derogations from labor law to promote exports or attract foreign investment from dispute settlement

FTA = free trade agreement; NAALC = North American Agreement on Labor Cooperation

the spring of 2003, the Bush administration signed FTAs with Chile and Singapore that also contain labor standards in the main text, subject to the same settlement procedures as commercial disputes, albeit with fines rather than trade measures as the principal enforcement mechanism.

These three agreements contrast with earlier trade deals that addressed labor issues through supplementary "side" agreements with separate dispute resolution procedures. The common element in all the trade agreements with labor provisions, however, is that they require parties to enforce their own labor laws, with no requirement that those laws be consistent with internationally agreed core labor standards.[13]

The first trade pact to address labor issues, NAFTA, which was negotiated by Canada, Mexico, and the United States in the early 1990s, was an unsuccessful attempt by the Clinton administration to assuage the fears of workers and unions about the consequences of an economic integration deal with a low-wage country. The Canada-Chile and Canada-Costa Rica FTAs signed later in the decade followed this precedent by placing labor issues in side deals with their own institutional structures and dispute settlement mechanisms that do not include trade sanctions.

The North American Agreement on Labor Cooperation (NAALC) and the arrangement under the Canada-Chile FTA establish a mechanism for ministerial consultations to deal with accusations that one of the parties has not adequately enforced its labor laws. If neither consultations nor an expert evaluation resolves the problem, the parties can appoint an arbitral panel to review cases involving a subset of technical labor regulations on minimum wages, health and safety, and child labor, and the panel may impose a monetary fine (Elliott 2001).[14] Allegations of forced labor and discrimination are subject to evaluation by a panel of independent experts but are not eligible for monetary penalties. Complaints involving violations of union rights go no further than ministerial consultations. Under the NAALC, US practices, particularly with respect to the treatment of migrant agricultural workers, have been challenged as have Mexican labor practices.

Unlike these two agreements, the labor agreement attached to the Canada–Costa Rica FTA provides for ministerial consultations on labor issues but does not authorize fines in the case of disagreements over adequate enforcement. Under all these agreements, however, disputes are referred

---

13. Although unfortunate because it potentially discourages improvements in local law, this approach is unlikely to change as long as the United States has itself ratified so few ILO core conventions.

14. In the case of a bilateral dispute between the United States and Mexico, bilateral tariff concessions can be withdrawn to the extent necessary to collect the value of the fine. But this provision is not regarded as authorizing trade *sanctions*. In disputes involving Canada, including under the Chile agreement, enforcement of the fine resides with the local judiciary.

for consultation or more dispute settlement only if there is a "persistent pattern" of failures to enforce relevant labor laws and if the violations are in trade-related sectors.

The US-Jordan FTA, which was completed in late 2000 by the Clinton administration, established a new precedent by including a section on labor in the main text that is subject to the same dispute settlement procedures and remedies as the rest of the agreement. The protectionist risk here arises not from the language on labor standards but from the vague language on dispute settlement procedures. If consultations, a dispute settlement panel, and the Joint Committee created to implement the agreement do not resolve a dispute, the complaining party is authorized "to take *any* appropriate and commensurate measure" (emphasis added)— broad discretion that could be abused.

But the US-Jordan FTA labor standards text is so weak that it is difficult to see any dispute getting that far. In section 6, the agreement requires only that the parties "*strive* to ensure" (emphasis added) that domestic laws are consistent with "internationally recognized labor rights," and that they do not "waive or otherwise derogate from . . . such laws as an encouragement for trade." The only "shall" in this section refers to the obligation of the parties to "not fail to effectively enforce its laws" on a sustained basis in a way that affects trade. However, other paragraphs preserve the discretion of governments to adopt, modify, and enforce labor laws and regulations so that a party will be in compliance with its labor obligations under the agreement if

> a course of action or inaction [in enforcing labor laws] reflects a reasonable exercise of such discretion, or results from a *bona fide* decision regarding the allocation of resources. [Section 4(b) of Article 6 of the agreement]

Despite this language, Republicans and the business community blasted the US-Jordan FTA as setting an unacceptably dangerous precedent. In the fall of 2001, the Bush administration argued in favor of the agreement on the grounds that it was important to support an ally in the war on terrorism and in the Middle East peace process. The Republican-controlled House of Representatives, however, approved the agreement only after US Trade Representative Robert Zoellick arranged for an exchange of letters with his Jordanian counterpart indicating that they did not anticipate using the dispute settlement provisions.

During the congressional debate over trade promotion authority, which allows the president to negotiate trade agreements that Congress cannot amend once embodied in legislation, Senate Finance Committee Chair Max Baucus (D-MT) insisted that all future trade agreements must meet the "Jordan standard" of having enforceable labor standards in the main text. After passage of the Trade Act of 2002, Baucus and other Democrats claimed that this is the correct interpretation of the labor provisions. But

Senator Charles Grassley (R-IA), the chair of the Finance Committee in the 108th Congress, adamantly disagreed.

Either way, it is clear that US trade negotiators cannot ignore labor issues in future negotiations. In the section of the Trade Act providing trade promotion authority, references to workers' rights and labor standards appear as an "overall" and a "principal" trade negotiating objective, as well as a "certain priority" that the president should promote to address and maintain US competitiveness. The key section, 2102(b)(11), essentially copies the language from the US-Jordan FTA in defining principal US negotiating objectives with respect to labor (and the environment), emphasizing the legitimacy of discretion in setting and enforcing one's own laws.

In a Trade Act amendment that muddies the enforceability question, however, Senator Phil Gramm (R-TX), a leading opponent of linking standards and trade, convinced his House colleagues to insert additional language barring retaliation "based on the exercise of these rights [to discretion in enforcement] or the right to establish domestic labor standards." But this provision appears contradicted by the next negotiation objective, on dispute settlement and enforcement, which requires US negotiators to "seek provisions" that treat all "principal negotiating objectives equally with respect to" the availability of "equivalent dispute settlement procedures and remedies."

In its first attempt to interpret this potentially conflicting language, the Office of the US Trade Representative developed a compromise for the bilateral FTA negotiations with Chile and Singapore that combines elements of NAALC and the US-Jordan FTA.[15] Like the Jordan agreement, labor obligations are in the main text of the agreements, making violations subject to the same dispute settlement procedures as commercial disputes; and there is no distinction among applicable labor standards, as in NAALC.

The Chile and Singapore FTAs follow the practice of basing labor obligations on the effective enforcement of each country's own laws in trade-related sectors. In a bizarre twist, they "recognize that it is inappropriate to encourage trade or investment by weakening or reducing the protections afforded in domestic labor laws" but then go on to explicitly exclude such derogations from dispute settlement.[16]

Like NAALC and in a departure from the Jordan FTA, these agreements limit enforcement measures in labor disputes to monetary fines,

---

15. This is based on the text of the Singapore FTA and a summary of the Chile FTA, both available on the Office of the US Trade Representative Web site at www.ustr.gov.

16. One explanation is that this provision was constructed this way to meet the Gramm language giving governments the "right to establish domestic labor standards." It is bizarre, however, because such derogations create exactly the sort of distortions that trade agreements typically address.

with the possibility of suspending tariff concessions if necessary to *collect* the fine (explicitly not a trade sanction). Unlike NAFTA, the fines would accrue annually if problems remain unresolved. In commercial disputes, the country in violation of the agreement could choose to pay a fine, but traditional trade retaliation would also remain an option. The Office of the US Trade Representative argues that while not "mirror images," the mechanisms for enforcement of labor and commercial disputes would be equally effective and therefore would meet the congressional standard of equivalence.

The outstanding question is whether any of these approaches affect labor standards on the ground. As of 2002, a number of studies and consultations had occurred under NAALC, but no complaint had gotten as far as an experts' committee, much less imposition of fines (Hufbauer et al. 2002). The process has directed attention to labor problems on both sides of the border. But independent unions still must battle to be recognized in the maquila sector in Mexico, and US firms can still use the threat to relocate to Mexico in bargaining with unions with virtual impunity (Bronfenbrenner 2000). The agreements reached thus far that include labor standards are with relatively small trading partners with little negotiating leverage and relatively good labor standards, and they may not provide precedents for trade agreements with larger countries.

The principal problem with many of these FTAs is that they have been largely concerned with finding politically acceptable trade-labor mechanisms that permit trade agreements to proceed, while doing little to ensure that labor standards improve. It is possible that experimentation with further regional agreements will produce useful and replicable compromises on trade and labor issues. These FTAs are also useful in setting a precedent for linking core labor standards with the further expansion of trade and investment.[17] But the link between trade and labor rights should not be limited to bilateral agreements. Multilateral agreements covering trade sanctions for improving standards are necessary, both to improve standards broadly and to limit possible protectionism associated with standards.

A Role for the WTO

Given the evidence that trade measures can contribute to improving labor standards, and that protectionist motivations have not captured the policymaking process when labor clauses are included in trade agreements, we believe that the WTO should include a provision allowing countries to retaliate against *trade-related* and egregious violations of the core labor standards.

---

17. See also Polanski (2002).

Our proposal differs from most social clause proposals in that it focuses on labor standards in the traded goods sector, for which the WTO and the world trading community are responsible, rather than seeking to move the general enforcement of labor standards from the ILO to the WTO or having the two organizations share broad enforcement power. In the nontraded goods, informal, and subsistence agricultural sectors, in which most people in poor countries work, the ILO should remain the primary organization charged with promoting and enforcing labor standards.

The starting point for WTO involvement in labor standards in the traded goods sector should be to adapt Article XX of the General Agreement on Tariffs and Trade (which was incorporated into the WTO). This article lists exceptional circumstances in which members can depart from their obligations under the agreement, including Article XX(e) permitting countries to ban imports of goods produced using prison labor. Article XX(h), which authorizes countries to impose otherwise prohibited trade measures if they are undertaken pursuant to an intergovernmental commodity agreement that "conforms to criteria" acceptable to member countries, might also be adapted to permit trade measures authorized by the ILO under its supervisory procedures.[18]

The WTO should build on Article XX(e) by adding a provision that allows countries to sanction the specific sector of a country that has violated core labor standards, if the ILO has determined that there is indeed a violation. As currently written, Article XX(e) allows members to take action only against imports implicated in the labor standards violation—not imports in unrelated sectors. This element should be retained to prevent any country from using labor standards problems in one sector of a trading partner to block LDC exports in unrelated, higher-value-added sectors with "good" jobs, such as electronics (Moran 2002).[19]

Similarly, to minimize the risks of protectionism, any revision of Article XX(e) should focus on egregious and narrowly defined violations of standards—based on ILO supervisory evidence, and subject to WTO review, just as actions under Article XX currently are. To define violations eligible for Article XX action, it would be natural to include, in addition to forced labor and the worst forms of child labor (which usually in-

---

18. Environmentalists have suggested broadening Article XX(h) to address potential conflicts between the WTO and multilateral environmental agreements that incorporate trade measures. This idea might also be adapted to avoid conflicts with the WTO if the ILO becomes more active in using trade sanctions under Article 33 of its own Constitution to enforce egregious labor standards violations (see the discussion of ILO enforcement in chapter 5).

19. We view this "targeted" sanctions feature as a major attraction of the Article XX approach. Staiger (2003), relying on a more traditional bargaining approach to WTO dispute settlement, minimizes this as an option because it might result in increased discrimination in trade. The alternative he proposes would, we believe, be unwieldy in practice and inappropriate in dealing with undemocratic regimes because it assumes labor standards reflect national preferences.

volve coercion), de jure national policies that discriminate on one of the prohibited grounds (i.e., gender, race, ethnicity, political opinion, religion, or social origin) that employers can exploit to promote exports. Such explicit, illegal discrimination appears to be rare, however, and the ILO approach emphasizes promotional measures, so we would not expect many disputes in this area.

It would be more difficult to identify actionable violations of freedom of association and bargaining rights. Guidelines should focus on the egregiousness of the violation and on its relation to trade. In addition to the examples of legal restrictions on unions in export processing zones, evidence that union organizers are de facto barred from entering such zones or are fired or arrested for trying to organize an exporting firm could be considered actionable.[20] In these and other cases, an additional useful criterion would be whether or not the country is cooperating with the ILO to remedy problems.

In addition to identifying the range of violations that would be actionable, there is the question of which agency should make the determination. One of the weaknesses of the current dispute settlement process for Article XX cases is that WTO panels with no expertise on environmental issues, for example, rule on the legitimacy of environmental claims. To avoid putting trade dispute settlement panelists in the position of having to investigate the legitimacy of claims on labor standards violations, the wealth of information produced by the ILO supervisory system should be used instead. Countries invoking Article XX(e) against a trade-related core labor standards violation should be required to present evidence from the ILO supervisory process, as described in the next chapter, before taking any action.

In cases involving forced labor (by adults or children) or discrimination where the targeted country has not ratified the relevant conventions, the country invoking Article XX should offer evidence from other independent sources, for example the UN Human Rights Commission or respected nongovernmental organizations such as Amnesty International or Human Rights Watch. In this case, the defendant country could appeal to the ILO to conduct an independent investigation, and if the claim of a violation is not upheld and the trade measure is not removed, the defendant country could then file a dispute with the WTO.

Experience with the WTO's Dispute Settlement Understanding and with trade-environment disputes suggests that multilateral trade rules provide safeguards that would prevent protectionists from exploiting the trade-labor link as a trade barrier (Elliott 2000a, 199–201). The Dispute

---

20. The big problem is what to do with respect to countries that either ban unions or enforce a trade union monopoly that is not independent and does not genuinely represent the interests of workers. These violations, though egregious, are almost always motivated by fear of political competition and not by competitiveness concerns, and a ban on *all* exports would be both costly and ineffective.

Settlement Understanding reduces the threat that protectionists could exploit an expanded Article XX in a number of ways. Restrictions on unilateral trade measures mean that trade threats cannot be used as a tool of "aggressive unilateralism," as they were on intellectual property, for example, to force countries to change their policies or to agree to negotiate new multilateral rules. The key is for the trading rules to limit government discretion and to require that trade measures related to social issues be subject to multilateral review and discipline.

The WTO settlement system has also demonstrated that it can protect small, poor countries from unjustified or arbitrary discrimination against their exports. Several LDCs have challenged US trade measures, including those based on environmental concerns, and have prevailed in the WTO, leading the United States to modify its policies. In one case, a panel ruling forced the United States to revise its clean air regulations on gasoline that discriminated against imports without a legitimate rationale. The appellate body ruling that allowed the United States to ban shrimp imports that threaten endangered sea turtles did not result in a proliferation of new trade bans for nominally environmental purposes.[21] Though not satisfactory to everyone, the WTO system in this and other cases has shown itself capable of distinguishing protectionist trade barriers from legitimate attempts to address environmental issues.[22]

Finally, the WTO could consider expanding the General Agreement on Trade in Services to cover the cross-border provision of "worker agency services." Workers' associations provide a variety of services that support markets. These associations alleviate market failures associated with collective action problems, workplace public goods, and imperfect information; and they discipline practices that border on coercion and create countervailing market power to the anticompetitive market power of firms.

Moreover, the services provided by workers' associations encompass not just bargaining over compensation but also workplace safety monitoring, grievance and dispute settlement, training and education, and management of other services, such as child care, pensions, and health insurance (Richardson 2000; Stiglitz 2000; Freeman and Medoff 1984). It would be consistent with the WTO's mission to encourage the liberalization of "trade" in such market-supportive services. The ILO could also provide advice on how to develop these rules and could assist in training workers' (and employers') organizations on how best to take advantage of them. Again, trade and labor working together can do more than either can do separately.

---

21. The United States has modified its application of the law that led to the shrimp-turtle dispute but is still struggling to find a solution that satisfies both the demands of its trading partners and the requirements of its domestic law.

22. Whether, and if so on what basis, the WTO should make such distinctions is a separate issue.

5

The ILO to the Rescue?

We renew our commitment to the observance of internationally recognized labor standards. The International Labor Organization (ILO) is the competent body to set and deal with these standards and we affirm our support for its work in promoting them.
—World Trade Organization, Singapore Ministerial Communiqué, 1996

To deflect demands for a social clause, globalization enthusiasts, LDC governments, and the world trading community have proposed that an international agency other than the World Trade Organization (WTO) deal with global labor standards—the International Labor Organization, or ILO. Until the battle over standards erupted in the 1990s, neither trade specialists nor labor economists paid much attention to the ILO. Even today, most reasonably informed people have little idea what the letters I-L-O stand for.

The ILO is the Methuselah of international institutions. It was created in 1919 and is the only League of Nations institution to survive World War II. It is also the only international organization that is not purely intergovernmental in its governance structure. Unions and employer-group representatives are part of each country's delegation and have the same right to vote as government representatives at Governing Body meetings and at the International Labor Conference, where delegates make policy in plenary sessions (for the details of the ILO's structure, see box 5.1). As of the end of 2002, the ILO's membership included government, worker, and employer representatives from 175 countries.

Historically, the ILO's major activity was to negotiate and promulgate conventions on labor standards that member governments could ratify. By

Box 5.1   ILO institutional structure and supervisory mechanisms

The ILO, founded in 1919, is a tripartite organization with 175 member states and 700 voting delegates, because each state delegation has two government representatives and one each representing employers and workers. In theory, the worker and employer delegates vote independently and are not bound by their government's position. Delegates gather annually at the International Labor Conference, where new conventions may be adopted and implementation of existing conventions is reviewed.

The *Governing Body* is the ILO's executive body, with responsibility for developing policy, electing the director general, overseeing the International Labor Office (see below) work program, and responding to complaints about inadequate implementation of the ILO's conventions. The Governing Body has 28 government members, with 10 of those slots "permanently held by states of chief industrial importance" (currently Brazil, China, France, Germany, India, Italy, Japan, Russia, the United Kingdom, and the United States) and the others elected every three years at the annual conference. The 14 employer and 14 worker members are elected by the employer and worker delegates, respectively.

The *International Labor Office,* headed by the director general, is the ILO secretariat, with headquarters in Geneva and branch offices around the world. The International Labor Office provides advisory services (e.g., on how to create or reform laws for social protection), carries out research projects, and conducts technical cooperation programs.

The *Committee of Experts on the Application of Conventions and Recommendations* (CEACR) reviews and comments on the routine reports submitted by members regarding the application of conventions they have ratified (Article 22) or efforts to ratify other conventions and the status of law and practices in those areas (Article 19).

The *Conference Committee on the Application of Standards* is a tripartite body formed at each International Labor Conference that reviews the CEACR report, selects a subset of problem cases identified in that report, and invites the government delegates from the countries involved to discuss them in open session.

The *Committee on Freedom of Association* deals with complaints alleging violations by a member state of this fundamental right. Because it is regarded as a constitutional obligation of membership, complaints about freedom of association violations can be brought against any member state, regardless of whether it has ratified Convention 87.

Sources: "About the ILO," www.ilo.org/public/english/about/index.htm and "International Labor Standards: How Are They Enforced?" at www.ilo.org (click on "International Labor Standards" on the homepage and then on "FAQs").

2002, the ILO had developed 184 conventions determining international standards for various aspects of work and employment. Some of the standards dealt with fundamental rights of workers, but most were narrow and technical, on issues of importance only to labor, management, or regulators in specific sectors, for instance, shipping or communications.

From 1977 to 1980, the United States withdrew from the ILO, seeing it as overly politicized, ineffective, and unwilling to distinguish between genuine unions and government-run sham organizations in the old Soviet bloc. Like other UN organizations, the ILO was also infected by the political poisons emanating from the Middle East conflict.

The ILO's institutional weaknesses aside, a simple comparison of its budget with those of the World Bank and IMF shows its relative status. In 2000–01, the ILO had a budget of $467 million, of which 25 percent came from the United States. This compares with the Bank's and IMF's hundreds of billions of dollars in lending authority.

Thanks to the debate over labor standards and globalization, however, the ILO has recently received more attention, political support, and resources than ever before. The organization has responded with new initiatives and a tougher attitude toward countries that violate standards (Charnovitz 2000). In 1998, the ILO approved a Declaration on Fundamental Principles and Rights at Work, which provided a consensus definition of the four core labor standards that have become the centerpiece of the global standards movement.

The ILO followed this declaration by approving a new convention calling for immediate action against the "worst forms" of child labor. It developed programs to ensure that reductions in child labor did not leave families worse off. In 1999, for the first time in its history, the ILO imposed penalties on a member state, in this case Burma for allowing forced labor. In 2002, it established a World Commission on the Social Dimensions of Globalization to explore ways to make economic globalization more inclusive.[1]

What tools does the ILO have to improve labor standards around the world? Will the countries that supported the ILO in lieu of the WTO to deal with labor standards work to strengthen the organization, or is their support just rhetoric? Will the United States continue to help the ILO become an active agent of change or return to an earlier stance of neglect or hostility? Can the ILO transform itself from the 90-pound weakling of UN agencies into an effective guardian of labor standards around the world?

The ILO's Tools

In 1999, the ILO elected Juan Somavia, previously Chile's permanent representative at the United Nations, to be its director general. Somavia grasped the opportunity offered by the labor standards debate to reinvigorate

---

1. The commission is cochaired by the presidents of Finland and Tanzania and made up of 19 prominent individuals from all regions of the world and from government, academia, the business community, and the labor movement.

the ILO. With a team of ILO officials, he visited institutions around the world to gather ideas on what an activist ILO could do.

At Harvard University, Richard Freeman offered a radical scheme: The ILO's director general and its other leading officials should identify a horrid violation of labor standards somewhere in the world, go to that factory or workplace, protest, and get arrested or attacked by the company's guards or police. This would put Somavia and the ILO on the front pages of newspapers and television screens around the world and give the organization instant credibility as the guardian of labor standards. People would say, The ILO? Oh yes, the part of the United Nations that stands up for workers' rights. Then whenever the ILO spoke out on standards issues in the future, the global community would pay attention.

Though the director general and his staff did not follow this far-out advice, they did shake up the ILO and strengthen its presence in the global economy. In response to the criticism that the costs of globalization and the burdens of financial crises and structural adjustment fall largely on the poor while the benefits go largely to the wealthy, the ILO developed a four-part strategy to improve the well-being of workers around the world. Under the heading "Decent Work," it promotes the four core labor standards and the need for job creation; supports the development and improvement of social safety nets; and calls for social dialogue among management, labor, and government. And in response to widespread concerns about child labor, the ILO also expanded its International Program on the Elimination of Child Labor (IPEC).

In addition to setting standards, the ILO has three tools for improving working conditions (Elliott 2000b). It supervises compliance with global labor conventions and publicizes violations of standards to shame countries into improving matters. It gives technical assistance to labor ministries and other agencies, unions, and employers' groups to improve the implementation of labor standards. And it can punish countries that do not comply with their commitments through an enforcement mechanism that, until the 1990s, the organization had rarely used. In response to activist campaigns for global labor standards and the desire of the trade community to divert attention from the WTO on these issues, the ILO has strengthened all three of these tools.

Supervising and Publicizing Country Performance

The ILO has extensive mechanisms for supervising the application of its labor conventions. Article 22 of the ILO Constitution requires member governments to routinely report on how they apply the conventions they have ratified.[2] Article 19 requires members to report periodically on why

---

2. To reduce the burden on member governments, the ILO now asks countries to report on each core convention they have ratified every two years and on other ratified

they have not ratified particular conventions and what they are doing to achieve the goals of those conventions. The Committee of Experts on the Application of Conventions and Recommendations, composed of 20 independent members, reviews these reports and prepares its own report to the International Labor Conference. When the committee detects a problem in implementing a convention, it makes an "individual observation" that draws attention to discrepancies between convention obligations and the law or practice in particular countries.

The annual International Labor Conference provides a public venue for directing attention to the success or failure of countries in complying with international standards. At that meeting, the ILO's Conference Committee on the Application of Standards reviews the experts' report, selects 20 or so of the most serious problems identified there, and invites governments to respond to them in public session. The Conference Committee then prepares its own report to the full Conference, highlighting areas of both progress and inadequate compliance. A separate section of the report lists cases in which there is a "continued failure to implement" or includes "special paragraphs" directing attention to the worst cases. A press release highlights these cases with the aim of shaming the violator into making reforms.

The ILO disseminates much of the information generated by its supervisory mechanisms on its Web site (www.ilo.org). ILOLEX, a searchable database, contains the ILO Constitution, all the conventions and recommendations, ratifications, Committee of Experts and Conference Committee reports, information on complaints under Articles 24 and 26 (see below), and more. In important functional areas, including the promotion of international labor standards, child labor, and occupational safety and health, the agency has created In Focus programs that pull together key information on the problem and on ILO programs to address it. The ILO has done a great deal in recent years to make its Web site more user-friendly but the sheer volume of information can overwhelm potential users, such as the media, nongovernmental organizations (NGOs), unions, and business groups in particular countries.

ILO officials believe that the increased transparency brought by increased attention and new technologies has had an effect on compliance. In a report assessing the impact of the specialized Committee on Freedom of Association, the ILO concludes that countries are

> finding it increasingly unacceptable that their failings and non-compliance with their international obligations are discussed in public, particularly at a time when new means of communication are making it possible for information to be disseminated more effectively than ever before. (Gravel, Duplessis, and Gernigon 2001)

---

conventions over a five-year cycle, rather than every year, as was originally required when the number of members and of conventions was far smaller.

The most important addition to the reporting and information toolbox, however, came in 1998 when the International Labor Conference approved the Declaration on Fundamental Principles and Rights at Work defining the four core labor standards. The follow-up mechanism for implementing the declaration requires member countries that have not ratified one or more of the eight conventions associated with these principles to report annually on what they are doing to promote the conventions and encourages employers' and workers' groups to comment on the national submissions. In addition, the Conference requires the director general to prepare a global report summarizing how each core standard is being implemented around the world.

The ILO appoints independent expert advisers to write an introduction to the compilation of country reports, to point out strengths and weaknesses in them, and to recommend how to make the reports more useful. In combination with the Article 22 reports the ILO requests from the signatories to conventions, this reporting mechanism means that *every* ILO member is obligated to report routinely on efforts to promote fundamental workers' rights.[3] But the ILO cannot force countries to fulfill their reporting obligations. In 2002, roughly a third of the required reports were not sent to the ILO, and 10 countries had not reported at all under the follow-up, mostly the poorest or weakest. Moreover, most country reports are more bureaucratic than informative and are filled with detailed discussions of legal provisions rather than with information on the actual implementation of standards.

The director general's global reports have more of an impact. They are succinct and easy to read. They summarize the key problems in implementing the core standards and identify countries with problems. The reports are prepared in a four-year cycle beginning with freedom of association (2000), forced labor (2001), child labor (2002), and discrimination (2003).

The purpose of the ILO supervisory mechanisms is to direct a spotlight on labor standards and improve compliance. One way to judge the potential power of these reports is that several countries tried to water down the declaration and to stop the director general from "naming names." In 1998, delegates from some of the LDCs that had argued that labor standards should be kept in the ILO and out of the WTO either left Geneva early or abstained from the vote on the declaration and follow-up mechanism, nearly denying it the quorum needed to gain approval. The countries of the delegates who abstained are listed in box 5.2. Some, such as Burma, have subsequently been identified as serious violators of labor standards.

---

3. An unfortunate discrepancy has been created, however, because the country reports under the Declaration follow-up are published on the ILO Web site while the Article 22 reports are kept on file at ILO headquarters, largely inaccessible to the public.

When the June 2000 International Labor Conference discussed the first global report, many of these countries criticized Director General Somavia for pointing to violations of freedom of association in Bahrain, Equatorial Guinea, Oman, Qatar, Saudi Arabia, and the United Arab Emirates, where worker organizations were either prohibited or so restricted as to be meaningless.[4] The report also highlighted the denial of the right to organize in countries with legislatively imposed official unions, such as in China, Cuba, Iraq, Sudan, Syria, and Vietnam.

Somavia rejected the criticism, noting that "it is difficult to see how the [International Labor] Office can do credible reporting unless countries are identified and facts are stated."[5] In fact, naming names helped shift the policies of some Middle Eastern countries. Saudi Arabia announced in 2001 that it would permit the formation of worker committees, and Bahrain decided to allow trade unions. These countries, along with Oman, Qatar, and the United Arab Emirates, also asked the ILO to provide technical assistance to help them make further progress.[6]

To avoid conflict with its members, the ILO has shied away from clearly prioritizing the violations or putting countries in categories by degree of violation. But there is nothing to prevent other organizations from using

4. The Gulf countries protested being singled out in the report and, privately, some ILO officials concede that the report should have been more sensitive to the particular problems of these countries, which are in an unusual position with respect to freedom of association because a huge proportion of their workforce consists of foreign workers.

5. "Reply by the Director-General to the Discussion of his Report," Provisional Record 25, International Labour Conference, 88th Session, Geneva, 2000.

6. ILO, "Decent Work in Asia," August 2001.

the ILO data in this way. In 1996 and in 2000, the OECD used ILO data and other documents to put about 70 countries into four categories based on their respect for the right to freedom of association. And a committee appointed by the US National Research Council has been studying ways to use ILO and other data to develop indicators of how countries are faring with labor standards.

In sum, with routine ILO reporting, the declaration follow-up mechanism, and efforts by other public and private organizations, such as the OECD, the International Confederation of Free Trade Unions, and corporations, the world now has much more information about labor standards than in the past.

Technical Assistance

Some LDCs lack the funding and knowledge to improve labor standards. Ministries of labor and other organizations seeking to raise standards are often weak bureaucracies unable to accomplish goals, such as reducing child labor or improving occupational health and safety. In such situations, even modest ILO technical assistance can help them accomplish their goals.

For decades, ILO technical assistance programs received only modest funding from wealthier member states, and the agency had a limited presence in LDCs. In the late 1990s, however, many countries, including the United States, responded to activist demands that the world community do more to improve labor standards by increasing their funding for ILO programs. US contributions, exclusive of assessed dues and money for child labor, went from zero in 1998 to $20 million in 2000 for technical assistance to promote the 1998 declaration.[7] As a result, overall spending on technical cooperation increased from an average of just above $90 million a year in 1998–2000 to $122 million in 2001 (International Labor Office 2002, 1).

Much of the increased money went to IPEC. From its launch in 1992, with a donation from Germany and 6 participating countries, IPEC has grown to 70 participating countries and 25 donor governments. In the space of 2 years (2000–01 to 2002–03), allocations for the child labor program increased from $64 million to $119 million (IPEC 2002b).

US contributions to IPEC were $3 million in 1998 and increased to $45 million by fiscal 2000. Canada, France, the Netherlands, and the United Kingdom also more than doubled their contributions in the late 1990s. Among the largest recipients of IPEC assistance in 2002–03 were Bangladesh ($11 million), India ($15 million), and Pakistan ($3 million). Central American countries received another $10 million (IPEC 2002a).

---

7. *ILO Focus*, Summer-Fall 1998, 14; Winter-Spring 1999, 12; Spring 2000, 7; and Spring 2002, www.us.ilo.org (various dates).

Having been bolstered by the increase in funding and political support, the ILO began to attack problems of raising labor standards more creatively than before. It worked with government, industry, and NGOs to address child labor in South Asia and West Africa (see chapter 6). And in 2001, it worked with El Salvador, Nepal, and Tanzania to develop new "time-bound" programs to eliminate the worst forms of child labor that take a systemic countrywide approach to identifying problems and finding holistic solutions to eliminate the problem. The ILO also worked with Cambodia and the US government to monitor conditions in Cambodia's garment sector, while training labor ministry inspectors, employers, and workers to enforce laws and settle disputes themselves.

Looking at the effect of some of these programs, IPEC reports that during the period 2000–01 it provided more than 300,000 "units of service" to children, more than double the number in the previous biennium. The beneficiaries include nearly 40,000 children removed from work or rescued; more than 50,000 children helped by ensuring safer working conditions or shorter hours; about 80,000 children provided with basic education or vocational or skills training; and more than 50,000 children mainstreamed into the formal education system.[8]

Although the number of children benefiting from these services is small in a world with about 250 million child workers (8 million of whom the ILO estimates are engaged in the unconditionally "worst forms" of child labor), it is a fruitful beginning. Overall, the assistance given these children cost less than $200 per "unit of service" provided, but much of this was start-up costs, suggesting that the marginal cost of aiding the children is less.[9]

To maintain or increase these levels of support, the ILO must demonstrate to donors and recipients that it spends the money wisely. This, in turn, requires that it become more transparent and undertake more systematic evaluations of its technical assistance. At the 2001 International Labor Conference, US employer delegate Ed Potter asked the organization to list all the countries acting to correct problems and the countries requesting technical assistance, and to provide more information on the assistance given those countries and criteria for assessing the impact of the assistance (International Labor Conference, 89th Session, Provisional Record 1). Behind this request was a concern that much ILO technical support involves seminars on freedom of association or collective bargaining, where it is difficult to assess success. At the least, the agency

8. These "units of service" appear not to correspond one-to-one with individual children because some might have been both withdrawn from work and enrolled in training. The IPEC report also implies, without being specific, that higher-value services may be worth more than one "unit" (IPEC 2002b).

9. This is calculated by dividing $56 million in actual expenditures by the estimated 300,000 service units.

could ask whether participants found the seminars useful and what could be done to make them better.

More broadly, the ILO could do more with its Web site to report organized information about technical cooperation. Its Technical Cooperation Committee regularly reports to the ILO Governing Body, but information on particular programs can be difficult to find. The ILO would also benefit from creating an office to independently evaluate its programs, as the World Bank and IMF have done in recent years in response to pressure for more transparency.[10]

Enforcement of Conventions and Standards

The most frequent complaint about the ILO is that it lacks enforcement power—that it is the proverbial toothless tiger. Article 33 of its Constitution gives it broad authority to take action against countries that are not in compliance with the obligations of membership. Until 2000, however, it had never invoked that provision. It encouraged compliance through the supervisory and technical assistance systems described above rather than seeking to sanction countries that violated standards.

The ILO has two ad hoc mechanisms to promote compliance with labor standards that focus attention on possible violations and that could eventually lead to Article 33 sanctions. The first, Article 24 of the ILO Charter, gives any worker or employer organization around the world the right to file a complaint alleging that a member government is not complying with a convention it has ratified or that a country has violated freedom of association (regardless of whether it ratified the relevant conventions). If these complaints are not resolved through informal consultation, the Governing Body can refer the "representation" to the Committee on Freedom of Association or appoint an ad hoc committee of its members, consisting of representatives of governments, workers, and employers. These committees analyze the situation, ask the government to respond, and make recommendations on what the government can do to comply.

If the problem remains unresolved, official delegates to the ILO can file a complaint under Article 26. Governments can raise complaints against another country only if they have also ratified the convention in question. This provision constrains the US government because it has ratified just 13 conventions and only 2 core conventions—Conventions 105 on the abolition of forced labor and 182 on the worst forms of child labor. But the US Council for International Business, representing US employers, and the AFL-CIO, representing American labor, can bring a complaint regardless of US ratification status. And as with representations, Article

---

10. For information on the IMF's Independent Evaluation Office, see www.imf.org/external/np/ieo/index.htm; and for the World Bank's Operations Evaluation Department, see www.worldbank.org/oed/.

26 complaints regarding freedom of association can be brought against governments that have not ratified either Convention 87 or 98.

Upon receiving a complaint under Article 26, the ILO Governing Body tries to resolve the problem informally. It can seek the member country's permission to send a Direct Contacts Mission to discuss the problem. If that leads nowhere, the ILO can appoint a Commission of Inquiry to investigate the charges. The commission reports its findings and recommends how the country can bring its laws and practices into compliance with the relevant convention. The target of the complaint can appeal the commission's finding to the International Court of Justice. If the commission's findings stand, the ILO will ask the country to report what it has done to implement the commission's recommendations.

Up to this point, ILO procedures are similar to those standards advocates propose for a WTO "social clause." But many advocates believe that the similarities end there, with the ILO having no power to enforce its findings. In fact, Article 33 of the ILO Constitution provides that, if a satisfactory resolution is not forthcoming, "the Governing Body may recommend that the Conference take such action as it may deem wise and expedient to secure compliance therewith."[11]

Until 1946, Article 33 provided that members could take "measures of an economic character" against another member that refused to come into compliance with the recommendations of a Commission of Inquiry.[12] A constitutional review undertaken after World War II broadened Article 33 to "leave the Governing Body discretion to adapt its action to the circumstances of the particular case." However, the amended language does not exclude the possibility of economic, or any other, sanctions.[13]

The ILO has rarely used its enforcement process, in part because the founding countries never intended this to be a major tool for improving labor standards. Article 26 was

> artfully devised in order to avoid the imposition of penalties, except in the last resort, when a State has flagrantly and persistently refused to carry out its obligations under a Convention. It can hardly be doubted that it will seldom, if ever, be necessary to bring these powers into operation.[14]

---

11. International Labor Office, "Measures, Including Action Under Article 33 of the Constitution . . . to Secure Compliance by the Government of Myanmar. . .," GB.276/6, 276th Session of the Governing Body, Geneva, November 1999.

12. International Labor Office, *Reports I and II and Constitutional Questions,* 29th Session of the International Labor Conference, 1946.

13. International Labor Office, *Reports I and II and Constitutional Questions,* 29th Session of the International Labor Conference, 1946. Also see International Labor Office, "Measures, Including Action Under Article 33 of the Constitution . . . to Secure Compliance by the Government of Myanmar. . .," GB.276/6, 276th Session of the Governing Body, Geneva, November 1999.

14. International Labor Office, *Reports I and II and Constitutional Questions,* 29th Session of the International Labor Conference, 1946, 4.

Between 1919 and 1960, there was only one Article 26 complaint. Since then, there has been an average of six complaints a decade. Throughout its history, the ILO has appointed only nine Commissions of Inquiry.[15] And despite weak implementation of the commissions' recommendations in some cases, the ILO never took the next step, invoking Article 33 of its Constitution—until 2000.[16]

The Burma Case

The ILO finally invoked Article 33 against Burma over a long-standing problem with forced labor. The problem grew worse after a military junta seized power in 1988 and initiated a massive infrastructure-building campaign to attract tourists and foreign investment. After years of comment by the Committee of Experts, worker delegates filed an Article 26 complaint against Burma in 1996. In March 1997, the ILO appointed a Commission of Inquiry. The commission completed its report in 1998 and called on the Burmese government to bring its laws and practice into compliance with Convention 29 by May 1999.

In June 1999, not having received a constructive response from Burma, the International Labor Conference approved a resolution that condemned Burma's refusal to comply with the Commission of Inquiry's recommendations, prohibited technical assistance except as necessary to implement the recommendations, and banned Burma from most meetings.[17] It also requested that the Governing Body consider whether further action under Article 33 might be justified.

Even these modest penalties attracted opposition from some LDCs. Cuba, seconded by Colombia, Mexico, and Venezuela, sought to separate the part of the resolution condemning Burma's noncompliance from

---

15. All but three of the complaints since 1960 addressed alleged violations of one of the four fundamental rights, usually freedom of association or forced labor. See "International Labor Standards: How Are They Enforced?" on the International Labor Standards sections of the ILO Web site at www.ilo.org.

16. One assessment finds that most governments accept the findings of commission reports. Poland, however, refused to cooperate with the Commission of Inquiry appointed to investigate a freedom of association complaint raised in the early 1980s, when the government was trying to break the Solidarity union movement. Germany also rejected the finding by a commission that it unfairly discriminated against public employees for political (anticommunist) reasons. In other cases, governments nominally accepted the conclusions of a commission but remedial actions often have been inadequate. See Romano (1996).

17. At the time of the resolution, Myanmar was not receiving any technical assistance and had received a total of only $1.5 million from 1991 through 1996. The ban on meetings is also more about symbolism than substance, because no member that is not in arrears on its dues can be barred from constitutionally authorized Governing Body and International Labor Conference meetings.

the portion imposing penalties. But a voice vote defeated this motion.[18] In March 2000, when Burma had still done nothing to remedy the forced labor situation, the Governing Body formally invoked Article 33 and recommended that the June 2000 International Labor Conference take action. It suggested that the conference call on member states "to review their relationship with the Government of Myanmar (Burma) and to take appropriate measures to ensure that Myanmar 'cannot take advantage of such relations to perpetuate or extend the system of forced or compulsory labour.'" It also recommended that the ILO call on other international organizations to consider whether their activities "could have the effect of directly or indirectly abetting the practice of forced or compulsory labour."

In May, the Burmese regime stopped denying that forced labor had occurred, and it invited the ILO to send a technical mission to discuss the problem. The regime admitted that forced labor had been a problem in the past but insisted it was no longer a problem and that Article 33 action was unnecessary. The technical mission, however, noted that the country had taken no concrete action to implement the Commission of Inquiry's recommendations. On May 27, just before the conference opened, the Burmese labor minister wrote to the director general, claiming that the country had taken steps against forced labor and would "take into consideration appropriate measures . . . to ensure the prevention of such occurrences in the future."[19]

Burma's East Asian neighbors seized on the apparent concessions and argued that the organization should delay a decision on Article 33 action and monitor the situation for another year. The workers' group at the International Labor Conference argued for immediate action. The employers' group proposed a compromise that called for conference approval of the measures proposed by the Governing Body but also for a delay in implementation until November 30, 2000, to test Burma's promise of more action. In October, Burma again tried to head off action by promising to change its laws, policies, and practices to end forced labor. But the ILO deemed this insufficient, and the Governing Body voted 52 to 4 to allow the June resolution to take effect, with only China, India, Malaysia, and Russia dissenting.[20]

By the spring of 2002, the Burmese regime had issued executive orders to bring its practices into compliance with Convention 29, but it still refused to amend the underlying law permitting forced labor. Bizarrely,

---

18. *ILO Focus,* Summer-Fall/Winter 1999, at www.us.ilo.org/news/focus/999/index.htm/ (May 9, 2003).

19. "Report of the ILO Technical Cooperation Mission to Myanmar," Provisional Record 8, International Labour Conference, 88th Session, Geneva, 2000.

20. *Washington Post,* November 17, 2000, Associated Press report.

the military argued that because it had not been democratically elected, it could not change the law. Despite ample evidence of continuing forced labor in many areas, particularly those in close proximity to military camps or facilities, the government also prosecuted no one for violations of the new orders.[21]

Later that year, Burma again headed off stronger action by agreeing to accept a permanent ILO liaison officer to oversee implementation of the forced labor ban. Unions, NGOs, and many others concerned with forced-labor in Burma remained frustrated that the problem continued. Yet as of the end of 2002, no government, international organization, or workers' or employers' group had informed the ILO that it had taken any action against Burma under the Article 33 resolution.[22]

The slow and tortuous response to Burmese intransigence underscores the unwillingness of the ILO membership to punish miscreants, even when the country in question is a small, poor, isolated one whose violations are egregious and well documented. The Article 33 resolution did not directly impose sanctions. It called on member governments and other UN organizations to take appropriate action, which for the most part they ignored.

In this respect, however, the ILO's authority does not differ much from that of the WTO, which also authorizes member governments to take action to remedy violations and does not directly impose them itself. Only the UN Security Council can *require* member governments to impose sanctions against another country. But countries have a greater incentive to enforce WTO rules than ILO ones. The complaining country in WTO disputes expects that its traded goods sector will benefit from improved compliance with WTO rules, whereas the main beneficiaries of compliance with ILO standards are primarily workers in the countries charged with noncompliance.

The ILO removed explicit reference to economic measures from its Constitution in 1946 for fear that newly independent LDCs would not join it if they could be threatened with economic sanctions. In addition, advanced countries felt economic sanctions had a limited ability to change behavior because progress would require a genuine commitment to change by domestic actors. The ILO viewed poor labor standards as primarily a problem of national law enforcement and favored international action to develop national capacity to implement labor standards.

The evidence from chapter 4 supports the skepticism that economic sanctions are a powerful tool for enforcing standards, particularly against large, powerful countries or on major problems such as the absence of

---

21. The report of the high-level team is available on the ILO Web site at www.ilo.org/public/english/standards/relm/gb/docs/gb282/pdf/gb-4ax.pdf (May 9, 2003).

22. Under pressure from a Burma-focused human rights campaign, however, a number of apparel manufacturers and retailers announced they would no longer produce in or import clothing from Burma.

freedom of association in nondemocratic countries. The lack of freedom of association in China provides a test of the ability of the ILO, and of the world community more generally, to improve labor rights in an economically important country through pressure and engagement without sanctions. China's arrests of workers seeking to form independent unions may generate reports but are unlikely to produce threats of Article 33 punishment. The $64,000 question is whether the combination of a spotlight on China's abuses and technical assistance in areas where China seeks to improve worker rights can raise other labor standards in the absence of genuine freedom of association. We return to this question in chapter 6.

The Role of the United States

The ILO's ability to deliver improvements in labor standards around the world depends greatly on the attitude and behavior of the United States. Americans, including American Federation of Labor President Samuel Gompers, helped create the ILO following World War I. But the US Senate's refusal to ratify the Versailles Treaty led the United States to postpone joining the ILO until 1934. The United States became increasingly frustrated by the politicization of the organization during the Cold War and withdrew again in the 1970s. It rejoined in 1980 and sharply increased its funding in the late 1990s, but there is already evidence that American enthusiasm is fading once again.

When the United States initially joined the ILO in the midst of the Great Depression, some politicians and labor advocates favored membership as a way around the Supreme Court's hostility to national regulation of labor markets. They believed an international treaty might override Supreme Court opposition to infringing states' rights in this area. Support for using the president's treaty power to strengthen federal regulation of labor markets faded once the Supreme Court upheld the Fair Labor Standards Act and other New Deal legislation. Instead, political concerns about international rules overriding state and local laws have prevented US ratification of most ILO conventions.[23]

After World War II, the ILO was incorporated into the UN system, where it became bogged down in Cold War and, later, Middle East antagonisms. The decision by the Soviet Union to rejoin the ILO (after having left in 1940) sparked a vigorous debate on the meaning of the ILO's

---

23. The United States has ratified 14 conventions (12 of which remain in force), half of them since 1988, and only two core conventions—105 on the abolition of forced labor and 182 on elimination of the worst forms of child labor. Half the conventions ratified relate to maritime issues (including the two that are no longer in force), which are regulated by the federal government, and the others are fairly narrow or technical.

tripartite structure. Labor and employer delegates are supposed to be free to vote as they please, regardless of the position of their government's delegates. But the ILO allowed the Soviet bloc countries to join and to send labor and employer delegates that followed their government's dictates, despite AFL-CIO President George Meany's strong opposition (Lorenz 2001, 126, 167–73, 194). Parts of the US business community, which had supported the ILO as "revolution insurance" in the aftermaths of the two world wars, also turned hostile to the organization. Postwar prosperity made revolution seem remote, and some US business leaders worried that the ILO's decision to expand standard setting beyond technical issues to such core principles as freedom of association might threaten their interests.[24]

In 1975, when the International Labor Conference voted to seat a Palestinian delegate while harshly criticizing Israel, Meany convinced US President Gerald Ford to announce that the United States would withdraw. This decision took effect in 1977 and reduced the ILO budget by a quarter. In response, the ILO sought to reestablish its credibility by condemning labor practices in Czechoslovakia (1978) and the Soviet Union (1979). President Jimmy Carter decided to rejoin in early 1980, and his successor, Ronald Reagan, turned to the ILO as a tool for helping workers in communist countries form free unions thereby undermining state control. In 1982, with strong backing from the United States, ILO conference delegates voted to initiate an Article 26 complaint against Poland for its treatment of the Solidarity trade union. That and strong support for black unions fighting apartheid in South Africa revived the ILO's credibility in the 1980s.

But the ILO did not move to the center of the globalization and labor standards debate until globalization enthusiasts seized upon it as a means to keep trade and labor issues separate. Bill Clinton's administration looked upon the ILO as a way to address US domestic union pressures on labor standards as it pushed free trade agreements. In its last few years in office, the Clinton administration sharply increased financial support for ILO initiatives. Being less concerned with the views of unions, George W. Bush's administration proposed sharp cuts in funding for the ILO and for promotion of labor standards in each of his first three years in office. But Congress maintained the appropriation for international labor standards at near-peak levels, at least in fiscal 2002 and 2003 (ILO Focus, spring 2002). At the Doha meeting of WTO ministers in November 2001 (held in relatively isolated Qatar to protect ministers against terrorists and to make it difficult for protesters and NGOs to converge in large numbers), the US Trade Representative gave tepid support to a European

---

24. ILO members approved Convention 87 on freedom of association in 1948, 98 on collective bargaining in 1949, 100 on equal remuneration in 1951, 105 on the abolition of forced labor in 1957, and 111 on nondiscrimination in employment in 1958.

Union proposal to encourage WTO participation in ILO discussions on the "social dimensions of globalization."

Thus strong US support for the ILO during Clinton's second term may prove to be a short-run blip in US-ILO relations. It reflected Clinton's desire to give something to labor and protesters in domestic politics as much as any fundamental commitment to the ILO's goals. The Bush administration's efforts to give something to labor took a very different turn: tariffs in the steel industry and support for construction of an Alaska oil pipeline. Following the successful launch of a new round of trade negotiations in November 2001 and congressional approval of "trade promotion authority" in 2002, the Bush administration's incentives to pay attention to the ILO faded further. Without US support and pressure to be more aggressive, the ILO's burst of activism also may fade.

Globalization and Labor Standards in Action

We didn't want foreign factories taking advantage of our workers either. And we wanted that quota increase—how else would we grow our economy?
—Cambodian Commerce Minister Cham Prasidh on the US-Cambodia agreement linking labor standards to apparel market access
(*Wall Street Journal*, February 28, 2000, 1)

Opposition by global enthusiasts and the absence of a social clause in trade agreements notwithstanding, trade pressures have contributed to improved labor standards in some less developed countries (LDCs). Having been threatened with consumer backlashes and trade restrictions due to child labor practices, Bangladeshi garment firms, Pakistani manufacturers of soccer balls, and cocoa growers in West Africa have worked with activists, governments, and international agencies to reduce child labor while providing better alternatives for the children. And Cambodia —promised increased access to the US market for apparel—has improved its enforcement of labor laws and international core labor standards. This chapter documents these successful cases of globalization and labor standards in action.

The chapter also examines the interplay between globalization and labor standards in China, the outcome of which we do not yet know. China's increased global engagement and entry into the World Trade Organization (WTO) have created both opportunities and risks in the market for standards. If pressures from global engagement induce China to improve standards more rapidly than otherwise, our case for the positive interplay of standards and globalization will be enhanced. But if China's joining the global economy buttresses repressive labor policies and pressures other countries to reduce standards, our case will be weakened.

The Bangladeshi Garment Sector

In the early 1990s, activists directed attention to the prevalence of child labor in Bangladeshi apparel production. In 1992, the NBC television news program *Dateline* ran a story showing children in a Bangladeshi factory sewing clothing destined for Wal-Mart (*New York Times*, December 24, 1992, D1).

At about the same time, the AFL-CIO petitioned the US government to suspend Bangladesh's eligibility for trade benefits under the Generalized System of Preferences (GSP) program, in part because of child labor. The interagency Trade Policy Staff Committee recommended against withdrawing GSP because Bangladesh was "taking steps" to rectify violations of internationally recognized workers' rights, but it stressed that child labor was indeed "the principal worker rights problem facing Bangladesh today." The committee also expressed concern about inadequate implementation of compulsory education legislation to give more children an alternative to work.[1]

What forced action on the child labor issue was the decision of Senator Tom Harkin (D-IA) to introduce in 1993 the "Child Labor Deterrence Act" to bar manufactured imports from any foreign industry that used child labor. The first response from Bangladesh was that the senator did not understand the situation: the children had to work to survive. Bangladeshi newspapers accused him of promoting child prostitution, for if children did not work in garment factories, they would be forced into the street (us.ilo.org/teachin/harkin.html, February 2003). And the initial response of Bangladeshi manufacturers, fearing they would lose access to a market that accounted for 43 percent of total apparel exports, was reportedly to fire an estimated 50,000 child workers. UNICEF and others investigating the case reported that many children were forced into worse situations, including prostitution and stone crushing (UNICEF 1997, 60). The fears of globalization enthusiasts that trade threats would end up doing more harm than good seemed justified.[2]

---

1. The Trade Policy Staff Committee "Worker Rights Review Summary" for Bangladesh (Case 008-CP-91) is available in the Office of the US Trade Representative, Washington.

2. We have been unable to track down an often-cited Oxfam report allegedly confirming the UNICEF findings. UNICEF's *State of the World's Children 1997* referred to "follow-up visits by UNICEF," local nongovernmental organizations, and the International Labor Organization finding children in prostitution and other hazardous activities, but offers no specifics and no citations for these reports. Some activists and nongovernmental organizations question the reports of mass firings and large numbers of girls being forced into prostitution. E.g., the International Labor Rights Fund reported in 1995 that

But the initial firing of the children was just the beginning of the response to the child labor issue. American nongovernmental organizations (NGOs), supported by the US ambassador to Bangladesh, pressured the Bangladesh Garment Manufacturers and Exporters Association to find a more constructive solution. The negotiations between the activists and the association took two years to conclude, waxing and waning depending on the seriousness with which the exporters viewed the threat of US sanctions (Harvey 1995). The Republican victory in the 1994 congressional elections stalled the talks, because the Bangladeshi manufacturers and exporters expected the Republicans to bury the Harkin bill.

In May 1995, members rejected the agreement negotiated by the trade association and decided to fire all underage workers within a few months to avoid any potential loss of exports. Shortly thereafter, however, the US Child Labor Coalition reluctantly notified its members and the American and Bangladeshi press that it would call for boycott of Bangladeshi clothing. This threat led to a resumption of negotiations four days later.

At this stage, the International Labor Organization (ILO) joined UNICEF in the negotiations. On July 4, 1995, the ILO and UNICEF signed a memorandum of understanding with Bangladeshi manufacturers and exporters that provided that all children working in the sector would be removed when schools were available for them, and that the firms would hire no new children. The parties also agreed on joint funding and a monitoring plan to be overseen by the ILO. The Bangladeshi employers committed about $1 million over three years, and the ILO and UNICEF contributed $425,000 in the initial year to ensure that the children would indeed benefit after losing their jobs. In the first year of the agreement, UNICEF reported that the program enrolled 4,000 children in school.

The program succeeded in nearly eliminating child labor in the Bangladeshi apparel sector and seems to have succeeded as well in creating better opportunities for the affected children. The proportion of factories using child labor dropped from 43 percent in 1995 to less than 4 percent by 2000. The number of children working in garment factories fell by 27,000, and about 8,000 children received educational or other rehabilitative services. In 2000, the ILO, the government of Bangladesh, and Bangladeshi garment manufacturers agreed to broaden the program to other core standards and health and safety issues under the technical cooperation program promoting the ILO Declaration on Fundamental Principles and Rights at Work.[3]

"informed sources agree that the children have simply been relocated to less visible factories, particularly small subcontractors" (*Worker Rights News*, Fall 1994–Winter 1995, 1).

3. See ILO (2001); IPEC (1999); US Department of Labor (1998, 89); and Vahapassi (2000, 3, 11).

Pakistani Soccer Balls

In 1996, an American activist group, the International Labor Rights Fund, launched the Foul Ball campaign to mobilize consumer and player pressure on Nike, Adidas, and other major marketers of soccer balls because the firms sourced from producers in Pakistan using child labor. The firms' trade association, the International Federation of Football Associations (FIFA)—worried about fan response to the image of youngsters in advanced countries kicking balls made by poorly treated child workers in LDCs—adopted a code of labor practices for all manufacturers of balls carrying the FIFA label. The FIFA code barred child labor and called for the manufacturers to protect freedom of association and adhere to other labor standards.

Although the International Labor Rights Fund claimed it was done to blunt implementation of the stronger FIFA code, the Sialkot (Pakistan) Chamber of Commerce and Industry (representing soccer ball manufacturers) signed an agreement with the ILO and UNICEF to reduce child labor and provide health and training services to the children removed from work.[4] The Pakistani Chamber of Commerce and the US Department of Labor funded the program, and the ILO was given responsibility for monitoring the agreement. Save the Children, a British NGO, and the Bunyad Literacy Community Council, a Pakistani NGO, agreed to provide health services, vocational training, and microcredit and savings schemes for affected workers (ILO 2001, 112).

The effort to reduce the use of child labor in the sector succeeded. In October 1999, the ILO's International Program on the Elimination of Child Labor reported that more than 90 percent of the production of soccer balls by participating manufacturers had moved to stitching centers subject to monitoring and that the monitors had found no children working in those stitching centers. In addition, the ILO reported that about 6,000 children had been enrolled in the village education and action centers created by the program (IPEC 1999).

There have been problems in implementation, however. A key part of the agreement created stitching centers where employers or officials could monitor who did the work. Previously, the stitching of soccer balls was often done at home by mothers and children working together. The stitching centers created problems for some women who had rarely worked outside the home or who had no one to take care of their children. The program addressed these issues by encouraging the manufacturers to

---

4. Not long after this agreement, two other projects were launched in Pakistan by the International Program on the Elimination of Child Labor. The first, also in the Sialkot region, targeted the use of child labor by subcontractors in the production of surgical instruments, and the second focused on small-scale carpet weaving in two districts of Punjab (Vahapassi 2000, 4–5).

create stitching centers in villages close to where the women workers lived, but it is possible that some adults were displaced. In addition, the International Labor Rights Fund argued that some production moved across the border to India and that the ILO report on outcomes in Pakistan was overly optimistic. An early assessment by the fund argued that some firms had moved production to nonparticipating facilities or subcontracted out production, potentially done by children (International Labor Rights Fund 1999). Still, there were no mass firings, and at least 6,000 children were educated who otherwise would not have been.

West African Cocoa

In the late 1990s and early 2000s, international agencies and the news media reported that cocoa farms in West Africa were using forced child labor. UNICEF reported in 1998 that recruiters were trafficking in children from neighboring countries and forcing them into labor on cocoa farms in Côte d'Ivoire. In July 2001, the US newspaper chain Knight-Ridder ran a series of investigative articles profiling young boys who were tricked or sold as slaves to Ivorian cocoa farmers. In that same year, Ivorian authorities stopped a ship trying to smuggle child workers into the country, producing headlines in newspapers around the world. Shortly thereafter, the ILO's global report on child labor identified West African trafficking in children as one of the most blatant violations of core labor standards.

These reports created a problem for chocolate makers in advanced countries, which feared lost sales from consumers associating child labor with their candies. Within days of the discussion of the child labor report at the International Labor Conference in June 2001, participants in the cocoa market moved to head off a consumer backlash. Côte d'Ivoire's prime minister declared that farmers must be paid more to eliminate child exploitation, and then announced a government campaign to reduce child labor. The US Chocolate Manufacturers Association said that it would fund a study of the problem by the US Agency for International Development. In Congress, Representative Elliot Engel (D-NY) attached an amendment to the fiscal 2002 agriculture appropriations bill to provide funds for the Food and Drug Administration to create a "no child slavery" label for chocolate products.

A few months later, the global confectionery industry developed a protocol listing the specific steps that it would take to address the problem. Representative Engel, Senator Harkin, and a number of NGOs, including the Child Labor Coalition and Free the Slaves, endorsed the protocol. The ILO agreed to serve as an official adviser to the initiative. Keeping pressure on the industry, the International Labor Rights Fund petitioned the US Customs Service to investigate cocoa imports under the US law that prohibits the importation of products made with forced child labor. The fund argued that "an investigation by US Customs will provide a strong incentive to the Côte d'Ivoire government and to the cocoa exporters to solve the problem of forced child labor."[5]

In July 2002, the industry announced the creation of the International Cocoa Initiative to act as a clearinghouse for information on forced child labor and on practices to resolve it; to support pilot projects in the field; and to "help determine the most appropriate, practical and independent means of monitoring and public reporting in compliance with these labour standards."[6] Shortly thereafter, the US Department of Labor and US Agency for International Development released survey results that found roughly 300,000 children working in hazardous conditions on cocoa farms in West Africa, most of them children under the age of 14 years, and all but 12,000 of them on family farms. Among the unrelated children working on cocoa farms in Côte d'Ivoire and Nigeria, the surveys reported that about 2,500 children had been trafficked from neighboring countries.[7]

In October 2002, the ILO began a three-year, $6 million effort to develop programs to remove children from forced labor and to provide them with education or other training, replace at least some of the income lost to the family, and build capacity among workers and inspectors to prevent forced child labor in the sector from recurring in the future (*ILO Focus*, Winter 2003, 15). The programs resembled those in Pakistan and Bangladesh. The US Department of Labor provided the largest share of the funding for this initiative. The rapid movement from investigation and discussion of the problem to action shows how trade links can improve labor standards quickly in a particularly egregious case.

All three of these child labor cases show the market for standards at work in essentially the manner described in chapter 2, with one extra element: financial support from international organizations or US government agencies to make sure that the changes in standards benefit the children. In these cases, the combined work of all the groups—activists, firms, LDC governments, the US government, and the ILO—produced improved standards and conditions.

The US-Cambodia Textile and Apparel Agreement

The use of trade pressure to raise labor standards in Cambodia took a different path. In the absence of an activist campaign targeting conditions

---

5. International Labor Rights Fund, June 27, 2002, www.laborrights.org/press/cocoa/ 053102.htm (May 2003).

6. See www.international-confectionery.com/issues.asp (May 2003).

7. The summary is available on the department's Web site, www.dol.gov/ilab/media/ reports/iclp/cocoafindings.pdf (May 2003).

in Cambodia, the US government took the initiative and offered a positive trade incentive in exchange for Cambodian compliance with the core labor standards. In 1998, the United States and Cambodia signed a bilateral trade agreement that included a US commitment to expand Cambodia's quota for textile and apparel exports to the US market by 14 percent if "working conditions in the Cambodia textile and apparel sector substantially comply with" local law and internationally recognized core standards.

In December 1999, US officials reviewed labor standards in Cambodia and concluded that although Cambodia had not achieved "substantial compliance," it had made progress. US trade officials offered a 5 percent quota increase if Cambodia would allow the ILO to monitor factories in the sector. Initially, the ILO was leery of undertaking the monitoring, but it agreed to the plan when US officials promised to provide $500,000 for a parallel program to provide technical assistance and training to the Cambodian labor ministry. The United States also provided $1 million of the $1.4 million cost of the three-year monitoring program with the Cambodian government and Garment Manufacturers' Association, splitting the balance (press release, Office of the US Trade Representative, May 18, 2000).

In May 2000, US officials granted the initial 5 percent quota expansion, and they added another 4 percent the following September in recognition of further improvements in workers' rights. The total 9 percent quota expansion was extended for 2001, but the United States withheld the remaining 5 percent potential increase as an incentive for continued improvement (*Inside U.S. Trade*, January 19, 2001). One estimate of the value of the 14 percent increase was $50 million a year, far in excess of the costs to the Cambodians of improving standards. Cambodian Commerce Minister Cham Prasidhthat said, moreover, that his country was interested in more than just the quota increase because "we didn't want foreign factories taking advantage of our workers either" (*Wall Street Journal*, February 28, 2000, 1).

But even though the United States and Cambodia were happy with the agreement, other LDCs and US importers opposed it and tried to discourage Cambodia from accepting the bargain because it set a precedent linking trade and labor standards. US importers claimed that Cambodia was benefiting little if at all from the agreement, because the initial quota level was set below that of other comparable exporting countries.[8] When the

---

8. *Inside U.S. Trade*, February 5, 1999, 13. It is difficult to test this claim, but data on quota levels elsewhere in Southeast Asia do not appear to support it. Using per capita textile and apparel exports under the Multi-Fiber Arrangement as a crude measure, the figure for Cambodia was 24 square meters per person, which compares with 8.2 for the Association of Southeast Asian Nations as a whole, 9 for Bangladesh, 12.4 for the Philippines, 21.3 for Thailand, and 5 for Indonesia (US Department of Commerce, Office of Textiles and Apparel, "Major Shippers Report," March 2001; International Monetary Fund, *International Financial Statistics*, for population figures).

United States did not grant the full quota increase, critics claimed that the US government was not sincere and that unions with protectionist motives were driving its decisions. But the Union of Needletrades, Industrial, and Textile Employees (UNITE) supported the partial quota increases granted in 2000 and 2001, and only the American Textile Manufacturers Institute, representing the industry, opposed it (*Inside U.S. Trade,* January 19, 2001).

The agreement appears to have improved conditions in the Cambodian garment sector. Wages and benefits rose, and the Cambodian government stepped up its monitoring of working conditions.[9] Perhaps most important, the incentives in the agreement, the presence of ILO inspectors, and the knowledge gained by the workers led some to form unions and demand changes in working conditions.[10] The AFL-CIO opened a Solidarity Center office there to provide training on how to set up and run a union. Since 1997, unions have organized 75 garment factories. And in July 2000, garment workers successfully pressured the government to establish Cambodia's first minimum wage ($45 a month) (*New York Times,* July 12, 2001).

The experiment also produced new standards for independent, transparent factory monitoring. By the end of 2002, the ILO had released its first four reports on conditions in the factories, including a follow-up report that summarized problems in individual factories and what managers had done to resolve them.[11] ILO monitors had inspected 129 of Cambodia's roughly 200 registered garment facilities, with an employment of more than 125,000 workers, most of them female (out of a total garment industry employment of roughly 200,000).

The monitors reported no evidence of child labor or forced labor. They found no evidence of sexual harassment in the first 30 factories inspected, but some evidence that harassment existed in the next 65. The most frequent violations of Cambodian labor law were incorrect wage payments and involuntary and excessive overtime work, but there were also problems with freedom of association in some facilities.

Even though ILO inspectors do not have enforcement powers, their identification of problems and recommendations for remediation nevertheless induced manufacturers to make some changes. On follow-up visits, the ILO determined that manufacturers had implemented 40 percent of the improvements the monitors had suggested. By the time of the follow-up visit, the most responsive facility had implemented 94 percent of the monitors' suggestions, and the least responsive only 6 percent.[12]

9. *Wall Street Journal,* February 28, 2000, 1; *Financial Times,* April 7, 2000, 5.

10. *Time* (Asian edition), July 10, 2000.

11. All the reports are available on the Social Dialogue section of the ILO Web site, www.ilo.org/public/english/dialogue/ifpdial/publ/cambodia.htm (May 2003).

12. These figures are calculated from the ILO's "Third Synthesis Report on the Working Conditions Situation in Cambodia's Garment Sector."

In early 2002, George W. Bush's administration negotiated a three-year extension of the bilateral agreement and retained a quota-growth incentive for Cambodia to continue to improve labor standards compliance. But the agreement did not bring the country's most rapidly growing exports under the quota, making it unclear how much of an incentive the in-quota growth bonus will have.[13] The ILO project director also reported "monitoring fatigue" in Cambodia because some factories had to submit to monitoring of multiple codes required by individual buyers. Factory owners or managers can share monitoring results with buyers if they wish, but the ILO cannot do so. And in the absence of a mutual recognition agreement among the various multistakeholder initiatives, such sharing of information may not be enough for some buyers.

Still, the Garment Manufacturers Association appears committed to the program of improving standards and monitoring results. It hopes this will give Cambodia a reputation for good standards and stable industrial relations that will appeal to brand-name buyers.[14] The test will be whether such a reputation enables Cambodia to carve out a niche for its exports after the Multi-Fiber Arrangement (MFA)[15]—which uses bilateral quotas to regulate international trade in textiles and apparel—expires in 2005.

Can Globalization Improve Labor Standards in China?

What happens in China is important for labor standards around the world. Because a large proportion of the global workforce is Chinese, changes in China's standards affect more people than changes in dozens of smaller countries. In the 1990s, the world rate of poverty fell substantially, despite rises of poverty in Africa, the countries of the former Soviet Union, Eastern Europe, and Latin America. The principal reason: poverty fell in China and India, with their huge populations. China's entry into the global economy and accession to the WTO also means that Chinese labor market developments will have large repercussions for workers elsewhere in the world. Policymakers and leaders in many LDCs worry that China

---

13. According to one source, Cambodia's uncontrolled exports in the fall of 2001 were two and a half times larger than its exports under the quota (*Inside U.S. Trade,* January 11, 2002, 15).

14. The source for this is a presentation by Lejo Sebbel, the Cambodian project director, to a workshop of the National Academies Committee on Monitoring Labor Standards.

15. Under the MFA, the United States and European Union restrict imports of textiles and apparel through country-specific import quotas. This has the effect of creating a competitive advantage for low-productivity countries that have unfilled quotas, whereas more productive suppliers cannot increase sales due to the constraints of the quota system.

will dominate world textile and apparel production when the Multi-Fiber Arrangement expires. Many are concerned that they will be unable to maintain wages and standards in their country if Chinese wages and standards fail to rise rapidly.

The Problem in China

China has a huge problem with labor standards, both in the contracting state-owned sector and in the growing private or semiprivate sector (see Hankin 2002). In the 1990s, the country dismantled large parts of the state-owned sector, laying off 25 million to 30 million workers and creating substantial unemployment and economic misery. In the prereform planned economy, state-owned enterprises provided not just jobs but also many of the benefits and protections that governments provide in capitalist economies: health care, housing, pensions, even schooling for the children of workers. The employees in these enterprises had lifetime job security.

As these enterprises have contracted, privatized, or closed down, they have not paid retirees or laid-off workers the amounts that they had contracted to pay and in many cases have fallen behind in paying wages to their workers. According to statistics from the All-China Federation of Trade Unions (ACFTU), nearly 14 million staff and workers were owed back pay in 1999, 7 percent of the urban workforce. An additional 3.6 million workers who had retired or resigned also were owed money. The number of staff and workers owed wages increased nearly sixfold from 1993 to 1999, while the number of retirees owed money increased nearly tenfold.[16]

Lost jobs and failure to be paid what they are legally due has led many Chinese workers to protest, marching in the streets, blocking railway lines, and surrounding government offices. The largest workers' protests reported by Hong Kong and the Western media usually have been about arrears, with workers angered at companies or the government reneging on promises to provide benefits. The protests are concentrated in such provinces as Liaoning, where there is little business growth to absorb the laid-off workers and where the government and firms lack the funds to pay retirees what their former state-owned enterprise had contracted to give them. As an indication of the rising tide of discontent, the number of labor disputes accepted by official arbitration committees grew from 8,150 in 1992 to 327,152 in 2000. The number of unofficial protests also increased greatly, although the only data we have are media reports.[17]

China's new and growing private sector has experienced a different set

---

16. Research Office of the All-China Federation of Trade Unions, *Chinese Trade Union Statistics Yearbook*, Beijing, various years.

17. All-China Federation of Trade Unions, *Yearbook of Labour Statistics*, various years. Also see Freeman (2002).

of problems. Chinese labor laws are comparable to those in advanced countries, save for the country's treatment of freedom of association.[18] If enforced, the laws would guarantee decent working conditions for most workers. But private-sector employers, including foreign investors, regularly flout labor laws. Many employers do not pay for required overtime work. Many ignore rules on occupational safety to the extent that China has one of the world's worst records in workplace fatalities and injuries. In the 1990s, China reported 133 fatalities per 100,000 workers in mining, compared with 50 in eight LDCs with comparable data and 24 in the United States (Freeman 2002, exhibit 4). Almost every week, the Chinese press reports on mine disasters. In Guangdong Province, firms flout China's labor laws by forcing hours in excess of the legal maximum, withholding wages due to workers, and abusing workers in diverse ways (Chan 2001).

One leading human rights vigilante group, the National Labor Committee, examined conditions in Chinese toy factories and reported mandatory daily shifts of more than 15 hours, 7-day workweeks, toxic paints and chemicals, 104-degree factory temperatures, and 16 workers sharing a single dorm room in the factory's living quarters.[19] The most poorly treated workers are almost always migrants from rural communities, who do not know their rights under Chinese law and who have no chance to bargain with management for better conditions. No one disputes the existence of horrific conditions in many private firms. The Chinese government recognizes the problem, as do most globalization enthusiasts.

With the exception of union rights, the problem in China is not one of deficient labor laws but of deficient enforcement. There are three main reasons for China's inability to enforce its laws. First, China's government-controlled trade union monopoly (the All China Federation of Trade Unions) is a major obstacle. The ACFTU is an old-fashioned "transmission belt" union movement, which follows the dictates of party leaders and local officials. At various times in its history, the ACFTU has sought greater independence from the state; but since the Tiananmen Square massacre in 1989, the government has kept it under strict control. ACFTU cadres and officials are generally sympathetic to workers' concerns, but they side with management and the state whenever workers have a serious problem.

In the fall of 2001, China enacted legislation to enhance the ACFTU's authority to organize private enterprises and to help enforce labor laws. But the law still puts the party's interests ahead of those of the workers that the organization nominally represents, requiring the ACFTU to "take economic development as the central task, uphold the socialist road, the people's democratic dictatorship, [and] leadership by the Communist Party of China" (quoted in Hankin 2002, n. 1).

---

18. See www.china-tradenet.com/english/a14.htm (December 2002).

19. See www.nlcnet.org/china/1201/toysofmisery.pdf (December 2002).

The second reason China cannot enforce much of its labor code is the widespread corruption in the government and ruling Communist Party. The businesses that violate labor rights range from foreign-owned firms to Chinese private enterprises. Many have links to local or national party or government leaders and most pay taxes to the local government. Transparency International gave China poor scores on both its Corruption Perceptions Index and its Bribe Payers Index. That China does so poorly on both rankings underscores the pervasiveness of its corruption, among both officials and firms, including China-based firms operating abroad.[20] In China's own assessments, corruption always comes up as one of its two or three major problems. Workers' protests are often motivated by the belief that the privatization of state-owned properties has been done for the benefit of corrupt managers and officials, who transfer the valuable parts of businesses to themselves and leave the state with a shell enterprise.

The third and most sensitive reason China cannot enforce its labor code is that the government is unwilling to allow workers to form independent trade unions for fear that such organizations would eventually challenge the state's authority. In 2002, the government was so worried about alternative sources of authority that it clamped down on a local initiative that would have improved labor standards and enhanced social stability. A former migrant worker tried to organize a "nonprofit, nonpolitical migrant workers' association" in a heavily migrant neighborhood to give workers a mechanism for resolving disputes with their employers. Local officials supported the idea as a means of lowering crime by disgruntled migrants with no connection to the local community.

After the migrant workers' association had successfully intervened on behalf of workers in a few disputes, workers eagerly joined. But as the association gathered steam and local officials encouraged the creation of similar groups in other neighborhoods and nearby towns, higher-up officials stepped in. Fearing that the associations might become a source of independent power outside their control, they moved to shut them down (*Washington Post*, October 15, 2002, A1). Because the most effective way to deal with low labor standards is to give workers the ability to defend their own interests, China has put itself in a box on this issue.

Roads to Improvement

Will China's growing global engagement encourage improvement in workers' rights, or will it legitimize an outmoded, internationally illegitimate system? What can activists in both advanced countries and China

---

20. See www.transparency.org/cpi/index.html#cpi (February 2003). In 2001, China ranked 59th in a list of 102 countries. China was rated as having less corruption than Russia, Bangladesh, Nigeria, and India, among larger LDCs. Chinese companies are widely seen as using bribes in developing countries as well. China was the second worst country in terms of using bribes, based on the Transparency International ranking of 21 countries.

do to pressure the country to improve labor standards and free workers to form their own organizations?

There is substantial debate over these questions among those concerned with the well-being of Chinese labor. In the late 1990s, the AFL-CIO opposed China's entry into the WTO, in part because of concerns about workers' rights. According to one spokesperson, "Our view is that once China comes into the WTO, we have no leverage to raise the worker rights problems anymore."[21] Similarly, the AFL-CIO and many other unions were appalled in 2002 when worker delegates to the ILO elected the ACFTU as a worker representative on the ILO's Governing Body.

In this vote, the ACFTU was supported by many LDCs, some of which had been courted by China and some of which wanted the Israeli Histradut removed from the governing body because of the Israeli-Palestinian dispute. The global federation of unions in the food sector denounced the ACFTU's accession to the ILO Governing Body as a "sellout" of China's workers.[22] In the aftermath of these events, some union and human rights activists continue to argue for limiting engagement with China because of its lack of freedom of association (Diamond 2003).

On the other side of this debate are other union and human rights activists, who favor increased engagement with China to strengthen Chinese efforts to improve labor standards. Our analysis suggests how increased trade with China and its greater engagement with the global community could be used to improve labor standards and hasten the time when the country's leadership will recognize that independent unions are more likely to enhance than reduce social stability and economic progress. Just as elsewhere in the market for standards, traded goods can become a lightning rod directing attention to low standards and efforts to improve them. Rather than reduce leverage to help Chinese workers, our analysis suggests that a larger role for China in the global economy will increase it.

Already, there is a two-pronged effort to move China along the road to higher standards. As the country's trade increases, human rights vigilantes are devoting even more attention to its working conditions. It is critical to identify and publicize violations of workers' rights and the Chinese government's suppression of dissidents, and to continue to support workers' efforts to organize independent organizations. The National Labor Committee and diverse human rights activist groups—those that produce the *China Labour Bulletin*, Human Rights Watch in China, and others in Hong Kong and the West—must continue to galvanize public opinion and bring transparency to the practices of firms operating there.[23]

---

21. See http://seattlepi.nwsource.com/business/chi09.shtml (December 2002).

22. See www.hartford-hwp.com/archives/55/293.html (December 2002).

23. See, among others, http://iso.hrichina.org/iso/ and www.china-labour.org.hk/iso/index.adp.

At the same time, there is also increased engagement with Chinese authorities by other groups and institutions with the purpose of strengthening the position of those in China who seek to improve standards and reform the outmoded ACFTU. Some observers believe that the labor law passed in the fall of 2001 opens up space for workers to form "bottom-up unions that are nominally affiliated to the ACFTU" (Hankin 2002, n. 20). As is discussed below, some NGOs and firms are already experimenting to test this proposition.

The ILO has the potential to play a major role in the engagement process. It suspended cooperation with China after the Tiananmen Square massacre, but it resumed technical assistance in 1996, engaging the ACFTU and employers organizations, as well as government officials. In 2001, the ILO signed a memorandum of understanding with Chinese authorities to promote a decent work agenda, including improvements in the core labor standards.[24] Although ILO technical assistance in the late 1990s focused primarily on employment creation, the projects contemplated under the memorandum include one "promoting workplace democracy and improved industrial relations," which has been approved by representatives of the government, employers, and the ACFTU and for which funding was being sought in 2002. Other priorities under the memorandum include creating and strengthening social safety nets and continued attention to employment creation. At the same time, ILO officials and experts continue to criticize China's policies on freedom of association and on the "reeducation" of political dissidents through forced labor.[25]

Multinational corporations also are taking steps to improve standards in their Chinese operations, though as National Labor Committee reports show, they have a long way to go. One route some corporations are trying is creating employee committees on health and safety, which give workers a say in conditions and provide an informal mechanism for addressing grievances. The Levi Strauss Foundation is also working with the Asia Foundation in China on projects focused on migrant women workers in the Guangdong area, including providing education and health services and legal aid.

Reebok went further in the fall of 2001. It worked with the Hong Kong Christian Industrial Committee and Jonathan Unger and Anita Chan of the Contemporary China Center at the Australian National University to organize and monitor a secret ballot election of union representatives at two footwear factories in Fujian and Guangdong. The factories are Taiwanese owned but were pressured by Reebok to hold open elections; local government officials went along because the Taiwanese investors

24. See www.ilo.org/public/english/chinaforum/download/chinamou.pdf (March 2002).

25. See the presentation by Anthony Freeman, director of the ILO's Washington Branch Office, before the Congressional Executive Commission on China, March 18, 2002; www.cecc.gov/pages/roundtables/031802/briefingnotes.pdf (March 2002).

are important employers in the region (*Financial Times*, December 12, 2002, 14).

According to Doug Cahn, Reebok's director of human rights programs, organizing the elections took months of negotiation with the Taiwanese managers, local officials, and representatives of the ACFTU. Cahn noted that Reebok has a code of conduct that includes respect for freedom of association and collective bargaining and added,

> [W]e can throw up our hands in China and say: "The ACFTU is government-controlled and therefore we can do nothing." Or we can engage in experiments like this in democratizing the union in hope that workers will take advantage of the opportunities this provides them. (*Financial Times*, December 12, 2002, 14)

Though an encouraging example, this union is still officially affiliated with the ACFTU, and it remains too early to tell whether management, local officials, and the ACFTU will respect the independence of the new union leadership in representing worker interests.

Activists both inside and outside China are also working in a variety of ways to support workers and raise labor standards without directly challenging the one-party state. Activists have set up help lines for workers, sometimes with the support of local government officials, and are educating workers about their rights (Senser 2002, 40). The Institute of Contemporary Observation in Shenzen, with support from Oxfam Hong Kong, has a labor hotline on which workers can get free legal advice on work-related problems (see www.ico-china.org).

Another Chinese group has a Web site that offers information on Chinese labor law and advice to workers.[26] Han Dongfang is a former political prisoner who is now exiled in Hong Kong because of his union organizing activities during the Tiananmen Square protests. He hosts a Radio Free Asia show and writes an Internet e-newsletter to inform workers of their rights and how to use the law to defend themselves.[27] He also notes that workers filing lawsuits for labor law violations against American and other foreign-owned companies may have the best chance because they can invoke the theme of unfair exploitation by foreigners in their behalf (*American Educator*, Winter 2002, 43). The US Congressional Executive Commission on China also has recommended increased US government financial and technical support for training labor lawyers and others to help Chinese workers use the law to protect their interests.

---

25. The source for this is a presentation by Yiu Por Chen at the Networked Labor Conference, London School of Economics and Political Science, London, December 6, 2000.

26. The *China Labour Bulletin* is available at www.china-labour.org.hk (February 2002). See also the Asia Monitor Resource Center at www.amrc.org.hk/home.htm (February 2002).

Finally, Chinese decision makers are as threatened by the potentially destabilizing effects of growing worker protests as by the nascent attempts by workers to form independent organizations to represent their interests. With both continuing pressure from activists and engagement by the ILO and multinational corporations, Chinese officials may be moved in the direction of giving the ACFTU greater independence in defending workers and, in some cases, of accepting bottom-up, local worker associations such as those formed indigenously by migrant workers in eastern China or encouraged by Reebok in southern China.

A Bottom-Line Assessment

This chapter's analysis of the developments in Bangladesh, Pakistan, Côte d'Ivoire, and Cambodia has demonstrated that trade pressure and incentives from consumers and governments can lead to improved labor standards in LDCs. It has also shown that cooperation from governments and international agencies, notably the ILO, has been important in ensuring that activist pressure produces the desired outcomes. The ILO's role in these cases suggests that it could do more to assist firms and consumers in sorting through the various codes and monitoring procedures, perhaps setting out some minimum standard for acceptable codes of conduct.

The interplay of trade and labor standards in China has yet to produce a clear direction of change in standards. The more China deals with countries through trade and investment flows, the greater is the potential for activists, corporations, and unions to move China along the road toward higher standards and eventual freedom of association. We anticipate that a mix of pressure from both domestic and foreign activists and from democratic governments concerned with human rights, along with technical assistance to the Chinese government on ways to improve standards, will eventually yield more evidence for our thesis that trade and standards together offer the best chance to improve the lives of workers in LDCs.

7

When Does Doing Good Do Good?

The moral face of these developed-country lobbies agitating for higher labor and environmental standards in the developing countries, whether they are labor unions or corporate groups, is little more than a mask which hides the true face of protectionism.
—Jagdish Bhagwati, Columbia University professor
and principal author of the Third World Intellectuals'
and NGOs' Statement Against Linkage (TWIN-SAL)[1]

How can it be considered protectionist to say that people deserve the same protection as companies? That is all that the proponents of labor rights at the WTO are asking for and why we want to see respect for core labor standards included within the WTO.
—Response to TWIN-SAL by the
International Confederation of Free Trade Unions[2]

The antisweatshop movement brought the labor standards issue to the fore in discussions of globalization. Activists have pressured firms to develop codes of conduct and have helped create a small industry of monitoring organizations. But have these successes in the battle for labor standards translated into improved working conditions? Or have they made it more difficult for poor countries to export to rich ones?

We conclude this book by assessing the accomplishments and failures of the antisweatshop campaigns and by suggesting ways to make the campaigns more effective in doing good in the global economy. We also recommend steps that the key international economic institutions can take to amplify workers' voices and to bring more balance to the globalization process—the bottom line in judging the battle for labor standards.

---

1. See www.columbia.edu/~jb38/twin_sal.pdf (April 13, 2003).

2. See www.icftu.org/displaydocument.asp?Index=9909161688Language=EN (May 6, 2003).

Assessing the Achievements of the Antisweatshop Campaigns

The aims of the antisweatshop activists are twofold: first, to stimulate consumer demand and create a "market for global labor standards"; second, to induce governments and international institutions to adopt social clauses that equate the protection given to labor with that given to capital and intellectual property. Less developed country (LDC) governments and officials of the international institutions fear that external pressures to raise standards will raise costs enough to lower LDC exports and thereby reduce the number of jobs available to poor workers. Worse, these officials fear that the push for trade sanctions to enforce standards masks a protectionist motivation that would lower LDC exports even further.

The evidence analyzed in this book leads us to reject the assertion that antisweatshop campaigns are disguised protectionism or that they have had adverse effects on workers. The human rights groups, students, and church groups that make up the activist community do not compete with low-paid workers in LDCs. If they succeed in their campaigns, they raise the prices of the goods they consume.

These groups also recognize that poor countries need more manufacturing jobs to improve people's lives and oppose shifting business from less developed to advanced countries as part of their campaigns. For instance, the United Students Against Sweatshops, which has close ties with the Union of Needletrades, Industrial, and Textile Employees (UNITE), opposes firms shifting production of college logo clothing to US factories (Moore 2000, 10). And the National Labor Committee mounts campaigns against firms not just for low standards but also for abandoning workers in LDCs when conditions in their suppliers come under criticism, as Disney did in Bangladesh and Haiti (www.nlcnet.org).

Whatever the motivation of the activists, globalization enthusiasts point to the firing of children by Bangladeshi garment manufacturers in the early 1990s as evidence of how campaigns can have unintended consequences. But this was not the intent of the activists, and their critics either do not know or ignore the part of the story in which the activists kept the pressure on until the manufacturers agreed to work with the International Labor Organization (ILO) and UNICEF to build schools and rehabilitate the children.[3] Indeed, chapter 6 documents other campaigns that have resulted in similar multistakeholder initiatives to remove children from work and to provide educational, rehabilitative, and other services for them and their families. Although a drop in the bucket of

---

3. Globalization enthusiasts Brown, Deardorff, and Stern (2003, 41–42) mention this case as a generally successful effort to address child labor. But they mention neither the role of trade threats nor the role of the activists in negotiating the agreement.

child labor, thousands of child workers have received these services, ensuring a positive outcome for the children.

More broadly, though activists have thus far failed in their goal of incorporating social clauses into trade agreements, they have begun to succeed in building a market for standards beyond just child labor. Human rights vigilante campaigns have catalyzed consumer sentiment sufficiently so that most major retailers and marketers have developed corporate codes of conduct that address labor standards. Many of the more visible brand-name firms have also put considerable resources into implementing and monitoring these codes.

Activist campaigns have also led firms and interested groups to create a monitoring industry that would never have existed otherwise. Although the Fair Labor Association is weaker than many activists would like, its creation and that of Social Accountability International's SA8000 standard are products of their campaigns, as are the procedural improvements adopted by the Fair Labor Association in April 2002. However personally committed Reebok managers are to human rights, it is doubtful that they would have put so much effort into organizing union elections in China in the absence of activist pressure.

Yet the successes have been limited. Campaigns to harness consumer demand for labor standards are inherently limited because they target conditions in the production of brand-name goods in export markets rather than conditions in the agricultural and informal sectors in LDCs, where workers are worse off. Consumers care most about the working conditions associated with products they personally consume and, in any case, they cannot directly affect conditions in nontrade sectors. Other limitations with antisweatshop campaigns arise from the nature of the supply chains in the garment industry. High-end retailers and marketers are both more vulnerable, because they have usually invested heavily in brand image, and better able to enforce compliance with standards, because they use a smaller number of stable suppliers. Activists have a harder time targeting firms selling unbranded generic varieties.

In addition, discount retailers, such as Wal-Mart, usually have much longer and more flexible supply chains. They also often use intermediary buyers to locate suppliers, making it harder for them to enforce codes of conduct—if they have them. But even the most successful activist campaign will improve standards for only a small proportion of workers because the export sector accounts for a relatively small share of employment in most LDCs.

Given this, the largest accomplishment of the activists in the battle over labor standards has arguably been to put the issue of labor standards on the international agenda, despite opposition by many globalization enthusiasts and LDC governments. The activists have convinced officials of governments and international agencies that the world must address labor standards in some fashion to maintain support for liberal trade policies. This has not produced a social clause in the World Trade Organization (WTO), but it has led governments to give more attention and resources to the ILO and to fund programs to improve implementation of the core labor standards, especially child labor. On the basis of its history, the ILO would never have penalized Burma for forced labor without the climate of opinion set by human rights activists.

Box 7.1 presents our scorecard for the battle over labor standards. We give the human rights vigilantes and their verifier allies a qualified thumbs-up. They have made progress on the terrain they have contested, and they have avoided the pitfall of doing more harm than good—into which their critics feared they would tumble. Their principal failure is that they have just scratched the surface of the problem of inadequate labor rights and poor working conditions around the world. They have focused more on improving conditions in existing jobs than on creating the millions of new jobs that are needed to address poverty and living standards more broadly. There is a long way to go before labor standards advocates can claim "victory" in the battle to improve standards.

Increasing the Effectiveness of Antisweatshop Campaigns and Spreading the Benefits of Globalization

What might the activists and other concerned groups—citizens, international organizations, businesses, and governments—do to further advance the cause of labor rights around the world? Our analysis suggests seven areas in which the labor standards movement can progress. The first three recommendations are intended for activist campaigners. The other four are primarily for international organizations, though they also suggest new goals for activist campaigns because continuing civil society pressures are necessary to induce international organizations to undertake new initiatives.

The principal theme for our recommendations is that improving the well-being of workers in LDCs requires both the implementation of global labor standards in those countries and increased market opportunities for them to compete in the global economy—our Siamese twins of trade and labor standards. This in turn will require both globalization critics and enthusiasts to work to shift more benefits of globalization to workers in LDCs.

This section examines each of our seven recommendations, while box 7.2 summarizes them briefly. They are (1) crediting firms for improved conditions, (2) increasing cooperation among monitors, (3) broadening the targets of antisweatshop campaigns, (4) doing social audits of development bank projects, (5) turning export processing zones into globalization

Box 7.1 Scorecard for labor standards campaigns

Successes

- Roused consumer concerns over sweatshop conditions in developing countries.
- Induced major multinational corporations to develop codes of conduct.
- Encouraged the development of monitoring organizations and triggered improvements in the professionalism of social auditors and monitoring agencies.
- Improved conditions for modest numbers of workers in sectors exporting brand-name goods.
- Put labor standards on the globalization agenda.
- Helped galvanize political and financial support to strengthen the ILO.
- Induced the United States to put labor standards into bilateral trade agreements.

Failures

- Failed to improve conditions for most LDC workers—those in agriculture, the informal sector, and domestic production.
- Played little direct role in altering World Bank and IMF lending policies.
- Played little role in improving LDC access to advanced country markets, particularly in agriculture.
- Failed to get the WTO to address labor standards even minimally and even in trade-related areas.

at its best, (6) targeting trade-related violations of core labor standards in the WTO, and (7) strengthening the ILO in the Internet age.

1. Crediting Firms for Improved Conditions

To harness consumer demand, the vigilantes and verifiers should continue demanding disclosure about firms' overseas operations and transparency in the monitoring process. But they also need to give credit to firms that have improved conditions and tell consumers that, yes, XYZ company (Nike? Starbucks?) has begun to do the right thing. Consumers need positive alternatives to products tainted by worker repression and abuse.

Some groups, such as the fair trade certifiers and anti-Nike activist Jeff Ballinger, are trying to do this by removing intermediaries and marketing "sweat-free" products themselves (see www.nosweat.com). But these initiatives are likely to remain a tiny part of the market for T-shirts, coffee, and other targeted items. Even though any large firm that produces or subcontracts to suppliers in LDCs will have some labor

Box 7.2   Recommendations for the labor standards movement and international institutions

1. Antisweatshop activists should applaud firms making good-faith efforts to raise standards, as well as expose those turning a blind eye. To expand the market for standards, activists should respond favorably to firms that seek to publicize legitimate improvements to attract additional sales from consumers.

2. Monitoring groups should work more closely together to keep the pressure on firms, to continue to improve their own transparency, and to reduce monitoring fatigue.

3. Antisweatshop activists should broaden the scope of their campaigns to deal with other development problems, including the need for reductions in LDC debt burdens, increasing access to markets for agricultural products, and improving institutions in developing countries. They should work *with* globalization enthusiasts to increase LDC access to advanced country markets.

4. Activists should demand that the World Bank and regional development banks require social audits on projects they fund, using a combination of suitably trained domestic nongovernmental organizations or trade unions, as well as accredited auditors. The banks should publish the results on how well contractors comply with labor standards.

5. The WTO and ILO together should collaborate on a project to document labor standards problems and industrial relations policies in export processing zones and use the information to turn these zones into models for promoting globalization and labor standards together.

6. The WTO should revise its list of exceptions for taking action against imports to include egregious violations of the core labor standards when they are intended to increase exports or inward foreign investment.

7. The ILO should continue to increase the intensity of the spotlight it shines on inadequate compliance with labor standards. It should also take advantage of the Internet to widely disseminate information to workers explaining their rights; to consumers, workers, and nongovernmental organizations on the actual state of conditions around the world; and to these groups, employers, and governments on effective ways to raise standards.

standards problems somewhere in the world, activists should develop lists of firms that are improving conditions and publicize those lists to consumers. This, in turn, will increase the pressure on firms not on the list to take action as well.

2. Increasing Cooperation among Monitors

Competition among the monitoring initiatives has strengthened them and improved disclosure. But as the demand for monitoring has increased, factories with multiple international buyers often must deal with code requirements and inspectors from several agencies. Monitoring agencies should work out some form of "mutual recognition" so that certification of a factory by one group for a particular buyer could be used by another buyer without having to duplicate the verification process. The convergence in code content and monitoring procedures makes this feasible. Since there will inevitably be disagreements among firms, monitors, and activists about what is actually going on inside some workplaces, it would be useful to create mediation mechanisms to resolve such disagreements, either under the guise of the ILO or the Permanent Court of Arbitration (see Zack 1999, 2003).

Another way to address the problem of monitoring fatigue is to press firms—beyond the relatively small circle that have thus far joined the Fair Labor Association or Social Accountability International—to sign up with one of the multistakeholder groups. This would reduce the number of individual company monitors that factories have to deal with. Expanding membership in the multistakeholder initiatives would also strengthen these groups and increase their credibility with consumers.

3. Broadening the Targets of Antisweatshop Campaigns

Antisweatshop activists should broaden the targets of their campaigns by joining with Oxfam America and the Jubilee movement to pressure advanced countries to reduce the debt burdens of poor countries, to open their markets for LDC exports, and to reduce subsidies to agriculture, which harm farmers in these countries. Even modest success in lowering LDC debt or in moving the international financial institutions from their rigidly orthodox policies has the potential for improving working conditions in LDCs on a broad scale. And if anyone can popularize these issues, it is the antisweatshop activists.

In addition, activists should work *with* globalization enthusiasts in one area where they have a mutual interest: increasing LDC access to advanced country markets, particularly in highly subsidized agriculture. Oxfam International launched a campaign in early 2002 to "make trade fair," emphasizing these themes. But activists have given this initiative a mixed reception. At the next WTO meeting, antisweatshop activists should join with Oxfam to demand that more of the benefits from trade go to LDCs and thus ratchet up the pressure on advanced country negotiators to offer those countries better terms.

4. Doing Social Audits of Development Bank Projects

Although the World Bank and regional development banks have not played a major role in our story, we believe they should also support the market for standards. These institutions fund projects throughout the less developed world, often without any assessment of whether project implementation is consistent with core labor standards.[4] They should require social audits on projects to make transparent what these projects do in the job market, and to pressure firms outside the multinational export sector to raise standards.

To develop guidelines for best practices for such social audits, the development banks should work with the ILO. To ensure transparency and auditors' independence, the banks should choose the auditors and pay them and should commit to publish all resulting reports on their Web site. They could also subsidize the training of auditors, either by the ILO or by independent organizations.

Given the limited supply of credible social auditors, such a policy would have to be phased in, with the audits focusing on projects or countries where the risks of workers' rights violations are highest. Over time, the scope of projects covered could increase, and other multilateral and bilateral donor agencies could begin to require social audits on their projects. Donor agencies have strengthened their audit capabilities because of concerns about corruption. They should do no less in the area of working conditions and labor standards.

Development banks are unlikely to develop social audits of their projects without continuing pressure from activists. We suggest that activists take the lead in demanding that the banks monitor labor conditions on their projects, just as the activists have done in the corporate sector.

5. Turning Export Processing Zones into Globalization at Its Best

Export processing zones (EPZs)—areas of countries given reduced tariffs and other incentives to produce for the global market—are the most readily identifiable face of globalization. EPZs offer tax holidays, duty-free imports, and dedicated infrastructure to attract foreign investment and create jobs.[5]

Traditionally, EPZs have had a weak record on labor standards. Some countries seek to attract foreign investment to EPZs by exempting them

---

4. For a detailed review of current multilateral development bank policies with respect to labor standards conditions in procurement contracts, see Social Protection Unit (2002). Just as we were going to press, we were told that Asian Development Bank officials had decided to include all four core labor standards in their standard procurement documents and contracts but that they had not yet determined how to enforce these provisions. This recommendation for social audits might be one way of moving forward.

5. According to the International Labor Office (1998a, 3), there were 845 EPZs around the world in 1997, more than half in North America (320) and Asia (225), and another 133 in Latin America and the Caribbean. The features of EPZs—whether they are physically isolated, industry specific, or more integrated into the local economy—vary from country to country.

from labor laws. Bangladesh and Pakistan exclude EPZs from coverage under at least some labor and industrial relations laws; Malaysia, Panama, and some other countries restrict the application of labor laws in EPZs, particularly with regard to freedom of association.[6] In 1994, Pakistan admitted that its exemption of EPZs from certain labor laws was the result of a "deal with foreign investors who have invested in this zone on the basis of certain exemptions provided to them."[7] The Bangladeshi Export Promotion Bureau advertises its "production-oriented labour laws," including prohibitions on unions and on strikes within the zones.[8]

Going beyond restrictions on workers' rights to attract foreign investment, LDCs often look the other way or collude with EPZ investors to discourage union organizing in the zones, and they make little effort to enforce national labor laws in these areas.[9] The worst abuses are concentrated in footwear, apparel, toys, and other products that are highly price competitive, labor intensive, and mobile.

Because EPZs are strongly identified with trade, they are the natural locale for the WTO to work with the ILO to demonstrate that trade and labor standards together can raise living standards in poor countries. The WTO should consider rules to prevent EPZs from giving exemptions on labor laws and implicit promises of low standards to foreign investors. Allowing violations of labor standards and laws in EPZs distorts trade and undermines the legitimacy of international trade rules.

Moreover, when the Multi-Fiber Arrangement (MFA) expires in 2005, many poor countries will no longer have a guaranteed market share thanks to the network of MFA quotas, and they will need to find new ways to compete, particularly with China. A joint WTO-ILO project to make EPZs a model of best practices in complying with core labor standards, funded by advanced countries and the World Bank, could assist poor countries in adapting to the MFA phaseout and moving up the development ladder.

A good starting point for turning EPZs into the poster children for globalization and labor standards would be a joint WTO-ILO baseline survey of standards in EPZs. The results of the survey could be publicized on a Web site that lists basic facts about EPZs in various countries

---

6. See International Labor Office (1998a); US Department of Labor (1989–90). The International Labor Office report also indicated there were concerns about Zimbabwe's treatment of EPZs but, according to ILO sources, the law in question has been amended. Bangladesh also reportedly will ease its restrictions on organizing in EPZs.

7. Individual Observation of the Conference Committee on the Application of Standards, 1994, available in the ILO database, ILOLEX, at www.ilo.org/ilolex/english/iloquery.htm. See also Complaint Against the Government of Pakistan, Case no. 1726, Report no. 2940, in the same database.

8. See www.epbbd.com/banEPZA.html (May 6, 2003).

9. US Department of Labor (1989–90); Romero (1995); International Labor Office (1998a); International Confederation of Free Trade Unions (1996).

—whether labor laws apply equally within and outside zones, unionization rates in zones and the rest of the country, average hours and wages,
accident rates, the percentage of women in the labor force, and so forth.
Improving the collection and dissemination of such data is already an
ILO objective. It would provide the world community, from governments
to consumers to human rights activists, with the information on which
they could base decisions.

Finally, EPZs or firms within them that egregiously violate core standards should face the threat of trade restrictions. This could be negotiated
in the ILO without WTO participation, as has occurred with various multilateral environmental agreements. But the WTO should also be involved,
because such violations are in fact distortions of trade.

6. Targeting Trade-Related Violations
of Core Labor Standards in the WTO

Violations of core labor standards to attract foreign investment or to promote
exports are a trade distortion as much as subsidies or other forms of aid
to traded sectors. That the WTO chooses to ignore them fits the worst
image of the organization as sensitive to violations of trade rules that
harm businesses but insensitive to distortions that harm workers. Because trade threats can contribute to the achievement of limited, carefully defined objectives, and safeguards can avoid protectionist abuse of
labor standards in trade agreements, there is no reason for the WTO to
shy away from targeting *trade-related* violations of core labor standards.

A simple way to do this would be for WTO members to interpret
Article XX(e) of the General Agreement on Tariffs and Trade, which allows countries to ban imports of goods produced using prison labor, as
also applying to other forms of forced labor.[10] This interpretation would
include coerced child labor and therefore go a long toward meeting the
requirements of ILO Convention 182 on the worst forms of child labor. But
addressing violations of the other core labor standards—freedom of association and the right to organize, and nondiscrimination—would require
formal amendment of WTO rules, along the lines laid out in chapter 4.[11]

---

10. A 1985 "wise men's" report setting the stage for the Uruguay Round of trade negotiations suggested that it was clear under General Agreement on Tariffs and Trade (GATT)
rules that countries could not be forced to import products made with slave labor. But
that interpretation is not binding, and it is not known whether a dispute settlement
panel would allow a country to take action against forced labor products under this
exception. The Business Roundtable (1999, 27), an association of CEOs that address
issues of public policy, www.brtable.org, has recommended that the WTO clarify this
ambiguity and also consider expanding Article XX(e) to cover the worst forms of child
labor as defined in ILO Convention 182.

11. The International Confederation of Free Trade Unions has proposed a way to avoid
the need for an amendment to GATT rules. This would take the form of having dispute

Our recommendation for amending Article XX(e) would allow WTO members to ban imports of goods whose production is directly linked to violations of any of the four core labor standards. The violations would have to be egregious, not amenable to remedy by other means, and trade related—part of an effort to either promote exports or to attract foreign investment. Sanctions would be limited to the specified imports. To further safeguard against protectionist abuse, countries invoking this provision would have to rely on the ILO for evidence that a problem exists. By focusing on violations of labor standards that distort trade, this proposal fits naturally under the WTO framework.

7. Strengthening the ILO in the Internet Age

Information is also power. It is essential in the market for standards. It is also essential in official enforcement of labor laws and standards. This is the ILO's great strength. The steps that the ILO has taken to improve the information that it collects and disseminates through its supervisory system are described in detail in chapter 5. Here we suggest ways for the ILO to become even more transparent and to better use Internet technology to empower workers, activists, and consumers to raise labor standards in the global economy.

One reason that the ILO remains vulnerable to the vagaries of US and other member government whims is that it has no constituency of its own on the global scene. The ILO does not represent workers or firms or governments. Its operations depend on agreements reached among those groups. With a limited budget, it lacks the big stick that financial institutions carry. When the ILO disagrees with the IMF or World Bank on economic policy, LDC governments are likely to listen to the ones with money, not to the ILO.

Because the major ways that the ILO affects labor standards are through moral suasion, information, and technical assistance, it needs to establish independent standing and presence with the public in both advanced and less developed countries. The most efficient way to gain that presence is through the Internet. The low cost of the Internet means that for the first time in its history, the ILO can directly reach the people it is supposed to help. The strength the ILO brings to the Internet is what in other settings is its weakness: the modus operandi of a staid international organization. This is no rabble-rousing organization that looks for

---

settlement panels interpret Article XXI(c)—which allows member countries to take actions to fulfill "obligations under the UN Charter for the maintenance of international peace and security"—as permitting trade actions authorized by the ILO as well. But this article is explicitly aimed at national security exceptions, and many regard it as already overly broad. It is also not clear that gaining approval for such an interpretation would be easier than amending the rules, given the breadth of Article XXI.

trouble. So when it speaks clearly and factually on an issue, its statement carries weight.

The ILO has made substantial improvements to its Web site in recent years, for example adding In Focus sections that pull together information on important topics such as child labor, and promoting the declaration on fundamental rights, and health and safety at work. But the Web site is still geared more toward professionals than ordinary citizens.[12] To reach workers and others not familiar with it, the ILO should create new, streamlined Web sites geared toward particular users: information on rights, international standards, and national laws for workers in one place; ratings of codes of conduct and monitoring systems for consumers in another (though the ILO has thus far been unwilling to do this); information on best practices in industrial relations for employers in still another; and information on legal codes and inspection systems for governments in still another.

The most user-friendly product that the ILO currently offers on compliance with core labor standards is the director general's global report under the Declaration on Fundamental Principles and Rights at Work. But this report could be improved as well. Now that the first four-year cycle of reports on each of the core standards in turn has been completed, the ILO should revise the report to sum up the progress—or regression—in all the core standards during the previous year. The Global Report might retain the rotating focus on one core area, but it should also monitor what countries with problems in other areas are doing to resolve them and in each case whether lack of progress is due to government policy or a lack of capacity. This would make the report more useful to outside observers and assist the Governing Body in identifying future priorities for technical assistance.

But the ILO also needs to demonstrate its worth to its core constituents to maintain and even increase its level of available financial resources. This means being more transparent about its own operations as well. It needs to provide more and better (or at least better organized) information on technical assistance. It also needs to do systematic independent evaluations of its programs, along the lines of the IMF's Office of Independent Evaluation and the World Bank's Operations Evaluation Department.

Unless it establishes an independent and broadly publicized presence on the Internet that allows it to reach the larger public, the ILO will need to depend on outside forces—protesters threatening global trade agreements, trade organizations and LDCs seeking to keep labor and

---

12. Information on the ILO Web site (www.ilo.org) is organized functionally but often under headings that are opaque to outsiders. "Standards and Fundamental Principles and Rights at Work" is clear, but would anyone think to look for the Cambodia garment industry monitoring project under "Social Dialogue"? Or to find information on gender discrimination issues under "Employment" rather than under "Fundamental Rights" or "Social Dialogue"? And even the In Focus pages can be difficult to find, because they are scattered throughout the site map and not highlighted in one easy-to-find place.

trade issues separate, US administrations with a particular debt to unions or protesters—to maintain its current prominence in the battle over labor standards. An effective use of the Internet could give the ILO a powerful mechanism to carry its message forward.

Final Thoughts

The evidence and analysis in this book have shown that enforcing global labor standards can improve the conditions of workers in LDCs. Ensuring this outcome requires concerted efforts by activists, forward-thinking multinational corporations, the ILO, and the world trading community, including the WTO, along the lines laid out in this chapter. Together, these actors can improve working conditions, increase the benefits of trade for workers, and promote growth in LDCs. Globalization and labor standards are not mortal enemies but complementary ways—Siamese twins, in our analogy—to make modern economic growth work better for all.

APPENDICES

Appendix A
US-Based Transnational Labor
Rights Activist Organizations

Name (Web site)	Special-ization	Year formed	Orientation
American Friends Service Committee (www.afsc.org)	General	1917	Religious
Asian Immigrant Women Advocates (www.corpwatch.org/feature/hitech/aiwa.html)	US Asians	1983	Ethnic
Asian Law Caucus (www.asianlawcaucus.org)	US Asians	1972	Ethnic
As You Sow Foundation (www.asyousow.org/index40.htm)	Shareholder activism	1992	Do-gooder
Bangor Clean Clothes Campaign (www.bairnet.org/organizations/pica/cleanclo.htm)	Code of conduct	1997	Do-gooder
Campaign for Labor Rights (www.summersault.com/~agj/clr/)	General	1995	Activist-left
Coalition for Justice in Maquiladoras (www.coalitionforjustice.net)	Mexico	1989	Do-gooder
CISPES (www.cispes.org)	El Salvador	1980	Activist-left

Name (Web site)	Special-ization	Year formed	Orientation
Co-op America (www.coopamerica.org)	General	1982	Do-gooder
Fair Labor Association (www.fairlabor.org)	Code and monitoring	1998	Do-gooder
Fair Trade Federation (www.fairtradefederation.org)	Codes/labels	1996	Do-gooder
Free the Children USA (www.freethechildren.org/main/index.html)	Children	1995	Do-gooder
Global Exchange (www.globalexchange.org)	General	1988	Activist-left
Global Kids (www.globalkidsinc.org)	Children	1989	Do-gooder
Human Rights Watch (www.hrw.org)	General	1978	Do-gooder
Human Rights for Workers (www.senser.com)	General	1996	Do-gooder
Interfaith Center for Corporate Responsibility (www.domini.com/iccr.html)	Shareholder activism	1971	Religious
International Labor Rights Fund (www.laborrights.org)	General	1986	Activist-left/do-gooder
La Mujer Obrera (www.mujerobrera.org)	El Paso	*	Activist-left
National Consumer League, Child Labor Coalition (www.natlconsumersleague.org)	Children	1989	Do-gooder
National Labor Committee (www.nlcnet.org)	General	1981	Activist-left
NY State Labor-Religion Coalition (www.labor-religion.org)	Codes	1980	Religious

Name (Web site)	Special-ization	Year formed	Orientation
National Interfaith Committee for Worker Justice (www.nicwj.org)	US	*	Religious
Nicaragua Network Education Fund (summersault.com/~agj/nicanet/index.html)	Nicaragua	1980	Activist-left
Press for Change (www.nikeworkers.org)	Nike	*	Activist-left
Resource Center of the Americas (www.americas.org)	Latin America	1991	Do-gooder
Rugmark Foundation USA (www.rugmark.org)	Child labor, carpets	1995	Do-gooder
Social Accountability International (www.sai-intl.org)	Code and monitoring	1997	Do-gooder
STITCH (www.stitchonline.org)	Guatemala	1992	Activist-left
Support Committee for Maquiladora Workers (www.enchantedwebsites.com/maquiladora/index.html)	Mexico	*	Do-gooder
Sweatshop Watch (www.sweatshopwatch.org)	General (mainly US)	1995	Activist-left
Transfair America (www.transfairusa.org)	Coffee	1996	Do-gooder
Transnational Resource and Action Center (Corporate Watch) (www.corpwatch.org)	General	1996	Activist-left
UNITE (union) (www.uniteunion.org)	Apparel	1994	Activist-left
US Labor Education in the Americas Project (www.usleap.org)	Central America	1987	Activist-left

Name (Web site)	Special- ization	Year formed	Orientation
USAS (www.umich.edu/~sole/usas/)	College apparel	1997	Activist-left
Verité (www.verite.org)	China, Asia	1995	Do-gooder
Vietnam Labor Watch (www.saigon.com/~nike/)	Nike, Vietnam	1996	Do-gooder
Witness for Peace (www.witnessforpeace.org)	Central America	1983	Activist-left
Witness Rights Alert (www.oddcast.com/witness/)	Human rights groups	1992	Do-gooder

* = year unknown

Sources: Global Exchange, *A Directory of US Anti-Sweatshop Organizations*; Internet search.

Appendix B
Timeline of Antisweatshop
Activities in the 1990s

1990	Charles Kernaghan becomes the director of the National Labor Committee, founded in 1981 to oppose the Ronald Reagan administration's policies in Central America.
1992	Levi Strauss develops the first code of conduct for suppliers following a US Department of Labor suit against contractors in Saipan over wages and other problems; a year later, Levi Strauss announces plans to withdraw from China because of the human rights situation there.
1992	US Senator Tom Harkin (D-IA) introduces a bill to bar imports of goods produced using child labor; he reintroduces it in each Congress until 1997, when he substitutes legislation calling for beefed-up enforcement of an existing law barring imports of goods produced with forced labor, including bonded or other forced child labor.
1993	Wal-Mart publishes Standards for Vendor Partners after televised revelations regarding child labor use by a supplier in Bangladesh.
August 1993	The Clinton administration negotiates side agreements on labor and the environment to accompany the North American Free Trade Agreement.

March 1995	The Clinton administration—criticized for "de-linking" human rights from most-favored-nation trade status for China in 1994—releases "model business principles" to encourage multinational corporations to adopt voluntary codes of conduct in their operations around the world.
August 1995	The US Department of Labor closes down a sweatshop in El Monte, California, after discovering immigrant Thai workers being forced to work in slavelike conditions; the incident gives momentum to Labor Secretary Robert Reich's campaign to combat US sweatshops.
December 1995	Under pressure from the National Labor Committee and the People of Faith Network over working conditions in El Salvador, the Gap agrees to independent monitoring of its contractor facilities.
Spring 1996	Kernaghan reveals Wal-Mart clothing—endorsed by television personality Kathie Lee Gifford—is produced under exploitative conditions, including child labor; Gifford vows to remedy the situation. A second scandal involving Gifford-endorsed clothing produced in New York sweatshops leads to collaboration with Reich on his No Sweat campaign.
August 1996	Clinton and Reich, with the involvement of Gifford, announce the creation of the Apparel Industry Partnership, bringing together retailer-importers, unions, and NGOs to address sweatshop issues.
March 1997	The management of a Phillips-Van Heusen contract facility in Guatemala recognizes a union, a first in that country's apparel export sector.
April 1997	An Apparel Industry Partnership report outlines a Workplace Code of Conduct and Principles of Monitoring.
August 1997	Duke University students form a group called Students Against Sweatshops; in subsequent months, the movement grows on campuses across the country, eventually becoming United Students Against Sweatshops.
October 1997	The Council on Economic Priorities, following consultations with companies and NGOs, publishes the SA8000

standard for workers' rights, and the following January the council launches an agency to accredit compliance monitors.

April 1998   Levi Strauss announces its return to China, arguing that the human rights situation has improved sufficiently so "that the overall environment now is such that the risks to our reputation are minimal" (*Financial Times*, April 8, 1998).

Spring 1998   Under pressure from a student group, Duke University releases a code of conduct for suppliers of apparel licensed by Duke to display the university name or logo. The code calls for independent monitoring of compliance, through the Apparel Industry Partnership, if appropriate, and it requires suppliers to disclose the names and addresses of all contractors and plants involved in producing Duke-licensed apparel.

Summer 1998   The Union of Needletrades, Industrial, and Textile Employees commits interns and resources to helping establish United Students Against Sweatshops on a national basis.

August 1998   A joint delegation of the National Labor Committee and United Students Against Sweatshops visits Central America to meet workers and NGOs.

November 1998   The Apparel Industry Partnership agrees on the creation of the Fair Labor Association and accreditation of independent monitors to monitor compliance with the AIP/FLA code.

December 1998   Phillips-Van Heusen closes its unionized plant in Guatemala, saying it lost a major contract and has excess capacity; production will continue at its nonunion plants elsewhere in Guatemala.

January 1999   UN Secretary General Kofi Annan, at the World Economic Forum in Davos, Switzerland, announces a new Global Compact calling on the business community to respect basic principles on human rights, workers' rights, and protection of the environment, but with no means for monitoring compliance. NGOs follow this compact a year later with a Citizens' Compact that rejects the

January 1999 (*cont.*)	"partnership" between the United Nations and the global business community and calls on the United Nations to make the principles mandatory with provisions for monitoring.
Early 1999	United Students Against Sweatshops criticizes universities for signing on to Fair Labor Association model for monitoring without consulting them; students hold sit-ins to demand a stronger code at several universities (Duke, Georgetown, Wisconsin, and North Carolina, and, for 226 hours, Arizona). In April, United Students Against Sweatshops releases detailed report on inadequacies of Fair Labor Association code and monitoring process and gives universities until October 15 to seek improvements.
October 7, 1999	Under pressure from United Students Against Sweatshops and universities, Nike discloses the locations of 41 factories producing licensed apparel for Duke, North Carolina, Georgetown, Michigan, and Arizona.
October 19, 1999	After rejection by the Fair Labor Association of their suggestions and passage of the 6-month deadline with no other action by universities, United Students Against Sweatshops announces an alternative Worker Rights Consortium and calls on universities to withdraw from the Fair Labor Association. Brown University is the first to respond, announcing that it will join the Worker Rights Consortium but also remain in the Fair Labor Association; others, including Phil Knight's alma mater University of Oregon, follow.
December 1999	Liz Claiborne agrees to independent monitoring at its supplier facility in El Salvador.
December 9, 1999	The Philadelphia City Council calls on area colleges and universities to join the Worker Rights Consortium.
Spring 2000	Nike, retaliating against Brown and the University of Oregon for joining the Worker Rights Consortium, terminates its contract to provide hockey products to Brown and ends its personal and corporate philanthropic relations with the University of Orgeon.

Appendix C
Workers' Rights Conditionality in the US Generalized System of Preferences

The US Generalized System of Preferences (GSP) program, originally implemented on January 1, 1976, waives import duties on eligible products for "beneficiary developing countries" (BDCs), subject to both "competitive need limits" (CNLs) and political conditions. The program was reauthorized in the Trade and Tariff Act of 1984 for an additional eight years, with new conditions tying eligibility to respect for workers' rights and the protection of intellectual property rights.

From 1993 through 2001, "pay-as-you-go" budget rules (requiring offsets for the tariff revenue lost from the preferences) made long-term extensions difficult. The program lapsed and was revived several times before being reauthorized for five years in the trade promotion authority bill of 2002. In 1999, more than 140 countries were eligible for GSP benefits on more than 4,400 individual items, about half the total number of tariff lines in the 8-digit harmonized tariff system. Another nearly 2,000 products can be imported duty-free from least developed beneficiary countries.

Commercial Limits and Political Conditions in the GSP Program

When GSP was reauthorized in 1984, Congress added language noting that the program was intended to "provide trade and development opportunities for BDCs *without adversely affecting U.S. producers and workers*" (GAO 1994, 24; emphasis added). This is achieved through a number of exclusions from eligibility based on import sensitivity and judgments about the competitiveness of certain exports. The limits on benefits include:

- exclusion of import-sensitive products, including most textiles and apparel;

- shipment directly from the BDC of eligible products, which must meet rules of origin (35 percent of the appraised value of the product, including the direct costs of processing, must have originated in the beneficiary country);

- graduation—that is, *permanent* exclusion—of particular products (from particular BDCs) from the program if the beneficiary country is determined to be "sufficiently competitive" in the export of that product that it no longer needs preferential treatment; and

- the possibility of temporary exclusion of particular exports from particular beneficiaries if they hit predesignated CNLs, based on the dollar value of exports or the exporter's import market share.

Table C.1 summarizes these limits and shows that about half the potentially eligible imports were excluded for various reasons in 1992 when the US General Accounting Office analyzed the program. Finally, whole economies can be "graduated" from the program once they hit a per capita income ceiling or if they are determined to be competitive exporters. Hong Kong, South Korea, Singapore, and Taiwan were graduated first, on January 1, 1989; Malaysia was removed in 1997; and Mexico was removed when the North American Free Trade Agreement entered into force at the beginning of 1994. Israel and the Bahamas were graduated in 1995 because they were over the per capita income ceiling.

In addition to the competitive limitations on benefits, the 1974 Trade Act also excluded communist countries, members of the Organization of Petroleum Exporting Countries (later eased), and countries that expropriate US-owned property without compensation. When Congress reauthorized GSP in 1984, it tightened the eligibility conditions, provided a specific per capita ceiling for country graduation, and introduced "country practice" standards relating to protection of workers' rights and intellectual property.

Workers' Rights in the GSP Program

When determining a country's eligibility for GSP benefits, the US administration is supposed to consider "whether or not such country has taken or is taking steps to afford to workers in that country (including any designated zone in that country) internationally recognized worker rights" (US House of Representatives 1997, 254). The law as amended by the 2002 trade bill defines "internationally recognized" workers' rights as including

Table C.1 Limitations on eligibility for the Generalized System of Preferences (GSP)

A. Import-sensitive products excluded by statute from the GSP program

Textile and apparel products subject to textile agreements
Footwear
Leather products, including handbags, luggage, and work gloves
Watches
Import-sensitive electronics, steel, and glass items

B. Imports excluded for other reasons, 1992

Reason	Value of excluded products (millions of dollars)	Percent of total exclusions	Percent of GSP-eligible imports
Administrative reasons[a]	9,076	56.4	25.4
Product graduation[b]	276	1.7	0.8
Competitive need limits[c]	5,827	36.2	16.3
Reduced competitive need limits[d]	905	5.6	2.5
Totals	16,084	100.0	45.0

a. These are most often failures to meet rules of origin. Mexico was the most frequent source of this type of exclusion and the frequency of administrative exclusions was expected to drop with Mexico's graduation from the program after implementation of the North American Free Trade Agreement.
b. This means that there was a determination that the beneficiary country is a competitive exporter of a particular product.
c. Automatic triggers based on a dollar value of $101 million in 1992 and an import share of 50 percent.
d. Reduction in the value of the automatic triggers for certain products from certain countries determined to be competitive relative to other beneficiaries; equal to $39 million in 1992 and an import market share of 25 percent.

Source: GAO (1994).

■ freedom of association;

■ the right to organize and bargain collectively;

■ freedom from coerced labor;

■ a minimum age for the employment of children, and a prohibition on the worst forms of child labor; and

■ acceptable conditions of work, including minimum wages, regulated hours of work, and occupational health and safety.

There is no reference to the International Labor Organization (ILO), and this list differs from the "core" labor standards enumerated in the ILO's 1998 Declaration on Fundamental Principles and Rights at Work, though there is substantial overlap.[1] In setting these standards, Congress recognized that their enforcement could legitimately vary with a country's level of development. The House Conference report on the 1984 Trade and Tariff Act stated:

> It is not the expectation of the [House Ways and Means] Committee that developing countries come up to the prevailing labor standards in the United States and other highly-industrialized developed countries. It is recognized that acceptable minimum standards may vary from country to country. (Quoted in Lyle 1991, 9)

When country practice reviews for workers' rights and intellectual property were added to the program in 1984, they were simply appended to the existing process for determining product eligibility. Under that process, private-sector groups, including businesses, unions, and nongovernmental organizations, can challenge the eligibility of beneficiaries on the basis of inadequate protection of workers or intellectual property. Petitions must be filed by June 1 of each year, and an interagency committee supervised by the Office of the US Trade Representative must decide whether to accept or reject them by July 1. Final decisions on the merits of the petition are announced the following April and must be implemented by July 1.

Advocates of workers' rights complain that the administrative process for reviews is too rigid. They argue that workers' rights cases, which involve negotiations with the beneficiary country to change *its* policies, are fundamentally different from the product eligibility cases, for which the decision-making process is internal to the US government. In workers' rights cases, the inflexible annual cycle may result in long lags between the time when violations occur and when they are reviewed.[2] In addition, this process has been disrupted in recent years because of the lapses in authority. Thus, 1997 was the first year since 1993 that new workers' rights petitions were considered. During the period 1994–96, ongoing reviews were continued or acted upon as appropriate.

---

1. The first three of the rights listed in the US GSP law are included in the ILO declaration, as is child labor. To address some of the concerns about the minimum age convention, the ILO adopted a new convention at its 1999 conference giving priority to the elimination of the "worst forms" of child labor. Minimum conditions of work and wages do not generally appear on lists of "core" standards, including the ILO declaration, whereas nondiscrimination in employment usually is included. See Elliott (1998) for a detailed discussion.

2. GAO (1994, 106) offers the example of Sudan, where a coup d'état occurred at the end of June 1989 bringing to power a government that abolished unions, forbade strikes, and detained and harassed union leaders. Because the period for submitting petitions had just closed, the human rights group Africa Watch and the AFL-CIO could not bring their petition for 11 months, followed by another 11 months for the review, meaning that Sudan's GSP eligibility was not suspended for nearly two years after the coup.

Table C.2 Value of Generalized System of Preferences to beneficiary countries, 1991–98 (millions of dollars)

Year	Total US imports (A)	Total US imports from beneficiary countries (B)	Duty-free imports from beneficiary countries (C)	(B/A)	(C/B)	(C/A)
1991	490,981	96,011	13,663	19.6	14.2	2.8
1992	536,458	109,656	16,735	20.4	15.3	3.1
1993	589,441	123,094	19,520	20.9	15.9	3.3
1994	668,590	103,974	18,379	15.6	17.7	2.7
1995	749,431	111,825	18,304	14.9	16.4	2.4
1996	803,239	124,120	16,922	15.5	13.6	2.1
1997	859,110	117,334	15,546	13.7	13.2	1.8
1998	905,339	119,616	16,336	13.2	13.7	1.8

Source: US International Trade Commission, The Year in Trade: Operation of the Trade Agreements Program, various years.

Implementation of Workers' Rights Conditionality in the GSP Program

Because of the numerous limitations on benefits, imports from eligible countries under the GSP program are small. In the 1990s, total imports from BDCs as a share of total US imports averaged only about 15 percent, and duty-free imports under GSP were only 2 to 3 percent (table C.2). Despite the relatively small size of the program, however, there were more than 100 petitions in the first decade after workers' rights conditionality was added to GSP. As is shown in table C.3, as of 1998, 47 of these petitions had been accepted for review and 35 had been rejected. The remainder resulted in the continuation of previously initiated reviews.

Unions, usually members of the AFL-CIO, submitted more than 70 percent of the petitions summarized in table C.3. Roughly half the petitions alleged violations of the "minimum conditions" of work, including lack of or inadequate minimum wages, but all of them list violations of the core right of freedom of association, and most include infringements on the right to organize and bargain collectively. Countries targeted in union petitions exported, on average, 40 percent less in the year the petition was filed than countries targeted in petitions without union involvement ($2.4 billion versus $4.1 billion). Table C.4 lists the top ten BDCs in 1998, only three of which had been the subject of workers' rights reviews; the other seven have never even been the subject of a petition.

Table C.3 shows that unions were more likely to have their petitions accepted for review than human rights groups. This may have to do

Table C.3 A portrait of countries challenged over workers' rights protections, 1985–96

Key characteristics	Petition rejected (35)	Share	Petition accepted (47)	Share
By petitioner				
Union (usually AFL-CIO member)	18	51	34	72
Union plus human rights groups	3	9	5	11
Human rights groups	11	31	4	9
Other	3	9	1	2
Respect for civil liberties				
Average Freedom House rating[a]	4		5	
Number judged "not free"	2	6	15	32
Number judged "free"	3	9	4	9
Rights targeted in complaint[b]				
Forced labor	3	9	9	19
Child labor	12	34	12	26
Subminimum working conditions	18	51	22	47
Average trade, size, and income				
Total target country exports (billions of dollars in year of petition)	11.0		8.7	
Percent of target exports going to United States	36		23	
Duty-free GSP exports as percent of total target exports (1992)	13		15	
Population of target (millions)	37		33	
Per capita income in target (dollars)	1,888		1,918	

a. Freedom House is a nongovernmental organization that ranks countries on two scales: political rights, such as the right to vote in free and open elections, and civil rights, including freedom of association and the right to form unions. Each scale goes up to 7, with 1 or 2 indicating that a country is largely free and 6 or 7 indicating a country is not free.

b. Either freedom of association or the right to organize and bargain collectively, and usually both, are cited in every petition.

Note: Four petitions were filed in 1997–99 that have not yet been added to the data set for this table: Belarus, Cambodia, Guatemala, and Swaziland. In late 2000, the Clinton administration suspended Belarus's eligibility.

Source: Elliott (2000d).

with the political sensitivity of the issues raised by the human rights groups, especially mistreatment of union activists, than with a desire to placate union interests. Table C.3 also shows that, though the majority of countries that have been the subject of a petition are classified as "partly free" by the New York–based nonprofit Freedom House, nearly a third of those selected for review are classified as "not free." These are the

Table C.4 Top beneficiary countries in the Generalized System of Preferences program, 1998 (millions of dollars)

Country	Total US imports from beneficiary country	Duty-free imports from beneficiary country	Duty-free imports as a percent of total
Angola	2,165	1,571	72.6
Brazil	9,922	2,186	22.0
India	8,190	1,355	16.5
Indonesia[a]	9,262	1,927	20.8
Philippines[a]	11,874	1,245	10.5
Poland	780	401	51.4
Russia	5,675	424	7.5
South Africa	3,053	552	18.1
Thailand[a]	13,363	2,693	20.2
Venezuela	8,420	546	6.5

a. This country has been the subject of a workers' rights review.

Addendum: In 1986, the top beneficiaries were Taiwan, Korea, Hong Kong, Mexico, Brazil, Singapore, and Israel, which accounted for 79 percent of duty-free Generalized System of Preferences imports in that year. All but Brazil have since graduated from the program.

Source: US International Trade Commission, The Year in Trade: Operation of the Trade Agreements Program, various years.

cases in which one would expect violations of internationally recognized workers' rights to be the worst and in which the defense of legitimate diversity in the level of standards would be least applicable.

Does Conditionality Improve Workers' Rights in Beneficiary Countries?

Ferreting out the effects of GSP conditionality on workers' rights in beneficiary countries is difficult. Assessing the results in these cases requires a two-stage process: first, determining whether there has been any change in conditions in the target country; and second, trying to attribute that change to various potential influences, including US pressure.

Although it is possible that a petition rejected for review could have some influence in the target country, the causal link to US trade pressures would be even more tenuous, and those cases are put aside for the purposes of this analysis. That leaves the 47 petitions that were accepted for review. Of those, 12 resulted in suspension or termination of GSP eligibility and 35 resulted in a finding that the beneficiary "had taken" or "was taking" steps to protect "internationally recognized worker rights." Seven of the cases in the latter category were excluded because the administration in office found the countries in compliance without making any demands for change.

Of the 40 remaining cases, respect for workers' rights appears to have improved in 58 percent.[3] For purposes of examining the utility of GSP conditionality, however, another eight cases are excluded because the improvement in workers' rights that occurred cannot reasonably be attributed to threats to withdraw GSP. The improvement in these cases followed a regime change or other political opening that resulted in improved respect for human rights generally. In some of these cases, the political change might have been due in part to broader sanctions imposed by the United States for other foreign policy reasons, but the specific linkage between GSP and improved workers' rights is difficult to discern.

It should be noted that, though many petitioners complain that the "taking steps" standard has been applied too loosely, we found only two cases for which we concluded that, despite a positive administration finding, the target had taken no steps at all that were responsive to the petition.[4] There were another eight cases, however, for which we concluded that the target was unable or unwilling to implement or enforce commitments to improve respect for workers' rights.

The bottom line is summarized in table 4.1 in the main text. The 32 cases analyzed are almost evenly divided between success (15) and failure (17), with the failures also being nearly evenly divided between those for which there was no discernible change in the protection of workers' rights and those for which promised changes were not made. The other information in table 4.1 suggests that GSP leverage is more likely to contribute to improved workers' rights

- when a human rights group is involved,
- when the target is relatively more politically open,
- when less politically sensitive labor standards are emphasized,
- the more dependent the target country is on the US market, and
- the greater the potential capacity the target country has to implement promised changes (as reflected in per capita income).

---

3. These assessments are based on analysis of the administration assessments, US Department of State, *Country Reports on Human Rights Practices* (reports submitted to the Senate Committee on Foreign Relations and House Committee on International Relations), various years; Freedom House, *Freedom in the World: The Annual Survey of Political Rights and Civil Liberties*, various years; and Harvey (no date).

4. In one of these cases, the country in question did take some action, allowing the administration to find they had "taken steps" to protect workers' rights, but the action taken did not respond to the complaints raised in the petition.

References

Aaronson, Susan Ariel. 1996. *Trade and the American Dream: A Social History of Postwar Trade Policy.* Lexington: University Press of Kentucky.

Aaronson, Susan Ariel. 2001. *Taking Trade to the Streets: The Lost History of Public Efforts to Shape Globalization.* Ann Arbor: University of Michigan Press.

Aidt, Toke, and Zafiris Tzannatos. 2002. *Unions and Collective Bargaining: Economic Effects in a Global Environment.* Washington: World Bank.

Amsden, Alice H. 1989. *Asia's Next Giant: South Korea and Late Industrialization.* New York: Oxford University Press.

Baker, James A. 1987. Remarks before a Conference sponsored by the Institute for International Economics. *Treasury News* (US Department of the Treasury), September 14.

Bardhan, Pranab. 2000. *Social Justice in the Global Economy.* Geneva: International Labor Organization.

Barenberg, Mark, and Peter Evans. 2002. The FTAA's Impact on Democratic Governance. Paper presented at the Inter-American Development Bank and Harvard University Forum, FTAA and Beyond: Prospects for Integration in the Americas, organized by Antoni Estevadeordal, Dani Rodrik, Alan Taylor, and Andrés Velasco. Punta del Este (December).

Barfield, Claude. 2001. *Free Trade, Sovereignty, Democracy: The Future of the World Trade Organization.* Washington: AEI Press.

Bayard, Thomas O., and Kimberly Ann Elliott. 1994. *Reciprocity and Retaliation in U.S. Trade Policy.* Washington: Institute for International Economics.

Benjamin, Medea. 1998. A Critique of Fair Labor Association (FLA), December. www.citinv.it/associazioni/cnms/archivio/strategie/doc_globalexchange.html (January 5, 2001).

Bernard, Elaine. 1997. Ensuring that Monitoring Is Not Co-opted. *New Solutions* 7, no. 4 (summer): 10–12.

Bhalla, Surjit. 2002. *Imagine There's No Country: Poverty, Inequality, and Growth in the Era of Globalization.* Washington: Institute for International Economics.

Braithwaite, John, and Peter Drahos. 2000. *Global Business Regulation.* New York: Cambridge University Press.

Bronfenbrenner, Kate. 2000. Uneasy Terrain: The Impact of Capital Mobility on Workers, Wages, and Union Organizing. Research paper submitted to the US Trade Deficit Review Commission. Washington (September).

Brown, Drusilla. 2000. *International Trade and Core Labour Standards: A Survey of the Recent Literature*. Labour Market and Social Policy Occasional Papers 43, DEELSA/ELSA/WD(2000)4. Paris: Organization for Economic Cooperation and Development.

Brown, Drusilla, Alan V. Deardorff, and Robert M. Stern. 2003. Child Labor: Theory, Evidence, and Policy. In *International Labor Standards: History, Theory, and Policy Options*, ed. Kaushik Basu, Henrik Horn, Lisa Román, and Judith Shapiro. Malden, MA: Blackwell Publishing.

Brown, Drusilla, Alan V. Deardorff, and Robert M. Stern. Forthcoming. The Effects of Multinational Production on Wages and Working Conditions in Developing Countries. In *Challenges to Globalization*, ed. Robert Baldwin and L. Alan Winters. Chicago: University of Chicago Press for National Bureau of Economic Research.

Business Roundtable. 1999. Preparing for New WTO Trade Negotiations to Boost the Economy. Washington: Business Roundtable.

Chan, Anita. 2001. *China's Workers Under Assault: The Exploitation of Labor in a Globalizing Economy*. Armonk, NY and London: M.E. Sharpe.

Charnovitz, Steven. 1987. The Influence of International Labour Standards on the World Trading System: A Historical Overview. *International Labour Review* 126, no. 5 (September–October): 565–84.

Charnovitz, Steven. 2000. The International Labor Organization in Its Second Century. In *Max Planck Yearbook of United Nations Law*, ed. Jochen A. Frowein and Rüdige Wolfrum. New York: Kluwer.

Charnovitz, Steven. 2001. Rethinking WTO Trade Sanctions. *American Journal of International Law* 95, no. 4 (October): 792–832.

Chowdhury, Sumaira. 1997. The Kathie Lee Gifford Sweatshop Scandal: "Shining the Light on Cockroaches." Institute for International Economics, Washington. Photocopy (August).

Cline, William R. 1997. *Trade and Income Distribution*. Washington: Institute for International Economics.

Compa, Lance. 2001. Wary Allies. *American Prospect* 12, no. 12 (July 16).

Compa, Lance, and Jeffrey S. Vogt. 2001. Labor Rights in the Generalized System of Preferences: A 20-Year Review. *Comparative Labor Law & Policy Journal* 22, nos. 2 & 3 (Winter/Spring): 199–238.

Connor, Melissa, Tara Gruzen, Larry Sacks, Jude Sunderland, Darcy Tromanhauser. 1999. *The Case for Corporate Responsibility: Paying a Living Wage to Maquila Workers in El Salvador*. Study for the National Labor Committee. Program in Economic and Political Development, School of International and Public Affairs, Columbia University, New York. http://www.nlcnet.org/elsalvador/sipareport.htm (December 2002).

Cooper, Richard N. 2001. Growth and Inequality: The Role of Foreign Trade and Investment. Paper prepared for the World Bank Annual Conference on Development Economics, Washington (April).

Deere, Carolyn, and Daniel C. Esty. 2002. *Greening the Americas: NAFTA's Lessons for Hemispheric Trade*. Cambridge, MA: MIT Press.

Diamond, Stephen F. 2003. The "Race to the Bottom" Returns: China's Challenge to the International Labor Movement. Comments for a Symposium on Workers and International Economic Organizations: Roles and Responsibilities in a Global Economy, University of California, Davis (March 7).

Dollar, David, and Roberta Gatti. 2000. *Gender Inequality, Income, and Growth: Are Good Times Good for Women?* Working Paper 1 for Policy Research Report on Gender and Development. Washington: World Bank.

Dollar, David, and Aart Kraay. 2001. *Trade, Growth, and Poverty*. Policy Research Working Paper 2615. Washington: World Bank.

Dollar, David, and Aart Kraay. 2002. Growth Is Good for the Poor. *Journal of Economic Growth* 7, no. 3 (September): 195–225.

Duong, Trinh. 2000. Codes of Conduct Don't Work: A View from the Factory Floor. In

Human Rights Dialogue (Carnegie Council on Ethics and International Affairs) 2, no. 4 (Fall): 5.

Elliott, Kimberly Ann. 1998. International Labor Standards and Trade: What Should Be Done? In *The Future of the World Trading System: Global Challenges and US Interests,* ed. Jeffrey J. Schott. Washington: Institute for International Economics.

Elliott, Kimberly Ann. 2000a. Getting Beyond No . . .! Promoting Worker Rights and Trade. In *The WTO after Seattle,* ed. Jeffrey J. Schott. Washington: Institute for International Economics.

Elliott, Kimberly Ann. 2000b. *The ILO and Enforcement of Core Labor Standards.* International Economics Policy Briefs PB00-6 (updated April 2001). Washington: Institute for International Economics.

Elliott, Kimberly Ann. 2000c. (Mis)managing Diversity: Worker Rights and US Trade Policy. *International Negotiation* 5: 97–127.

Elliott, Kimberly Ann. 2000d. Preferences for Workers? Worker Rights and the US Generalized System of Preferences. www.iie.com/publications/papers/elliott0598.htm.

Elliott, Kimberly Ann. 2001. *Fin(d)ing Our Way on Trade and Labor Standards?* International Economics Policy Briefs PB01-5. Washington: Institute for International Economics.

Elliott, Kimberly Ann, and Richard B. Freeman. 2003. White Hats or Don Quixotes: Human Rights Vigilantes in the Global Economy. In *Emerging Labor Market Institutions for the 21st Century,* ed. Richard B. Freeman, Joni Hersch, and Lawrence Mishel. Chicago: University of Chicago Press for the National Bureau of Economic Research.

Elliott, Kimberly Ann, Debayani Kar, and J. David Richardson. Forthcoming. Assessing Globalization's Critics: Talkers Are No Good Doers??? In *Challenges to Globalization,* ed. Robert Baldwin and L. Alan Winters. Chicago: University of Chicago Press for National Bureau of Economic Research.

Elliott, Kimberly Ann, and J. David Richardson. 1997. Determinants and Effectiveness of "Aggressively Unilateral" U.S. Trade Actions. In *The Effects of U.S. Trade Protection and Promotion Policies,* ed. Robert C. Feenstra. Chicago: University of Chicago Press for National Bureau of Economic Research.

Esty, Daniel C. 1994. *Greening the GATT: Trade, Environment, and the Future.* Washington: Institute for International Economics.

Feenstra, Robert, and Gordon Hanson. 2001. *Global Production Sharing and Rising Inequality: A Survey of Trade and Wages.* NBER Working Paper 8372. Cambridge, MA: National Bureau of Economic Research.

Fields, Gary. 1995. *International Labour Standards: A Review of the Issues.* Paris: Organization for Economic Cooperation and Development.

Flanagan, Robert J. 2002. Labor Standards and International Competitive Advantage. Paper prepared for a conference on labor standards, Stanford University, Stanford, CA (May).

Fogel, Robert William. 1989. *Without Consent or Contract: The Rise and Fall of American Slavery.* New York: W.W. Norton.

Foner, Eric. 1988. *Reconstruction: America's Unfinished Revolution, 1863-1877.* New York: Harper Collins.

Frankel, Jeffrey A., and David Romer. 1999. Does Trade Cause Growth? *American Economic Review* 89, no. 3 (June): 379–99.

Freeman, Richard B. 1993. Labor Market Institutions and Policies: Help or Hindrance to Economic Development? In *Proceedings of the World Bank Annual Conference on Development Economics 1992.* Washington: World Bank.

Freeman, Richard B. 1994. A Hardheaded Look at Labor Standards. In *International Labor Standards and Global Economic Integration: Proceedings of a Symposium.* Washington: Bureau of International Labor Affairs, US Department of Labor.

Freeman, Richard B. 1996. International Labor Standards and World Trade: Friends or Foes? In *The World Trading System: Challenges Ahead,* ed. Jeffrey J. Schott. Washington: Institute for International Economics.

Freeman, Richard B. 1997. Working for Nothing: The Supply of Volunteer Labor. *Journal of Labor Economics* 15, part 2 (January): 140–66.

Freeman, Richard B. 1998. What Role for Labor Standards in the Global Economy? United Nations, New York. Photocopy (November 13, 2002).

Freeman, Richard B. 1999. Spurts in Union Growth: Defining Moments and Social Processes. In *The Defining Moment: The Great Depression and the American Economy in the Twentieth Century*, ed. Michael D. Bordo, Claudia Goldin, and Eugene N. White. Chicago: University of Chicago Press for National Bureau of Economic Research.

Freeman, Richard B. 2002. China's Labor Issues: The Disconnect Between China's Labor Market and Labor Institutions. National Bureau of Economic Research, Cambridge, MA. Photocopy.

Freeman, Richard B., and David L. Lindauer. 1999. *Why Not Africa?* NBER Working Paper 6942. Cambridge, MA: National Bureau of Economic Research.

Freeman, Richard B., and James L. Medoff. 1984. *What Do Unions Do?* New York: Basic Books.

Freeman, Richard B., and Joel Rogers. 1999. *What Workers Want*. Ithaca, NY: Cornell University Press.

Frost, Stephen. 2000. Factory Rules Versus Codes of Conduct. In *Human Rights Dialogue* (Carnegie Council on Ethics and International Affairs), series 2, no. 4 (Fall): 3.

Fung, Archon, Mary Graham, and David Weil. 2002. The Political Economy of Transparency: What Makes Disclosure Policies Sustainable? Institute for Government Innovation, John F. Kennedy School of Government, Harvard University, Cambridge (Winter).

GAO (US General Accounting Office). 1994. *International Trade: Assessment of the Generalized System of Preferences Program*. GAO/GGD-95-9. Washington: GAO.

Gravel, Eric, Isabelle Duplessis, and Bernard Gernigon. 2001. *The Committee on Freedom of Association: Its Impact over 50 Years*. Geneva: International Labor Office.

Green, Francis, Andy Dickerson, and Jorge Saba Arbache. 2000. "A Picture of Wage Inequality and the Allocation of Labor through a Period of Trade Liberalization: The Case of Brazil." University of Kent, Department of Economics, Working Paper 00/13, December.

Hankin, Mark. 2002. Testimony Presented to the Congressional Executive Committee on China. American Center for International Labor Solidarity, AFL-CIO, Washington. Photocopy (March 18).

Hanson, Gordon. 2003. What Has Happened to Wages in Mexico since NAFTA? Working Paper No. 9563. Cambridge, MA: National Bureau of Economic Research.

Harrison, Ann. 1996. Openness and Growth: A Time-Series, Cross-Country Analysis for Developing Countries. *Journal of Development Economics* 48: 419–47.

Harrison, Ann, and Gordon Hanson. 1999. Who Gains from Trade Reform? Some Remaining Puzzles. *Journal of Development Economics* 58, no. 2 (April): 315–24.

Harvey, Pharis. 1995. Historic Breakthrough for Bangladesh Kids Endangered by Industry Inaction. *Worker Rights News*, no. 12 (August): 1.

Harvey, Pharis. No date. U.S. GSP Labor Rights Conditionality: "Aggressive Unilateralism" or a Forerunner to a Multilateral Social Clause? www.laborrights.org/h-library/cfrgsp.html.

Hoberg, George. 1999. The Coming Revolution in Regulating our Forests. *Policy Options* (Montreal), December: 53–56.

Holzer, Harry J., and David Neumark, eds. 2003. *The Economics of Affirmative Action*. Northampton, MA: Edward Elgar.

Hufbauer, Gary Clyde, Jeffrey J. Schott, and Kimberly Ann Elliott. Forthcoming. *Economic Sanctions Reconsidered*, 3d ed. Washington: Institute for International Economics.

Hufbauer, Gary Clyde, Jeffrey J. Schott, Diana Orejas, and Ben Goodrich. 2002. North American Labor Under NAFTA. www.iie.com/publications/papers/nafta-labor.htm (September 2002).

ILO (International Labor Organization). 2000. *Your Voice at Work*. First Global Report Under the Follow-Up to the Declaration on Fundamental Principles at Work. Geneva: ILO.

ILO (International Labor Organization). 2001. *Stopping Forced Labor*. Second Global Report Under the Follow-Up to the Declaration on Fundamental Principles at Work. Geneva: ILO.

ILO (International Labor Organization). 2002. *A Future Without Child Labor*. Third Global Report Under the Follow-Up to the Declaration on Fundamental Principles at Work. Geneva: ILO.

International Institute for Sustainable Development and World Wildlife Fund. 2001. *Private Rights, Public Problems: A Guide to NAFTA's Controversial Chapter on Investor Rights*. Winnipeg: International Institute for Sustainable Development and World Wildlife Fund.

International Confederation of Free Trade Unions. 1996. *Behind the Wire: Anti-Union Repression in the Export Processing Zones*. Brussels: International Confederation of Free Trade Unions.

International Confederation of Free Trade Unions. 1999. *Building Workers' Human Rights into the Global Trading System*. Brussels: International Confederation of Free Trade Unions.

International Labor Office. 1998a. *Labor and Social Issues Relating to Export Processing Zones*. Report for Discussion at the Tripartite Meeting of Export Processing Zones–Operating Countries, TMEPZ/1998. Geneva: International Labor Organization.

International Labor Office. 1998b. *Overview of Global Developments and Office Activities Concerning Codes of Conduct, Social Labelling and Other Private Sector Initiatives Addressing Labor Issues*. Report to the Governing Body of the Working Party on the Social Dimension of the Liberalization of International Trade, GB.273/WP/SDL/1(Rev. 1), 273d Session. Geneva: International Labor Office.

International Labor Office. 2002. *The ILO's Technical Cooperation Programme 2001–02*. Governing Body Document GB.285/TC/1. Geneva: International Labor Office.

IPEC (International Program on the Elimination of Child Labor). 1999. *IPEC Action Against Child Labour: Achievements, Lessons Learned, and Indications for the Future, 1998–99*. Geneva: International Labor Organization.

IPEC (International Program on the Elimination of Child Labor). 2002a. *IPEC Actions Against Child Labour: Highlights 2002*. Geneva: International Labor Organization.

IPEC (International Program on the Elimination of Child Labor). 2002b. *IPEC Actions Against Child Labour 2000–2001: Progress and Future Priorities*. Geneva: International Labor Organization.

ILRF (International Labor Rights Fund). 1999. Child Labor in the Soccer Ball Industry: A Report on the Continued Use of Child Labor in the Soccer Ball Industry in Pakistan. www.laborrights.org/projects/foulball/index.html (May 2003).

Jeffcott, Bob, and Lynda Yanz. No date. Voluntary Codes of Conduct: Do They Strengthen or Undermine Government Regulation and Worker Organizing? Paper prepared for Workers in the Global Economy Project, International Labor Rights Fund. www. laborrights. org/projects/globalecon/jeffcott.html (May 2003).

Kahneman, Daniel, and Amos Tversky. 1979. Prospect Theory: An Analysis of Decision Under Risk. *Econometrica* 47, no. 2: 263–91.

Keck, Margaret E., and Kathryn Sikkink. 1998. *Activists Beyond Borders: Advocacy Networks in International Politics*. Ithaca, NY: Cornell University Press.

Klasen, Stephan. 2000. *Does Gender Inequality Reduce Growth and Development? Evidence from Cross-Country Regressions*. Working Paper 7 for Policy Research Report on Gender and Development. Washington: World Bank.

Klein, Naomi. 1999. *No Logo: Taking Aim at the Brand Bullies*. New York: Picador USA.

Kletzer, Lori G. 2001. *Job Loss from Imports: Measuring the Costs*. Washington: Institute for International Economics.

Kucera, David. 2001. *The Effects of Core Worker Rights on Labour Costs and Foreign Direct Investment: Evaluating the "Conventional Wisdom."* Decent Work Research Program, Discussion Paper DP/130/2001. Geneva: International Labor Organization.

Lancaster, Kelvin. 1979. *Variety, Equity, and Efficiency: Product Variety in an Industrial Society*. New York: Columbia University Press.

Lawrence, Robert Z. Forthcoming. *Crimes and Punishments.* Washington: Institute for International Economics.

Leipziger, Deborah. 2002. *SA8000: The Definitive Guide to the New Social Standard.* London: Financial Times/Prentice Hall.

Levine, Ross, and David Renelt. 1992. A Sensitivity Analysis of Cross-Country Growth Regressions. *American Economic Review* 82, no. 4 (September): 942–63.

Liubicic, Robert J. 1998. Corporate Codes of Conduct and Product Labeling Schemes: The Limits and Possibilities of Promoting International Labor Rights Through Private Initiatives. *Law and Policy in International Business* 30, no. 1 (fall): 112–58.

Lorenz, Edward C. 2001. *Defining Global Justice: The History of US International Labor Standards Policy.* Notre Dame, IN: University of Notre Dame.

Lyle, Faye. 1991. *Foreign Labor Trends: Worker Rights in U.S. Policy.* FLT 91-54. Washington: Bureau of International Labor Affairs, US Department of Labor.

Margolis, Joshua Daniel, and James Patrick Walsh. 2001. *People and Profits? The Search for a Link Between a Company's Social and Financial Performance.* Mahwah, NJ: Lawrence Erlbaum Associates.

Marymount University Center for Ethical Concerns. 1999. The Consumers and Sweatshops. www.marymount.edu/news/garmentstudy/overview.html (January 5, 2001).

Maskus, Keith E. 1997. *Should Core Labor Standards Be Imposed through International Trade Policy?* Policy Research Working Paper 1817. Washington: World Bank.

Maskus, Keith E. 2000a. *Intellectual Property Rights in the Global Economy.* Washington: Institute for International Economics.

Maskus, Keith E. 2000b. *Regulatory Standards in the WTO: Comparing Intellectual Property Rights with Competition Policy, Environmental Protection, and Core Labor Standards.* Working Paper Number 00-1. Washington: Institute for International Economics, January.

Massie, Robert Kinloch. 1997. *Loosing the Bonds: The United States and South Africa in the Apartheid Years.* New York: Doubleday.

Moore, David. 2000. Speaking with a Unified Voice: Student Consumers Make Targeted Change. In *Human Rights Dialogue* (Carnegie Council on Ethics and International Affairs), series 2, no. 4 (Fall): 10–11.

Moran, Theodore. 2002. *Beyond Sweatshops: Foreign Direct Investment and Globalization in Developing Countries.* Washington: Brookings Institution Press.

Morici, Peter, and Evan Schulz. 2001. *Labor Standards in the Global Trading System.* Washington: Economic Strategy Institute.

Noland, Marcus, and Howard Pack. 2003. *Industrial Policy in an Era of Globalization: Lessons from Asia.* Policy Analyses in International Economics 69. Washington: Institute for International Economics.

OECD (Organization for Economic Cooperation and Development). 1996. *Trade, Employment, and Labour Standards: A Study of Core Workers' Rights and International Trade.* Paris: OECD.

OECD (Organization for Economic Cooperation and Development). 2000. *International Trade and Core Labour Standards.* Paris: OECD.

O'Rourke, Dara. 2000. Monitoring the Monitors: A Critique of Price Waterhouse Coopers (PWC) Labor Monitoring. Massachusetts Institute of Technology. http://web.mit.edu/dorourke/www (October).

Paul-Majumder, Pratima, and Anwara Begum. 2000. *The Gender Imbalances in the Export Oriented Garment Industry in Bangladesh.* Background Paper for World Bank Policy Research Report, *Engendering Development.* Washington: World Bank.

Polanski, Sandra. 2002. *Trade and Labor Standards: A Strategy for Developing Countries.* Trade, Equity, and Development Working Paper. Washington: Carnegie Endowment for International Peace.

Portes, Alejandro. 1994. By-Passing the Rules: The Dialectics of Labour Standards and Informalization In Less Developed Countries. In *International Labour Standards and*

Economic Interdependence, ed. Werner Sengenberger and Duncan Campbell. Geneva: International Institute for Labour Studies.

Revenga, Ana. 1995. *Employment and Wage Effects of Trade Liberalization: The Case of Mexican Manufacturing*. Working Paper 1524. Washington: World Bank.

Richardson, J. David. 2000. The WTO and Market-Supportive Regulation: A Way Forward on New Competition, Technological, and Labor Issues. *Federal Reserve of St. Louis Quarterly Review* (July/August).

Robbins, Don. 1994. *Worsening Relative Wage Dispersion in Chile during Trade Liberalization and Its Causes: Is Supply at Fault?* Harvard Institute for International Development Discussion Paper 484. Cambridge, MA: Harvard Institute for International Development.

Robbins, Don, and T.H. Gindling. 1999. Trade Liberalization and the Relative Wages of More Skilled Workers in Costa Rica. *Review of Development Economics* 3, 140–54.

Robertson, R. 2000. Trade Liberalization and Wage Inequality: Lessons from the Mexican Experience. *World Development* 23, no. 6: 827–49.

Rock, Michael T. 2003. Public Disclosure of the Sweatshop Practices of American Multinational Garment/Shoe Makers/Retailers: Impacts on their Stock Prices. Forthcoming in *Competition and Change*.

Rodriguez, Francisco, and Dani Rodrik. 2001. Trade Policy and Economic Growth: A Skeptic's Guide to the Cross-National Evidence. In *NBER Macroeconomic Annual 2000*. Cambridge, MA: National Bureau for Economic Research.

Rodrik, Dani. 1996. Labor Standards in International Trade: Do They Matter and What to Do About Them. In *Emerging Agenda for Global Trade: High Stakes for Developing Countries*, ed. Robert Z. Lawrence, Dani Rodrik, and John Whalley. Policy Essay 20. Washington: Overseas Development Council.

Rodrik, Dani. 1999. *The New Global Economy and Developing Countries: Making Openness Work*. Policy Essay 24. Washington: Overseas Development Council.

Rodrik, Dani. 2000. Comments on "Trade, Growth, and Poverty," by D. Dollar and A. Kraay. http://ksghome.harvard.edu/~.drodrik.academic.ksg/rodrik%20on%20dollarkraay.pdf (May 2003).

Rodrik, Dani, Arvind Subramanian, and Francesco Trebbi. 2002. Institutions Rule: The Primacy of Institutions over Geography and Integration in Economic Development. Discussion Paper no. 3643. London: Center for Economic Policy Research. Photocopy (November).

Romano, Cesare P.R. 1996. The ILO System of Supervision and Compliance Control: A Review and Lessons for Multilateral Environmental Agreements. International Institute for Applied Systems Analysis, Laxenburg, Austria. Photocopy (May).

Romero, Ana Teresa. 1995. Labour Standards and Export Processing Zones: Situation and Pressure for Change. *Development Policy Review* 13: 247–76.

Rothstein, Richard. 1996. The Starbucks Solution: Can Voluntary Codes Raise Global Living Standards. *American Prospect*, no. 27 (July–August): 36–42.

Sabel, Charles, Dara O'Rourke, and Archon Fung. 2000. *Ratcheting Labor Standards*. Social Protection Paper 11. Washington: World Bank.

Scheve, Kenneth F., and Matthew J. Slaughter. 2001. *Globalization and the Perceptions of American Workers*. Washington: Institute for International Economics.

Senser, Robert A. 2002. Growing Worker Activism Pushes Envelope in China. *American Educator* 26, no. 4 (Winter): 39–41.

Srinivasan, T.N., and Jagdish Bhagwati. 1999. Outward-Orientation and Development: Are Revisionists Right? Festschrift in honor of Anne Krueger. Photocopy (September). www.columbia.edu/~jb38/Krueger.pdf (May 2003).

Staiger, Robert W. 2003. The International Organization and Enforcement of Labor Standards. In *International Labor Standards: History, Theory, and Policy Options*, ed. Kaushik Basu, Henrik Horn, Lisa Román, and Judith Shapiro. Malden, MA: Blackwell Publishing.

Stiglitz, Joseph. 2000. Democratic Development as the Fruits of Labor. Keynote Address, Industrial Relations Research Association. Boston (January).

Tallontire, Anne, Erdenechimeg Rentsendorj, and Mick Blowfield. 2001. *Ethical Consumers and Ethical Trade: A Review of Current Literature.* Policy Series 12. Chatham, UK: Natural Resources Institute.

UNICEF. 1997. *The State of the World's Children 1997.* London: Oxford University Press for UNICEF.

University of Maryland. 2000. *Americans on Globalization: A Study of Public Attitudes.* Program on International Policy Attitudes. www.pipa.org/onlinereports/globalization/global_rep.html (March).

US Department of Labor. 1989–90. *Foreign Labor Trends: Worker Rights in Export Processing Zones.* FLT 90-32. Washington: Bureau of International Labor Affairs, US Department of Labor.

US Department of Labor. 1998. *By the Sweat and Toil of Children: Efforts to Eliminate Child Labor,* vol. 5. Washington: Bureau of International Labor Affairs, US Department of Labor.

US House of Representatives. 1997. *Overview and Compilation of U.S. Trade Statutes.* Committee Print WMCP 105-4, Committee on Ways and Means. Washington: US House of Representatives.

Vahapassi, Antero E.E. 2000. *Workplace Monitoring in Asia to Combat Child Labour.* Prepared for the Asian Regional High-Level Meeting on Child Labour, Jakarta. Geneva: International Labor Organization.

Varley, Pamela, ed. 1998. *The Sweatshop Quandary: Corporate Responsibility on the Global Frontier.* Washington: Investor Responsibility Research Center.

Wade, Robert. 1990. *Governing the Market: Economic Theory and Taiwan's Industrial Policies.* Princeton, NJ: Princeton University Press.

Weil, David. 2000. Everything Old Is New Again: Regulating Labor Standards in the U.S. Apparel Industry. In *Proceedings, 52d Meeting of the Industrial Relations Research Association.* Champaign, IL: Industrial Relations Research Association.

Winston, Morton. 2002. NGO Strategies for Promoting Global Corporate Social Responsibility. In *Justice in the World Economy: Globalization, Agents, and the Pursuit of Social Good,* ed. Robin Hodess. New York: Carnegie Council on Ethics and International Affairs.

World Bank. 2001. *Engendering Development through Gender Equality in Rights, Resources, and Voice.* World Bank Research Policy Report. New York: Oxford University Press.

Yanikkaya, Halit. Forthcoming. Trade Openness and Economic Growth: A Cross-Country Empirical Investigation. *Journal of Development Economics.*

Zack, Arnold. 1999. Proposal to Director-General Juan Somavia for an ILO Corps of Mediators. Photocopy (on file with author).

Zack, Arnold. 2003. Alternative Dispute Resolution and the Settlement of International Labor Disputes: A Proposal for Conciliation through the Permanent Court of Arbitration. Permanent Court of Arbitration, The Hague. Photocopy.

Index

Who's Bashing Whom? Trade Conflict in High-Technology Industries   Laura D'Andrea Tyson
November 1992   ISBN 0-88132-106-0
Korea in the World Economy*   Il SaKong
January 1993   ISBN 0-88132-183-4
Pacific Dynamism and the International Economic System*
C. Fred Bergsten and Marcus Noland, editors
May 1993   ISBN 0-88132-196-6
Economic Consequences of Soviet Disintegration*
John Williamson, editor
May 1993   ISBN 0-88132-190-7
Reconcilable Differences? United States-Japan Economic Conflict*
C. Fred Bergsten and Marcus Noland
June 1993   ISBN 0-88132-129-X
Does Foreign Exchange Intervention Work?
Kathryn M. Dominguez and Jeffrey A. Frankel
September 1993   ISBN 0-88132-104-4
Sizing Up U.S. Export Disincentives*
J. David Richardson
September 1993   ISBN 0-88132-107-9
NAFTA: An Assessment
Gary Clyde Hufbauer and Jeffrey J. Schott/ rev. ed.
October 1993   ISBN 0-88132-199-0
Adjusting to Volatile Energy Prices
Philip K. Verleger, Jr.
November 1993   ISBN 0-88132-069-2
The Political Economy of Policy Reform
John Williamson, editor
January 1994   ISBN 0-88132-195-8
Measuring the Costs of Protection in the United States
Gary Clyde Hufbauer and Kimberly Ann Elliott
January 1994   ISBN 0-88132-108-7
The Dynamics of Korean Economic Development*   Cho Soon
March 1994   ISBN 0-88132-162-1
Reviving the European Union*
C. Randall Henning, Eduard Hochreiter, and Gary Clyde Hufbauer, editors
April 1994   ISBN 0-88132-208-3
China in the World Economy   Nicholas R. Lardy
April 1994   ISBN 0-88132-200-8
Greening the GATT: Trade, Environment, and the Future   Daniel C. Esty
July 1994   ISBN 0-88132-205-9
Western Hemisphere Economic Integration*
Gary Clyde Hufbauer and Jeffrey J. Schott
July 1994   ISBN 0-88132-159-1
Currencies and Politics in the United States, Germany, and Japan
C. Randall Henning
September 1994   ISBN 0-88132-127-3
Estimating Equilibrium Exchange Rates
John Williamson, editor
September 1994   ISBN 0-88132-076-5

Managing the World Economy: Fifty Years After Bretton Woods   Peter B. Kenen, editor
September 1994   ISBN 0-88132-212-1
Reciprocity and Retaliation in U.S. Trade Policy
Thomas O. Bayard and Kimberly Ann Elliott
September 1994   ISBN 0-88132-084-6
The Uruguay Round: An Assessment*
Jeffrey J. Schott, assisted by Johanna W. Buurman
November 1994   ISBN 0-88132-206-7
Measuring the Costs of Protection in Japan*
Yoko Sazanami, Shujiro Urata, and Hiroki Kawai
January 1995   ISBN 0-88132-211-3
Foreign Direct Investment in the United States, 3rd Ed. Edward M. Graham and Paul R. Krugman
January 1995   ISBN 0-88132-204-0
The Political Economy of Korea-United States Cooperation*
C. Fred Bergsten and Il SaKong, editors
February 1995   ISBN 0-88132-213-X
International Debt Reexamined* William R. Cline
February 1995   ISBN 0-88132-083-8
American Trade Politics, 3rd Ed. I.M. Destler
April 1995   ISBN 0-88132-215-6
Managing Official Export Credits: The Quest for a Global Regime*   John E. Ray
July 1995   ISBN 0-88132207-5
Asia Pacific Fusion: Japan's Role in APEC*
Yoichi Funabashi
October 1995   ISBN 0-88132-224-5
Korea-United States Cooperation in the New World Order*
C. Fred Bergsten and Il SaKong, editors
February 1996   ISBN 0-88132-226-1
Why Exports Really Matter!* ISBN 0-88132-221-0
Why Exports Matter More!* ISBN 0-88132-229-6
J. David Richardson and Karin Rindal
July 1995; February 1996
Global Corporations and National Governments
Edward M. Graham
May 1996   ISBN 0-88132-111-7
Global Economic Leadership and the Group of Seven   C. Fred Bergsten and C. Randall Henning
May 1996   ISBN 0-88132-218-0
The Trading System After the Uruguay Round*
John Whalley and Colleen Hamilton
July 1996   ISBN 0-88132-131-1
Private Capital Flows to Emerging Markets After the Mexican Crisis*   Guillermo A. Calvo, Morris Goldstein, and Eduard Hochreiter
September 1996   ISBN 0-88132-232-6
The Crawling Band as an Exchange Rate Regime: Lessons from Chile, Colombia, and Israel
John Williamson
September 1996   ISBN 0-88132-231-8
Flying High: Liberalizing Civil Aviation in the Asia Pacific*
Gary Clyde Hufbauer and Christopher Findlay
November 1996   ISBN 0-88132-227-X